THE FAMILIAR

ASH FITZSIMMONS

THE FAMILIAR

FORTUNE'S CHILD, BOOK TWO

THE FAMILIAR. Copyright © 2024 by Ash Fitzsimmons.

Print Edition ISBN: 978-1-949861-65-5

Cover design by MiblArt.

www.ashfitzsimmons.com

CHAPTER 1

One tends to underappreciate how lovely it is to walk into a place and be greeted as a friend until that event becomes a rarity.

"Hi, Jane!" Tabitha Bradley called from behind the counter as I hauled a carton of lotions and bath soaks into Ragged Gap Apothecary. She'd pulled her box braids into a thick ponytail that morning, keeping her hair from her face while she worked. "Go nuts over there. I've got to finish this up."

I'd installed a small three-tiered shelf of my products in Tabitha's pharmacy about two months prior, after Bitsy Prescott dropped me from the Mercantile's vendor list, killing a good chunk of my foot-traffic sales. The Apothecary wasn't in nearly as plum a location—Tabitha leased a spot in the strip mall with the grocery store, compared to the Mercantile, which commanded half a block downtown, prime tourist real estate—but I appreciated the business. Tabitha liked and trusted my products, she recommended them, and she didn't loathe me, which was more than I could say for Bitsy.

"Restocking your lotion display," I told Tabitha. "I brought in a few bags of bath soak—"

"*Ooh*, nice."

"And I've got some lavender sugar scrub in the truck, if that's something you'd be interested in."

Tabitha looked up, a gleam in her dark eyes. "Is that the one you sold last year?"

"The same."

"Wonderful. Put up whatever you've got—I like what that one did for my legs."

Tabitha and I had worked out an arrangement whereby I sold my wares on commission, but I still ran my products by her before I put them on the shelves. She had yet to reject any of my proposals, but it was her store and reputation, and I didn't want to overstep my bounds.

I returned to my truck and pulled out the sugar scrub, a pale lilac concoction with tiny bits of dried lavender flowers in the mix. It was only early November, but given the proliferation of dry skin in the colder months, I suspected that the jars would sell well.

"Just a thought," said Tabitha as I came in out of the morning chill and continued tidying the display, "but have you considered doing any of your stuff with almond oil?"

"I was actually trying to source a good supplier a few days ago," I told her, crouching by the shelves. "Got a couple leads, but I want to be confident in the product."

"Let me know if you get stuck. I might be able to help you."

I turned to her, grinning. "Someone likes almond, hmm?"

"*Someone* wouldn't mind," she replied, glancing toward the ceiling tiles with a *Who, me?* expression.

"Got it. I'll put you on the list for testers."

As I straightened up the lotions—the goat's milk formula also tended to do well during the winter—the door chimed as a customer walked in. "Hi, Mrs. Talcott," said Tabitha. "Just let me finish this right quick, and I'll get your prescription."

Geraldine Talcott was one of my repeat customers, and I smiled at her as she lowered herself into one of the well-padded waiting room chairs. "Good morning, ma'am."

"Morning, Jane," she replied, wincing as she shifted position. Geraldine was a tough old bird, but she was still old, and the years weren't getting any kinder.

"Chilly enough for you yet?"

She peeled off her soft gloves. "Unfortunately. I hate these early cold snaps. A word of advice, young lady: never develop arthritis."

"Noted, and I'm sorry." Pointing to the Keurig Tabitha had set up in the corner for customers, I asked, "Cup of coffee?"

"If you'd be so kind. Two sugars, please."

I started the machine and slipped out to my truck to bring in the last of the load and my notebook so I could tally up the delivery. As I dropped a box of shea butter bath bombs on the thin carpet, Geraldine commented, "Glad I have occasion to come out here. I thought you might have gone out of business."

"Not just yet." I grabbed her drink as its brew gurgled to an end and carried the insulated cup to her. "Sorry for any trouble. If you want, I deliver in the area…"

"I'll bear that in mind." She cupped her hands around her coffee, warming them as the steam rose toward her cold-pinked cheeks. The day *was* unseasonably raw, about fifteen degrees below normal, and the thick, damp fog that left water droplets clinging to my hair had yet to lift. "I grew accustomed to finding your lotion at the Mercantile," Geraldine continued, "and then you stopped selling there all of a sudden. You really should start again," she said, and sipped. "It's so much more convenient."

I smiled tightly. "You know, the Mercantile wanted to go in a different direction, and that was that."

"But they've got other bath products," she pointed out.

"I think Bitsy wanted to open up to some new vendors," I fibbed. "It's a big store, but even so, there's only so much shelf space."

Geraldine harrumphed into her cup. "Pity, if you ask me, but no one does. Ah, thank you, dear," she said as Tabitha came out with a white paper bag for her. "One moment…"

Tabitha waited as Geraldine opened her pocketbook—and it was most definitely a pocketbook, a tan leather clutch easily a couple decades my senior—and wrote out a check for her prescription. She lingered a few minutes longer, chatting with Tabitha as she finished her coffee, and then she made her way back to her old Cadillac to continue her errands.

"I'm guessing she doesn't have a debit card," I remarked as Geraldine drove away.

"Oh, she does," said Tabitha, cracking her back. "She just doesn't trust it. Thinks paying me by check is a better way to ensure that I get my money." Taking in my display, she asked, "All set?"

"That'll do it. Want to square up now or next week?"

"Well, since you're here," she teased, and returned to the back, where the computer and cash drawer sat. With a few clicks, she'd printed off an itemized list of sales, dates, and fees for October. "Picking up, I think," she said as I reviewed it. "Word's getting around."

"I appreciate it—"

"Hey, I'll take the customers, too." Smirking, she asked, "Electronic transfer okay, or would you like a check as well?"

"I trust the computer gremlins." As Tabitha pulled out her phone to pay me, I likewise reached for mine and opened the calendar. "So...when are we redoing your bathroom?"

She finished the transfer before answering me. "That depends on your schedule, I should think."

"Next weekend, maybe? Later this month? I can squeeze you in before Thanksgiving, no problem."

"Oh, that's great! What do I need to buy?"

"Just like last time," I replied. "I need material samples. Paint, tile, hardware, et cetera. And you'll want to buy light fixtures," I added with an apologetic wince. "I don't trust myself with wiring quite yet."

Tabitha rubbed her hands together and grinned. "Can do. You're sure you don't mind wasting a Saturday?"

"Hey, it's good practice for me. No worries."

Gathering the empty cartons into my arms, I pushed open the door with my butt and tensed at the unpleasant blast of cold, damp air. "Give me a call once you've got your swatches and such, and I'll be by."

All my life, my dad had stressed to me the importance of subtlety—a sorcerer could do remarkable things with a little effort, but the constant goal was to avoid humans finding out about it. This was one reason why I lived in a two-bedroom cottage and not a showpiece home. But while Tabitha was unquestionably human, I'd decided I could trust her. She'd caught a peek behind the curtain back at Labor Day, after all, and hadn't run screaming for the hills. While she generally kept her questions to herself, I tended to volunteer snippets of information the more comfortable I grew with our altered relationship.

Tabitha wasn't just my business mentor any longer— she was a confidante, someone I could count on to, say, babysit a bunch of potion-drugged wannabe witches in a pinch. As a Wiccan, she'd believed in the potential for magic long before she moved to Ragged Gap. Now having seen a sampling of what I could do, she accepted it almost as a matter of course and kept her mouth shut.

Some people show their gratitude with bottles of wine or boxes of fine chocolate. I realized that a more meaningful gift for Tabitha would be assistance with the odd home improvement project, so since mid-September, I'd volunteered to help her repaint her kitchen, put up garage shelving, and deliver a dryer when hers broke. Creating matter from thin air took work and concentration, but the exercise was good for me, and as long as I had references for what Tabitha wanted done, I could save her time and considerable money.

She wasn't greedy. Tabitha always insisted that I didn't need to help her, that she'd pull the cash together and get her hands dirty, but honestly, I enjoyed it. Being able to openly cast in front of another person was a novel and freeing experience…and besides, Tabitha always repaid me with dinner. Since she was a darn good cook, I'd have been a fool to let her renovate alone.

More than that, Tabitha was the closest thing I had to a real friend around Ragged Gap in those days. I'd never counted myself among the most social of creatures—and having been homeschooled, I didn't have lifelong friendships with the folks my age in town, who'd never been my classmates—but since the Oil of Life debacle, even acquaintances had turned as cold as that wet November wind.

Let me set the scene.

You're involved, deeply or tangentially, in the New Age community. Perhaps you dabble with reiki. Maybe you bought a few crystals because they're pretty, and though you don't *entirely* believe they'll bring you love or money or serenity, part of you keeps hoping. Or you could be all in. Mystic Mountains, Ragged Gap's witchiest boutique, is welcoming to novices and experts alike.

One day, you're invited to a seminar guaranteed to change your life. When you arrive, the owner of the store, a woman you like and trust, gleefully introduces a beautiful young woman who promises power beyond your wildest imaginings. Katarina is blonde, she's polished, and with a whisper, she can summon items from across the room into her manicured grip. *She* is the real deal. And she, full of so much love and light, promises that this power, this *magic*, is yours for the unlocking. She's made a special blend of essential oils that will help you channel your inner abilities—abilities you knew you had all along, you've *always* known you could tap if only someone would show you the way. A few little dabs or sips, some meditative exercises, and suddenly, your fingertips will glow with a thought. And that's only the beginning, Katarina insists, merely the first sign that you're about to have everything you've ever wanted.

Her oil is criminally cheap, barely above cost, because she so wants to share this with you. She is goodness and joy, the greatest teacher you've ever met. You'd follow her wherever she held her seminars, but lucky you, they're always right here in Ragged Gap.

After a few weeks, with your control improving, Katarina gives you the wonderful news that you're ready to progress to the strongest level of oil. This is it—soon enough, you'll be doing real magic, and everyone who ever doubted you, who scoffed at your openness to powers and energies beyond science's understanding, will have to eat their words. Your moment of triumph and actualization is at hand.

Maybe you start to feel a little fuzzy in the head. You chalk it up to the oil at work, or the weather, or your crappy mattress.

Maybe you're too far gone to notice.

But the next thing you clearly know, you're lying on the floor in the workshop space at Mystic Mountains, dirty, disoriented, and streaked with something you suspect is vomit. You're missing time. The black woman with the gray-threaded box braids watching over you—the pharmacist, you vaguely remember, the one from Savannah—tries to explain that you were drugged and kidnapped, and that the junk you took has been neutralized.

You try to make your fingers light up. They don't so much as flicker.

Soon, you realize that the biggest asshole of a witch in north Georgia has killed your nascent power and driven Katarina away. The oil is gone, and so is your shot at magic.

And only one person is to blame. One selfish, greedy person who couldn't bear the thought of being eclipsed as the town's sole true practitioner.

Me.

Had Stephanie Love put on her big-girl panties and explained the situation, her flock might not have hated me quite so severely. The owner of Mystic Mountains had been suckered in by the promise of power, and she'd acted as an unknowing accomplice in the grift. She, too, had been left a zombified drudge by the potion she'd ingested, but unlike some of her posse, she had a fragmented memory of her time at Katarina's compound, where she'd been put to work for her new mistress. Deep down, Stephanie *knew* she'd been had.

She also knew that I'd busted up in there, set the building on fire, and rescued her sorry ass.

She came to my home a few nights later to confront me, and I was more or less honest with her: the things Katarina could do—and that *I* could do—couldn't be taught to people like her, and no essential oil in the world would confer great power upon her. Katarina had lied through her pearly teeth and preyed upon Stephanie and her gullible friends.

Stephanie told me I was mean to them, a rude showoff who rubbed my talent in their faces. I countered that *she* was the one who'd tossed me to the curb when I was thirteen, came to her for guidance, and made the mistake of demonstrating a touch of genuine power. I told Stephanie that I wasn't trying to supplant her in her own weird hierarchy—I was just me, and if people came to me for help, that was my business.

She could have been woman enough to explain to her fellow victims that Katarina had been a monster, that she'd been wrong and everything had been a beautiful lie, and that I wasn't the one to blame for their condition. But that would have meant admitting fault and losing face, so instead, she left it up to the others to decide for themselves what to believe.

Opinions varied. A good chunk of the Mystic Mountains crowd weren't sure what had transpired at the cabin in Whitford, but they knew I was involved, and they feared me. If we passed on the street or in the grocery store, they nodded tensely and said as little as possible. Those like Stephanie with actual memories of their time in drugged servitude tended to have a better sense of my role in the incident. Though they hated the fact that their blossoming power had withered, they knew that I'd saved them from *something*, even if the details were hazy. And then there was the handful who would have catapulted me into an erupting volcano, had they the means. Never mind that we'd found Penny Oglethorpe and given her neutralizer before she could be abducted; never mind that we'd counteracted the potion as Bitsy seized on the floor. As far as they were concerned, I was the worst thing to ever happen to them—pretty rich, considering what their fate could have been.

I'd hoped that Bitsy, at least, would come around. A seizure had to be terrifying, and she was surely scrambled when Tabitha drove her home to recover. Yes, she'd cussed me and told me to collect my wares, but I'd crossed my fingers that this was only her immediate fear talking.

No such luck.

I'd waited until five days after the rescue, giving Stephanie a chance do the right thing—unnecessary, as it turned out—then drove down to the Mercantile for a word with Bitsy that Thursday morning. We never made it as far as a conversation. When I pulled up, I discovered half a dozen mismatched cardboard boxes loosely taped shut and stacked by the stockroom door behind the shop, each labeled BITCH in black Sharpie, and a quick peek inside the topmost confirmed that she'd filled the cartons with my products.

If I said that didn't hurt, I'd be lying. Bitsy had become a friend since she'd moved to Ragged Gap. We'd talked about her cheating husband and her mountain renaissance over bottles of local wine, and I'd thought I'd found a kindred spirit. Rejection stung at the best of times, more so when it was unwarranted. But I wasn't stupid, and I wasn't planning to beg. I'd collected my boxes that day and drove home, and in the nearly two months since, I'd yet to darken the doorway of the Mercantile.

While I'd lost that shop, however, one of Bitsy's neighboring merchants had recently seized the opportunity. Two blocks up from Mystic Mountains and the downtown square was The Robin's Nest, which sold all manner of small, often kitschy home goods and knickknacks. The owner, Juanita Kowalski, was a fixture at First United Methodist and a sweet old lady, the sort of person who keeps a bowl of suckers by the cash register and deems all children worthy of candy, no matter what terrors they might be. Just before Halloween, Juanita had gone to Tabitha about an ointment and found my display rack, and with Tabitha's blessing, she'd called me to see about getting my wares back in the thick of traffic. The Robin's Nest didn't do half the business of the Mercantile, and Juanita didn't have nearly as much space, but she was an enthusiastic partner who'd made a few sales for me with a well-placed tester and a load of small-town charm, and I was grateful to work with her.

Juanita had called to ask about restocking before the weekend. Friday morning was cutting it close, but the leaf-peeping crowd wouldn't be out in full force until Saturday...and since the trees were definitely on the decline, they'd have plenty of time to browse downtown. As spaces behind The Robin's Nest were at a premium and I didn't have much to schlepp, I pulled into the public lot by the square and grabbed the box of requested items.

Out of habit, or perhaps an unmet need to torture myself, I glanced toward Mystic Mountains as I crossed the street. The shop was open, the door propped with a brick despite the weather, and Stephanie had taped a pair of flyers to the inside of the glass—yoga and a beginner's class on crystal use, I figured, judging by the clipart. Her templates seldom varied, unfortunately, and her design skills left much to be desired. A group of older women in sweaters and rain jackets wandered in out of the fog, takeout coffees clutched against the cold and shopping bags dangling from their arms. For a fleeting second, I entertained the wild thought of following them in and having a quick browse. What would Stephanie do? Call the cops on me for trespassing? She'd never officially banned me, just strongly discouraged my presence. Or would she or whichever of her minions was on duty sit frozen on the stool behind the register, hoping I left without turning them into frogs?

(I couldn't have rendered them frogs had I wanted to. Sorcerers have a natural affinity for inanimate objects. I could mask my truck to look like a Ferrari and copy cans of paint for Tabitha, but working magic on living things took considerable effort. Dad had taught me that elves' talents went in the opposite direction, but even still, nothing in his considerable collection of grimoires suggested that true transmutation of a human into an amphibian was possible.)

Pushing that thought aside, I turned and headed up the sidewalk to meet Juanita, neither looking back nor trying to pick the Mercantile out of the mist ahead.

It wasn't fun being on so many shit lists, and I wondered if our relationships would have time to thaw before Market Day season resumed and we all tried to play nice for the tourists, but that was a problem for the summer. For now, I could keep my head down and plow on.

My phone vibrated in my bag, and I shifted the carton to my left hip so I could dig for it. Illuminating the screen, I saw a text message written in gobbledygook and smiled to myself.

My cousin, who didn't speak a word of English, was asking for a chat.

Once I was squared away with Juanita, I hurried back to

my truck and called Canna. "Hey, there," I said in Pactish as I pulled out. "Sorry, had my hands full. How's it going?"

"*Busy*," she replied, and chuckled. "I've had patients since the moment I walked in today, and I'm just now taking a break."

I glanced at the clock on the dash—quarter past eleven. "Ouch."

"I know. Hitting the caffeine hard while I catch my breath. But I thought you'd appreciate this," she said, slipping into the conspiratorial tone I'd come to know over the past few weeks. "Secretary came in first thing."

"Laws takes *secretaries* into the field?"

"No, this was for a non-work incident, but we don't mind handling those," she explained. "Anyway, his daughter read some article about making your own soaps, and she gave it a try, then offered him a tester bar. Of course, he's going to support his kid, so he goes into the bathroom and lathers up this morning..."

"Uh-oh."

"Yeah. The bar was scented with dried lavender. Guess who has a lavender allergy and never mentioned it to his family?"

I groaned as I approached a four-way stop. "That was *dumb*."

"Right? Maybe this is just me, but if I were allergic to purple flowers and saw bits of purple petals in my soap, I might ask questions. Anyway, the poor man's red and itchy from the neck to his knees."

"At least he didn't wash his feet..."

"I'm going to pretend that was an aberration and move on," Canna said primly. "Got him a potion to counteract the reaction and reduce the inflammation, but *that* is why we read labels."

"Absolutely." When I was starting out, Dad and Tabitha had both stressed the importance of an accurate ingredient list, and assuming my customers could read, they knew precisely what they were getting. "Weekend plans? Sleep?" I teased.

"Ever better. Pars is taking me on a real vacation," she replied, a slightly giddy note in her voice. "His parents are watching the kids, bless them."

"*Ooh.*" I wasn't sure what she appreciated more, a trip out of town or a few days without four small children underfoot. 'Where are you going?"

"He found a cabin near Acori. Four days of hiking and sleeping in…" She sighed happily. "There's a daily catering service, but beyond housekeeping and meal delivery, we'll have the place to ourselves."

I racked my brain, trying to slot their destination into my admittedly hazy conception of Pactlands geography. "Sorry, you're going…where?"

"Ananila. It's in the Edoli Mountains," Canna explained.

"And the Edoli Mountains are…"

She laughed. "Jane, you're asking *me* to map our locations onto the outside?"

"I mean, you knew that Beukal is near Richmond."

"Only because of Pars's work. There's little need to send healers out," she reminded me. "But make a note, and when you finally come over, you two can sit down with his atlas and plot all you like."

My cousin had decided that I *would* find a way into the Pactlands. Precisely how or when were as yet undetermined variables, but she was convinced that we'd have a chance to meet in person. While I didn't entirely share her faith that I'd ever get an invitation, I didn't try to temper her enthusiasm. Canna had looked up to my long-absent mother, Essa, and having not seen Essa in nearly thirty years, she was eager to forge a relationship with me in her stead. Since September, the two of us had chatted by phone every two or three days, getting acquainted. Between tidbits about her work, her kids, and her devoted husband, Canna had offered me glimpses of the maternal family I'd never known. Thanks to her, I'd learned that

Essa was one of five sisters, that her parents were still alive, and that I had a passel of first cousins ranging in age from six months to sixty-three years…none of whom had any clue as to my existence.

I wasn't supposed to have power. Had Dad—who was, technically, my adopted dad—done his job properly, he'd have given Essa the death draught when she ran off with my human father. Instead, he'd opted not to condemn her to a quick death, and they'd produced me, half sorcerer, half human, and a pyromancer to boot. Yes, I supposed I could call one of the handful of people I'd met in the Pactlands, get one of them to sneak me in, then announce my presence to the magically built pocket world and hope for the best. But doing so would reveal that Dad had broken the law in letting Mom go without the draught, and I'd be damned if I left him to rot in jail on my account. Dad had even offered to take me and turn himself in, but I'd refused. As much as I wanted to see the Pactlands and meet my extended family—who might not actually want to meet me—my priority was protecting the man who'd raised me as his own.

This was, naturally, complicated by the fact that our secret had spread. Dad's detective buddy from the Division of Laws, Liogh Birrid, knew how to keep mum, but when the Oil of Life incident kicked off, they'd called in reinforcements from the Division of Plants and Potions to assist in the investigation. The ones chosen were unlikely to give me up: Annie Humphries and Rose ti'Dana had been raised human, Yven ti'Ansha was Rose's fiancé, and Pars Mera was, among other things, Canna's husband. Unfortunately, something about me had drawn the attention of Rose's great-grandfather, the head of the Division of Intelligence, and the notion that a *well-*connected elf with the ability to see the future was casually peeking in on me didn't exactly boost my confidence in my ability to maintain the status quo.

But in the eight weeks since the agents had left, there

had been no black Jeeps in the night, no strange calls alerting me that we'd been outed, no officers busting down Dad's door to drag him away. Perhaps this was merely the calm before the storm, but I clung to it while it lasted.

I wished Canna a great trip and promised to call once she was back to get the highlights, then hung up and let her return to work as I made my way home. Having made my deliveries, I'd cleared my schedule, and the rest of that Friday was mine to enjoy. Not even the fog could dampen my mood on *that* count.

A quiet Friday evening was just what I needed.

True, it hadn't been a particularly rough week. I'd made a few batches of candles and soap, then planned my garden for the spring—plenty of herbs, all of which would end up in my products. I'd gone to Dad's as usual on Wednesday night for the brewing lessons he'd been giving me for the last month and a half, but he was starting me on easy potions, the kind that didn't require all-night babysitting so as not to end in fireballs. No one had come to me seeking magical assistance since Labor Day, and I hadn't found any fresh corpses on my property—well, nothing but the remains of a squirrel, and a garbage bag had fixed that.

Resolving to atone for my sins with a long hike in the morning, I flopped down on my couch with a large meat lover's pizza, primed for a Netflix binge.

And then the damn doorbell rang.

CHAPTER 2

Of all the people I could have anticipated finding on the welcome mat on a random Friday night, Warner Cavanaugh was so low on the list that he barely bore consideration. While the two of us weren't enemies, the guy wasn't anywhere in the neighborhood of what I'd consider to be a friend. Frankly, I thought he was a rich asshole who hadn't bothered to buy himself any manners.

Warner Cavanaugh—the sixth of his name, as if his family were heirs to a freaking Appalachian duchy—had inherited the old homestead in Whitford, the next town of any size to Ragged Gap, though that wasn't saying much. From what I'd gathered, a good chunk of Whitford had once been Cavanaugh land, and while the familial estate had dwindled to a large farmhouse and about twenty acres, the money endured. Warner didn't *work*, per se, that being an activity beneath his dignity, so the family trust paid the bills and granted him a relatively indolent lifestyle.

It didn't bother me one way or another if he wanted to live out his life in the recliner, eating Doritos and playing video games—that wasn't any of my business. Unfortunately, I met Warner at Mystic Mountains during some of my few visits as a young teenager, and what I saw of him then put him on my permanent roster of people to avoid.

Folks talk about having a sixth sense—not the "I see the ghost of Great-Aunt Sally!" variety, but rather the little alarm in the back of your mind that starts blatting in the presence of someone hinky. I trusted mine, and no one I'd met in Ragged Gap put my internal warning system on red alert as strongly as Warner did. In fairness to him, there was nothing I could particularly point to as evidence of criminal behavior—I mean, he didn't drive around in a white panel van, offering candy to unsuspecting children—but two things about him set me on edge.

First, Warner got *way* too close to younger women. He was only about a decade my senior, putting him in his early twenties when I ventured into Mystic Mountains at thirteen. I was no great beauty at that age—gawky, really, too tall for my jeans and still somewhat boyish—but Warner spotted me at the events we attended, and he *stared*. That's what I noticed immediately about him: he was a dark-haired man with piercing blue eyes who always wore a black duster and stared at me. I couldn't understand his interest, especially since he didn't deign to strike up a conversation. Over the course of my visits, I realized that Warner was prone to stare at all of the young women who attended Stephanie's lectures, and while he never approached me, he made a point of sitting beside the prettiest attendees and demanding their attention, no matter how hard they tried to ignore him. To put it bluntly, he was a creep, and even as inexperienced as I was, I recognized that his behavior was obnoxious at best.

Second, Warner claimed to be a great warlock.

A few of the Mystic Mountains crowd called themselves practicing witches, which didn't really bother me. Hell, Tabitha cast the odd spell and performed the occasional ritual, and she hurt no one. As a born sorcerer, someone who could change my face and create fire at will, I didn't see the *point* in the sort of witchcraft that was heavy on intention and didn't generate immediate results, but if it made people feel better to sit around and chant over a brazier of herbs or whatnot…weird, but no skin off my nose.

Warner was different. He bragged about being a warlock, for one, stressing that he could curse anyone and make it stick. He claimed to possess abilities far beyond those of the other practitioners in town—not a high hurdle, to be sure, but one that I suspected he couldn't actually surmount. Even at thirteen, I'd learned enough from my dad to know that curses weren't the sort of spells one casually cast, especially not at the frequency Warner described, and I soon surmised that the dude was full of hot air and desperate to impress *someone.*

Since my unofficial banishment from Mystic Mountains, I hadn't had much occasion to chat with Warner, but I saw him around town: always single, always in that black duster, and still prone to stare at people in checkout lines or on the street. He didn't buy moonshine from Dad, and he certainly didn't buy my products, so our interaction in the last fourteen years had been minimal— not that I was complaining.

Before I could so much as ask if he was lost, Warner swept his duster back, shoved his hands in his jean pockets, and smirked at me. "So. Jane Fortune."

"Uh, yeah?" I replied, fighting the urge to retreat a step into the safety of my house.

"I understand that you've grown into a practitioner of…some ability," he said, giving me a slow once-over.

Yep, that stare was still creepy at close range. "Says who?"

"Stephanie Love. She gave me your address," he added. "But I've heard stories for a *long* time. Whispers. Stephanie actually looked a little nervous when she told me where to find you, so I suspect we may have more in common than I'd realized." He chuckled deep in his throat. "Not every day you meet another warlock, especially one of the female persuasion."

"And today is *not* your lucky day, I'm afraid," I said, glaring back at him, "as I'm not a warlock. What do you want?"

Please, I begged any merciful deity within range, *not a date.*

To my relief, he didn't immediately suggest a night of passion. "Your secret's safe with me," he said, faintly smiling, "but if you want to play coy, that's fine. I have a proposition for you."

"Oh? Business?"

Warner cocked his head as if I'd uttered an unfamiliar word. "I suppose you could say that," he replied after a moment's consideration. "More like an offer from one practitioner to another."

"I don't curse people, so if that's what you're after—"

"No curses. Just hear me out, hmm? What do you have to lose?" When I didn't immediately protest, he asked, "Are you going to invite me in, or would you rather shiver in the doorway?"

Damn it.

Reminding myself that I could set him on fire if he tried to get handsy, I showed him into the den and grabbed the pizza box before he could get any ideas about dinner. "Something to drink?" I called over my shoulder as I headed for the kitchen.

Warner didn't miss a beat. "Your father makes 'shine, does he not? How is it?"

"Decent."

I poured him a single, topped up my iced tea, and returned to find him sitting back with his heels propped on my coffee table. "Here you go," I said, and though manners forced me to smile, I fought the urge to kick him in the shins.

Warner swirled the amber liquid—I'd brought him a drink from an oak-aged bottle—then sniffed and sipped. "Not bad," he decreed after swirling the liquor around his mouth. "Not Johnnie Blue, but not bad."

In fairness to Dad, I hadn't opened one of the *really* good bottles for Warner. "Need water?"

"No, this is fine neat." He sipped again, smiling to himself, then sighed contentedly. "Cozy place you have here."

"It suffices," I said, and took a seat at the other end of the couch. "Now, what's on your mind?"

"As I said, a proposition." Warner glanced at his drink, then finished the moonshine in one long gulp and set the glass aside. "I have something I think you might be interested in purchasing."

I frowned. "Land?"

He waved off the suggestion as if it were preposterous. "Nothing so mundane. How would you like to own a familiar?"

"A…familiar?" My bemusement only deepened at the question. "What, have you started breeding black cats or something?"

"Don't be absurd. It's beneath our dignity," he retorted, shooting me a look of disdain.

"Well, you're going to have to give me a hint, then, because I'm not following."

Warner tucked his hands behind his head and crossed his ankles atop my table. "A familiar, Jane. A creature bound to your will—"

"Yes, I'm aware of the concept," I snapped, "but what sort of familiar are you trying to sell me?"

"A rare kind. For the last thirteen years, I've kept a demon captive in my home."

"I'm sorry, *what?*"

"A demon," Warner repeated. "It was a gift to me from my…*patrons*. You understand how those sort of gifts can be challenging, yes?"

I was sorcerer enough to know that there was no damn way Warner had found a dark god to serve as his patron— Dad's grimoires had taught me enough to know that the relationship he spoke of simply didn't happen. If the sort of creature he claimed to serve truly existed, it would be far more likely to eat him than do him favors. But what, then, was Warner's "demon"?

"What makes you think it's a demon?" I asked.

"Oh, it's obvious," he said dismissively. "Anyway, I've

been using it to do chores around the house, but I find these days that the creature costs more in upkeep than it's worth to me. That's why I'm giving you the opportunity to buy it."

"Why me?"

"You're a woman of business, are you not? Put it to work. It's trainable, if not the brightest creature, and it will serve you."

I stared at him, clutching my tea and trying to decide whether I should call the police or a priest.

"Look," said Warner, sitting up and taking his boots off the table, "I don't want it anymore. Under other circumstances, I'd just banish it to whatever hell it came from, but I *really* don't want to upset my patrons by tossing their gift back at them. Frankly, I'm tired of dealing with it. I'll sell it to you for far less than it's worth."

I suspected that he'd somehow captured a faun. Though they were strong and long-lived, their only inherent magical talent was the ability to brew potions— they couldn't cast. It wasn't inconceivable that Warner had managed to lock a faun in his basement, and considering their goatish aspects, I could see where he might mistake a faun for something demonic. What a faun was doing in north Georgia, *unmasked*, was another matter, but if he'd kept one imprisoned for thirteen years…

Well, at least I had a contact at the Division of Laws. I didn't like to think of what Liogh Birrid would say if I called to report yet another faun in my town, but I appreciated having the detective in my phonebook.

"Let me see this demon of yours before I agree to anything," I said.

Warner smiled. "That's fair," he replied, and pushed himself from the couch. "Come on, I left it in the truck."

As he rose from the couch, I grabbed sneakers and a fleece jacket against the chill. November wasn't a terribly harsh month in other parts of the state, but up in the mountains, it had teeth, and the forecast warned of an overnight freeze. Thus insulated, I picked up a small flashlight from the hallway table and followed Warner outside. He'd parked a chrome-plated monstrosity of a pickup truck beneath my security light, a pristine black dually that I suspected had never hauled or towed a damn thing. Squeezed in beside it, my ten-year-old F-150 looked as hard-used as a farm truck. But *something* was in the bed of Warner's ride that night, or so the tarp lashed across the back seemed to suggest.

Our shoes crunched over the gravel as we drew near, and Warner patted my shoulder. "Why don't you wait here? Let me draw the demon out."

I wanted to tell him where he could go stick that condescending smile of his, but I played nice and stopped a few feet away from the vehicle. "Sure you don't need a hand?"

"Never," he scoffed, and swept toward the rear of the truck. Instead of releasing the tarp, he unlocked the tailgate and lowered it. "Come out. *Now.*"

Curious, I flicked on my flashlight and aimed it at the bed, and what I saw in there chilled my blood.

The face of the creature huddled at the far end was *young*, female, and on first glance, human. Had she not been in Warner's possession for thirteen years, I'd have doubted she was a teenager. She flinched and squinted at the light, shrinking into a ball.

"Come out," Warner ordered, then hoisted himself onto the tailgate and reached into the bed. I thought he might be grabbing for her arm until I heard the clank of metal.

A chain. He'd put a fucking *chain* on the girl.

"Get out of there," he snapped as he climbed down, then gave the chain a sharp tug like a dog owner with a leash. "Don't you make me go in after you."

The chain jingled, and I heard a scrabbling sound from within the bed as the girl crawled toward the tailgate...and then, as she appeared in the glow of the security light, I got a better look at what Warner had brought me.

The child was pale as a cave-dwelling creature, with matted dark hair falling to her mid-back in an irregular cut. She wore a stained, oversized white T-shirt and a long denim skirt that could have come from the closet of one of Ragged Gap Baptist's modest matrons. Instead of shoes, she wore black galoshes, or perhaps rubber farm boots. She was thin—no, not thin, *scrawny*—and given her general disheveled state, I wondered when she'd last bathed. In any case, she was grossly underdressed for the weather, and she huddled beside the tailgate, hugging herself.

The chain in Warner's hand was connected to a thick iron collar around her little neck.

"This way," he said, giving the chain a jerk, and led her toward me. She walked with a pronounced limp, I noticed, and as she drew nearer, I could see the terror in her eyes.

"Behold," said Warner, pulling the girl close to him. "My familiar."

In all my freelance magical work since returning to my hometown, I'd never killed anyone, though I'd certainly been tempted. Spouse beaters and child abusers challenged my self-control. That night, watching that kid shiver in my driveway, was the closest I'd yet come to homicide. This wasn't a job for a sorcerer, but rather for the cops, the sheriff, and CPS. I mean, Warner had blatantly admitted that he'd kept that girl for *years*, and I pushed down thoughts of what he might have done to her. If I let myself consider those possibilities, he'd end up so charred that the pathologist would need to pull his dental records.

I couldn't just *buy* a kid off of Warner. Wasn't that textbook human trafficking? But if I said no and sent him away, what would he do with her? Keep her? Hide her somewhere new? Or would he get spooked and sell her to someone else?

Or worse. He'd said that he didn't want to send her back to Hell...would he *kill* her?

I wanted that monster off my property, but I couldn't risk letting him go with the girl still in his possession, and I couldn't risk attacking him outright. Something told me the son of a bitch would have no qualms against employing her as a shield.

"She's little, isn't she?" I said, trying to sound blasé about the whole fucked-up situation.

"A lesser demon, to be sure," said Warner, "but she has her uses. Cleaning, manual labor. Her cooking has improved, but it's nothing great."

"Mm. And you say she's more trouble to you than she's worth?"

He slipped his hands into his duster's pockets against the cold. "I don't need much menial work done. You do. Bottling, packaging, am I right? Or you'd find other tasks for her, I'm sure. She can chop firewood. Personally, I prefer to buy mine."

"Huh." My fingers itched to ignite, but I kept the flames at bay. "What do you want for her?"

Warner didn't hesitate. "Five thousand dollars."

I laughed in his face. "For *that* little thing? I wouldn't give you five hundred."

"She's quite useful—"

"Not to you. I'd be doing you a favor by taking her off your hands," I countered. "Saving you money and keeping you in your *patrons'* good graces."

He huffed. "One thousand."

"Two hundred. Mine is a cottage industry—I don't need a freaking demon to keep up with my orders. This is me doing you a favor as a fellow practitioner."

His jaw clenched, but he didn't walk away. "Five hundred."

"Three hundred, and I throw in a bottle of aged 'shine. Final offer," I said, and held my breath.

Warner hesitated, but to my relief, he gave me a curt nod. "Deal. Cash?"

"Venmo?"

"Fine."

"Wait here," I said, and hurried back into the house. I grabbed a fresh bottle of moonshine and my phone, then returned and opened the app. "Where do I send the money?"

He walked me through the transfer, telling me to keep the transaction private and say it was for dinner. Though I cringed internally at the notion of anyone thinking I'd gone on a date with him, I did as he said and handed over the booze. "And my demon?"

"All yours," he replied, dropping her chain into my outstretched hand. "Here's the key to the collar," he added, fishing it from his deep pocket. "In case you ever need it. I find it simpler to keep the creature collared at all times. Safety first." Dropping me a wink, he retreated toward his truck. "Pleasure doing business with you, Jane. See you around."

"Right," I said, and clutched the chain as he gunned the engine and pulled out into the night.

Once the truck had vanished down the mountain, I turned to the child I'd just purchased, who continued to hug herself and stared up at me with saucer eyes. "Come on, hon," I said as gently as I could. "Let's get you in out of the cold."

I thought I might have to physically coax her, but once I opened the front door and the warm air wafted out, she lingered on the porch for only a moment before limping inside.

CHAPTER 3

The security light wasn't flattering, but the interior lights told the truth, and it was worse than I thought.

The girl was pale, yes, but she was also filthy. Her clothes were stained and stank, and I wondered whether it had been days or weeks since she'd brushed her hair. Up close, her face seemed gaunt, little more than big green eyes and dark brows.

The tremor in her jaw was certainly from more than just the weather.

"It's okay, sweetie," I said. "Why don't we go into the kitchen and...oh, *shit*," I muttered, realizing the end of her chain was still in my hand. "Here, uh...you hold on to this, okay?"

She shrank away as I approached, but when I didn't move to strike her, she took the chain from me.

With a little more persuasion, I convinced her to follow me into the kitchen and take a seat at the table. "First things first," I said, pulling out the chair beside hers, "let's get that collar off. Do you know where the keyhole is?"

She nodded.

"Can you point it out to me?" I asked. When she reached around and tapped the back of her neck, I said, "Okay. I'm going to need to move your hair to get to it. Is that all right? May I touch you?"

Though she tensed up, she nodded, and I smiled. "You're being so brave, honey," I murmured, and slowly walked behind her. Pushing her hair aside—given its sad state, I wondered if the poor kid had lice or fleas—I found the tiny keyhole and jiggled open the lock. "There we go," I said, pulling the halves apart. "How's that?"

The area where the collar had been was cleaner than the rest of her neck, demarcated by old scars where the top and bottom edges had rested and chafed. I suspected that Warner had removed it rarely, if ever.

"May I have that chain, please?" I asked.

She released her grip, then watched in silence as I opened the back door and tossed the chain and collar out into the yard. "We can get rid of that properly in the morning," I told her as I closed and locked the door, "but I don't want it in the house overnight. Stay right there, now. I'll be back."

She didn't seem to have moved a muscle by the time I returned with an old blue electric blanket, which I plugged in and dialed up. "Let's get you warm," I said, wrapping it around her thin shoulders. "That shirt's not doing you any favors. Is this okay?"

Clutching the edges of the blanket closed in front of her, she nodded.

"How about something to drink? Would that make you feel better?"

Again, she nodded, though the way she cringed as she did so hurt my heart.

I made her a mug of instant hot chocolate in the microwave and chucked in a few mini marshmallows, the best I could do on short notice. "I'm sorry, I don't have any of the good stuff right now," I said as I put it on the table beside her. "The good mix, I mean. This is kind of the cocoa of last resort, but it should get you a little toastier…"

As I sat, she dared to reach for the mug, then lifted it to her lips and sipped. Her eyes widened with surprise, and she drank again.

"You like it?"

She nodded enthusiastically.

"Have you ever had that before?"

When she shook her head, I rose and returned to the pantry. "Don't you worry. Let me get another mug ready for when you finish that one."

By the time the second round was prepared, she was licking the chocolate and marshmallow residue off her lips, and I chuckled and brought her a napkin with the fresh cocoa. "It's not going anywhere. You take your time."

Apparently, the kid only had one drinking speed, as she gulped down her refill and stifled a belch. She clung to the empty mug, looking to me as if awaiting directions, and I remembered the pizza I'd been about to enjoy before Warner dropped in. "When did you last eat?" I asked.

She frowned, then glanced toward the ceiling as if trying to do the calculations.

"Never mind. Are you hungry? Want some dinner?"

She nodded.

"Is pizza okay? It's meat lover's..."

She cocked her head in query, and I fought the irrational urge to call Warner back to the house just so I could deck him.

"Pizza," I said, and got up to retrieve the box from the stovetop. Plopping it between us with a stack of paper napkins, I opened the lid and pulled free a slice. "Give that a try, eh?"

She mimicked me and tentatively raised the slice to her mouth, then took a bite and grinned.

"Is that good? You can have as much as you want."

Wrapped in the electric blanket, she hunched over the pizza box and inhaled a third of the pie before she groaned from a full stomach. "I'm just putting the rest in the fridge for later," I promised her, and gave her another look when I returned to the table. Her mouth had picked up a layer of grease and crumbs, but there was pink in her cheeks, and her jaw had stopped shaking, which I took as progress.

"So," I said, pulling my chair a little closer to hers, "can you tell me your name?"

"Sage," she whispered.

"Sage. *Just* Sage?"

The girl nodded. "That's what Master calls me," she replied in a soft rush, her voice childishly high. "But if…if you don't like it, Mistress, you can—"

"Whoa, *whoa*," I interrupted. "I'm Jane, not 'Mistress.' Okay?"

She cringed. "I'm sorry—"

"No, honey, don't be sorry. You haven't done anything wrong. *Warner*, however, has a lot of explaining to do, and I'm going to get to the bottom of this mess."

Her head tilted again. "Warner?"

"The guy who brought you here. Uh…Master," I said with distaste. "His real name is Warner."

"Oh. I'm sorry, I didn't know."

"Nothing to be sorry for. You want a Coke? Please tell me that asshole introduced you to soft drinks."

He had, it seemed, and Sage happily accepted a can while she continued to toast in her blanket cocoon. I joined her with a can of my own, as the alternatives were alcohol and arson. "How old are you, Sage?"

"Thirteen, Mis—uh, Jane."

As I'd feared. The kid looked closer to ten. She was probably a little under five feet tall and maybe seventy pounds wet, and from what I'd seen, she wasn't wearing so much as a training bra beneath her T-shirt. It was possible that she had a medical condition that stunted her growth, but the much stronger probability was that she'd been severely underfed.

"I'm sorry," she said yet again. "Master told me that I was supposed to call you 'Mistress,' and—"

"Listen to me," I said, gently gripping her wrist through the blanket and holding her worried stare. "You are not in trouble, Sage. I am *not* upset with you."

"Sorry…"

I let it go. "Where did you come from? Who are your people? Your family?"

Sage shrugged. "I've always lived with Master."

"You don't remember your mom and dad?"

"I...I don't think I have a mom and dad. Master says I don't..."

"Did he tell you where you were born?"

She shook her head. "He said I was sent to him. From one of the hells. I don't remember what it was like, though. All I remember is living with Master..."

Her eyes began to film, and her mouth twisted as she tried to stop a rising sob.

Of course she was upset. The only home she'd ever known was with Warner, and he'd sold her to me and driven away. Even if he'd been "Master" to her, even if he'd starved her and chained her by the neck, he was still the closest thing she had to a parent...and here she was, abandoned with a stranger.

"It's going to be okay," I said, and took Sage's Coke can out of her hands before I reached over and hugged her. She stiffened in my arms—I suspected she was unaccustomed to touch like that—but when I started rubbing her back, she relaxed enough to let herself cry. "Let it out," I murmured as my shoulder dampened. "That's a girl. It's all right, Sage."

Once she calmed and her sniffles began to slow, I brought her a box of tissues and let her dry her reddened face. "Sage, honey, I need to ask you a very serious question," I began, and quickly added, "You've done nothing wrong," as fear flickered in her puffy eyes. "Uh...has Warner ever been, um...shit, how do I put this?" I muttered, wishing I had a doll handy. "Did Warner ever touch you...down *there*?" I asked, gesturing toward her blanket-wrapped body. "Or make you touch his private bits?"

Fortunately, Sage caught on through my fumbling. "No, no," she said vehemently. "Master doesn't like to see me with my clothes off. He...he brings home ladies sometimes, but I've never seen what he does with them, so I...I don't know..."

Suddenly horrified that Warner might have a murder room on the old homestead, I pressed, "Do they leave in the morning? These ladies?"

"Oh, yes," said Sage, and my guts unknotted. "And they don't come often. I'm not sure he's ever brought the same lady twice, but I never really get a good look at them."

"He made you hide?"

"I guess. I live...I *lived*," she corrected, a note of sadness in her voice, "in the barn, see, and he always took them to the main house."

"He made you live in the *barn?*"

Sage shrank from the sharpness of my tone, and I kicked myself. "I had a stall and everything," she reassured me. "Master gave me fresh hay every few weeks. There's a broken board in that stall, so I could peek at the house at night. That's how I saw him and the ladies."

"You never tried to sneak in?" I asked.

She shook her head.

"Too scared?"

"Yes, ma'am. He warned me not to make noise. And my chain wouldn't go that far, anyway."

There would be time later, I reasoned, for me to deal with the knowledge that Warner had chained that baby in the barn every night, but I had to maintain my composure for the moment.

As I wrestled for control, Sage asked, "Um...ma'am? Could you tell me what my chores are, please?"

I frowned. "Chores?"

"Yes, ma'am. I want to be good, but Master didn't tell me what you needed me to do. I...I can sweep and mop, and dust, and Master lets me polish his silver—"

"Honey." I held out my hands, and Sage tentatively let me take hers. "I didn't buy you from Warner to put you to work, okay? I paid him for your freedom."

Sage's brow knit as she struggled to understand. "But...but Master said—"

"He says a *lot* of things, and he's a liar. But I promise you this, Sage: he's never going to hurt you again. I'm not quite sure how yet, but I'm going to get you back to your real family."

I squeezed her little hands, which had warmed considerably, and she didn't flinch.

"Who are my real family?" Sage asked.

"Don't know yet. But you had to have come from somewhere, and you probably have a mom and dad out there. Or…you know, maybe two moms and a sperm donor, or two dads and a surrogate, or…look, there are possibilities," I said as Sage's confused expression deepened. "What I'm getting at is that you have genetic progenitors out there, and we need to find them. Figure out how you ended up with Warner in the first place."

"How do we do that?"

"*That*," I said with a sigh, "is a question for tomorrow morning. For tonight, we need to figure out what we're doing with you in terms of a bed."

"If you have some hay…" she began.

"Absolutely not. Here's the problem." Releasing her, I pointed down the connecting hallway toward the other end of the cabin. "This house has two bedrooms, but I've been using one as a glorified storage closet ever since I moved in. I'll fix it up for you, but that's also a project for tomorrow. Would you mind taking the couch tonight? It's pretty comfy, I swear." Having magically upgraded it, I could attest to that. "I've got plenty of extra blankets, and you'll be nice and warm—"

"You'll let me sit on the *couch*?" she asked in disbelief.

"As much as you want," I said. "We'll get you a real bed, but for tonight—"

"Master never let me sit on the couch."

"Because he's a monster. Here, come with me. We'll leave your blanket plugged in for now."

Sage carefully draped the electric blanket over the back of her chair and limped after me into the den. "Try it out,"

I said, gesturing toward the couch. "Tell me what you think."

She hesitated, her expression suggesting that she was wrestling with the idea of doing something naughty, and then she lowered herself onto the nearest cushion. Her eyes widened in surprise as she sank in, and she grinned at me. "It's squishy!"

"But not too squishy, I hope. I don't want you to wake up with back pain. How firm do you like your pillow?" I asked. "I've got a variety…"

"I…don't know. Master never gave me one."

Or cushions. Or a mattress.

If Warner had been in my house at that moment, he'd have crawled out a bloody mess, at *best*.

"Tell you what," I said, "I'll fix up the couch for you and bring in some pillows you can try out, and while I'm doing that, why don't you take a bath? Let's get some of that grime off of you, eh?"

She perked at the mention of a bath, but to my dismay, she pointed toward the kitchen door. "Is the washtub out there, ma'am?"

"Follow me."

Shuffling along, Sage waited in the hall until I flipped on the bathroom light, revealing the deep soaking tub, glass-walled shower with double heads and mood lighting, and dual white marble vanity counters. The bathroom had been my big magical splurge in my cabin renovation; drywall and paint I could handle, but removing the old avocado tile, rust-stained tub, and discolored laminate would have been beyond my skill set, even with online videos. The master bath was far too nice for the cabin, and I had no idea how I'd ever explain it to a realtor, should I opt to sell, but it was my space, and I told myself I deserved the occasional treat.

"Wow," Sage breathed behind me. "That's…*huge*."

"But not so big that we can't get it good and steamy," I replied, ushering her inside. "How about a soak first? I've got just the thing to make your skin feel soft."

She watched with interest as I plugged the tub and ran the hot water, then pulled one of my bath bombs from a plastic box beneath a sink and chucked it in. "Did Warner tell you that I make bath products and such?" I asked.

Sage nodded. "Yes, ma'am. He said you would probably make me work on those."

"Negative—and you're very polite, sweetie, but you don't have to call me 'ma'am.'" Though I'd been raised by a sorcerer with no ties to the region, I'd grown up southern enough to deploy my *ma'am*s and *sir*s as needed...and to cringe a little when someone younger than me deemed me old enough to merit deployment in turn. "Just 'Jane' is fine."

"I'm sorry—"

"Don't worry about it," I soothed, and smiled at her.

To my relief, Sage smiled back—a shy smile, to be sure, but it seemed genuine.

"So, the bath bomb I just dropped in has lavender to help you relax and shea butter to soothe your skin," I explained. "The fizzing is just baking soda and citric acid, nothing crazy. Do you like bubbles? I've got a lavender bubble bath, too."

She nibbled her lip. "I...I don't know..."

"Mm. Want to try?" I pulled the bottle from its spot beside the bomb box and let her look. As she turned it over in her hands, a little wrinkle formed between her eyebrows. Hoping I wouldn't upset her, I asked, "Can you read, Sage?"

"Some," she admitted. "Master taught me for a while, but he stopped years ago. I can sound things out," she offered, and pointed to the large type on the front label. "La...lav...laveen..."

"Lavender," I murmured, and patted her shoulder. "We can work on your reading, if you like. Maybe not *tonight*, though. Bath first."

She looked relieved when I took the bottle back and

squirted a healthy dollop into the tub. It foamed immediately, and Sage reached in to run her fingers through the bubbles as the bathroom began to fill with the floral scent.

"I'll give you your privacy," I said, putting the bubble bath away. "Shampoo and conditioner are right there on the ledge...uh, shampoo is pink and goes first, and follow that with the purple conditioner. The third bottle is body wash. Let me get you a washcloth and towel, and some sheets..."

As I rummaged through the linen closet, Sage asked, "What is, uh...sham..."

"Shampoo? Hair cleaner. Put some in your hand, then rub it all over your scalp and in your hair, and rinse. That plastic cup on the ledge is for rinsing, or sometimes I just hold my breath and go all the way under. If you prefer, you're welcome to hop in the shower after you soak."

"And, um..."

"Conditioner makes your hair softer and more manageable. Same procedure as with the shampoo." I turned around and considered her dark snarls. "You don't have naturally curly hair, do you?"

Sage shook her head. "I haven't brushed in a while."

"That's what I figured. Okay, here's a set for you," I said, putting her towel and washcloth beside the tub, then checked the water level and cut off the faucet. "That should be high enough, but add more if you want or if you get cold. I'll leave you to it, but before I go, could I ask you something silly?"

"Yes, ma'am?"

"Why on earth would Warner call you a demon?"

She regarded me bemusedly, as if I'd asked her a trick question. "Because I'm a demon?"

I folded my arms over the sheet set I'd chosen and leaned against the doorframe. "I'm not going to stand here and pretend to be an expert in the mysteries of the universe, but if demons exist, you are *absolutely* not one of them."

"But Master says that's what I am."

"And as I told you, Warner says a lot of things that aren't true. You seem like a sweet girl to me. Did he ever tell you *why* he thinks you're a demon?"

Again, Sage chewed her lip, and she stared at the floor as she spoke. "I...I've got a little power. It's been getting stronger."

I forced myself not to show alarm. "What sort of power?"

"Um..." She glanced up at the counter, and the hairbrush I'd left there that morning floated across the room to land in her hand. "Like that," she whispered.

Oh, this was *bad*. Warner had locked an untrained baby sorcerer in his barn.

"That's very impressive, sweetie," I said. "Who taught you to do that?"

She shrugged. "No one. It just happened one day and...you know?"

I did, actually, but I decided not to spring my own abilities on her just then. "Well, it's nothing to worry about tonight, and it certainly doesn't make you a demon. You enjoy your bath, hon."

I'd turned to go when Sage mumbled, "I'm not human."

True—not if she was a sorcerer—but that was no time for technicalities. "Why do you say that?" I asked.

Sage sat on the edge of the tub, her long denim skirt rising a few inches to reveal the black rubber of her oversized boots. She reached for her right foot, then hesitated, and I saw the fresh fear in her eyes.

"Sweetheart, you can tell me," I murmured. "I'm not going to be upset. Promise."

Even with my reassurances, it took her a few seconds longer to screw up her courage, and then she slowly eased her boot off.

For the record, I kept my promise. My eyebrows rose,

but I didn't freak out when I saw what the boot had been hiding.

Sage's feet were *hooves*—not goat hooves like a faun's, but rather equine hooves, and hers were in terrible shape. The one on display wasn't long enough to spiral, thank goodness, but it curved out and upward, explaining both her need for the big boots and her pronounced limp. Above the hoof, the little of her leg that I could see was thin and covered in black hair.

"Oh, you poor kid," I managed. "When did Warner last trim your hooves?"

"I don't know," she said softly, clutching her boot.

Considering their state, it could have been years. "We'll get them trimmed tomorrow, okay? That'll be our first stop. I don't want you in pain."

I started to leave again, but Sage said, "Jane?"

When I turned back, she was watching me, holding her boot like a teddy bear and tucking her denuded leg behind its mate. "You get clean, Sage, and let's put you to bed. We've got a big day ahead of us."

Leaving her to soak in peace, I tidied the kitchen, then made up the couch as well as I could with the oversized sheets. I plugged in the electric blanket and covered it with a light fleece, and I found a firm pillow and a softer one in my closet and put pillowcases on them both. And then, once I'd fussed and straightened all I could, I stopped and allowed the night's events to wash over me.

I'd bought a teenager who looked like a child. Warner had apparently kept her chained up in his barn. She had no real name, no family, and obviously no papers, and her education was surely minimal. The bit of magic she'd demonstrated was standard beginner fare—Baby's First Sorcery, as it were—but if Sage had sorcerer in her, that surely wasn't *all* she was.

Her feet were definitely horse hooves. I'd been around Dad's equine clients enough to recognize the shape, and I'd seen overgrown hooves on some of the rescues that wound up in his barn for trimming. If what I'd seen of her leg was any indication, her horse-like qualities didn't end at the ankle.

Half sorcerer, half *horse?*

There was one possibility. While I'd never met a centaur, Dad had told me that they lived in the Pactlands. Maybe Sage was a deformed centaur...

No, that didn't work. Centaurs weren't inherently magical creatures. Long-lived and naturally adept at growing plants, yes, and a few possessed preternatural skill as healers, but they couldn't cast or brew. What Sage had demonstrated was unmistakably the fumbling of a young sorcerer.

Which led to a somewhat disconcerting conclusion—

Nope. I'd had quite enough for one evening without ruminating on the potential weirdness in Sage's conception, *thank you.*

After about forty-five minutes, the bathroom door creaked open, and Sage emerged, once again dressed in her dirty clothes and shod but pinker and smelling of soap and flowers. "Feel better?" I asked.

"Yes, ma'am. Um..." She held up her washcloth and towel. "I didn't know where to put these..."

"Let me have them. We'll get you fresh ones in the morning," I said, and dumped them into the washer. "How's your hair?"

She turned around to show me, and the mats were cleaner but still tangled. "May I work on it for a bit? I've got a good detangler spray."

Sage settled in at the kitchen table, and though she whimpered on occasion, she let me pick apart her snarls. By the time I finished, I had a better idea of the damage. "Did Warner cut your hair?" I asked, trying to sound casual.

"No, ma'am. I did."

Ah. "Would you like me to even it out? I'm not a beautician, but—"

"Yes, please."

I draped a fresh dishtowel around her shoulders and started trimming. The bottom few inches of Sage's hair were split beyond salvaging, and with her permission, I trimmed her hair to just below her shoulders. Her new 'do wasn't fancy, but at least I could run a brush through it, and Sage beamed when I gave her a mirror. "There," I declared. "Now, I think it's time for you to get some sleep, and I'll sweep up in here. Do you want to borrow some pajamas?"

Sage rose and shook her head. "No, ma'am. Thank you. I...I don't think that's a good idea."

"Okay, no problem." If she wanted to sleep in something familiar, I wasn't going to take that away from her. "Let's see how the couch works for you."

She didn't want to take off her boots at first—she feared tearing the sheets, she explained—but I convinced her to swap the boots for a thick pair of fuzzy blue socks with grippers. With her hooves thus protected, she snuggled down, opting for the firmer pillow, and I turned up the electric blanket again to keep her warm. I put a glass of water on the coffee table for her, just in case, then plugged in an old night light. "I'm going to sweep the kitchen," I told her, "and then I'll be down the hall in my room. Come get me if you need *anything*, okay?"

"Just, um, one thing, Jane?"

"Sure, honey."

"Is there a bucket I could use?"

I frowned. "A bucket? For what?"

She started to stammer. "I, uh...I drank a lot, and, um..."

It hit me then what she was asking about, and my desire to give Warner an amateur nose job returned with renewed vigor. "Did Warner not let you use the bathroom inside?"

"No, ma'am."

"I see. Come here."

Sage pushed back her blankets and followed me down the hall, her hooves muffled by the non-skid socks. I pushed open the bathroom door again, briefly noted the dark ring around the tub—I'd fix that before going to bed—then showed Sage to the toilet behind the inner door. "Don't take this the wrong way, but do you know how this works?"

"Yes. Master made me clean his."

"Well, I'll handle the cleaning. Use this one or the little one off the den."

Giving Sage some privacy, I swept up the leavings of her haircut, then noticed the short white flames dancing up and down my arms as I dumped the dustpan into the trash. With a few deep breaths, I forced the fire to die, and I was back to normal when Sage returned. "Thank you, Jane," she murmured, and smiled at me before heading to bed.

I tucked her in and smoothed her damp hair from her forehead. "Things will be better tomorrow," I whispered, and set off to clean the filthy tub.

I had to do something, I mused, as I scrubbed away the dirt Sage's bathwater had left behind. *Many* somethings. A long list was growing at the back of my mind, though the physical work of the cleaning was at least giving my anger an outlet.

But the first stop, without question, would be Dad.

CHAPTER 4

I awoke Saturday morning, not to sunlight in my face—Friday's cloud cover was forecast to linger through the weekend—but rather to the smell of bacon. Confused and still half asleep, I bolted upright in bed, momentarily convinced I'd been visited by a burglar intent on ransacking the fridge, then remembered my new houseguest and threw on my bathrobe to investigate.

I found her in the kitchen, tending a skillet. "Hey, Sage," I said through a yawn, "what are you doing?"

She cringed, shrinking back from me with the spatula in hand, and I hastened to reassure her. "No, it's okay, you're not in trouble. Really," I insisted, and her shoulders loosened.

"Just thought I'd get started on breakfast, ma'am," she mumbled.

"That's awfully nice of you, and if you're hungry, you're welcome to eat, but you don't need to be cooking breakfast. That's my job…unless you're just dying to whip something up, I mean. I'm not trying to police the kitchen…" As she stood there uncertainly by the sizzling pan, I said, "Why don't I finish this? Do you think you could set the table? Plates are in that cabinet by the sink."

She nodded and relinquished her spatula, and I chided myself. The kid was far too jumpy, and since her instinct at the first hint of possible criticism was to cower, I suspected I knew how Warner had kept her in line. I hadn't asked her about the old bruises on her bare arms the night before, but frankly, I didn't think I needed to.

While Sage rooted through the silverware drawer, I turned my attention to the food: two fried eggs and two strips of bacon. The whole-wheat loaf was sitting on the counter, so I assumed she'd planned to make toast, but the quantity of food raised my suspicions, and when I turned to see that she'd put only one plate on the table, by the chair I'd used the previous night, my heart clenched.

"You know," I said, trying to be careful with my words, "this is a really good beginning, and it smells *great*, but I'm thinking we could use a few more eggs and maybe the rest of that bacon pack. It's getting close to its expiration date, anyway."

Sage froze, a single set of silverware clutched in her fist. "I'm sorry, I didn't know how much you liked to eat, and I didn't want to waste food—"

"And that's very responsible of you, but from now on, we're cooking for two, okay?" Sage's brow scrunched, and I asked, "What did Warner normally feed you?"

"Toast, sometimes," she said, eyeing the loaf. "Leftovers."

"Real leftovers or scraps?"

"He let me finish the leftovers on his plate," she explained.

"Those are scraps, and that's absolutely not enough for a growing girl," I said. Hell, that wasn't enough for the average lapdog. "You're getting real meals from now on. At least three a day, maybe more until I see some meat on those bones."

Her eyes brightened. "Really?"

From the tone of her voice, I might have just suggested a Disney vacation instead of bacon and eggs. "Promise. Get yourself a plate, too, and I'll fix the rest."

I doubled the eggs and finished off the bacon—maybe a little much for two people, but it was good for the soul—while I made toast. I caught myself before I could float the kettle across the room to fill up at the sink, my usual bit of morning laziness, and did it myself, grabbing a couple mugs, a teabag, and another packet of hot chocolate mix. Sure, sugar and cocoa wasn't exactly *nutritious*, but if Sage liked it, that was good enough for me.

She was standing by the table when I brought over the platter of food, and I told her to have a seat and dig in while I got the drinks and condiments. When I returned, she'd helped herself to a single egg and a piece of toast, and I shook my head. "Nope. That's not fair. Do you like bacon?"

"Yes, ma'am."

"Good, because my arteries don't need all of this," I said, sliding four pieces and another egg onto her plate. "Dig in, honey."

And she did. For a skinny little kid, she could tuck it away, and she cleaned every crumb and streak of yolk from her plate. I pushed the leftover bacon on her and most of the toast, and she inhaled whatever I put in front of her. "It's not going to run away from you," I said as she looked up at me, cheeks bulging with bread. "You can take your time, Sage. There's no rush."

She nodded but kept up her rapid eating, and I wondered whether that was the result of hunger or of Warner's training.

Once the last of the food had vanished and my tea had taken effect, I said, "So, let's talk about the plan for today."

"What would you like me to do?"

"Nothing. You're coming with me."

She stiffened in her chair, then pointed toward the front windows, which had begun to lighten with the gray morning. "Out *there?*"

"Yes…" I began, then realized the problem—and it wasn't her feet. "Did Warner never take you anywhere?"

Sage shook her head. "Not until yesterday."

That the child had spent her entire life on the Cavanaugh farm was more fuel for my anger, but I pushed down the flames before they could ignite. "Will you give me your hand?" I asked. Hesitantly, she put hers in mine, and I squeezed it lightly as I held her stare. "I'm not going to let anything bad happen to you," I murmured. "If it's too much and you get scared and want to come back here, that's fine. You just have to tell me. Deal?"

She cracked a little smile. "Deal."

"Good." Releasing her, I said, "I thought we'd start at my dad's house. He's only a few miles away, not too far," I reassured her. "Dad's had training as a farrier…uh, someone who knows how to work with hooves," I explained, seeing her blank look. "He normally works with horses, but I bet he could trim yours, make it easier for you to walk. Would that be okay?"

She'd perked at the idea of a trim, but her expression rapidly clouded. "What would he say if you brought a demon to him?"

"Honey—"

"That's why Master never let me leave. Because people would be upset if they saw a demon…"

"Sage, sweetie," I said, cupping one hand against her cheek, "you are *not* a demon. Maybe a little different, sure, but then so am I."

"Master said you're a…a warlock, too, right?"

"*No*, and I'll let you in on a little secret," I said, sitting back in my chair. "Warner doesn't have the first drop of magical ability."

Sage looked stunned. "But he…he says he can curse people, make them hurt—"

"He's full of shit, and I'd tell him as much to his face. *You* have real talent. He's a poseur in a stupid coat. Trust me," I told her, "you're not a demon, and my dad isn't going to be upset."

Well, I mentally amended, he wouldn't be upset once I filled him in. At least not with me.

I took Sage back to the bathroom and pulled a spare toothbrush from my collection of dentist goody bags. Fortunately, it wasn't her first encounter with such a device—Warner had made her brush her teeth, at least, even if he'd never given her proper dental care—and while her smile was crooked and stained, her teeth didn't seem to be rotten. Leaving her with a hairbrush and a fresh washcloth and towel, I took my phone and slipped out the back door to call Dad.

Stepping onto the patio, I leaned against the wooden cabin and dialed. My eyes landed on the discarded collar and chain, now damp from their night outdoors, and I made a note to chuck them in the bear-proof garbage can before Sage noticed.

The phone rang three times before Dad answered. "Hi, Janie," he said cautiously. "You're up early."

"Morning, Daddy—"

"Uh-oh."

I sighed. "Is it that obvious?"

"I know you, girlie. What's wrong?"

"Are you busy?" I asked.

"I mean, I'm brewing, but it's nothing that can't be left alone for a bit if I need to come pay your bail."

Though I'd never had occasion to ask Dad to spring me from custody, it was nice to know he had my back. "Nothing so dire. I need a farrier."

Dad paused. "Janie, sweetheart, please don't tell me you just bought a horse."

"Heck, no. Where would I keep one? But I did, uh...kind of buy a kid last night," I said in a rush, "and she—"

"Whoa. You *what?*"

"Short version, there's a child in my house right now who's almost certainly part sorcerer, and I think there may be some centaur in the mix. She *badly* needs a hoof trim."

"O...kay," Dad murmured, taking that in. "Tell me more."

Quickly, I recapped the events of the previous night: Warner, Sage, the collar, her enormous appetite, her filthy condition, and finally, her hooves. "I don't know how far up the equine bits go," I explained, "because I only saw to about mid-shin, if that. But her hooves are in bad shape, and she's limping. If I brought her by—"

"Of course," he replied. "Bring her as soon as you can. It's just me and the potions here today. Can she sit normally?"

"What do you mean?"

"Like, in a chair. How do her legs bend?"

I hadn't even thought of that. "Uh...she can sit. I guess she's got standard knees..."

"I ask because sitting is unnatural for horses—the anatomy of the rear legs complicates the process. Centaurs have the same issue, which is why well-equipped meeting spaces keep mats for them."

"Well, I haven't seen much of her legs, and I'm not pushing her right now," I said. "The kid's been through hell, and Warner's told her she's a demon, so she..." I paused, watching Sage cringe in my mind's eye. "She's going to need a gentle touch."

"Absolutely. You just get her here, Janie. I'll be waiting."

I hung up from Dad and hastily carried the collar and chain to the outdoor bin, then returned to the house to find Sage with her teeth and hair brushed, her face still damp from the sink. "Ready to go?" I asked. "Two seconds, let me put on some real pants."

Once I was dressed, I wrapped her in a spare fleece jacket—it swamped her, but at least her arms were covered against the cold—then led her out to my truck. "Hop in. Dad's expecting us...oh, no, sweetie," I said as Sage headed for the tailgate. "No, why don't you ride in the cab with me? Much nicer."

I opened her door, and she hoisted herself inside. Once I was situated behind the wheel, I showed her the seatbelt and helped her adjust it. Her clunky boots dangled slightly above the floormat, and as she gripped the door, I wondered whether she was more afraid of the journey or the destination. From what little I'd gathered, this was only her second ride in a vehicle.

"Don't be scared," I said, reaching over to pat her knee. "I'm a good driver, I promise."

Sage smiled tensely, and I flipped the radio on, as my truck wasn't fancy enough for Bluetooth. She gasped at the first riff from the classic rock station, then stared at the controls, her eyes lit with delight.

"You like that?" I asked. "If there's a station you prefer—"

"No, ma'am, this is great," she assured me. "Sorry, I didn't...I didn't know..."

"Sit back and relax. I'm guessing you've never had a look around Ragged Gap, huh?"

"What's Ragged Gap?"

"My town. Warner lives over near Whitford, It's pretty hilly around here, and the best of the leaves is past, but...you know, it's kind of atmospheric with the fog," I said, shifting into drive. "Slightly spooky. I don't mind it."

Sage tensed again as the truck started moving, but by the time I reached the bottom of the mountain, her death grip on the door had begun to relax. "Dad's not too far away," I said, hoping to distract her. "He's got property without close neighbors, so we'll have plenty of privacy. And he'll know how to help your feet."

"You think so?"

"He trained as a farrier long before I was born." As he'd explained it, he'd thought it a good and useful thing to know how to care for horses, and so he'd worked with a farrier on the side when he was a young man...back in about 1905, when it was still a highly practical skill set. That had led to lessons with a blacksmith, and now, in his middle age, he was well seasoned in both areas. Then again, since Dad had better than a century and a half under his belt, he'd had plenty of time to practice.

Soon enough, we pulled up to my childhood home, and I spotted Dad waiting in a rocker on the porch, wearing his potion-stained jeans and a wash-faded UGA sweatshirt. I hopped out and waved, then went around to help free Sage, who slid to the ground and hugged herself. Wrapping my arm around her shoulders, I led her to Dad, who smiled and put his travel mug of what was surely strong coffee on the ground. "Morning, girls," he said, pushing himself from the chair. "I understand someone needs a pedicure."

Sage slunk closer to me, and I tightened my grip on her. "That's right. Maybe not toenail polish today, but…"

"Oh, I don't know, Janie, you've probably left a dried-out bottle around here *somewhere*," he teased, then cocked his head toward the barn behind the house. "Shall we?"

As Sage and I followed him, I asked, "Do you need me to, uh…babysit anything?"

"It'll keep. I was thinking that you could hang out with us and maybe give me a hand."

Sage seemed to brighten with the realization that I wasn't going to leave her alone with Dad, and I made a note to thank him.

Dad led us into the drafty barn and pointed to a metal folding chair. "Sorry, this isn't exactly luxurious. You see fancy spa pedicures on TV with the soaking tubs and the flower petals and whatnot, and…well, I've got what you see. You want fancy foot soaks, go raid Janie's workshop," he added to Sage in a stage whisper, and she grinned to be in on the blatant conspiracy. "Now, little lady, why don't you have a seat right there and shuck off those boots? I'll get my tools."

She sat and looked to me, and I nodded reassurance.

When Dad returned, bucket of nippers and picks in hand, he took one look at Sage's hooves and whistled low. "My goodness, kid, those are some *very* overgrown toenails. No wonder you've got such big boots."

"Master says they're hooves, sir," she mumbled as Dad pulled up a short stool.

"Well, yes, they are, but hooves and nails are both

made of keratin," he said, and patted his knee. "Could you pop one of your feet up here, sweetie?" Hesitantly, she did as he asked, and Dad nodded. "It's Sage, right?"

"Yes, sir," she whispered.

"And I'm Yacovi. You can call me Coby if it's easier—folks around here do. Now, let's have a look…" As he gently rotated her hoof back and forth and examined the bottom, he said, "You know, physically, hooves like these are fascinating. You're basically carrying your weight on a single toe, did you know that?"

Dad kept up a conversation while he worked, doing most of the heavy lifting at first until Sage began to acclimate. He explained the names and uses of his various tools and stopped at points to talk to her about the anatomy of her hooves and how to care for them…and to my relief, he didn't say a peep about her hair-covered legs. Once he'd clipped the worst of the overgrowth away, he had Sage stand up and walk around as he fine-tuned the trim, and by the end, her limp had almost entirely vanished.

"You, my dear, are going to need some smaller boots," he teased, and thumbed one hand toward the house. "Want to go inside for a minute? I need to have a quick word with Janie, and since you've been *so* patient with me, how would you feel about a bowl of ice cream while the grownups chat?"

That suggestion met with Sage's immediate approval, and Dad doctored up a generous serving of vanilla with sprinkles and chocolate sauce for her. As Sage scarfed it down, he and I stepped into his hidden brew room, and he closed the door behind us.

"Wow." Dad muttered, switching to Pactish for additional privacy. "Poor little thing."

"I told you her hooves were in bad shape."

"You didn't mention that she's skin and bones." He leaned against the lab bench, behind which three vats of a sickly-sweet-smelling liquid simmered atop their heaters on the floor. "Thirteen, you said?"

"That's what Sage told me."

"I wouldn't have guessed she's ten. *Feed* her, now, and I bet you'll be looking at a massive growth spurt. But with a delay like that…"

"Do you think she's okay?" I asked. "Mentally? I know, right, first impression, and she's shy, but from what I've seen…" I trailed off, hoping for reassurance.

To my relief, Dad nodded. "Layman's opinion, of course, but she seems sharp enough to me. Sweet kid. I'm sure she's overwhelmed. But first things first, let's talk about her hooves."

"Damaged?"

"Surprisingly, no. She seems sound, and what I could feel of her feet didn't set off any alarms. She doesn't appear to be limping anymore, but if that changes, or if she has any discomfort, call me." Scowling, he asked, "How the hell do you let hooves get that overgrown? I see it in rescues sometimes, but I still don't get it, and that's with horses. How do you let a *child* get to the point that she's hobbling for want of a trim?"

"Ever met Warner Cavanaugh?" I countered.

"Wouldn't know him if I saw him, but from now on, he has a punchable face," he muttered. "What do you know about Sage's background?"

I grimaced. "Little. She doesn't remember anything before Warner, and the bullshit story he told me had her coming to him as a gift from his *patrons*," I said, wiggling my hands sarcastically. "Whatever dark gods or demons or boogeymen he claims to work for…which *is* all bullshit, right?" I asked, suddenly unsure.

Dad grunted. "Never yet met a pure human with actual talent, and I can almost guarantee you that this kid won't change my mind."

"He's not a kid, Dad. He's, like, in his thirties."

He waved off my protestation. To my father, anyone under about fifty was still practically college-age.

"Whatever. What I'm more concerned about is how he really got his hands on Sage, and *when*. If she doesn't remember a family before him, then he may have found her as a baby, for all we know."

"She has no memory of parents," I said. "Didn't think she had any. Since Warner told her she was sent up from Hell…"

Dad softly swore. "Her parents may be a…*complicated* issue."

"Do you think I'm right about her? Part centaur, part sorcerer?"

"Yeah, that would be my guess. If I'm right, I'd expect a half-and-half presentation. Think a faun with horse legs. I've seen it before," he explained, absently rubbing a knot in his shoulder. "Guy I worked with in the greenhouse for a while. Sorcerer mother, centaur father."

"How was he?"

"Oh, nice enough. Competent. He could cast with middling ability, I'd say—not a great talent, but respectable. Had to have his pants custom-made, but he laughed that off. I don't think he had any major health problems, just the obvious physical issues. I mean, take the lower half of a centaur and compress it into a single pair of legs…"

From what Dad had told me, centaurs, like fauns and nagas, typically wore nothing over their lower halves. I could imagine where a guy with equine…*attributes*…on a more hominid framework could run into complications if he opted to leave the house in just a shirt.

"But crosses like him, and like Sage probably is, don't happen often," Dad continued, "and when you see one, it's usually evidence of a crime."

My guts churned. "What do you mean?"

"Well…centaurs typically find partners within their species. *Occasionally*, you'll find one in a mixed couple, but it's rare. To put it delicately, intimacy can cause issues, you understand. Same reason you don't see a lot of trolls coupling up with gnomes, yeah?"

The latter was more like pairing off a mastiff and a chihuahua, but I didn't need elaboration.

"A sorcerer and a centaur can produce viable offspring—*fertile* offspring, oddly enough—but that's just not a combination you see every day on the street," said Dad. "Usually, when a cross like that occurs, he wasn't consensually made. My colleague seldom talked about his family, but I know his mother was a sorcerer, and his father was in custody."

He didn't have to spell out the problem for me: Sage, who'd just begun to accept that she might have parents out there, might not like what she found if she went searching.

"What are your plans for Sage?" Dad asked. "One way or another, Laws needs to know."

"I agree, but does Laws need to find out today?"

He frowned. "She may have been kidnapped…"

"Or she may have been abandoned, or any number of things, but…look, I've had her less than twenty-four hours," I said, "and just being in my house has to be a massive change for her. Remember that part about Warner keeping her chained in the barn?"

"I did notice the scars on her neck," he said softly.

"Yeah. So, can't we give her a little time to breathe before dragging DOL into this? Especially if their investigation might add to her trauma."

One of the potions began to boil behind us, interrupting our conversation. Dad wheeled around to investigate, then relaxed as the heat automatically dropped and the surface of the liquid calmed. "Kid's going to need a therapist."

"Sure," I said, "but let's prioritize food and sleep while she transitions. From what I've gathered, she's had zero autonomy all her life. Let me keep her for a few weeks, help her acclimate to a world without Warner beating her, and *then*, when she's ready, we'll call Liogh. Okay?"

"Okay," he replied after a moment, though he didn't

seem altogether sold on the plan. "I'm sending you home with some healing potions for her."

Even for a brewer, those weren't cheap. "Sage doesn't seem to be in pain—"

"For the scarring. She may be hiding bruises, too."

"She's got some old ones," I admitted. "On her arms. I don't know about the rest of her…"

"So, dose her for the next few days. Have her drink it instead of dabbing it on, unless you find open wounds— treat those first." Pushing himself off his lab bench, he said, "Another thing. Can she mask?"

I made a face. "Kind of doubt it. Everything she knows is self-taught, and I haven't even broached the concept of masking with her. Haven't mentioned that I'm a sorcerer yet, either…"

He grunted. "Slipped your mind, girlie?"

"Trying not to dole out all the shocks at once. I could mask her until she gets the hang of doing it herself," I suggested. "The jewelry I've made should be sufficient. But…"

"But?" he prompted.

"You were never a teenage girl. She's grown up thinking she's demonic, she told me that Warner didn't like to see her body, and now I'm supposed to help her cover everything up? I don't want to give her another complex."

"And having been the father of a teenage girl, I do appreciate that, but it's not safe to let a half centaur wander around Ragged Gap," Dad countered. "Suggest it, eh? See how she takes it." Nodding toward the kitchen, he asked, "Think she's polished off that ice cream?"

"She's inhaled her food to this point, so…"

He headed for the door. "Well, then, I'm sure I've got some extra bags of chips you could have for the road."

Sage thanked Dad profusely, and he saw us out to my truck. As she buckled in and Dad slipped off to babysit his brew, I said, "Now that we've got your feet in good order, we have two options."

"What are they?" she asked, anxiety in her eyes.

"Nothing bad. We can go back to the house and hang out, or if you want, we can go for a drive. Since Warner didn't take you anywhere, I thought you might want to see more of the area," I explained. "But that's up to you. If the truck makes you nervous, or if this is all too much—"

"I think I might like a drive. If that's okay," she hastily added.

I grinned and patted her knee. "Wouldn't have suggested it if it weren't. Get comfy," I said, and flipped on the radio. "How about we start with Ragged Gap, and if we're out long enough, we could pick up burgers for lunch. Would that be good?"

"*Really?*"

"Play your cards right," I said with mock solemnity, "and I'll throw in milkshakes."

For the rest of the morning, we drove around town and out to the neighboring areas. I avoided Whitford—the last thing I wanted was for Sage to think I might be taking her back to Warner—but I cruised through Blairsville and Blue Ridge and Ellijay, varying my route between the necessary arteries and the more scenic roads. We drove by apple orchards and wineries, all of which were past their peak and somewhat dreary with the leaden skies, but Sage kept her nose to the window, drinking it all in as if I'd taken her to some exotic wonderland. She sounded out the shorter signs we passed, and as she started to relax, she began asking me questions...which gradually turned into a firehose of enquiries. The child knew *nothing*—she had only the vaguest of ideas what it meant when I said she lived in Georgia, and I had a devil of a time trying to convey to her the relative locations of the states named on the tourist license plates that zoomed past us—but she seemed eager, almost desperate to learn, and so I drove and talked until my throat was too parched to withstand the temptation of a cold Coke.

Since Sage was only a careless flip of the skirt away from revealing her secret, I opted to get our lunch via drive-thru. While I wanted her to pick her own meal, her questionable literacy complicated matters, so I rattled off a few options and ended up buying us both quarter-pounders, fries, and chocolate shakes. When I presented her with an entire paper bag of food, she looked like an awestruck kid on Christmas morning.

I forced down my rage at Warner with a handful of fries, reminding myself that open flames weren't a great thing to unleash around a gasoline-powered vehicle.

By the time we made it home, Sage was flagging, the last melted dregs of the milkshakes were long gone, and I had work to do. "How about a nap?" I suggested, shepherding Sage through the front door. "This is prime napping weather. We should have rain before dinner."

She cut her eyes to the couch, which she'd tried to tidy that morning, then back to me. "Is there not something I can do for you?"

"Not right now. Appreciate it," I said, "but I've got to go through my crap and figure out what moves where, and you've had a big day. Take it easy," I suggested. "Turn on the TV, if you like. I'll just be digging through boxes in the spare room."

Sage tugged off her boots and burrowed down beneath the electric blanket. When I returned from the back fifteen minutes later with the first load of cartons to move out to my workshop, she was sound asleep. One of her feet had slipped out from beneath the covers, and the hoof twitched as she ran in a dream.

CHAPTER 5

I was, admittedly, a mediocre cook, able to follow box directions without burning the house down but uncomfortable trying to freestyle without a recipe. Still, I could competently whip up chicken breasts and pre-made mashed potatoes, and if Sage didn't care for it, I couldn't tell. She ate every bite put in front of her, then the second helping I offered, and finished dinner with a satisfied groan.

As I pulled out the slightly freezer-burned ice cream sandwiches from their hiding place—it really was past time to go grocery shopping—I said, "We need to have a little talk."

Sage immediately stiffened to attention. "I'm sorry—"

"Honey, you've done nothing wrong," I insisted. "This isn't a bad talk. I'm just putting my cards on the table, as it were." She regarded me blankly, and I amended, "Coming clean with you. There's something you need to know."

I returned to the table with dessert, and she unwrapped the top of hers and took a bite before I could think better of giving her old ice cream. "So...Warner claimed that he had magical power, right? That's what he told you?"

Sage nodded and swallowed hard. "He said that if I didn't obey and beatings weren't enough, he had...other ways," she mumbled.

I gripped her free hand. "And I swear to you that he's full of shit. Warner has no power—he's a mean man, but he can't curse you, or whatever he threatened. He plays dress-up and tells people he's a warlock, but I don't believe it for a second."

"You're sure?" she asked, her green eyes wide with worry.

"Positive," I said, and leaned toward her. "Because *I* am the real deal. Not a warlock," I hastily added as Sage froze. "There's no such thing. I'm a sorcerer. Partly. For practical purposes…"

"I, uh.. I'm sorry, I don't know what that means."

"That's okay." Releasing her, I sat back and started on my dessert "Sorcerers look human, but they're not. They live longer—about three hundred years, give or take—and they can do interesting things with magic. Like this," I said, and muttered under my breath until the freezer door opened and the rest of the box of ice cream sandwiches flew to the table.

Sage's face lit up. "You can do that, too?"

"Give it a try."

Abandoning her food, she stared at the fridge for a moment, her forehead scrunched in concentration, until the door cracked open. "Sorry," she said, rubbing her temples, "I'm not very good at it—"

"But you've got the talent, hon. I mean, it's a baby talent, but it'll grow."

"You think so?"

"Sure. I went through the same thing, only I had Dad to teach me what to do. He's a sorcerer, too," I explained. "Let's get you settled in, and then I'll dig out my old wand and work with you on your focus."

"So, then I'll be able to—"

"Eventually," I cautioned. "You've got a ways to go. But there's no reason that you can't learn. Here's the thing," I said as she returned to her melting sandwich, "Dad and I had a chat, and we both think you're part sorcerer. That's actually what I am—my father was human. Not Dad," I clarified, "my biological father. He died when I was a few weeks old, my mom dumped me with Dad and ran, and Dad raised me."

She paused, ice cream halfway to her mouth. "Why would your mom dump you?"

The best answer I could give her was a shrug, since I *really* didn't want to get into Pactlands politics and the ramifications of the death draught that night. "She didn't say, and I've never spoken to her. It's complicated, but...you know, she'd just had a baby, and her husband was murdered, and she was suddenly broke and on her own. Probably got to be too much for her. Maybe she didn't know how to be a mom, and she didn't have anyone to help her. But she managed to pick a great dad for me," I said, "and he wants to help you."

"With magic?"

"More than that. We want to help you find your parents, wherever they are."

Sage perked briefly, but her excitement faded almost as quickly as it had bloomed. "What if they don't want to be found? Like...maybe they dumped me, too."

"That's a possibility," I allowed. "I'm not going to lie to you and tell you it's not. But it's far from the only possibility. Could be you were kidnapped. Maybe they didn't have a choice. In any case, you shouldn't have been left here, and we want to figure out where you came from. But if it's all right with you, we want to wait a little while before starting that process. You've had one hell of a time with Warner, and you need a chance to start recovering. Rest, heal...eat."

"That sounds nice," she said with a grin.

"And you could stay here with me, if you want."

Sage's smile widened as she fervently nodded.

"Perfect. Room for another?" I asked, offering her the ice cream box. She pulled a second sandwich free, and I sent the rest back to the freezer. "So, you eat up, and Dad sent some healing potions to help with your bruises and such—"

"*Potions?*"

"Real potions. He's a brewer, so he knows how to

make them work. And, uh…there's one other thing."

"My chores?" Sage guessed.

"Baby, you can help out if you want, but this is *recovery* time," I said, holding her gaze. "You worry about yourself for now and let me handle the housekeeping. No, I…" I hesitated, hoping I could find the right words, then said, "I want you to know that there's nothing wrong with you, okay? Your body is a little different, but it's not *bad* or evil."

She nibbled her lip as she unwrapped the ice cream. "Can you tell me why I have hooves, then?"

"I can't give you firm answers, but Dad and I think that the parent of yours who wasn't a sorcerer may have been, uh…a centaur."

Her head tilted. "What's that?"

"*Ah*. Just a second…" I plucked my phone off the counter and called up an illustration from a page on Greek mythology. "This."

Eyes bugging, Sage stared at the screen. "Whoa. He's, like…"

"Kind of horsy from the waist down. Humans think they don't exist because the last of them fled into…well, this other place a few hundred years ago. The Pactlands. I'll explain later," I told her, fearful of dropping too much on her at once. "*I've* never met one, but Dad has. He also knows someone who had a centaur and a sorcerer for parents, and that guy seems to be built a lot like you are."

I paused, letting Sage absorb that, then said, "I'm not trying to make you ashamed of your body or anything. *Please* know that I'm not. But with that said…one of the things we can do as sorcerers is mask. Do you know what I'm talking about?"

"No, ma'am…"

I closed my eyes and concentrated briefly, calling upon one of the minor alterations I'd used on occasion in college, and heard Sage gasp as the mask coalesced. "Like that," I said, flipping my hair—formerly blonde, now bright purple—over my shoulder. "Much easier than box dye, let me tell you. Anyway, that's a little mask," I said, allowing it to fall apart, "but we can make much bigger ones. Change our faces and more."

"*I* can do that?" Sage asked incredulously.

"In time. For now, though...if someone can't mask and needs to, the alternative is masking jewelry. It's usually a necklace or a ring. I can't make rings—nothing you'd want to wear—but I can make decent pendants. If you're interested."

Her brow knit with concern. "You think I need to hide from Master? Change my face?"

"No, and not your face. I was, uh...I was thinking about your feet."

To my great relief, Sage's face broke into a wide smile. "Can you make them normal?"

"I can make them look like human feet. It's not permanent," I cautioned, "but as long as you're masked, no one will be able to tell. Now, I am *not* suggesting this because I want you to cover up. This is purely for blending in. But if you don't want to—"

"I *want* it, Jane," she insisted, her eyes misting. "*Please.* If I could just look like everyone else..."

I stood and pulled her into a hug. "Don't you cry, sweetheart. I'll work on it tonight. Okay?"

When she pulled away, her face was damp, but she was smiling once more. "Thank you."

"Of course. Better finish your ice cream before it melts."

As Sage returned to her second dessert, I said, "There are two ways to go about masking jewelry. If you know what you're doing and you're comfortable with your piece, you can sort of freestyle your mask each time. If you're newer to masking or like to have one appearance, however, you can 'preset' a mask, if you will. I think that would be easier for you. All you would need to do would be to trigger it, and you wouldn't have to think about the rest."

"That sounds great," she replied around a bite. "You really don't mind?"

"Not at all. But there's one more consideration."

Sage swallowed and put the paper aside. "Yes, ma'am?"

"If I'm going to build this mask properly, I need to know what I'm working with underneath. How much I need to cover. I want to keep this as minimal as possible—you're very pretty, and there's no need to do a full-body mask."

She smiled at that, seemingly surprised, but then I supposed that Warner wasn't one to pass compliments.

"I know this is a weird request," I continued, "but will you let me see your body? Not the private bits," I quickly clarified, "but, say, your legs…"

Before I could finish, Sage had removed her gripper socks and was rising, her hands going to the drawstring waist of her long skirt.

"Let's do this in the bathroom," I said, mindful of the windows at the front of the house. My concern was probably nothing more than unnecessary paranoia, given the quiet of my street, but still, I followed Sage back to the privacy of the master bath and closed the door.

She hesitated only for a second before she untied the drawstring and let her skirt fall. "So…uh…is it too bad?" she mumbled.

As Dad and I had expected, she was centaur-esque in build below the navel, as if someone had removed the front legs of a horse and grafted them onto a little girl's torso. Her legs seemed passably equine—thin and knobby, and covered with a short, dark coat of hair—but her pelvic area was oddly formed, the result of taking a quadrupedal blueprint and compressing it. She had wrapped graying strips of old cloth around herself for modesty, and when she turned, I saw why standard underwear wouldn't work for her: a thin tail, its hair shorn to about an inch all over.

"No, it's not bad at all," I told her. "Um…if I may ask,

what happened to your tail?"

Glancing over her shoulder as she flicked it, she replied, "It gets matted, so Master makes me keep it short."

"Do you prefer it like that?"

"I...don't know," she admitted. "It's always like that."

"You're welcome to grow it out. I think it'd be nice," I said. "But that's your call. Would you give me a slow twirl, please?"

Sage acquiesced, and as she pivoted away from me, I asked, "Could you raise the bottom of your shirt up a little? I'm trying to see where the transition point occurs."

"Yes, ma'am." She hiked her T-shirt halfway to her armpits, and I saw a short, fuzzy stripe of dark hair rising up her spine—a mane.

"That's great, Sage. Thank you." As she reached for her skirt, I suggested, "Why don't you get a bath and sleep? I know you had a nap, but something tells me you could use the rest."

She frowned. "But I bathed last night."

"I know. Baths are kind of a daily thing around here. Is that all right?"

It turned out that she had no problem with cleanliness, but rather was concerned that I'd notice the waste of water and become upset. Warner had filled a metal washtub for her about once a week, so the chance to soak in a warm bath for two nights in a row was an unimagined luxury.

I rummaged through my drawers and grabbed a pair of scissors and my sewing kit while Sage was busy, and when I heard the drain begin to gurgle, I knocked on the bathroom door. "Sweetie? Can I come in?"

"Um...yes, ma'am," she called.

I poked my head through the door to find her wrapped in a bath sheet. "Sorry to interrupt. I was wondering if you'd let me wash your clothes before we go out tomorrow. Brought you some pajamas," I offered, holding out the clean and only slightly wrinkled alternative. "The pants are going to be big on you, but if you roll the waist, I think they'll do for tonight."

I'd found one of my freshman UGA T-shirts and a pair of plaid flannel pants, which now sported a long hole in the back that I hoped would accommodate Sage's tail. "I don't have any underwear that'll fit you, but if you'd like me to toss your clothes in the washer…"

As a decently trained sorcerer, I *could* use magic to get the grime and stench out, but frankly, when it came to laundry, I trusted Tide Pods over my casting.

Now that I'd learned her darkest secret, Sage wasn't nearly so attached to her leg-hiding skirt, and she gladly handed over her lone outfit. I left her to dry off—not the simplest of tasks with that much hair, which was why I'd given her the biggest towel I could find—and once I'd started the load of clothes, I heard her hooves clopping on the floor and turned to find her smiling in the kitchen, slightly swimming in my shirt and holding up her grossly oversized pants. "I think they're a little big," she said.

I tried to stifle my laughter and ended up snorting, which set Sage off, and she carefully followed me to the couch as I apologized for the state of her borrowed pajamas. "Tomorrow, I *promise* you, we'll go shopping," I said as I tucked her in. "I'm going to work on your pendant in the kitchen. Do you want me to turn the TV on?"

"Would it be okay if I go to sleep?"

"Absolutely, hon. Yell if you need me," I added, and retreated to the next room to start a pot of coffee. Sure, I could make masking jewelry, but programming it as well meant I was staring down the barrel of an all-nighter.

"Thank you, Jane," Sage called from the den.

"No sweat," I fibbed, and filled the carafe.

Through force of long habit, Sage was an early riser, and she caught me napping with my head on the placemat before dawn Sunday morning. "Jane?" she whispered, cautiously nudging my shoulder. "Are you okay?"

I groaned, sat up, and rubbed my neck. "Hey, there. What time is it?" I mumbled, tasting the ghost of old coffee.

She glanced around the kitchen for the answer. "About seven-thirty, ma'am."

"Really?" Waking my phone, I saw the discrepancy and grunted. "Closer to six-thirty. The Daylight Saving shift happened overnight. Do you need something?"

Sage retreated a pace from the table. "I...I thought you might be hungry, and I'm awake, so..."

"Don't worry about it. Sit down," I said, pulling out the chair I was beginning to think of as hers, and rose. "Is oatmeal okay?"

"Yes, ma'am."

"You're sure? If you don't like it, just tell me. I could make muffins."

"I'm not too picky."

My morning fog lifted enough then for me to realize the stupidity of what I'd just asked, and I patted her shoulder as she sat. "Oatmeal, then, because it'll stick to your ribs, but for future reference, please tell me if there are foods you hate. I don't want you going hungry."

As I dug out a pot and the Quaker cannister, Sage asked, "Is this the masking pendant?"

I turned, and she pointed to my work from the night before, which I'd finished sometime around two. It wasn't gorgeous by any means. Dad said there were elves and sorcerers in the Pactlands who created masking pieces as nice as anything you'd find in a jewelry store, but I was an amateur in north Georgia without a massive cash flow, and so my supplies tended to come from a beading shop outside of Ellijay. Having forgotten to ask Sage for details like her favorite colors before she passed out, I'd done my best with the supplies I had on hand, an oval azurite-malachite focal pendant I'd been saving for inspiration to strike and gold-plated beads to cover the cord on which I'd strung it. I'd have preferred to work with a metal focal piece—my spells seemed to take more easily when I used them—but this was a rush job, and I only had so much in my kit.

"That's it," I replied, putting the oatmeal on the counter. "If you hate it, I can make another—"

Before I could finish, she'd snatched it up and was examining it in the yellow glow of the kitchen lights, grinning as she twirled it between her fingers. "Is it okay?" I asked.

"It's *beautiful*," she declared. "And it's really mine?"

Cognizant of the likelihood that Sage had never owned jewelry, I'd tried to make the pendant more than merely utilitarian, and her wide smile reassured me. "All yours. May I help you with the clasp?"

Duly bedecked, she ran back to the bathroom, holding up her pants and skidding on her hooves, to admire it in the mirror while I measured out oats and pulled toppings from the pantry. She was still delighted when I called her to the table, double portion of oatmeal and mug of hot chocolate at the ready, and I chuckled as she tucked in. "Let's eat, and then I'll show you how it works."

With the rate at which she inhaled food, she was soon scraping her bowl, and I sent her to the stove to get herself seconds while I finished mine. I didn't want to keep her waiting, however—she was practically bouncing in her chair—and so I shoveled down the last of my breakfast as quickly as I could. "All right," I said, scooting away from the table, "pull your chair out this way to face me. I want to make sure the mask is solid."

Sage did as I asked. "Should I stand up, or—"

"No, you're going to sit for this. I don't want you taking a tumble if you lose your balance." Once she was in position, I said, "There are some pieces of masking jewelry that you can activate just by wearing. All you have to do is think about how you want to look. But *I'm* not that good at this yet," I admitted, "so to turn your pendant on and off, you'll need to touch it with two fingers and say the magic word...which I will tell you in a minute," I added as her mouth opened. "As I said last night, your pendant is preset with a mask, so you have nothing to worry about—it's either on or off. Got it?"

"Yes, ma'am. What's the magic word?" she asked, leaning toward me.

I smiled. "Banana."

"*What?*"

"First lesson: there are no true magic words, but rather words to which the individual sorcerer gives meaning. Words are focusing tools," I explained. "All of my so-called magic words are in English, nothing fancy. No need to complicate your pendant, right? That's an easy word to remember, and you're unlikely to accidentally say it if you start playing with your necklace."

"So...all I do is..."

"Two fingers on the stone—yes, like that," I said as she touched it with her right hand— "and say 'banana.'"

Sage scrunched her eyes closed and whispered the command, and in the blink of an eye, the mask coalesced. While I couldn't see her legs with the voluminous plaid flannel around them, I noticed that her feet had shifted shape to better fill out her socks. Startled, she patted her legs, then pulled off a sock to look at the result: a perfectly passable human foot, pale like the rest of her but equipped with the standard number of digits.

"Oh, *wow*," she whispered, wiggling her toes. "This is..."

"Weird?"

"Yes, ma'am. Good weird," she added, "but...oh, you can move them in different directions..."

"I knew a girl in college who could pick up a pen and write with her toes," I said. "Drunk party trick. Anyway, want to stand?"

I held out my hands and braced Sage as she tried to

find her footing. "Take your time," I urged her as she started to walk and almost face-planted. "With hooves, you're striking on a toe. You strike completely differently with feet like these. Let me demonstrate…"

It took us a solid hour before Sage was comfortable enough to walk across the kitchen, but her confidence grew with practice. Around eight-thirty, I retrieved her clothes from the dryer and sent her to the bathroom to brush her teeth and dress, and she returned to announce that her tail was gone. "It's still there, just hidden," I reassured her, and headed for the back door with my phone. "Need to make a call. I'll be right back."

While Sage started cleaning the oatmeal pot I'd left to soak, I shivered in the morning wind and dialed Tabitha's number. She picked up on the second ring, and to my relief, she sounded alert. "Hey, Jane. What's up?"

"I didn't wake you, did I?"

"Nope. Just got back from a walk. Is everything okay?"

"Uh…yes and no. May I come over, please? There's someone I need you to see."

Tabitha sucked her teeth. "Don't tell me there's another potion emergency—"

"No, nothing like that. But I could really use your expertise…and this is *absolutely* secret."

She didn't hesitate. "Come on over. And who would I tell, the Mystic Mountains true believers?"

"Thanks. Be there soon."

I stepped back inside to find Sage hard at work over the sink. "Leave that, hon, it'll keep. We're going to go see a friend of mine."

She put the pan down and added soap to let it soak again. "A friend?"

"Someone I trust. We'll get you new clothes after we visit her, okay?"

With that promise made, Sage grabbed my old fleece jacket and hopped into the truck, marveling at how much better her still oversized boots fit.

CHAPTER 6

Tabitha's cozy two-story home reflected its owner's personality: tidy, well-kept, and unobjectionable from the road, fronted by a welcoming porch with a pair of wooden rockers, but if you knew where to look, you'd find hints of its more interesting facets. Her lawn—or what little lawn would grow with the tall oaks overhead—was always weedy because she refused to use pesticides. She'd nailed up lattices on both ends of the porch, over which she'd coaxed flourishing honeysuckle vines. Her front beds were filled with native wildflowers: black-eyed Susan, mountain laurel, Georgia aster, ironweed, and bluebells. Her shutters and the ceiling of her porch were painted pale blue—"haint blue," she'd once explained to me, alleged protection against evil spirits. While Tabitha wasn't entirely sold on either said spirits' existence or the paint's properties, she kept the family tradition going, just as she'd installed a bottle tree decorated with mismatched blue glass bottles when she moved in—a structure of twisted, branching steel she'd commissioned from my dad, not bought online. I had no idea where she'd found so much cobalt glass, and some of the bottles looked like antiques. There were other bottle trees dotting the mountains, loaded with rainbow-hued glass and generally originating in China, but if any of them could be said to be efficacious against spirits, I'd put money on Tabitha's alone.

While she was not a sorcerer by any stretch of the imagination, Tabitha was wise in the ways of folk magic. Some lessons she'd picked up from the grandmothers and great-aunts back in Savannah who went to church two or three times a week but still wholeheartedly believed in the power of conjuring, the elder matrons who kept bottles of holy water and vials of graveyard dirt in the same cupboard. Other lessons Tabitha had learned from her extracurricular reading in high school, books sneaked home from the dusty corners of the public library because she knew damn well that her mama wouldn't approve. She'd studied herbs and folk remedies as a complement to her required pharmacy classes, making careful notes of what was said to work and why. Though she'd become a Wiccan during her college years, that corpus of ritual and belief was distinct from the sort of magic tolerated in her home community, and Tabitha never forgot her roots.

But while I appreciated Tabitha's knowledge of herbal teas and tinctures, I went to her that day because I needed someone with a decent medical background, and because I could trust her not to lose her composure.

I hoped.

The wind chimes hanging from a hook in the porch ceiling gently tinkled as I slid out of the truck, and I walked around the vehicle to find Sage considering them with interest, her head gently tilted in thought. "You like those?" I asked.

"What are they?"

"Chimes. They're for decoration." Giving her back a little pat, I steered her up the porch steps and rang the bell.

Tabitha soon appeared, sporting a much-loved Georgia Tech sweatshirt and leggings, and having pulled back her braids with a bright pink scarf. "That was quick," she said by way of greeting. "You know we have these things called speed limits, right?"

"I do, and that's why the truck is ensorcelled against police radar. Mind if we come in?"

She stepped back to admit us, and once she'd closed the door, I glanced at Sage, who was regarding Tabitha with wide eyes. "Tabitha, this is my new friend, Sage," I said, nodding to the girl. "Sage, this is Tabitha Bradley. She's safe."

"Hey, there," said Tabitha, smiling down at Sage. "Where'd you come from?"

"Um...uh..." Sage stuttered, and looked to me for help.

"Whitford," I said to Tabitha, "and I'll explain everything, but you've got to swear you won't tell a soul."

She folded her arms. "Not a word. Now that you've piqued my curiosity—"

"I really like your hair," Sage blurted.

Mentally, I kicked myself for not anticipating Sage's reaction. I didn't know what sort of movies and magazines she'd been allowed out on the Cavanaugh farm, and if she'd grown up with only lily-white Warner for company...

To my relief, Tabitha was gracious. "Thanks," she said, pulling her braids over one shoulder.

"Did you do all those yourself?"

She chuckled. "No way. I've got a lady who braids in Blue Ridge—this takes hours."

Sage looked up at me. "Could you do my hair like that, Jane?"

Tabitha hissed through her teeth. "Probably not the best idea, hon," she said, taking in Sage's straight black locks. "Your hair looks pretty fine, and you'd need extensions. But if you just want a few braids for the day," she continued as Sage's shoulders slumped, "heck, that's no trouble. I bet even Jane could do it," she added in a conspiratorial stage whisper, then turned her attention back to me. "Y'all come on in and sit down. What's going on?"

She led us to her den, made cozy with a plush gray sectional and built-in bookcases, and Sage perched carefully on one end as I took a seat beside her. "So," I said, "this is going to sound weird—"

"I expect nothing less from you," Tabitha replied with

a snort. "Hit me with your worst."

I exhaled slowly. "Okay. Uh…well, Friday night, Warner Cavanaugh came over and sold Sage to me—"

"Sorry, *what?*" she snapped, her back straightening.

"I was afraid he was going to hurt her, so I paid him," I hastily explained. "I'm not in the habit of buying children, yeah?"

"I should hope not. So, why are y'all here instead of with the police? They're open seven days."

"It's complicated."

"No, it's not," Tabitha protested. "That's human trafficking! And how the fu"—she caught herself, cognizant of her young guest—"how the hell did Warner get his hands on her?"

I grimaced. "Technically, it's not human trafficking."

She jabbed one hand toward Sage. "You literally just told me that you bought that kid."

"Right. But she ain't human."

Tabitha gave Sage a long, pointed look, then glanced back at me. "*Oh?*"

"Sweetie," I said, turning to Sage, "could you unmask for a minute, please? So Miss Tabitha here doesn't call the cops?"

Though Sage didn't seem thrilled with the request, she touched her pendant and mumbled, "Banana."

Given the girl's long skirt and oversized boots, the effect wasn't immediately evident, and I asked, "Would you mind taking one of your shoes off?" Sage looked at me uncertainly, and I said, "Miss Tabitha's a friend, I promise. She's not going to hurt you."

"No, of course not," Tabitha insisted, leaning closer to us. "Honey, if you're in trouble, I just want to help."

Thus reassured, Sage reached down and shucked off her right boot, revealing her trimmed hoof and equine leg.

"Dad and I think she's half centaur," I explained as Tabitha silently goggled. "Her other parent is probably a sorcerer—she's got the rudiments of talent—but…well, there's a reason she's got that skirt on. I can mask her, and we're going to buy other clothes today, but—"

"What the *fuck*?" she whispered.

Sage shrank under her stare and quickly put her boot back on. "Jane, may I—"

"Go ahead," I told her, and Sage reactivated the mask with relief. "And that's why we're here and not downtown with the police," I said to Tabitha. "I'm going to try to help Sage find her family, but first, she needs a chance to recover. Warner kept her chained up in the barn."

Tabitha's jaw clenched as she took that in. "For how long?"

"Always," Sage murmured. "Unless he needed me to do chores in the house. He put the chain back on my collar at night."

She held her composure, but the look in her dark eyes spoke of blood. "*Collar?*"

"Could you tilt your head, Sage?" She did as I asked, showing the pale band demarcated by scars, and I nodded at Tabitha. "Kid's been abused as long as she can remember. Warner gave me a bullshit story about how she's a demonic familiar sent to him from Hell as…I don't know, a bonus, but that's obviously not the case. She's thirteen—"

"*Thirteen?*" Tabitha echoed. "Holy…" She covered her mouth but held it together. "How is that baby thirteen?"

"Hasn't been fed properly. I thought I'd keep her with me for a while, let her put on a little weight and heal before I notify the authorities…*elsewhere.*"

"Pactlands?"

"Yeah. Only place I know where you'd find centaurs. Anyway," I said, "we're here because I obviously can't take her to a doctor in town. She doesn't have any ID or papers, not to mention the slight problem of her species…"

"Jane, I'm no doctor," Tabitha protested, "and I don't know the first thing about centaur biology."

"Understood, but you're the only healthcare professional I can trust here. I've got a cousin in the Pactlands who's a healer, but she doesn't have the credentials to get out, so—"

"I mean, I'll do what I can, but there's going to be a *lot* of guesswork."

"That's fine. I'm more worried about her stunted growth than anything."

Tabitha grunted and pushed herself from the couch. "This, uh, mask. Will it hide problems in her…real body?"

"It shouldn't," I replied. "I can't make guarantees, but it should map pretty faithfully."

"That'll do." Turning to Sage, she asked, "Mind if I take a look at you? We can go in the bathroom for privacy."

I waited in the den while Tabitha took Sage down the hall, mindlessly scrolling on my phone to pass the time. About fifteen minutes later, they returned, Sage seemingly relieved to be freed and Tabitha grim-faced. "What do you think?" I asked, rising.

"Nothing incurable," said Tabitha, folding her arms. "Not that I can tell, anyway. Those bruises of hers are healing."

"Dad gave me something to help that along."

She nodded. "This is going off of what I know of children, yeah? I'm no specialist, but I'm one of six siblings, and we were the eldest of two dozen cousins. I've done my share of babysitting," she added with a quick shudder. "That said, Sage doesn't look anywhere near thirteen to me. Immature, underdeveloped…and that's not meant as an insult," she said, glancing at Sage. "You can't help it. Your body hasn't been getting enough nutrients to grow properly."

"What can we do besides feed her?" I cut in.

"Well, that's the main cure for it," Tabitha replied. "Feed her well. Protein, carbs, good fats—there are weight-gaining diet plans online if you need suggestions.

Now, her stomach is probably small, too, so you're going to want to see that she eats multiple smaller meals until it starts to grow. Other than that?" She shrugged. "A nutrition shake, if she can handle it, something like Ensure."

Sage perked at that. "A shake?"

"It's more like a thick drink, but hell, milkshakes are fine. This is the kind of diet where dessert is encouraged," she said, grinning. "And you'll want vitamins, just in case."

"What kind?" I asked.

"A multivitamin, certainly. It doesn't have to be anything fancy. I might consider calcium supplements, too, especially if she starts a growth spurt. Don't go overboard, but it's something to consider."

I nodded, adding vitamins to my grocery list. "Anything else?"

Tabitha made a face. "I'd be remiss if I didn't stress the importance of vaccinations. Sage doesn't remember ever receiving any, and all things considered, I'm not surprised. She tells me she's never seen a doctor."

"That's probably right."

She sighed. "Not sure how much good human vaccinations would do for her, but still, I don't like it. We're heading deeper into flu season…" Her eyes narrowed, and she looked at me more sharply. "*You've* had your shots, right?"

"Yeah. Dad thought it couldn't hurt."

"Good," she muttered. "If y'all want, I've got a friend at the grocery pharmacy who might be able to start getting Sage caught up. The lack of papers or insurance is a problem, but he's dealt with his share of teenagers sneaking in to get vaccinated. Heading to college," she explained, "or just old enough to question why their parents never took care of it for them." Rolling her eyes, she said, "There are folks around here who believe that the MMR vaccine is basically the Mark of the Beast, and don't get me started on HPV. Anyway, he left his family and their cult church years ago, and he understands that some things need to be done off the books. If you think it won't hurt Sage…"

"I'll talk to Dad and let you know," I replied.

"Let me give you his contact info—I'll warn him that you might be in touch," Tabitha offered, and stepped into the kitchen, returning with an ancient Rolodex and a notepad and pen. While Tabitha's cell phone contact list was perfectly functional, she'd been through enough technology failures to keep a hard backup against even a cloud catastrophe. Flipping through the tabs, she located a business card and began jotting down the information.

Glancing at Sage, I found her watching with interest, and another thought occurred to me. "Tabitha, do you still volunteer with that tutoring program?"

"Yep. Here you go," she said, ripping off the page for me. "Why—*oh*," she murmured, looking at the girl. "Oh, *right*. Can you read, hon?"

"A little," Sage replied. "Not as good as I should, I guess…"

"And that's not your fault, either," Tabitha said gently, then turned back to me. "One of the classes offered around here is adult literacy. Let me get some materials for you, and I'll bring them by."

"Thanks," I said. "Just tell me what I owe you."

"You don't. We don't charge for those classes, anyway. I tutor in chemistry and physics," she explained, catching Sage's questioning look, "but I can get my hands on books for you."

As Tabitha escorted us to the door, she asked, "So, where are we going shopping, hmm?"

"Thought we'd start at the Walmart in Blue Ridge," I replied. "It's not high fashion, but we need basics."

"Mm. She paused, hand on the doorknob, then glanced down at her attire and shrugged. "This'll do. Wait there, I'll get my purse."

"You want to come?" I called after her as she retreated

into the house. "I don't mind driving."

"Works for me."

When she returned, having slipped on a water-stained pair of Uggs as well, she smiled at Sage and shooed her onto the porch. "Come on, hon. I need a good fashion show."

Sage didn't know what a fashion show entailed, but her face lit up when we brought her to the juniors' section and told her to grab anything she liked. Soon overwhelmed by the racks—the concept of choice was still foreign to her— she stuck close to me as Tabitha and I made a methodical sweep of the area, selecting jeans, sweaters, shirts, khakis, dresses, pajamas, and an armful of bralettes for her to try. I went ahead and opened a package of underwear before she began—the rags she'd been wearing simply wouldn't do— and as she marveled at the fit, I sorted her clothes and stepped out to give her space, telling her that we'd be waiting when she found something she liked.

A few minutes later, she shyly popped her head out of the dressing room, and Tabitha beckoned her forward. "Come on, let's see," she coaxed. "How's the fit?"

The jeans were enormous on her thin frame—she held them up as she walked toward us—but the pink cardigan sweater was cute, albeit dearly in need of an undershirt. While Tabitha ducked out to find smaller pants, I helped Sage style her top, and she'd gotten the hang of it by the time Tabitha returned in triumph. The second pair was much better, if still a touch on the baggy side, but as Tabitha reminded me, if Sage was going to grow, she could do with some wiggle room.

"Okay," I told Sage as we left her to undress, "put all of that in a pile to take. We'll be waiting for your next outfit."

"Huh?"

I stepped inside again to find her neatly folding the

cardigan. "All of these are to try, sweetie," I murmured. "You're going home with more than one pair of jeans."

She froze, surprised, then broke into a wide grin. "*Really*?"

"Anything you like," I assured her, and retreated to join Tabitha.

She patted the bench in invitation. "We might want to check the girls' department, too. I hate to put her in kids' clothing, but honestly, if we're worried about size…"

I nodded and sat down. "She thought we were just taking the one outfit."

"Shit," Tabitha muttered.

Resting my head on my fingertips, I quietly said, "That bastard left her with the clothes on her back. Well, that, plus the collar locked around her neck. Not even a trash bag of possessions. Kid didn't have a toothbrush to her name."

She mulled that over in silence for a moment. "Your policy is still no killing, right?"

"If I told you I'm tempted to reconsider it, would you think ill of me?"

"No. Might give you a hand."

I grunted. "You're supposed to be the mature one talking me off the ledge."

"Yeah, well, I'm right there with you. Son of a bitch…ooh, yes, let's see," she said, raising her voice as Sage emerged. "Yes. *That's* cute. Give us a twirl, work it, that's it. You like it?"

She nodded emphatically.

"Me, too. Put it in the take pile. How about that purple knit dress?"

As Sage disappeared into the dressing room, I whispered, "That was meant to be a cropped sweater she was wearing, right?"

"Details. Look, she can throw on a shirt beneath it if she blossoms before spring."

By the time we made it to the grocery side of the store,

Sage was pushing a buggy of clothes, shoes, boots, and accessories. Tabitha had helped her pick out a purse, and we'd found a selection of toiletries for her: coconut-scented shampoo and body wash, an electric toothbrush like mine, a brush and comb, and a few packs of elastics, headbands, clips, and scrunchies. Once we reached the self-checkout, Tabitha commandeered Sage's haul and insisted on paying, and she sat in the back of the truck with her on the drive home, teaching her the basics of braiding and promising to take her shopping for makeup another day. "Girl, you've got great pores, but if we play up your eyes, shape those brows, a little lipstick..."

"Nail polish," I volunteered.

"Absolutely. Ooh, there's an Ulta in Greenville... maybe next Saturday?"

"What about your bathroom remodel?"

"Oh, that'll keep. And Ulta's got a salon, so we could get Sage a professional haircut."

"Jane cut mine on Friday," Sage told her.

"Yes," Tabitha slowly replied, "I can see that." She met my eyes in the rearview mirror and winked.

Tabitha declined to come to lunch with us, saying she had work to do around the house before the weekend ended and a lasagna to prep for dinner, and so, feeling a bit guilty about my questionable parenting choices, I once again grabbed drive-thru burgers, picked up some groceries, and took Sage home to unpack her haul.

By the time I had the food unloaded and stowed away, Sage had sorted her things into piles on the couch and coffee table. While her folding was clumsy, she'd made the attempt, and she stood anxiously by her work as I entered the den to check on her. "Is this right, Jane? Do you have a box or something I could use, just to get everything out of the way?"

I cracked my knuckles. "Oh, I think we can do better

than that. Come with me."

I'd emptied the spare bedroom, leaving the scuffed off-white walls and old beige carpet that I hadn't bothered redoing in my home improvement spurts. The room was small, only twelve by ten, but the rear-facing window was large enough to admit plenty of afternoon light, even with the woods behind the cabin. The closet was nothing to write home about, just a metal bar behind folding doors. Still, I reasoned, it had to be a step up from Warner's barn.

Flipping the switch beside the door triggered the ceiling fan and its bulbous overhead light, a dated thing into which a quintet of ladybugs had managed to crawl and die. "So…think we could make some improvements?" I asked.

Sage looked up at me questioningly. "This is for me?"

"Exactly. Can't have you keep sleeping on that couch."

"It's really comfortable—"

"Sure, but wouldn't you prefer a bed?"

She frowned. "I…I don't know, really. I don't think I've ever had one. Maybe when I was little, but I don't remember. But this is very nice," she hastily added. "If I could maybe borrow a blanket or something—"

"Honey," I murmured, gently gripping her shoulders, "let's make you a real room. There's no need for you to nest on the floor."

Though she still seemed nervous, as if she feared I'd grow angry with her for the audacity of considering the luxury of a *bed*, she nodded. "What would you like me to do?"

"Your job is to pick colors," I replied. "Maybe give the odd test flop. I'm going to do the heavy lifting."

Grateful for the practice I'd had of late at Tabitha's house, I began by muttering until the ancient carpet vanished, and Sage gasped beside me. "We're just getting started," I said, patting her shoulder for reassurance, and cast my next spell, which covered the plywood underlayment with new hardwood planks matching the rest of the cabin. "All right, first big decision: what color are we painting the walls?"

Sage blanked, overwhelmed, and I recalled that she'd already had quite a day. "Tell you what, how about a light sandstone?" I suggested, and mumbled the fresh paint into existence. "That'll work with just about anything."

"Okay," she said, gawking at the renovated room.

"And if you live with it for a few days and *hate* it, let me know—we can do any color you want. Now, let me fix the trim…"

I whitened up the baseboards and window frame, replaced the bent aluminum blinds with a cellular shade, then covered the old water stain on the ceiling and squinted at the fan. "So, confession time: I'm not great with electronics and mechanical things. We can go to the hardware store and pick out a new fan and some lamps, okay? Safer that way."

Sage voiced no complaint, and as I cast a white, full-sized sleigh bed into existence, I glanced at her in time to catch the excitement in her eyes. A little concentration produced a box spring and pillow-topped mattress, and I gestured toward it in invitation. "Give that a shot."

She scampered across the room, then gingerly hoisted herself onto the bare mattress and beamed. "It's so soft!"

"Too soft? Or too firm? I can adjust it. Why don't you stretch out and see?"

Kicking off her boots, she slid fully onto the bed and starfished beneath the slowly spinning fan. "This is *great*."

"Glad to hear it."

"Like, this is the best bed ever," she said earnestly, and sighed as she closed her eyes.

I chuckled. "Not finished yet, hon. Hop off and give me a hand, okay?"

She did as she was told, waiting for instructions, and I grinned. Creating basic white sheets was no problem, and a cream blanket was unobjectionable, but as I threw on a thick comforter, I said, "We need some color. What do you think?"

"I…" Her brow knit as she pondered the problem. "I…don't know…"

A thought struck me, and a moment later, the comforter shifted to grayish green. "How about sage?"

She smiled and nodded, and I added pillows in deep brown and pale blue. As Sage sprawled atop her new bed, I pulled together a dresser and nightstand, added a thick blue rug, and redid her closet to incorporate a shoe rack and storage bins. With that accomplished, Sage helped me bring in her new things, and I produced hangers as needed.

It wasn't a showstopper of a bedroom, I mused upon completion. The walls were far too bare for a teenager's space, the fan really was sad, and she'd need at least a couple lamps to warm up the room. But Sage hugged me before I could suggest more decoration, murmuring her thanks, and I reminded myself that it didn't have to be perfect.

"You're very welcome," I said. "Put on something new, and let's go check out our lighting options."

CHAPTER 7

Two weeks later, it wouldn't have been accurate to say that Sage was a new child, but as she jumped out of my truck in her purple zip-up fleece and jeans, clutching the Thanksgiving grocery list, I couldn't deny the improvement.

She looked healthier. Dad's stock of healing potions had cleared up her cuts and bruises, and topical application had even begun to treat the worst of the old scars around her neck. Beyond that, two weeks of regular feeding had left their mark on her; she'd gained four pounds, and while she hadn't yet inched up past the line I'd made on the bathroom door, her face seemed fuller, the angles softer and younger. As her appetite hadn't flagged, I had hope to see growth by the end of the year.

True to her word, Tabitha had organized an afternoon at Ulta the weekend prior, and the three of us had driven to South Carolina to get Sage a professional haircut and a makeup lesson. Armed with a palette of mostly neutrals, she'd practiced every day since, and her application of her purple eyeliner had come a *long* way. She'd begun to experiment with her new wardrobe as well, mixing and matching pieces but always coming to me for inspection. I encouraged it—Lord knew she needed to boost her confidence—and soon, she'd figured out how to do more than pull clothes from the closet and hope for the best.

Sage continued to offer to do chores, but once Tabitha brought over workbooks and easy readers, I sat Sage down and informed her that her only task was to study. Having been homeschooled myself, I still had the books Dad had used for me, and I tried to assess her skill set. By my approximation, she could read at about a first-grade level—she had a decent grasp of phonics but little familiarity with the many exceptions to English's bizarre rules. She could add and subtract, she understood the concepts if not the execution of multiplication and division, and to my surprise, she had a decent grasp of fractions, which she'd apparently acquired through cooking for Warner. Her social studies knowledge was virtually nil, she knew almost nothing of history, and while she could tell me that the lights in the sky at night were the moon and stars, she didn't know *what* they were. Fortunately, Sage was hungry to learn, and she struggled through her worksheets with care, doing more than what I assigned her and beaming at my praise when I reviewed her progress in the evenings.

I did my best to get her out of the house, even as November chilled. She accompanied me on some of my delivery drives, especially when I went to Tabitha's pharmacy, and I took her to Dad's to give her a better place to run around than my sloping backyard. On rainy days and in the evenings, I sat with her in front of the television for a mix of educational programming and kids' movies. History specials were a bit outside her comfort zone, considering her general unfamiliarity with the timeline, but nature documentaries were a hit, a solid mix of action and soothing narration. I even pulled up the old *Schoolhouse Rock* shorts Dad had shown me when I was a kid, which she seemed to like. But Sage's favorite thing by far was my battered old MP3 player, the one Dad had bought me for my tenth birthday and that I had filled with hundreds of tracks (some of them even legally acquired). She knew little of music beyond the snippets she'd heard played in Warner's house, and I often caught her lying atop her bed on her stomach, earbuds in, working through a reader and humming my weird mid-aughts mix of nineties boy bands, pop country, and tracks I liked on the oldies station Dad put on while he brewed.

But I hadn't limited Sage's remedial education to mundane matters. The previous weekend, after we returned from South Carolina, I dug out my childhood wand and gave Sage her first lesson in casting basics. That she had innate talent was obvious to any experienced sorcerer, but hers was late-blooming and untutored, stunted like the rest of her. She'd only known of its existence since July, a few weeks after her thirteenth birthday, when she was loading Warner's dishwasher and a mug came floating across the kitchen into her outstretched hand. Sage had assumed at the time that the self-proclaimed warlock would teach her what to do with her gift, or would at least be pleased by its appearance, but Warner had told her not to use it and left the matter at that. I made up for lost time as well as I could, reviewing my student grimoires for easy exercises and walking Sage through the theory and practice of bending reality to her whim. Sure, she was leagues behind where I'd been at thirteen, but for a novice, she showed real promise.

I planned to work with her on focusing that night, but first, there was matter of braving the pre-Thanksgiving grocery store melee.

As a Pactlands native, Dad had never grown up with Thanksgiving—and in fairness, he predated its establishment as a federal holiday—but he'd lived in the U.S. long enough to appreciate the appeal of a day spent stuffing oneself and kicking back with televised football. He'd always handled Thanksgiving dinner for us when I was kid, which had been a combination of frozen casseroles and those dishes Dad trusted himself to make, but now that I'd grown up and moved out, I'd volunteered to take on the bulk of the cooking duties. Though no chef myself, I could follow instructions, and I was sorcerer enough to buy a frozen turkey the day before and have it thawed in minutes. I'd tasked Dad with a few of the simple dishes, then pulled out my binder of assorted recipes and made a grocery list, with Sage sitting beside me, doing her best to sound out the longer words and asking me questions about the more unusual ingredients.

I'd offered Sage an out if she didn't feel like getting stuck in the holiday shopping madness, but she wanted to help, and she strode toward the automatic doors with me, her jaw set and her arms loaded with reusable bags.

As far as shopping companions went, Sage wasn't the most useful, seeing as she hadn't been to the grocery store enough to be given half the list and let loose. But she stuck close to my side, offering company if nothing else, and wove around the loaded buggies and slower shoppers to grab the items to which I directed her.

After about fifteen minutes of perusing the produce and the end displays of chicken stock and canned pumpkin, we reached the aisle with baking necessities, and I slid in front of the muffin mixes to avoid the run on the spice racks. "Okay, let's see," I said, reading through my list, pen in hand. "We're going to need some spices, but give that a minute. I need a bottle of vegetable oil, sherry vinegar, a can of Pam, and some olive oil."

"On it," said Sage, ducking into the fray.

I pulled the sherry vinegar—the kid couldn't have been expected to pick that one out—but she found the vegetable oil and Pam with ease, and plucked a good-sized bottle of olive oil from a middle shelf. "This is the one, right?" she called down the aisle to where I waited with the buggy. "There's a couple with this picture on the label—"

Before I could take a closer look, a woman on a *mission* sideswiped Sage in her effort to get past an elderly couple perusing the spices. While Sage had figured out the trick to balancing on human feet quickly enough, she wasn't exactly graceful yet, and the bump sent her stumbling. She fell to her knees on the tile. The plastic bottle and the spray can landed unscathed, but the glass bottle of olive oil shattered on impact.

Sage froze, her face a mask of panic, and mumbled, "No, no, *no*," over and over, as she fumbled with the pieces of broken glass. Her jacket having been stowed in the buggy in the warm store, she bent and tried to use the hem of her shirt to mop up the spreading puddle, and when that failed, she grabbed for the glass shards as if she could reassemble the bottle. By the time I reached her, she'd cut her fingers, and little swirls of blood mixed with the viscous liquid.

"Baby, it's okay," I said, crouching beside her. "It's just an accident. We'll get this cleaned up…"

Her eyes were wide and frightened, and her tears began to spill as she babbled, "I'm sorry, Jane, I'm so sorry, I didn't mean to, I'm sorry—" Her rising voice cracked and hitched with a sob. "I'm sorry, I'm sorry, I'm—"

"*Honey.* Come on." I pulled her off the floor, her hands and clothing slick with olive oil, then grabbed my purse, left the groceries, and headed for the bathrooms by the floral department. The single-stall family bathroom was unlocked, and I hustled her inside for privacy. "Let's wash your hands," I said, turning on the warm water. "Oil's a pain to get off. I think I can clean your shirt right now, but let's get some soap on those cuts."

"I'm sorry," she managed through her tears, her face red and wet.

"It was an accident," I soothed, guiding her hands under the tap. "I'm not upset, Sage."

But she was inconsolable in her terror, and once I'd gotten the worst of the oil off of her, I sat on the padded bench by the fold-down changing table and pulled her into my lap. "It's okay," I said, holding her while she curled in on herself and cried. "Sage, sweetie, it's okay. This happens. You don't need to cry over a silly bottle of oil. Take a deep breath, now."

By the time she'd calmed enough to stop trembling, she was a splotchy, snotty mess, and I held cold paper towels on her face to hide the worst of it. With her shirt clean and her hands no longer bleeding, she followed me out of the bathroom and back to our abandoned cart, where an employee was mopping up the last of the oil. "Sorry about that," I told him, reclaiming our groceries. "She got knocked off her feet."

He leaned on his mop and smirked. "Not the worst thing I've cleaned up this weekend. Are you okay?" he asked Sage.

She nodded silently, and I coaxed her onward.

We made our slow way around the rest of the store, waiting in traffic jams of flustered holiday cooks. I kept my tone light and tasked Sage with holding the shopping list, hoping that giving her something to do would distract her, but she remained quiet and skittish, shying away from other customers and walking with her shoulders hunched and tense.

In the dairy aisle, I finally realized she was waiting for the blow. Bending to her ear, I murmured, "You're a good kid, and I'm not upset. We're almost finished."

As soon as I could, I got us out of there, loaded the truck, and started home. Sage sat in silence beside me, hugging herself even with the heater blasting, and I turned on the radio and let her be while I drove.

She helped me carry in the groceries and unpack without saying a word, and once the cold items were stowed, I took her hand and said, "Let's talk."

I led Sage back into the den and sat on the couch, then patted the cushion beside me until she joined me, stiff with fear and braced for my anger. "Listen," I said softly, squeezing her hand, "I am *not* upset with you. Not in the slightest. And even if I were upset, I will *never* beat you, sweetheart. Not ever."

Once again, her eyes filled. "Please don't throw me out, I'll do better, I'm sorry—"

"Baby girl, I'm not throwing you out, and I won't abandon you...oh, Sage," I said with a sigh as she cried, "no. *No.* Come here, it's okay."

Of course she was afraid, I thought, rubbing her shuddering back as she sobbed against my shoulder. As shitty of a parent as Warner was, he'd still been the closest thing Sage knew to a father...and then he'd up and dumped her on me out of the blue. I didn't know what she feared more, being beaten or being abandoned again.

"I know you're afraid to make mistakes," I said as she began to calm. "You don't have to be scared. Look, I made *tons* of mistakes growing up, and my dad never threw me out. What Warner did to you...that's not normal, Sage. Evil, really. I won't do that."

I sent her to the bathroom to wash up while I finished unpacking, then put on a movie and made a bag of popcorn. When Sage returned, still sniffly but better controlled, I wrapped a blanket around her shoulders and sat beside her. After a time, she risked leaning against me, and I absently stroked her hair until I noticed she'd fallen asleep, worn out by fear and heartbreak. As I studied her puffy, sleeping face with its streaks of mascara and shaky, smudged eyeliner, my anger rose again, a simmering cauldron nearing a boil.

I propped pillows up in my place to support her for a minute and stepped out back with my phone. "Hey, Dad," I said to his greeting. "Do you have plans tonight? I could really use a babysitter."

"An errand?" Sage asked, glancing out the windows at the darkness. "*Now?*"

"Just for a little bit," I said, trying to keep my voice bright. "I'll be home in a couple hours, max."

"Can I come?"

"Not this time—*ah.*" Saved by the sound of tires on the gravel out front, I headed to the door and unlatched it as Dad appeared with a large pizza, a box of garlic bread, and a loaded tote bag. "Ooh, that smells good," I said as he drew near.

He leaned over the pizza to kiss my forehead, then swept past me into the house. "If there's any left, I'll put it in the fridge for you. And *there's* Miss Sage! Hi, hon. You hungry?"

"Dad's going to hang out with you tonight while I'm gone," I explained. "So you don't get bored."

Or anxious and panicky, I mentally added, keeping that to myself.

Though she'd been clingy all afternoon, the scent of warm pepperoni pizza drew Sage like a moth to a bonfire. "This is for me?"

"Well, I thought we might share," said Dad, putting his bounty on the kitchen table. "Maybe make milkshakes for dessert, if that'd be okay. And I brought some games with me," he continued, unpacking his tote bag.

I smiled to myself. When it came to my toys, Dad had been something of a packrat, storing everything in plastic totes on the off chance that I'd need it again. Sensitive to Sage's reading level, he'd brought over Battleship, Trouble, and a checkers set.

"Only if you want," Dad told her. "I don't mind finding a movie, either." Turning to me, he asked, "You sure you don't want to join us, Janie?"

The lock in his eyes told me he suspected I was up to no good, and though he wasn't going to attempt to dissuade me in so many words, he was offering me an out.

"It sounds like you've got a perfect evening for two planned," I replied, and gave Sage a quick hug. "I'll be back as soon as I can. Sage, keep him in line."

Leaving her with the comfort of company, I climbed into my truck and glared at the night.

I could almost feel the flames licking just beneath my skin as I headed for Whitford.

Ragged Gap, so named for the break in the mountains permitting settlement, occupied the larger of a pair of valleys. Over the peak to the northeast lay a smaller area of relatively flat land, where Whitford had sprung up in its neighbor's shadow. While Ragged Gap was never a large town, lacking even a rail line, it had built a foundation on tourism and artisanal crafts, catering both to the families who came to hike and hang out on the water and to couples looking for knickknacks, fall color, and haute couture pork belly. While Whitford also had its share of rental cabins, it continued to serve as the nucleus of a loose cluster of farmers and ranchers, offering groceries, a handful of eateries, a bank, a drunk tank, and a volunteer fire department—the basics, really. I'd seen the odd police SUV with the town name painted on the side, but if the Whitford PD were called upon for more than speeding and the occasional domestic violence incident, I'd have been surprised.

The Cavanaugh homestead was located on the western edge of the valley, a scenic lot far from both the relative bustle of the town and the questionable off-the-grid community of East Branch to the north. I knew the place for the same reason I knew my way around much of the area: give a bored teenager a vehicle and gas money, and she'll explore. The long road that ran by the Cavanaugh property was winding at best, a narrow two-lane track bordered by a creek on one side and woods on the other, and in the dark that night, I kept my speed under forty-five and my high beams engaged. Hitting a deer wasn't part of the evening's itinerary.

The turn-off to the old farmhouse was marked by a pair of concrete lions affixed to low, limewashed brick podiums, a decorating quirk of one of the previous five Warner Cavanaughs. Neither podium had been marked by anything as detracting as say, oh, a lantern or a reflective strip, so I turned carefully to avoid hitting them and bumped my way up the private road. Another Warner Cavanaugh—perhaps he of the lions, for all I knew—had decided to pave the half-mile driveway, but time and hard freezes had done a number on the asphalt, and none of his successors had bothered to patch the ruts and potholes. The jostling ride only fueled my displeasure toward the current Warner Cavanaugh, which, frankly, was the last thing he needed.

The only lights on the property were within the house, and I wondered about Sage's time spent chained in the barn—had Warner given her so much as a flashlight, or had she sat out there in the darkness? As tiny flames began to spark around my wrist, I chided myself to focus. First things first, we needed to have a little chat.

I parked beside Warner's ridiculous dually, blocking him in unless he deigned to drive on the scrubby grass, then marched up the porch steps and rang the bell. He hadn't bothered to install a smart doorbell, I noticed, nor had he turned on a porch light, which was perhaps why he was foolish enough to open the door.

He tensed upon finding me on the mildewed welcome mat, but he recovered quickly and plastered on a smirk as his blue eyes narrowed. "Well, well. To what do I owe the pleasure?"

"I'm here about Sage," I said.

Brushing back the open sides of his unbuttoned duster, he shoved his hands into his pockets with casual nonchalance. "I'm afraid she's your problem now. You bought her fair and square, so the little demon—"

That sentence ended in a high-pitched yelp as I flung him across the foyer with a burst of force, leaving him pinned against the faded floral wallpaper with his bare feet kicking for purchase a few inches above the ground. I let Warner thrash and squeal for a moment, all pretense of the powerful warlock abandoned, then stepped over the threshold and slammed the door behind me. Cutting my eyes to the left, I saw the frozen picture on his widescreen TV—some sort of first-person shooter—and a half-empty bottle of Mountain Dew.

On the one hand, cliché. On the other, what sort of

idiot sat around the house gaming in his warlock cosplay coat?

As Warner began to call for help, I stepped closer to him and snapped, "Shut your mouth, you craven piece of shit, or I'll do it for you."

He had sense enough to do as I asked.

"That's better. Now, I should break every bone in your useless body for what you did to Sage," I said, pushing up my sleeves. "Hell, I'd enjoy listening to you scream. But I'm feeling merciful tonight, so I'm going to give you another option."

My bare forearms ignited.

Warner cried out again, scrabbling against the wall as if he could escape me, and the front of his jeans began to darken.

"Pissing your pants isn't going to help you," I continued, "though I admit it's a nice touch. What a *brave* warlock you are."

"Don't hurt me," he begged. "Please don't hurt me, I—I'll give you whatever you want. Money? My truck? You can have it, the keys are on that hall table there—"

"I want answers," I interrupted. "*Now.*"

He screamed when I released my grip, dropping him to the wooden floor. By the time he realized he was on the ground again, I was standing over him, and he shrank away from me with fear in his eyes. "Where did you find Sage?" I murmured, letting the flames lick along my skin.

Warner's mouth flapped like that of a dying bass for a few seconds while he processed the question. "I found her on the porch."

"Bullshit."

"I swear," he whined. "Came out one night to get a bottle of bourbon I'd left in my ride and found her lying there. She was wrapped in a blanket. No note."

"You didn't see someone drive up?"

"I was in the back of the house on the treadmill with the TV on. Didn't see or hear a thing—I'm serious," he insisted as I continued to stare down at him. "Just walked out for a drink and found a fucking baby."

"And you kept her?"

"Have you seen her? *All* of her? That thing's a monster—"

"She's a kid," I barked. "A starved, scarred, undersized, barely educated *child*."

"With hooves! I thought she might actually be a demon! What the hell was I supposed to do with her?"

"Not chain her in the barn, you son of a bitch!"

He whimpered as the fire on my arms briefly intensified. "I didn't know! She didn't come with a note or nothing—"

"If you thought she was a demon, why not give her to a priest?"

The shifty look he gave me spoke volumes. "Thought she might be a gift from my patrons."

"You don't *have* patrons, you moron!"

"Yes, I do!"

Glowering down at him, I said, "As the only one of us in this building with actual talent, I beg to differ. So…what, you thought Sage might have landed there as your dark minion?"

"I had to train her first," he mumbled. "Maybe I was being tested. Got her old enough to understand me and do what I told her."

"Yeah, you raised her. You raised a child," I said slowly, "and instead of acting like her father, you enslaved her."

"I taught her to be my *servant*—"

"With a collar around her neck? Eating scraps? Sleeping in a pile of hay? Dogs get better treatment than that. So, let's think about this," I said, planting my fists on my hips. "You have a little girl on your hands. Can't let her get the wrong idea about you loving her or anything silly like that, so you beat her into obeying? Chain her up so she can't run? She told me you threatened her with curses. A big, scary warlock like you, and the best you can do is curse a kid?"

"She's got power!" he blurted. "Real power! Shit started flying around her!"

"I'm aware. Been training her."

I think, at that moment, it truly sank in for Warner that whatever Sage could do, I was orders of magnitude *worse*.

"I...I got scared, okay?" he babbled. "Is that what you want to hear? I can't do the physical stuff she was doing, and I was afraid she'd turn on me, so I thought I'd make her your problem."

I grunted. "And if I hadn't bought her from you? What was your backup plan?"

Warner stared at me, silently pleading for a reprieve.

"What," I repeated, each syllable barbed, "was your backup plan?"

He swallowed hard. "Wait until she went to sleep, then..." He anxiously licked his lips. "Old Yeller her, you know?"

"And what about your precious patrons?"

"I, uh...I told myself they'd understand. Just returning her to them. But you took her, so she's fine, yeah? Look, I'll pay you back the money. I drank the hooch, but I'll make you whole—"

"Get up," I ordered.

"Please, Jane—"

"*Get up.*"

He scrambled to his feet, doing his best to keep his distance from me and my fire. "You can have whatever you want," he tried again. "Take it. I won't say a word—"

"Outside."

"Please—"

"Get you sorry ass outside, or so help me..."

Warner scurried for the door, and I grabbed his truck keys before following him. Frightened as he was, he didn't bolt for the trees, instead freezing on the porch like a little boy caught red-handed.

"Walk," I said, pointing to the stairs, and Warner hastened to the bottom. I directed him about ten yards from the house, and once he was safely away, albeit barefoot, I focused on the building and set it ablaze.

Warner cried out as his inheritance burned, and old as the wooden structure was, it went up easily. I shot another blast of fire toward the barn, though I didn't bother with the rest of the outbuildings. I'd made my point.

He almost dropped his keys when I underhanded them to him, and he looked back at me with confusion, the firelight flickering in his eyes. "You have until dawn to get out of the county," I murmured. "I won't follow you."

He nodded frantically.

"But you've heard of the Rule of Three, haven't you? Whatever you put out into the world is retuned to you thrice over?" I shrugged. "Not sure if I believe it, but in this case, let me be plain: if I ever see you again, I'll return to you threefold everything you did to Sage." I pointed to our trucks. *"Git."*

And he ran. Coat flapping, unshod feet probably insensate to the debris in his path, he sprinted for his vehicle, threw open the door, and had started the ignition before he was buckled in. I stood aside and watched as he off-roaded across the lawn, avoiding both me and the driveway, then turned left past the lions with a squeal of tires and roared into the night.

A crash drew my attention back to the burning farmhouse, and I looked over my shoulder to find that the roof had caved in. I stood there for another ten minutes, until I was sure the place was unsalvageable, then retracted the fire and watched the blackened remains of the upper floor collapse. As satisfying as it might have been to burn the place to ashes, I didn't have all night, nor did I want to leave the fire unchecked and risk igniting the trees.

Still, I slowed as I approached the lions and shattered both before I turned onto the road toward home.

"Janie?" Dad called from the kitchen as I let myself in. "Is that you?"

"Were you expecting someone else?" I teased. "Candygram?"

I found the two of them seated at the table, the Trouble board between them and, if I wasn't mistaken, Sage in the lead with the blue pegs. She had a can of Coke beside the board and a bag of barbeque chips within reach, and I surmised that the evening hadn't been terrible.

"You okay, girlie?" Dad asked, giving me a once-over from his seat. "Is everything all right?"

"It is now. Any pizza left?"

"About a third of it. Fridge." As I headed across the kitchen to satiate my growling stomach, Dad said, "You look tired."

He wasn't wrong. Despite my natural affinity for fire, a wild talent Dad didn't share, employing it to the extent I had that night wore me out. Training would have helped, but finding a safe, secluded place in which to do so presented a challenge.

"Nothing pizza can't fix," I replied. "Ooh, and garlic bread. Perfect."

While I loaded up a plate, Sage asked, "Where did you go?"

I took my time and slipped my dinner into the microwave, then returned to the table and crouched beside her chair. "I went out to Whitford to see Warner."

Fear crossed her face, and though I wondered whether she thought I was trying to return her like defective goods, she kept her cool. "What did he say?"

"Nothing for you to worry about. And I promise you this," I said, taking her hand and giving it a firm squeeze. "He will *never* hurt you again. Trust me. Everything's under control."

CHAPTER 8

Around ten the next morning, as I did the books on my laptop at the kitchen table and Sage plowed through a reader in her room, the doorbell rang.

I glanced up, startled. Dad and Tabitha always called before coming by, and I wasn't expecting visitors, so a midmorning summons to the door couldn't bode anything good. Heck, I hadn't bothered to dress beyond throwing a sweatshirt over my pajamas, and I'd yet to shower...though I *had* brushed my teeth, I recalled, grateful for at least a small step in the direction of presentability as I tightened my ponytail and crossed the cabin to see who'd come. It wasn't Girl Scout cookie season, I'd never been visited by a Mormon or a Witness, and the ladies of Ragged Gap Baptist knew I was a lost cause...

I unlatched the door, hoping for an early UPS run.

The man on the porch wasn't wearing brown, or even the blue of the mail carrier. While he *was* wearing blue, it was a much deeper shade, almost black, a collared shirt with a matching tie and trousers over black boots. Above his left breast was pinned the sort of gold shield I'd have recognized anywhere as law enforcement, even if I hadn't seen the speaker microphone clipped at his shoulder or the pistol holstered at his belt. A name strip had been affixed across from the badge, but my eyes skipped over that as I considered his face. Young, I thought, probably not much older than thirty. His dark brown hair was wavy, just short enough to be professional but still somewhat reminiscent of the floppy style favored by teenage boys with baseball caps and pickup trucks. Olive complexion, clean-shaven— figured, for a cop—and with a mole near his left temple that probably bore observation. His eyes, though, drew my attention, large and deep brown, with the sort of thick lashes I could only achieve through multiple passes with a mascara wand. He stood about six feet tall, and though he didn't have a linebacker's physique, he seemed solidly built.

My mind raced, but I tried to play it cool. "Uh…can I help you?"

He took off his hat. "Good morning, ma'am. Are you Jane Fortune?"

Oh, shit.

"Yes, sir," I replied, internally cringing at the upward lift at the end that made my answer sound like a question. "Yes," I tried again, "I'm Jane."

"Connor Willow," he said with a nod, and smiled tightly. "I'm the chief of the Whitford Police Department. May I come in?"

This was *exceedingly* not good, and as all the times Dad had joked about me needing bail money swarmed to the forefront of my memory, my helpful brain managed only an incredulous, "*Chief?*"

He chuckled briefly, looking almost boyish as he did so, and rubbed the back of his neck. "My predecessor retired last year, and the rest of the force was two guys and a K-9. Stiff competition for the job, but enough folks in town thought I was the least of the bad options."

"What about the other officer?"

"Oh, he didn't want the gig. It was me or Sam, and while Sam has the charisma, he doesn't have thumbs. Hard choice."

He grinned, and while part of me was certain that this was an attempt to get past my guard, the part that kept fixating on his admittedly pretty eyes was eating it up.

"There was a fire last night," he continued, sobering. "Could I ask you a few questions?"

"Am I under arrest?"

"No, ma'am, and you can tell me to take a hike," he replied with a shrug. "But I *will* mention that my dad's old boss owns the hardware store in town, and he's got a security camera with a good view of the intersection of Main and Dogwood."

Dogwood, unfortunately, was the road I'd taken into Whitford the night before. "Oh?"

"Yeah. I had him pull the recording first thing this morning, and I saw a truck that looked an awful lot like yours on there."

"A blue F-150?" I countered. "Come on, Chief, they're a dime a dozen around here."

"Oh, sure. But the camera got your plate, and I ran that, so...' He spread his hands. "Can we chat? Maybe inside?"

I hesitated, trying to decide what course of action was least likely to land me behind bars.

"I'm not here to arrest you," the officer said quietly. "Promise. And unless I have reason to believe you killed Warner Cavanaugh—"

"Wait—he's *dead*?" I demanded, fear clenching my stomach like a fist.

"Missing. Wasn't home when the fire department showed up last night. Of course," he allowed, "by the time they arrived, the fire was out—which is weird, not going to lie—so he might have poured some gasoline and left town. Kind of doubt it, though. But what I was saying is that unless I learn you've killed him, I'm not planning on taking you in."

When I continued to waffle, he said, "I just want to talk, Ms. Fortune. Please."

Damn those pretty eyes.

Against my better judgment, I stepped back and nodded toward the couch, praying that Sage would stay in her room.

"Thank you," he said, and took a seat on the far end,

leaving me plenty of space. As I closed the door and sat, he put his hat on the coffee table, then turned off his speaker microphone.

I arched a brow. "Should I be recording this?"

"No need. This ain't exactly police business," he replied. "Well...I suppose it is, technically, but I won't be writing a report."

He paused and slowly released a breath, and it occurred to me that the guy with the gun might actually be *nervous*.

"So," said Connor, drumming his fingers on his knees, "this area—Ragged Gap and Whitford, I mean—we've had an uptick in fires in the last few years. House fires, mostly, but some burned-out vehicles. Most of those fires are perfectly explainable, lightning strikes and space heaters and such, but a few...you know, the fire investigator never seems to find the cause. And when it's an unexplained fire like that, the property owner doesn't rebuild."

Truth be told, there were more fires than he knew about. I'd reconstructed a handful of porches and such after scaring off particular inhabitants of shared dwellings.

"My old chief thought it might be a firebug, some damn arsonist getting his jollies," he said, holding my gaze. "But there was a pattern, see? When I started quietly asking questions, it turned out that every one of those weird fires was connected to domestic violence. Someone beats on a partner or a parent or a kid, there's a fire, and poof, the assailant leaves town. And when I asked the right people," he continued, his voice low, "I kept hearing your name."

I remained silent, waiting for him to spring the trap.

"The one fire that didn't fit the pattern happened in September. Rental cabin burned, but the woods around it were unharmed. I didn't see any evidence of DV—the owners said they'd rented it to a nice young couple for a few months, folks from out of town. Thought it might be a fluke until I stopped in at the bar one night and ran into

Ernie Flores. You know him?"

"Vaguely," I replied, which wasn't untrue. Ernie worked in the café at Mystic Mountains, and while I'd never had a conversation of more than a few words with the man, I knew his face. With the help of an agent from a law enforcement agency with *zero* jurisdiction in Georgia, I'd given him a dose of neutralizer to counteract the Oil of Life potion that had rendered him a virtual zombie. I knew Ernie had contacted Tabitha after the neutralizer left him puking in the smoothie blender and bereft of his newfound ability to make his fingertips light up, but I didn't know who else had heard his story. If Ernie was telling tales in public…

"He was pretty damn drunk," said Connor. "Several shots in. Football Saturday down at Eight Ball's."

That was Whitford's only watering hole, as far as I knew, a sketchy joint with boarded-up windows and regular pool tournaments.

"I took a stool next to him at the bar, and during the halftime report, he asked whether he could press charges against you for stealing his magic." Smirking, Connor said, "I had to break it to him that state law doesn't recognize the existence of magical powers, let alone the theft of such, but I did buy him a round to make him feel better."

I made a mental note to march down to Mystic Mountains and chew Ernie out at the next opportunity, but I pushed that to the back burner and focused on the cop in my house.

"Ernie seemed pretty low about the whole thing, so I asked him for details. He told me this…well, *insane* story about a witch or something selling oil that gave people power. Said you got jealous, stole all the power from everyone else, and ran her out of town. Burned down the house where she was living and almost killed her."

"You believe that?" I asked with what I dearly hoped sounded like nonchalance.

Connor shook his head. "Not all of it. But I did want

to ask you about something."

"Oh?"

"Do you have the touch?"

I frowned, puzzled. "Sorry…what?"

"The touch," he repeated. "That's what my parents always called it. They didn't have it, but some of my kinfolk do." Seeing my deepening confusion, he said, "That little spark of magic, I mean."

Before I could deny it or feign incredulity at the notion that magic was real, Connor glanced around the den until his gaze landed on a half-burned jar candle I'd left by the TV. He reached for it, whispering under his breath, and the candle rose and floated across the room into his grasp.

Well, *that* was unexpected.

"Holy shit," I muttered.

He grinned and put the candle on the coffee table by his hat. "Surprised?"

"What *are* you?"

Shrugging, he said, "Just myself. A guy with a weird talent. Like I said, a number of my relatives have the touch to one degree or another. They're out at East Branch."

"The, uh…" I paused, unsure of how to phrase my question. Anyone native to the area had heard the rumors about the veritable holler known as East Branch, a place to which even the sheriff gave a wide berth. Supposedly, they had neither electricity nor running water, and if you strayed too close, the inhabitants would shoo you back to the main road with shotguns. Whether they were a cult or just primitive homesteaders was up for debate, but the banjo jokes abounded, especially as the people living out there were reported to be a little too genetically close to each other.

"The compound?" Connor volunteered.

"Sure, let's go with that."

He rolled his eyes. "It's…something. My parents left when they got married and settled in town, but we used to visit every now and then to see folks. There's people in there with the touch, some stronger than me."

My thoughts whirled. Humans did *not* have magical abilities. They just didn't. But now here was Connor, sitting on my couch, casually demonstrating talent…

Was East Branch a community of sorcerers? Or maybe people like me, folks with human blood mixed in? Were these refugees who hadn't made it into the Pactlands, or were they the descendants of sorcerers like my mother who'd left for love?

"That said," Connor murmured, "I know how to keep my mouth shut. If you've got the touch, believe me, I understand not wanting to talk about it. But I've also got a town to consider and a brand-new mystery fire on my hands, so…want to tell me what happened last night?"

The implications of living beside an entire community of potential sorcerers could be dealt with later, I decided. I didn't have the bandwidth quite yet to wrestle with *that*, though I supposed I could put the officer's mind at ease.

"I, um…you could say I have the touch, I guess. If that's what y'all call it. Folks around here…" I began, then sighed. "Look, I screwed up and showed talent to the owner of Mystic Mountains when I was a kid—"

"What, that New Age store?" he asked, brow crinkling.

"Yeah." My cheeks began to heat. "She talked a good game, and I thought she might actually have abilities, but then I basically showed her what you just did, and she freaked out. I've had a reputation ever since, and…" I paused, unsure of just how far I could go with a freaking *cop*, then threw caution to the wind. "Sometimes, people get in trouble, and when the law can't help them, they look for alternative solutions. They come to me."

He nodded. "And you do what, exactly?"

"What you think. Run off the problems. I've never killed anyone," I hastily stressed, "though I'd be lying if I said I've never wanted to. But a little light property damage can do some good, you know?"

The corner of his mouth twitched. "We tend to call

that 'arson,' Ms. Fortune."

"Po-*tay*-to, po-*tah*-to."

"Uh-huh. And these people who need alternative solutions…"

I cocked my head. "Just how well do restraining orders work, really?"

Connor grunted at that. "What happened to Ernie?"

"That oil he was using was the magical equivalent of a party trick. He thought he was developing power, but he was being strung along. Him and a lot of other people," I explained. "They got tricked into taking a potion that left them acting like drones, and the woman behind the whole thing had rented that cottage. I did run her and her crew out of town"—well, or had them carted off by magical law enforcement, which was close enough—"but I made sure I got everyone out of the house before I let the fire do its thing."

"So…you *are* the firebug, then?"

Sighing, I reached for the jar candle, and a tiny burst of will sent a stream of flame from my fingertip to light the wick.

"I'll be damned," he murmured. "That's impressive."

"That's the answer you were looking for?"

"One of them. Let's talk about last night's fire." Reaching into his breast pocket, he pulled out a small notepad and a stubby golf pencil, then flipped to a page covered in chicken scratches. "Warner Cavanaugh…the sixth. Clean record but for a few parking tickets, no known romantic entanglements, no known employer. What's your beef with him?"

"You ever met him?" I asked.

"*Oh*, yeah. The weirdo who always wears the long black coat."

"He bills himself as a warlock."

"Seriously?" said Connor with a snort. "You're not going to tell me he has the touch, too, are you?"

"Not in the slightest. But, uh…he was keeping a kid

captive out there."

The cop sobered in a heartbeat. "What do you mean?"

"Just what I said. About two and a half weeks ago, he came out here at night and offered to sell her to me."

He ran one hand over his face, processing that. "What did you do?"

"Bought her, naturally."

"And you didn't think to call the local PD? Or us?"

"It's complicated—"

"It's *trafficking*! Shit, this is the kind of thing we call in to the GBI—"

"Not in this case," I interrupted, staring him down. "Not with this victim."

His eyes narrowed. "She in trouble with the law?"

"No. Look, I know it's a lot to ask, but can you please trust me that I've got it under control?"

"I can get past the house fire," he replied, "but if that creep's been trafficking girls, then no." Softening, he said, "I appreciate what you're trying to do, but there are specialists for these sort of cases."

"Not like this one." I pushed myself off the couch and scowled down at him. "If I show you why I don't want you setting off an investigation, will you promise not to freak out?"

"I'll...do my best," he said, bemused.

"And what you see doesn't leave this house? You don't tell another soul?"

"*If* it's as weird as you say and you can convince me not to call the GBI...then yes, I can keep a secret."

That would have to do. Leaving the skeptical cop on the couch, I knocked on Sage's door and poked my head into the room. She pulled off her headphones and grinned at me as she pushed her book away. "Hey, Jane! Need me to do something?"

"Actually, yes, if you don't mind," I said, and slipped fully inside as she slid off the bed. "There's a police officer in the house," I whispered. "He's got some talent, too, but

I don't know what his deal is."

She looked up at me in alarm. "Are we in trouble?"

"Not just yet, but I need to show him why we shouldn't be parading you around human law enforcement. Could you, uh…could you slip on a skirt and unmask for a moment?"

"Sure," she replied, though she sounded anything but certain. "And that'll make him go away?"

"It'll put him on our side," I told her, hoping I was right.

Leaving Sage to change clothes, I returned to the den and said, "Give her a minute."

"You're not sending her out the back, are you?" Connor asked, and though his tone was light, it sounded forced.

"No. Patience."

A moment later, Sage peeked out from the end of the short hall to her room, then shuffled into the den, having traded her leggings for a flowy knee-length skirt but still barefoot. She hugged herself and watched the newcomer with hunted eyes.

"Hi, there, little lady," said Connor, going to his feet. "I'm Chief Willow. What's your name?"

"Sage," she whispered.

"Well, that's pretty," he replied, and smiled. "Ms. Fortune here told me you were being kept at the Cavanaugh place."

She nodded.

"For how long?"

A shrug answered that. "I dunno. Always, I guess. It's only ever been Master and me."

He cut his eyes to mine, and I could practically see his antennae rise. "And who is *Master*?"

"That would be Warner," I said. "Still peeved at me for burning down his house?"

"No, but why am I not calling for reinforcements from the state, again?"

"For one, Sage has the touch."

"Touch or no, this case—"

"You didn't let me finish. Sage, honey, could you please show him?"

Though clearly nervous, she felt for her pendant and whispered, and in an instant, the mask fell away.

To his credit, Connor didn't start screaming. He stood very still by the far end of the couch, slowly blinking as he considered Sage's unmistakably equine legs. I let him gawk for a moment, then said, "Thanks, sweetheart. You can mask again if you want."

She did so with relief, but she continued to lurk at the edge of the room, hunched and avoiding Connor's stare.

"Do you understand now?" I asked him.

It took a few seconds for him to find his voice. "I...no?"

"What don't you get?"

"Uh..." He gestured toward Sage, struggling for words, then recovered sufficiently to recognize her discomfort. "Sorry, I...I'm sorry," he told her, "I don't mean to..."

"Do you understand why we don't want to get the law here involved?" I tried again.

"That, yes. Everything else..." Pulling himself together, he walked across the room, took Sage's hand, and coaxed her into an overstuffed chair. Crouching beside it, he said, "I'm not going to hurt you, okay? But I do need some answers."

Sage glanced at me, and I nodded.

"Where did you come from?" he asked gently. "Do you have a family out there?"

"I don't know," she mumbled.

When Connor turned to me in query, I said, "We're working on that. I'm pretty sure I know where she came from, but Warner told me she was abandoned as a baby, and he kept her until he realized she has power. Getting real answers for her could mean opening up a massive can of worms, so I've kept Sage here for a while, letting her…decompress…before we take any next steps."

"What did he do to her, exactly?"

"He didn't give me the play-by-play, but it sounds like he used her as a servant. Told her she was a demon. Kept her chained up in the barn."

Anger rippled across his face, but he controlled it and turned back to Sage. "I'm going to leave this up to you. We can search for Warner, arrest him for false imprisonment and human trafficking…there's a special state unit that prosecutes those sort of crimes."

"I'm not human, though," she pointed out.

"You look human enough right now—"

"Because she's masked," I cut in. "I guarantee that if you tried to sequence her DNA, she'd come back with all sorts of abnormalities. For what I assume are obvious reasons, we don't want there to be any risk of her information ending up in a database."

"No…I do understand that," he allowed. "But if we're talking sex crimes—"

"We're not."

Sage shook her head. "Master always said I'm disgusting. He likes women, but not me."

Still, his jaw remained tight. "So…*just* false imprisonment and forced servitude? For how many years?"

"About thirteen," I said. "Sage looks younger than she is. Warner…he didn't feed her well. I'd say there's a clear case here for child abuse, but to prove that, wouldn't there be doctors involved? People poking into Sage's background and examining her?"

"Shit," he muttered, and stood. "And you didn't kill the bastard?"

"Last I saw of him, he was in his truck, flying toward the northeast end of the valley. Still had his life, if not his dignity. I told him get out of town and not come back."

Connor nodded. "Well, Ms. Fortune, clearly, I'm not arresting you for the act of God that burned down the

Cavanaugh house. But if Sage doesn't want me to try to find Warner and bring him in…"

She shook her head.

"I was afraid of that. In that case…shoot, is there anything I can do?" he asked, looking between the two of us before landing on me. "If you know where her people are and you need help getting there or something…"

"Appreciated," I said as his voice petered out. "Actually, yeah, a little help might be nice."

"What do you need?"

I paused, choosing my words carefully. "If Sage decides to search for her people, I'll have to get in touch with some folks from…*elsewhere*. I don't know what, if anything, they'll want to do here, but if they need to go out to the Cavanaugh property and poke around…"

He reached into the pocket where he'd kept his notepad and extracted a business card. Flipping it over, he scrawled a number on the back, then passed it to me. "That's my cell. Should these friends of yours need a hand in Whitford, you let me know. I can make excuses."

"You're sure?"

"Pretty confident. And if it means getting that kid back where she belongs, I'm happy to help coordinate." As he glanced at Sage, he must have internally replayed that last statement, as he quickly amended, "Not that there's anything wrong with you, hon. I just meant that I hope you find your family."

"Thanks," she said softly, and flashed a small smile as he rose to go.

While Sage retreated to her room, I saw Connor out to his vehicle, a souped-up Ford Explorer with the city logo on the sides. But as he stepped off the porch, he turned back to me. "One more question."

God, he *did* have pretty eyes.

"And what's that?" I replied.

"You asked me what I am. What are *you*, other than a firebug?"

I smirked. "Just myself."

"That so?" He laughed once, low in his throat, and started off again—and with the way he filled out those pants, I didn't mind the view. "You be safe, now, Ms. Fortune."

"Jane," I blurted.

Connor glanced over his shoulder and quirked a brow. "Yeah?"

"Yeah."

"Well, then," he said, opening the driver's-side door, "later, Jane."

CHAPTER 9

Once Connor had disappeared down the mountain, I returned to the cabin and found Sage curled up on her bed, hugging her knees. She'd changed back into her leggings, and she watched in silence as I let myself into her room. "I'm sorry about that," I said, keeping my distance. "He showed up and started asking questions, and I knew that if he didn't see for himself, he was going to bring in more cops."

She sniffed but said nothing.

"That…wasn't fair to you," I continued. "You deserve to have the final say over your own body. Thank you for going along with me, but I'm sorry to have put you in that position." I paused, trying to gauge her reaction. "Can we still be friends?"

Though she nodded, her grip on her legs didn't relax.

"That officer's not going to hurt you, baby. He's gone. And if he gets any *ideas* and comes back, I can take care of you. Promise, cross my heart," I said, making the gesture. "Heck, if it comes to it, I'll get you out of town…" When she continued to stare mutely at me, I risked a step closer to her bed and asked, "What's wrong? You can tell me."

She licked her lips before she spoke. "Did you hurt Master last night? When you ran him off?"

"Maybe a little," I admitted. "I threw him against the wall and held him there, and then I dropped him, so he might be bruised today. Didn't break anything, as far as I know. He'll need to wash his pants, but I didn't bloody him up, if that's what you're asking."

"*Could* you have hurt him?"

I hesitated, unsure whether the truth or a reassuring lie would be better for Sage's mental state, then opted for the former. "Yes," I said plainly. "I may only be half sorcerer, but I got the talent in spades. There's quite a bit I could have done to him, but I didn't."

"Why not?"

"Because that's not who I want to be. Because when someone with talent uses it like that and no one can stop her, she's not helpful anymore—she's a danger to the community. I have no problem setting a house on fire if it drives bad people out of here," I said, "but I've never left anyone to burn." Nodding to the foot of her bed, I asked, "Mind if I join you?"

Sage allowed it, and I sank slightly into the mattress. "I did make Warner give me some information," I told her. "He said he found you in a blanket on the porch, no note, no sign of how you got there. Assuming he's telling the truth, and I think I may have scared it out of him, it sounds like he didn't kidnap you."

"So, that means I was abandoned," she murmured.

"Or that someone else snatched you and dumped you here. Either is possible," I replied, though frankly, Sage's conclusion was the more plausible of the two. "Listen, honey…if you don't want to go in search of your parents, I understand. I *get* it. My mom abandoned me, remember, and I've never had so much as a postcard from her in all the years since. But if you do want to start looking, then I'll make some calls."

Sage held her knees more tightly and watched me over the top. "If they abandoned me, what good would it do to find them? They left me with Master, and he's…he was…"

"A monster?"

She nodded, her face contorting with the sudden tears she tried to hold in, and I scooted up the bed to hold her as she cried. "If they did abandon you," I said once her breathing began to calm, "even if they had good reasons, they've got a hell of a lot to make up for. You don't have to forgive them."

"But what if they didn't want me?" she mumbled into my shoulder. "What if they just didn't care? If I found them, they *still* wouldn't want me."

"That's a possibility," I allowed, "but at the end of the day, you're part sorcerer, and you've got a growing talent. Even if you don't have a loving family waiting in the Pactlands, you'd get a much better education there than anything I could give you."

Sage sniffled as she considered that. "It's a separate place, though, right? The Pactlands?"

I'd given her the simplest explanation, as trying to explain the magical underpinnings of a sorcery-created pocket world would have overwhelmed her. "Yes, but there are ways to get in and out. The nearest gate is about an hour away in South Carolina."

"So, I could go to school there and still live with you?"

I sighed and rubbed her thin back. "They'd probably find a place for you to live there if you couldn't stay with your parents. That'd be one heck of a commute. But like I said, you'd get a great education…and maybe a therapist. Someone who can help you work through all your feelings about Warner and your parents."

When Sage looked up at me, her eyes were watery again. "I can't stay here?"

"Oh, *honey*," I said, pulling her back against me as she hugged me with all she had. "If you want to stay, you can stay. I'm not trying to get rid of you, *please* know that. But I wouldn't be a good friend if I didn't try to do the best thing for you, and that probably means taking you to the Pactlands. That doesn't mean you have to go today, however. Want some lunch?"

She nodded and swiped at her eyes.

"Go wash your face, hmm? I'll make grilled cheeses."

As I was buttering the bread, Sage emerged, still puffy and flushed but seemingly feeling better. "Okay, before I get this going, let's talk toppings," I said. "I like ham on mine—do you want some?"

"Yes, please." She opened the cabinets and began setting the table.

"Why don't you get some soup bowls, too? I'll put on a can of tomato."

The sandwiches had just begun to sizzle when Sage joined me at the stove and said, "If you think we should look for my parents...I guess that'd be okay."

"Sure." I gave her a side hug with the arm not attached to a spatula. "I've got the phone number of a detective in the Pactlands. They'd probably know where to begin looking."

Sage's brow knit. "They?"

"Some nymphs are non-binary...not male or female," I explained, and she nodded. "This one is an old friend of my dad's. They'll help us." Checking the color of the underside of my sandwich, I said, "I could give them a call after we eat, if that'd be all right."

"Yeah," said Sage. "Yes, ma'am. I think...I think that could be good."

In truth, my misgivings persisted about the whole matter. We could speculate all we liked, but until someone went digging, we wouldn't know why Sage was left on Warner's doorstep. While I suspected that she might feel better having real answers, the flip side of that coin was that the answers she found could be devastating.

I knew well enough what it meant to be unwanted. Sure, by all accounts, my parents had been happy to have me, but with my father murdered, my mother had dipped out of my life a few weeks later. Perhaps she'd wanted me once—or the idea of me—but she'd never signed up for single parenthood, and I guessed she'd cut her losses. My cousin Canna insisted that she hadn't sneaked back into the Pactlands to start over with a new family, but that didn't mean she hadn't made another life for herself here, maybe with an unsuspecting human husband. I could have half siblings on the other side of the continent, for all I knew. Hell, maybe she'd gone abroad and built a life in some remote corner of the world where I'd never find her.

As far as our relationship went, my mother held all the cards. She knew where Dad lived, and he hadn't moved since she ran away. If she'd wanted to reach out to me, she could have done so. But she'd offered no forwarding address, nothing but a weak apology for dumping her baby on him, and so I'd been left to grow up with one eye on the mailbox, hoping she might send word. A letter, pictures, assurances that she loved me but somehow couldn't keep me—*something* to calm the mind of a kid who, deep in her core, feared that the dad who absolutely loved her might one day walk away, too. Dad didn't owe me anything, the little voice in the shadows of my soul whispered. Mom had owed me so much more. So, if she could leave, what was stopping him?

Dad hadn't sent me to therapy when I was a kid. He had no papers establishing himself as my guardian, and so he did his best to keep me under the radar until I was a legal adult. But I think he knew what was going through my mind in those years after I really understood what had become of my biological progenitors, when I screwed up or frustrated him and shrank away with frightened eyes. He'd reassured me that he loved me, that kids were supposed to make mistakes and get on their parents' last nerves from time to time, and that no matter what I did, he'd always be my dad. I hadn't internalized that message overnight, but Dad was patient with me.

As an adult, I could see just how greatly I'd lucked out. Here was a man who'd never married or had the slightest interest in children, yet the moment he was left with a baby in his arms, he'd stepped up to the plate and done his best. Perhaps ours wasn't the most orthodox of parent-child relationships, but I couldn't have asked for a better father.

Warner Cavanaugh hadn't wanted a child, either, but instead of doing right by the baby on the porch, he'd raised her to serve him, controlling her with fear instead of guiding her with love. Sage desperately needed a guardian who acted like a damn parent, and though I didn't mind stepping into that role, I also knew that I couldn't touch the resources that would be available to her in the Pactlands. That kid *needed* therapy, and while I was woefully unequipped to help her unpack her trauma, I couldn't take her to a child psychologist in north Georgia, whose first call upon hearing that Sage had been kept chained in a barn would be to the police. Plus, I was well aware that my education in magic was deficient by Pactlands standards—had I lived there, I'd still be in school. I could teach Sage what Dad had taught me, but in light of her severe academic deficits to that point, she needed the sort of tutoring that I didn't know how to provide. Yes, Dad had figured out how to homeschool me, and I could plan something, but…it was a *lot*.

On the other hand, Sage was fragile, and if she got to the Pactlands and found confirmation that her parents had thrown her away without the first care for her well-being…

There was no telling why she'd been left with Warner. Maybe a family member had decided she was an aberration that needed to vanish and kidnapped her. More likely was that she was the product of assault. The last thing I wanted to do was retraumatize a rape victim—my guts knotted at the thought—but someone had to advocate for Sage.

And so I pushed my misgivings aside, went out to my workshop shed, and called Liogh Birrid.

The Division of Laws was headquartered in Beukal, the Pactlands' capital, which was apparently located somewhere near Richmond…well, yes, in a pocket world, but had that pocket shattered, it would have appeared in east-central Virginia. Importantly for me, Beukal adjusted its clocks to Eastern time, so I knew I wasn't calling Liogh in the middle of the night.

They picked up on the second ring. "Jane?"

"Hi, Detective Birrid. Uh—"

"Are you all right?" they demanded in rapid Pactish. "Is Yacovi—"

"Dad's fine," I hastily replied, "and so am I. No bodies this time."

They released a breath on the other end. "Good. Great. Okay." Chuckling, they said, "Sorry, assume the worst and hope for the best. What can I do for you?"

"Do you have a few minutes?"

"I do .."

"So, uh…" Unsure quite how to begin, I settled for blurting, "I've got a kid here who's probably a sorcerer–centaur cross, and she was abandoned as a baby—"

"*Whoa*," they interrupted. "Slow down, start over. I'm taking notes."

I did as they asked, recounting how I'd come to purchase Sage, what we'd done over the last couple of weeks, and how I'd sent Warner packing. "I know this has got to be sensitive," I concluded, "but if there's someone over there who could help us find her family…"

They whistled as I came up for air. "You're right, this is probably going to be messy, but of course we'll search. Whether she was abducted or abandoned is immaterial— either case falls under DOL's purview." An alarm faintly beeped on Liogh's end, and they grunted. "That's my warning. I'm tied up in meetings all afternoon. Could I come by in the morning?"

"Sure. When should I expect you?"

"Let's say nine-ish. The outbound portals aren't terrible at rush hour, but better to be on the safe side. Your place or Yacovi's?"

"How about we meet you at my house?"

"Perfect. See you then, Jane—and tell Sage we'll get to the bottom of this."

Once I hung up from Liogh, I pulled Connor's

business card from my pocket and considered the number on the back.

I didn't *know* this man. Just because he was a cop didn't mean I could trust him—hell, in a lot of respects, that counted against him. But he'd been frank with me, and he'd shown me his talent, which meant he knew as well as I did how important it was to keep certain secrets around our respective towns. And he'd offered to help...

Before I could talk myself out of it, I dialed and waited through two rings, and then I heard the telltale cavernous sound of a phone call taken through a car speaker. "This is Willow."

"Hey," I said, "it's Jane Fortune. Can you talk?"

"One sec." After a brief pause, he said, "Okay, radio's off, and I'm alone in my vehicle. What's up?"

"I reached out to some folks...*elsewhere*...about Sage, and a detective is coming by tomorrow to start searching for her family. I don't know what they're going to need, but in case they want to stop by the Cavanaugh place—"

"I can make arrangements, sure."

"Do you want to sit in?"

"You're inviting me?" he asked, surprised.

"Well, seeing as you're covering up my string of arsons..."

He laughed low in his throat. "True. Yeah, all right. What time?"

"Nine, my place. I take it you still have the directions."

"Absolutely. See you then, Firebug."

He hung up before I could protest the label, but in truth, he wasn't wrong.

I'd just put on a fresh pot of coffee at ten of nine Tuesday morning when I heard the crunch of tires over my mostly gravel driveway. First to arrive was Connor, once more in uniform, and he again removed his hat as he entered the house. "Morning, Jane," he said, and glanced past me at

Sage, who remained at the kitchen table, her feet wrapped around the legs of her chair as if she were anchoring herself to the furniture. "Morning, Miss Sage. How're we doing?"

"Okay," she said, and sipped her hot chocolate.

"Little nervous," I whispered, and Connor nodded.

"Can't say I'm entirely at ease myself," he said, taking the seat I offered him on the couch. "Now, who's this fellow meeting you here today?"

"A detective. Someone I trust. Helped me out with the woman in the cabin after Labor Day."

"Huh. And *where* is this detective from, again?"

"Nowhere near here," I replied. "The place where I suspect Sage was born."

Those pretty brown eyes regarded me thoughtfully. "Kind of skimpy on the details, aren't we?"

"Some things are on a need-to-know basis, Chief. You should understand that."

"Absolutely, but if this concerns my town—"

"The connection is tangential at best. I don't know whether anyone needs to investigate in Whitford, but in case—"

The sound of another vehicle pulling up interrupted me, and I headed to the door. "Be right back."

Parked behind Connor's SUV was a nondescript black Jeep with Virginia plates, surely one of DOL's fleet. The person who slid out and strolled around the hood, squeezing between the vehicles, was unusual for Ragged Gap: tall and lanky, built a bit like a dancer, with a brown complexion reminiscent of southern Asia or the Middle East and a long black ponytail. Their eyes, like Connor's, were brown, though of a darker shade, and their nose had a slight bend, the mark of a past break. In contrast to Connor's getup, they sported khakis and a thin blue sweater that I suspected was cashmere, and they carried a brown satchel on one shoulder.

"Jane," said Liogh with a brief smile. "Good to see you

again, youngling."

I shook their hand as they reached the porch. "Thanks for coming," I said in Pactish. "Before you go in, I've got company."

They cut their eyes to the Explorer. "I was going to ask..."

"He's the police chief over in Whitford, where Sage was abandoned. I asked him to come today in case DOL needs to poke around...well, what's left of the house where she was kept. It's still being treated as a crime scene until the fire investigator finishes his work, but Connor can get you in."

"Mm. Connor..."

"Willow. And there's another thing," I murmured, though I could have shouted; the two still in the house didn't speak a word of Pactish, as far as I knew. "He's got talent."

Liogh's brows rose. "How so?"

"Object levitation at the very least. He comes from a commune of sorts and says that some of his cousins have talent, too, so I'm thinking there may be human–sorcerer crosses in the next valley over."

The detective stroked their bare chin. "*Yikes*."

"I mean, it's a problem for another day—"

"Of course, but I'm just wondering why nothing can be simple with you," they replied, and patted my shoulder. "I'll behave. Lead the way."

With that, I pushed the door open and escorted Liogh inside. They wiped their loafers on the mat, then spotted Connor, who'd begun to rise from the couch. "Ah, hello," they said, segueing into English. Liogh could affect a surprisingly good American accent, though it bore no trace of Georgia in its clipped vowels.

Connor briefly sized them up—Liogh had a few inches on him—then stuck out his hand. "Connor Willow, Whitford PD."

They met his hand without hesitation. "Leo Beard. Jane

says you're the…chief of police?"

He sighed as he released Liogh. "I know I'm young, but it was a process of elimination after my predecessor stepped down, and our office is tiny. Sorry, I didn't catch who you're with."

Liogh smiled. "Because I didn't say. Division of Laws."

"Dare I ask *whose* division of laws?"

I met Liogh's questioning look and shrugged.

"A place called the Pactlands," they told Connor, using the translation. "And my interest here is solely—oh, hello," they said as Sage crept into the room. "You must be Sage."

She nodded.

"Splendid. As I was saying, Chief, my interest here is purely the girl…but Jane did mention that you have talent of a sort."

"A bit," said Connor. "Take it you do as well."

"Me?" They grinned again. "Nothing like Jane's, if that's what you're thinking. I can't start fires, so put your mind at ease."

He hesitated, then pointed to his hat on the coffee table, crooked his finger, and whispered something that sounded decidedly like *Come here*, and the hat rose and floated to him. "Like I said," he murmured, tucking it under his arm, "a bit. It's the touch."

"Interesting. Sorcerers in the family?"

"Come again, now?"

"Never mind. Perhaps we can discuss your…touch, was it?" Connor nodded, and Liogh said, "Another time. I'd like to get started with Sage."

"Sure, sure," Connor replied. "And look, I'm not trying to get all up in your investigation. Not my case. But if your people need to do anything on the ground in Whitford, Jane has my number. Just give me a call."

"Much appreciated, Chief." Liogh stepped aside as Connor started for the door. "And, uh…thank you for your discretion."

"Absolutely." Looking back as he pulled the door open, he said, "Have a good one, Jane," and saw himself out.

Liogh waited until Connor's Explorer drove off, then chuckled to themself.

"What?" I asked.

"The male of the species, in my experience, tends to be somewhat transparent," they said, giving me a knowing look. "I don't believe that young Chief Willow's interest here is solely professional, if you know what I mean."

I rolled my eyes. "He came by to talk about arson, not to ask me on a date."

"The two aren't mutually exclusive. Now, then," they continued, smiling at Sage, "let's get down to it, shall we? Pleased to meet you, Sage," they said, extending their hand.

She stared at it, unaccustomed to the gesture, then gingerly clasped the detective's. "Yes, sir," she began, then caught herself. "Wait, uh...um..."

"That's fine," said Liogh. "It's difficult when you only have two sets of honorifics, isn't it?" Sage nodded vigorously, and they laughed again. "You don't know any Pactish, do you?" they asked, releasing her hand.

"No, sir."

"Don't worry about that now. And since Jane's friend has left, I'm actually Liogh Birrid, but I'll answer to quite a bit." Stepping back, they gave her a careful look. "Jane told me some things about you. I suspect you're masked right now, eh?"

"Yes, sir," she mumbled.

"Would you mind showing me your true appearance? And I know that can be a big ask," they said, "so if you like, I'll go first."

Her eyes widened. "You're masked, too?"

"Oh, *my*, yes. They'd never let me out of the Pactlands if I didn't mask up." Reaching beneath their sweater, Liogh pulled out a thin silver chain from which hung a nondescript disc pendant, the sort of jewelry that might be mistaken for a saint medallion at a distance. "See? Necessary evil around here." They glanced over their shoulder at the windows, and then, satisfied, they gripped their pendant and muttered under their breath.

The result was instantaneous and striking.

I knew what nymphs *were*—Dad had taught me that much—but I'd never seen one unmasked until that moment. Liogh's facial features remained much the same but for their hue. Their dark tan had shifted to pale green, their black hair and brown eyes to vibrant blue. Their only feature that seemed to have changed in shape was their ears, the long tips of which now rose at least a couple inches higher than the rounded-off version had.

"*Wow*," Sage whispered, too stunned to mind her manners.

Liogh laughed in earnest at her reaction. "You see why the mask is necessary, yes?" they said, and looked at me. "You seem surprised, Jane."

"Just, uh…not the coloration I was expecting," I mumbled.

They cocked their head. "I did tell you I'm a water nymph, yes? Green, blue, or violet complexion. We've got a limited range, but then again, since you're all shades of beige, brown, or black, you don't have much room to talk. I tried for something in the middle when I designed my mask," they explained. "No offense, but off-white has never really done it for me."

They turned around at the sound of Sage running away. "Something I said?"

"She's changing clothes," I replied. "Doesn't want to rip those jeans."

"*Ah.*"

We sat on the couch and waited, and Sage soon reappeared in the skirt she'd thrown on for Connor the day before, barefoot. "Okay," she announced, then touched her necklace and turned off her mask.

Liogh didn't gasp, but they went very still and studied Sage's suddenly equine lower limbs. "I'm certainly not going to ask you to raise your skirt," they said to Sage, "but does the transition happen around your navel?"

She shifted her weight from hoof to hoof under their stare. "Yes, sir."

"I see. Thank you."

"Can I mask again?"

"Oh, sure." They did likewise, then gestured toward a chair, and Sage, once more fully human in appearance, settled in. "Well, I'll say this for Jane: she described you well."

"I wouldn't have made that up," I protested.

"No, but I needed to be thorough. See for myself."

"And there you have it. So, what now?" I asked. "What do we do?"

They leaned back and folded their arms. "We seldom see abandoned children, but the protocol is to take a blood sample and run it against those we have on hand. If that doesn't work, the next step is more complicated, but it's essentially a spell that uses the child's blood as a compass to locate the parents."

"Whose blood would you have on hand?"

"It's an assortment," they replied. "Agency heads, representatives, anyone sufficiently high in government to be considered a kidnapping risk. Parents of missing children, though fortunately, there are precious few of them in the system. And a selection of others—I know Annie and Wylan are both in there because of the Roulette research. I'm not, but it wouldn't surprise me if Rose is."

Annie and Rose I'd met back in September. Annie, a trainee agent with the Division of Plants and Potions, had been an ordinary human until she was dosed with a novel potion and left stuck in the Pactlands for her own safety. Though she'd been cured, she'd wanted to stick around, which wasn't an option for humans…but since her husband was, as Rose had put it, "a primal sink of magic," he'd managed to make her one of the Wild Hunt. I hadn't met Wylan yet, but I knew I didn't want to tangle with him in a dark alley. As for Rose, she was of mixed heritage, the highly talented, farseeing daughter of two half-human, half-elven parents who'd lucked into nearly all of her parents' elven genes. While she could pass without a mask, she was possessed of a wild talent so rare that DPP had made a position for her, despite her youth and imperfect education. If I was missing a few lessons in magic, Rose was missing whole classes, as she hadn't had the first clue what she was until she was twenty-six.

"Anyway," Liogh continued, "we can compare Sage's sample to what we have on hand, and if that doesn't work, we'll move to plan B. Given what I've seen here, I'd like to bring Sage over as soon as possible and get started. *But.*"

"But?" I echoed.

They sighed. "This is the sort of thing I need to run up the chain. The director will need to give her permission to bring Sage through the portal—and I assume you'll want to come with her, yes?"

I nodded. "If that's possible without getting Dad in trouble…"

"Should be. I have a plan. If Director Erenani balks for some reason, I suspect a quiet call to DOI could fix the problem."

The fact that the head of the Division of Intelligence— Rose's great-grandfather and another farseer—knew of my existence didn't give me the warm fuzzies, as my talent was proof that Dad had committed a crime. Granted, said crime was not forcing my mother to take the draught, but still, I didn't want to be the reason he landed in custody.

"I'll start making the arrangements," said Liogh, "and I'll call as soon as everything is in place." Rising, they said, "Don't worry, Sage, we'll figure this out. Jane, might I have a word?"

I followed them onto the porch, then walked them to their Jeep. "Thanks for coming," I said in Pactish.

"Absolutely. That poor child is *tiny*."

"I'm feeding her—"

"I don't doubt it, but she may always be small. And I think I saw the scars you mentioned." They shook their head. "I'll take this to the director straight away. Give me a day or two, and I think we'll have permission. A quiet visitor's pass, as it were."

"Much appreciated," I replied. "So...what'd you think of Connor?"

Liogh grinned. "I mean, if you're fond of beige males—"

"*Seriously.*"

They sobered. "He could very well be like you. Maybe not a direct sorcerer–human cross, but if this commune you mentioned has multiple talented people—"

"And strong rumors of inbreeding."

"Ooh." They sucked their teeth. "Well, that would keep the sorcerer genes in play and concentrated. Under that scenario, perhaps he has multiple sorcerers in the family— he could be several generations removed but still exhibit talent. It warrants further investigation, most certainly, but for now, I think we need to prioritize Sage."

"Agreed." I stepped back while they climbed inside the vehicle. "Safe trip, Detective."

"Try to keep that officer of yours on your good side, eh?" they said with a wink, and started the engine as I groaned.

CHAPTER 10

Thanksgiving had always been a two-person affair for Dad and me, but that year, we'd doubled our numbers: Sage, naturally, but also Tabitha, who had no family in the area and had offered to bring a pecan pie. "I got the recipe from my cousin in New Orleans," she'd told me, "and it tastes like pralines and happiness." I'd have been a fool to turn that down, and so Sage set the table for four while I finished dinner preparations that afternoon.

Dad, who'd been warned in advance about my guest list, greeted Tabitha at the door. "Ooh, I've heard about *this*," he said, taking the pie from her as she sloughed off her coat. "How've you been?"

"Busy," she replied with a smile. "Yourself?"

"Always." Heading to the kitchen with dessert in hand, he said, "Follow me. Holiday libations are this way."

Said libations were a bottle of Dad's *good* moonshine, one recently decanted from the cask in which it had been maturing for most of my life. As he poured a generous double for Tabitha, she eyed the dark amber liquid in the unmarked bottle. "I don't mean any disrespect, Coby, but I've got to ask a question."

He handed her the glass. "Shoot."

"Well...*oh*, this is lovely," she murmured, lifting the drink to her nose, but didn't taste it. "Knowing what I do about what went on at Labor Day...what's in this?"

To my relief, Dad didn't seem offended. "That is one hundred percent pure moonshine, just aged for twenty-five years."

"Really?" She sipped then, and her dark eyes widened. "Whoa, that's smooth. And how much do we charge for this particular hooch?"

"Special customers only," he said, grinning. "You're on my list, don't worry. But for your peace of mind, I never adulterate my 'shine. The brewing and distilling ends of my business are kept separate."

Tabitha smirked back at him. "And am I to understand that you're not brewing beer up there?"

He spread his hands, a *guilty as charged* gesture. "Jane said she'd filled you in."

"To a degree." She sipped again. "You're a sorcerer out of the Pactlands, right?"

"That's the gist of it. Come here, Sage," he said, beckoning the girl closer with the bottle. "Want a taste?"

"Dad," I warned from the stove, where I was trying to coax my gravy into thickening.

"Oh, don't be a killjoy, Janie. Special occasion." When I didn't argue with him, he pulled a jelly jar glass from the cabinet and poured Sage about half a shot. "Ever had alcohol before?" he asked her.

She eyed the glass warily. "No, sir…"

"Then take this slowly. Little tastes, not big gulps. You're going to feel warmth going down—"

"And since you've got the tastebuds of a teenager, it's entirely possible that you'll hate it," I interjected. "Dad won't get his feelings hurt, will he?"

"Don't you worry about me," he said, and passed the drink to Sage. "Give it a go, kid."

I glanced over in time to see her face screw up at the taste of moonshine and laughed. "It's okay, Sage. Want a Coke? Just put that in the sink."

"Yes, ma'am," she said gratefully, and headed for the fridge.

Dad and Tabitha traded glances. "More for us," he said, and clinked his glass against hers.

Twenty minutes later, after we'd settled in with plates

loaded from my makeshift countertop buffet, Tabitha asked, "So, Sage, how're we doing? Any thoughts yet about hunting down your family?"

She smiled over her turkey. "Yes, ma'am. And things are good. Jane burned down Master's house."

Tabitha and Dad turned to me with a clatter of cutlery. "I'm sorry, *what* was that?" Dad asked.

"It needed burning," I muttered.

My friend made a face. "I mean…where's the lie?"

"I don't disagree," said Dad, "but the risk…"

"I've got it under control," I insisted. "And to answer your question, Tabitha, I've been in touch with a detective in the Pactlands—Liogh, Dad. They're making the arrangements to start the search process for Sage."

"And the other detective says he's willing to help," Sage volunteered.

One of these days, I mused, I was going to have to have a talk with Sage about choosing her audience. For the moment, however, I had to deal with Dad first.

"What other detective?" he demanded.

"Sorry, he's a police officer," Sage amended. "Over in Whitford."

"*Whitford?*" Dad echoed, staring me down. "Janie, I've warned you—"

"It's fine," I said, cutting him off. "He had questions, I answered them—"

"Without a lawyer?" Tabitha asked, aghast.

"He's got talent. Says a bunch of his relatives in East Branch co. I think there are sorcerers in the mix over there, or maybe there were a few generations ago."

Dad, who'd stiffened in alarm, began to relax. "So, he sought you out with questions about magic?"

"Not…exactly," I confessed. "He came to talk about some fires. Magic was incidental. But he says I'm not under investigation, and he does want to help Sage."

Tabitha picked up her roll and tore it in two. "Cute?"

"He's not bad," I allowed, declining to mention his

pretty eyes.

"That's the *least* of our concerns," Dad began, but Tabitha waved him off.

"Now, how many sorcerers do you know in Georgia?" she said, fixing him with a no-nonsense look. "If he's close and cute—is he nice?" she asked me.

"Seems nice enough, I guess."

"All right, so close, cute, and not a complete asshole. Personally, I've never had a thing for men in uniform, but if he floats Jane's boat—"

"Can we talk about something else?" I interrupted, rising and turning away to hide my flush. "Like, I don't know, who wants more potatoes? Sage made them."

Second helpings went around, the junior chef was complimented by all present, and Sage beamed at the praise. As I topped up tea glasses, Sage asked, "Miss Tabitha, are you a sorcerer, too?"

"*Me?*" She chuckled and lifted her lowball of moonshine. "No. I'm a Wiccan—a practicing witch, if you like—but what I do…" After a brief pause, she said, "To the extent that it works, it's not nearly as immediate as what Jane can do. Or Coby, I suppose," she added, nodding to Dad. "Spells for luck, healing, clarity…I don't set out to hurt anyone, and I don't believe I have. But, say, something like your necklace? That's beyond my ability."

Sage frowned in thought. "But you brew, right? Jane said you grow your own herbs."

"I do," said Tabitha, "but that's largely for personal use—and for a few friends," she said, cutting her eyes to me. "I'm a pharmacist by trade. That means I can mix up medicines and sell them to people with prescriptions from doctors," she explained. "Kind of like cooking, I guess, but with drugs. See, there are lots of medicines available on the shelf, but sometimes, people need something customized. Maybe what's in stock isn't strong enough, or it tastes awful and they need to convince a child to drink it, or it contains an allergen…lots of possibilities. That's where I come in."

"But it's not magic?"

"Not in the least," she said, and sipped. "I'm just your average, ordinary human."

Sage smiled at her. "We can still be friends, though, right?"

"Absolutely, sweetie."

A moment later, Sage excused herself to the bathroom, and Dad turned to Tabitha. "I wish that were the common sentiment."

"Wish what were?"

"That we can be friends," he said quietly.

She chuckled. "I'm not the 'torches and pitchforks' kind, Coby. Anyway, they'd come for me as easily as they would for y'all. You know, I'm not exactly a member in good standing at the Baptist church downtown."

"It took a while before they finally gave up on me," he replied, shaking his head. "Persistent, I'll give them that. Even the ones buying from me tried to invite me to Sunday services."

She smirked. "Suppose I lucked out, then. I'm not pale enough to warrant their notice."

"A right pity, that."

The two snickered, and Dad raised his nearly drained glass to Tabitha in salute before he polished off his 'shine.

"Look," said Tabitha, who was almost ready for a refill herself, "I realize that I'm not supposed to have peeked behind the curtain, but thanks for not flipping out on me and...I don't know, scrambling my brains or whatever it is you people do. I need everything in here," she joked, tapping her forehead.

Dad snorted. "I was involved with that Oil of Life business, and I know what you did. You've got a good head on your shoulders, Tabitha, and...well, in all honesty, I'm glad there's *someone* in this town Jane will listen to whose first impulse isn't to set the problem on fire."

Rolling my eyes, I said, "I can handle my shit, Dad.

Not a child."

"Yeah, yeah, girlie. Come see me at your centennial, and we'll talk then."

Tabitha arched a brow at me in query.

"Explain later," I muttered as Sage returned to the room.

With the main course behind us, Dad rose to top up drinks while I gathered the plates and started to cut into Tabitha's pie. Before I could free the first piece, however, my phone rang, and I glanced at its resting place by my purse in annoyance. "Sorry," I said, hurrying across the kitchen to silence it, then noticed who was calling. "Oh, wait, it's Liogh. Excuse me."

"I've got the pie under control," Tabitha called after me as I ducked into the privacy of my bedroom and took the call.

"Hey, Detective," I said, closing the door.

"Hi, there. Bad time?"

"No, this is fine," I fibbed. "What's up?"

"Good news: I just got off the phone with the director, and I have permission to bring Sage *and* you over."

My guts clenched. "Uh...what does your director know about—"

"It's all right," they soothed. "I thought about how to approach this with her, and then I decided to do the wise thing and seek advice first. Rose got me in to see Lord ti'Dana."

"She *would* have an in with him..."

"She's moved into the family mansion, apparently, so I would hope so. I told him what was going on out there, and he called Director Erenani today. Can't tell you precisely what was said on that call, since I wasn't invited," they continued with a hint of annoyance, "but it must have been a decent talk, as I got summoned upstairs at the end of the day. Word from the top is that DOL is not inclined to press charges against Yacovi for any...irregularities, shall we say?"

I released my breath, my limbs suddenly leaden. "You're sure?"

"Absolutely. Now, for the time being, we're keeping the truth about you quiet. There's no need to announce the details of your existence just yet, eh?"

"Not at all."

"Good. So, how soon do you want to begin? I can pick you two up in the morning, if that works."

"Um...sure," I said, trying to process the sudden news that I was on my way to the Pactlands. "Yeah, that'd be great. What time should we be ready?"

"Let's say eight," they replied. "Pack for a few days' stay, won't you? I'll see you then."

I returned to the kitchen, slightly dazed, and found that Tabitha had not only cut up the pie but had also located the spray can of whipped cream in the fridge and done the honors. "Is everything okay?" she asked, stabbing her pie with her fork.

Nodding, I sank into my chair. "We're cleared," I said, looking at Sage, then Dad. "Liogh's coming to get us bright and early."

Dad's eyebrows rose. "*Both* of you?"

"Yup. They said the directors of Intelligence and Laws had a chat, and..." I paused, unsure of how much to say with Tabitha at the table. "There will be no prosecution concerning Essa Nerin."

The tension in his face smoothed—he was off the hook for the matter of my mother. "You're certain?"

"Liogh was convinced."

Smiling, Dad dropped his folk and squeezed my hand, and I couldn't miss the sudden sheen in his eyes. "This is great news, Janie. *Great* news." He sniffed, then glanced away and cleared his throat. "I...oh, heavens."

I nodded, thrilled for him but trying not to clue in the rest of the table.

"And this could be the start of something really good for you," he said. "If they arrange for you to stay in the

Pactlands—"

"I have a good thing going on here," I pointed out.

"So does Sage," he countered, "but you're trying to do better by her, right? This is an opportunity for you, too, girlie," he said, leaning toward me. "Don't say no to opening doors before you know what's waiting behind them."

"And hey, I don't mind swinging by the place and checking up on it while you're gone," Tabitha offered. "Or if you need to make deliveries next week, just send the boxes with me. I can pitch in."

I thought of the stack of cartons in the workshop ready to go to the post office for the early Christmas orders. "Are you sure?"

"Wouldn't offer if I weren't."

"And as soon as I'm back, we're doing that bathroom reno," I said, and tried the pie. "Oh...oh, *wow*, I'm going to need this recipe."

The next morning, as I emerged in the predawn shadows to make myself a cup of tea, I found Sage already dressed and waiting by the front window, looking out at the dark mountain road. "It's going to be a while, hon," I croaked, then muttered at my mug until the water heated. "You want some breakfast? Tabitha left the rest of the pie."

While ours certainly wasn't the healthiest of meals, Sage ate every bite, then returned to the window to keep vigil. Anxious myself but trying not to show it, I cleaned up and dressed, and I'd joined her in the den with my duffel and the rolling weekender I'd loaned her to wait. I'd helped Sage assemble outfits after Dad and Tabitha went home, and though I'd cautioned that there might not be a way to charge it, she'd slipped my MP3 player into her luggage along with her workbooks.

A few minutes before eight, Liogh's borrowed black Jeep slowed and turned into the driveway, and Sage hurried to grab her things. I met the detective outside and lifted a hand in greeting. "Morning. Need the facilities? Coffee?"

"I'm set, but thank you," they replied. "And you? Ready?"

They helped Sage stow her bag and get situated in the back while I locked up—I'd given Tabitha a spare key the night before—and I hopped into the front seat. "So," I said, keeping the conversation in English for Sage's benefit, "how does this work?"

Liogh smiled. "You sit back and enjoy the ride, and I endeavor not to wreck."

"No, I mean how do we get into the Pactlands? Dad's never shown me the portal."

"*Ah*. It's nothing special," they replied, pulling back onto the quiet road. "The nearest portal is slightly west of a town called Central—"

"In South Carolina, yeah."

They glanced at me, and I suspected that I was doing a poor job of hiding my nerves. "Correct. There's an undeveloped area near a lake."

"I could be wrong, but I think that belongs to Clemson University."

"If they object, I've never heard it," Liogh said with a shrug. "The portal itself is inside the remains of an abandoned house. There are spells on the place keeping it upright and hidden unless you know what you're searching for. Drive around the back, and the rear wall is large enough to admit passenger vehicles."

"Sneaky."

"It works." Checking the rearview mirror for Sage, they said, "Nothing to worry about, youngling. We'll have you there long before lunchtime."

Liogh didn't have a lead foot, but they stayed slightly above the speed limit all the way, and I kept my eyes peeled for the turnoff as we drove through the northwestern tip of South Carolina. In less than an hour, we'd reached civilization, and then we crossed the lake to Clemson and turned north. The woods weren't exactly scenic, especially in late November, but Liogh navigated the back roads without consulting a map, and soon, they turned off on a dirt track that seemed to dead-end into the pines. "Where are you—*oh*!" I exclaimed as the magically hidden house appeared as if from a fog. "How the heck do you remember the way back to this place?"

"Practice," they said, and crawled around the crumbling building. As they'd said, much of the back was missing, perhaps the victim of a tornado or merely of time, but I couldn't see anything inside the house beyond debris and weeds.

Liogh parked and tapped a button on the Jeep's console with a pair of concentric circles on it. I'd thought it was a representation of a tire or something, but almost immediately, a female voice came over the SUV's speakers in Pactish: "Name and location?"

"Liogh Birrid, Central," they replied, "with two passengers authorized by Director Erenani. The forms should be in the system."

I held my breath until the speaker said, "You're clear, second in the queue. Portal should open in three minutes."

"Now we wait," they explained. "All of the external portals come through at the same location in Beukal, and some drivers are quicker than others to understand the importance of clearing the landing space. Don't worry about this—I'll do the talking."

"I think you'd better," Sage piped up behind them, "since I didn't understand any of that."

Liogh hissed. "Yeah, I know. We need to give you a language potion, but just let me handle the portal first."

Right on schedule, rainbow flashes of light began to spark within the house, and a small, bright pinprick at the center of the optical storm quickly ballooned into a hole in the fabric of the world perhaps six feet wide—not huge, but big enough for the Jeep to pass. On the other side, I could see what appeared to be the interior of a building—a garage, perhaps, or a warehouse—with a seeming tollbooth and an arm directly ahead.

"Here we go," said Liogh, and I wondered if the cheery note in their voice was meant to reassure Sage, me, or the both of us.

They slowly drove through and idled at the checkpoint, where a brunette in a dark green uniform awaited. "Good morning," she said, drawing closer to the driver's-side window. "Credentials, please?"

Only once Liogh handed her their badge did I notice her distinctly pointed ears. She nodded, satisfied, and smiled, revealing unusually sharp teeth.

An elf, I realized. That was an honest-to-God *elf.*

Technically, yes, I'd met elves. Rose was significantly elven, and Yven was full-blooded. But aside from Annie, who'd given me a brief peek of her true face, the agents who'd come to town in September had kept their masks firmly in place around me. And yet here was an elf, telling Liogh to have a nice day and raising the arm to give us passage.

"See?" Liogh said, heading for the exit. "No problem." They dug beneath their shirt for their masking pendant and disengaged it, and I wondered briefly if removing the mask once they were safely home offered the psychic equivalent of unhooking a too-tight bra.

"Okay back there?" I asked, turning to Sage, whom I found staring at her surroundings with wide eyes. She seemed superficially calm, but she worried her bottom lip with her teeth, giving herself away.

"Yes, ma'am," she managed…and then she gasped as we exited the building. "Oh, *look!*"

I straightened in my seat and saw what had so shocked her: the skyline of a city rising in the near distance, its tall glass spires glinting in the morning light. Having made periodic visits to Atlanta, I wasn't nearly so moved by the sight, but considering that the biggest city Sage had seen to date was Greenville, I could understand her excitement.

Glancing back again, I noted the exterior of the portal building, a nondescript circular structure with a brown domed roof. The opening through which we'd left also doubled as the entrance, as two lanes of traffic ran side by side through a hole perhaps thirty feet wide and just as tall. There wasn't any grand sign on it, no THIS WAY OUT tacked above the door in flashing neon, but then I supposed that anyone with permission to leave the Pactlands knew enough to recognize the exit.

The area through which Liogh drove us was manicured, if boring, nothing but winter-browning fields of grass that eventually gave way to the outskirts of the city proper. As we passed yet another grassy stretch—a park, perhaps, judging by the pair of joggers I spotted on a gravel track—I recalled the problem with the soil. The Pactlands being an artificial world, little grew well without significant magical assistance linking the land to the outside, which was a major reason why the inhabitants hadn't simply cut ties and sealed the gates. Dad had told me about the agricultural districts created and maintained to feed the populace, and there was a nature preserve similarly anchored with complex spells in which trees and shrubs grew to their normal proportions, but otherwise, the best anyone could do for landscaping was a healthy lawn and stunted trees that grew no more than hip high.

"Are we going into the city?" Sage asked, leaning forward in her seat.

"We certainly are," said Liogh, slowing to a rolling stop at a deserted intersection. "See the tallest skyscraper? That's where we're heading."

"What *is* it?"

"DOL headquarters…uh, the Division of Laws," they explained. "Police, investigators, counselors for the Pact, and such. We needed room downtown, and since horizontal space was at a premium, we went vertical."

"You needed *that* much?" I asked.

They shrugged. "There's room to grow, most certainly. But we're ten stories taller than DPP, and that never ceases to annoy them, so I suppose the building serves its purpose."

Frowning, I said, "I thought Laws and DPP were partners."

"Oh, sure. They're like our sibling agency. Our *little* sibling agency," they added with a sly grin. "I've been liaising with DPP since the sixties. Good people. But we do have our fun." Glancing in the mirror at Sage, they said, "I'm sorry I can't give you a proper driving tour right now, youngling. We're expected, so the sightseeing will have to come later."

As we approached the heart of the city, I found myself staring out the windows as badly as Sage was, and I hoped the tinted glass was dark enough to hide my gawking. It wasn't the architecture that truly drew my eye, or the unusually clean city streets, but rather the *people*. A pair of white-haired, three-foot-tall gnomes approached us, pushing a tiny stroller. A knot of young-looking men and women wearing sleeveless embroidered robes over their dress shirts and trousers crossed the street in front of the Jeep, talking animatedly and laughing. Only two of the group could have passed for human; another pair were elves, while the remaining three had to be nymphs, judging by their long ears and deep red or blue skin. An SUV closer to the size of a tank pulled up beside us at a light, and I found a dark blue, tusked creature with a black mohawk behind the wheel—a troll, I knew, though given the species' relative lack of sexual dimorphism, I couldn't hazard a guess as to their gender. Trolls, Dad had told me, were almost as bad as nymphs in that regard, though you could usually figure it out after a few minutes' conversation. Gendering a nymph, on the other hand, was a crapshoot unless you understood nymphic naming conventions.

Rounding a corner, I spotted what looked to be the

muscular tail of a giant anaconda hanging from the back door of a taxi, but then the rest of the body popped out, revealing the torso of a bald woman in a fuzzy pink sweater who'd reached in to grab her purse. A naga, I knew from Dad's lessons, humanoid to the waist but able to unhinge their jaws to swallow larger meals. Dad said he'd been friends with one in school, a guy who was quiet and bookish until provoked. When some older kids had started picking on a runty sorcerer in their class, the naga had struck, wrapping himself around the biggest of the group and squeezing until the bully passed out. They were constrictors, Dad had taught me, and ambush predators by nature. A naga could secrete powerful pheromones that incited lust in *many* species, and when the sex-addled unfortunate came hunting for the source...well, at least he got a last hug out of the deal.

We were only two blocks from the DOL tower when I saw a centaur, and judging by the soft, sharp gasp behind me, Sage had noticed, too. She was tall, dwarfing the goatish faun who trotted along beside her, with a head of neatly styled blonde waves. What little I could see of the rest of her body—her waist and front legs—bore a coat of the same shade. Both she and the faun wore long black robes, sleeveless but unadorned, and while the centaur's hung open in the front, it covered her back and fell nearly to her hooves. Beneath the robe, she sported only a pale blue blouse...but then again, the faun had also eschewed pants, so I supposed there was nothing scandalous about their attire.

"Is that..." Sage murmured.

Liogh nodded. "The centaur? That's Cennis Paf, one of our counselors. *Terrifying* in front of a tribunal. I'll be shocked if she never becomes a judge, though I suppose she has more fun in her current role. The faun with her..." They paused, squinting as we slowly drove past the pair. "I *think* I've seen him around, but he's new. Probably fresh from his internship. He must be shadowing Cennis. The tribunal building is that way," they added, cocking a thumb over their shoulder, "the domed building behind us. "It's only four blocks, so we usually walk it."

After one more red light—the traffic lights turned blue instead of green, I noted—Liogh pulled into a garage entrance in the DOL tower and headed down two floors to find a free space. "Morning crowds are the worst," they remarked, locking the Jeep. "Come with me, there's an elevator."

Luggage in hand, I followed them down the row, wondering why the spaces were so wide until I found a troll-sized vehicle parked in one. Trolls weren't impossibly large—maybe only eight or nine feet tall, per Dad—so while they could squeeze into many conventional vehicles, I understood why they might prefer better proportioned options.

I realized I had no idea how centaurs and nagas got to work, but that would be a question for another time.

We stepped into the elevator, and Liogh pushed the button for the twentieth floor. "First stop is with the healers," they explained. "We're expected."

Sage's eyebrows scrunched. "Healers?"

"Doctors," I offered.

"More or less," said Liogh. "I could be mistaken, but I don't believe the human version have any skill with magic. Healers do, or else they work in teams with other healers who can cast and such."

"But I don't feel sick," Sage protested, "and Mr. Coby has been giving me potions to make the scars better."

"Oh, this isn't for treatment," Liogh assured her. "The healer will probably want to examine you—I don't doubt Yacovi's skill as a brewer, but you may have issues that he and Jane haven't noticed. And the healer will be the one to take the samples we need to start tracking your family."

She tensed, and I took her hand. "I'll be right here," I promised. "Don't be scared, hon."

"Am I going to have to unmask?" she mumbled.

Liogh smiled wanly. "Probably just for a little while. But really, our healers see *everything*. No one will recoil in horror," they teased.

Sage tightened her grip on me, and I held on as the elevator came to a stop.

When the doors opened, Liogh escorted us down an ordinary, institutional tiled corridor past rows of doors. Some were open, revealing medical beds of various sizes; another door appeared to lead to a pharmacy. We made a turn, and the doors grew smaller and closer together—offices, I realized, trying to read the Pactish placards as we passed. As Sage and I stepped aside to give room to a faun pushing a medicine trolley, Liogh hurried on ahead and rapped at one of the doors.

It opened almost immediately, and a pretty woman in a purple lab coat slipped into the hall. A few inches taller than me, with soft green eyes and brown hair pulled up with a claw clip, she turned toward the sound of our footsteps and beamed. "Jane!" she cried, brushing past Liogh, her open coat flying behind her as she sped our way.

While I didn't recognize her face, I knew my cousin's voice from our phone calls. "*Canna?* Hi! What are you doing—"

"I work here, silly," she said, and I released both Sage and my bag to hug her. "Did they not tell you I'd be here?" she asked, cocking her head back toward Liogh.

"I thought it'd be a nice surprise," the detective replied, joining us. "The director knew we needed a healer and assigned Ms. Nerin to this matter. I suspect we all know why."

It didn't take a genius to see the wisdom in the director's choice. Canna knew of my existence—her husband, Pars, had been among the agents Liogh had pulled from DPP to assist in September, and Rose had called Canna as soon as she made the connection.

At first blush, there wasn't any great similarity between

Canna and me—I was blonde to her brown, brown-eyed to her green—but something about our noses seemed familiar, and I knew I'd seen her smile in the mirror. Strange, I thought, to be inches away from blood kin for the first time in twenty-seven years. But even if my mother hadn't wanted me, Canna grinned like I'd just waltzed in with a box of puppies and a chocolate cake, and she hustled us into her office after giving me another quick hug.

Her space wasn't anything to write home about, a windowless room outfitted with a metal desk, a counter crammed with bottles and cannisters between gray cabinets above and below, and a pair of folding chairs that had probably seen better decades for company. The only decoration was of the homemade variety: pictures of Pars and four small children, plus finger paintings and crayon scribbles, all neatly taped to the upper cabinets in a gallery of sorts.

"I'm so sorry," she began, "these offices are tiny, but let's give our special guest a seat. It's all right, darling," she said to Sage with a gentle smile. "Why don't you pop into a chair there, and let's have a chat before we get down to the fun part."

Sage looked at her blankly, and I explained, "She doesn't speak Pactish."

"*Oh*," said Canna, taken aback. "I'm so sorry…has Yacovi not given her a language potion?"

"We've had other priorities."

She grimaced. "I see. Fair, but…well, if we can get her fluent before I start working with her, that'll be easier. We won't need a translator that way, and once the investigation kicks off, in case she needs to be interviewed…"

Liogh considered it, then nodded. "Canna's right," they told me. "It'll push us back a few days while Sage recovers and adjusts, but better sooner than later."

"What's going on?" Sage asked me, unable to follow

the conversation. "Should I unmask?"

"Not yet. Have a seat," I said, and waited until she gingerly lowered herself into one of Canna's chairs. "This is my cousin Canna," I continued, nodding toward the expectant healer. "She's going to be the one handling this part of your case, but she doesn't speak English, and you don't speak Pactish."

Sage smiled up at her helplessly. "Hi. Sorry, um…"

"It's okay," I assured her. "They've developed a potion here that can make you fluent in a language pretty quickly…like, in a matter of days, I think."

At that, Liogh saved me from myself. "It doesn't hurt, though the taste isn't great," he told Sage. "It's how I acquired this language, in fact. Anyone in the agencies who goes outside takes a language potion at least once in their career. The problem is that you may feel a little sick after taking it—"

"What are they saying?" Canna whispered to me.

"Trying to explain the potion," I replied in kind.

Rolling her eyes, she said, "And that would be *my* job," then interrupted Liogh. "I talk, you translate, yes?"

They agreed, and with Sage watching the pair like a tennis spectator, Canna stepped into professional mode. "The language potion is highly complex, but the effects are permanent. The flavor is…unfortunate, but I can give you something to wash away the taste. Side effects upon taking it vary and are rather unpredictable. You may feel a little worn-down and sick to your stomach, or you may pass out for a few days. No way of knowing how you'll handle it until you take it for the first time. But I'll serve as the linguistic donor for the potion, and once your mind settles, you'll be as fluent as I am in terms of words and meanings. Idiomatic phrases may still be a challenge, and don't ask me for adolescent slang, but you'll be in a much better position than you are now. Any questions?"

Sage nodded. "How long does it take to work?"

"Well," she said after Liogh repeated the question for

her, "for adults, about seven days, and about five for children. Much faster than taking classes, though, right?"

"Will I be able to read?" she asked hopefully.

Upon receiving the translation, Canna looked to me, puzzled. "Her literacy is pretty minimal," I murmured. "She's been working on it with me, but she's got a long way to go.'

"Ah." Turning back to Liogh, she said, "Tell Sage that she may not be able to read perfectly, but it will probably be easier for her to read in Pactish than in English once the potion kicks in."

Grinning at the news, Sage told Liogh, "I'll do it."

Canna opened one of her cabinets and extracted a small bottle of thick, puce-colored liquid. She unscrewed the cap, closed her eyes and took a few deep breaths, then spat into the bottle. Before I could ask what *that* was all about, she muttered a spell, and the potion began to glow, its soft pink light reflecting off the polished countertop.

"Um…why did she spit in there?" Sage asked.

Liogh quickly translated, and Canna, who'd recapped the bottle, gave it a vigorous shake as she explained, "That's how you get the donor's language into the potion. It seems gross, but it won't hurt you." She waited until Liogh passed this on to Sage, then handed her the bottle. "All right, dear, if I were you, I'd hold my nose and knock that back."

Though Sage eyed the glowing liquid with mistrust, she did as Canna suggested, then slammed the bottle onto Canna's desk and stuck out her tongue. "Oh, *yuck*, that tastes spoiled…"

Liogh caught her as she lost consciousness and slumped forward, saving her from hitting her head, and I helped them lower Sage to the floor. "This is normal?" I asked Canna.

"Completely." She tossed the used bottle into a translucent plastic bin on the counter and resealed the lid. "I don't think you want to keep her here while she sleeps it off," she said to Liogh. "Pars and I have a spare room, and you know he can be trusted. Let me take Jane and Sage home with me, eh? I'll bring them back in as soon as Sage can converse."

Liogh mulled that over, then nodded. "Not as if I can't find you should the need arise," they said with a smirk. "Do you want to take a blood sample while she's unconscious?"

Canna's answer was immediate and firm. "No. I don't work on patients who can't consent unless it's an emergency. She'll be ready for you in a week or less, Detective. Surely you have another case to occupy you in the meantime."

Seeing that Canna was not to be moved, Liogh resigned themself to the new plan and took their leave, and I pointed to the sleeping girl on the tile. "So...what now?"

My cousin whispered until Sage rose from the floor, then stepped out, leaving her hovering. She returned with a wheeled stretcher, and with practiced motions, she soon had Sage strapped down for transport. "Come on," she said, pushing Sage out of her office. "Let's get her to bed."

I followed Canna toward the elevator. "Are you going to get an agency vehicle? I saw the hidden compartment on Liogh's..."

"No need. I've got something better."

Considering that Liogh's loaner back in September had come with a lab bigger than Dad's brew room, I had my doubts about that. "Oh?"

"Yep." The elevator chimed, and she pushed Sage aboard. "A minivan."

CHAPTER 11

Canna's version of the dreaded "mommy-mobile" was blue and fairly clean outside, and littered with crumbled cereal and crayons within—the expected for a parent of four. The bench in the first rear row bore a pair of car seats, while the bench behind it sported matching boosters. I considered the seats and the general detritus for a moment, wondering where we could put Sage, but then Canna opened the back hatch.

Apparently, in the Pactlands, extra storage came standard. From the outside, the trunk area seemed maybe a foot long, but its true length was closer to seven feet. Canna folded the stretcher and levitated it into the van, then strapped it in place with bungee cords. "Not exactly regulation transport protocol," she muttered, closing the door after I'd stowed our luggage beside the stretcher, "so we'll drive slowly and keep this between us, okay?"

I hopped into the front, dropped a half-eaten baggie of what appeared to be Cheerios into the cupholder, and buckled up. "You said you live in Beukal, right?" I asked Canna.

"Technically, yes, but not in any of the exciting bits," she replied, watching the camera as she backed out. "We moved to Old Farm when Dieta was a baby. Don't get me wrong, I liked our apartment downtown, but it's lovely having *space*, especially with four underfoot." Guiding the minivan through the garage, she said, "I grew up in an apartment in the city, but my mother's dental practice was close by, and my father taught upper-level classes—still does, I should say—so he was always at school when I was growing up. My parents preferred the convenience, but Pars and I wanted the kids to have room to run around."

Canna had mentioned her mother, Dahlia, my maternal grandfather's little sister. I'd asked once about her name, which struck me as unusual for a sorcerer, and Canna had laughed; her grandmother had worked for DOL as a young woman and so had been exposed to some of the outside world's foreign terminology. She'd liked the flower and its name, and so she'd bestowed the moniker upon her daughter. "It happens," she'd told me. "Look at Pars. To this day, I don't know what his parents were thinking."

It was then I'd learned that Pars was legally "Parson," but those closer than casual acquaintances seldom used more than his nickname.

"What does your dad teach?" I asked, bracing myself for a long explanation about a niche field of magic to which I'd yet to be exposed.

She pulled out into traffic, her windshield darkening against the morning glare. "Ethnomusicology."

"Come again?"

"It's the study of music within a culture—less about the music from a technical or performance standpoint than about how it functions in context. He specializes in twentieth-century human musical forms. Actually got permission to go out and do field research when I was little," she added with a smile.

"That's...*really* broad," I said, thinking of the variety even a casual sweep of the radio dial would offer.

"Oh, I'd believe it. Are you familiar with jazz?"

I paused, considering that. "I know what it is, but I'm not an expert."

"Mm. That's Dad's particular focus. We named Coltrane for his favorite artist," she added in a conspiratorial tone. "Dad *adores* his recordings. Saxophonist. Did you know there was a religious group that worshipped him for a time after his death?"

"Uh…no."

"Truly. They consider him…what's the word…a *saint* now," she said, her English oddly accented. "Fascinating stuff all around, but don't get Dad started, or he'll tell you more than you ever wanted to know. Anyway, he teaches electives to older students. Not everyone needs intensive magical theory."

Canna drove us out of the downtown area and into a residential zone, a neighborhood of one- and two-story homes with tidy lawns and bush-like trees. "This is Old Farm," she said, slipping into tour guide mode. "When Beukal was smaller, this was the main agricultural district for the city. But it grew, and we needed more housing, so the farmlands were moved farther out, and Old Farm popped up in its place. Unfortunately, when the farms were removed, so were the anchors to improve the soil, but at least the grass grows, right?"

I wondered what Canna, born in a veritable prairie, would think of my cabin halfway up a tree-covered mountain. She'd seen mountains—the designers of the Pactlands had put in a range, the Edolis, where she'd vacationed only weeks before—but my mountains were far older and wilder, somewhat tamed by tourists but alive with deer and hawks and the occasional bear.

Canna wove through quiet Old Farm, then slowed in front of a neat two-story house with white siding, a modest porch, and trim green shutters. Like its neighbors, it sat back from the street, separated from the asphalt by a swath of short brown grass. The lack of other landscaping bothered me—I could envision a mature oak in the front with a swing, or maybe a sprawling pear tree—but I kept my thoughts to myself as we pulled into the driveway.

"We'll have a few hours of peace, at least," she told me. "Dieta and Maliul are in school, and the twins are at daycare. Pars will pick them up on his way home, and then chaos will reign here once more, but for now, let's get Sage to bed."

I grabbed our bags and waited as Canna magically coaxed the stretcher out of the back, then held open the side door while she maneuvered sleeping Sage into the house. The stretcher rolled toward the front, then collapsed enough to float up the staircase, with Canna right behind it. By the time I made it upstairs, the stretcher had reached the guest room, a cozy space dominated by a wide, pillow-laden bed that seemed to swallow Sage's little body as Canna tucked her in. Three of her could have slept there comfortably, I estimated, and parked her borrowed luggage by the foot of the bed as Canna slid the stretcher beneath the frame to make room. "Let's go downstairs," she whispered, though there was no need for quiet; Sage hadn't stirred.

Canna led me back through the den, which was strewn with dolls and oversized plastic blocks for small hands, and into the warm kitchen. "Tea?" she asked. "I could do with a cup."

"Sure, thanks. Hey, if you need to get back to work, I'll sit with Sage—"

"I'm taking the day. Got to keep an eye on my patient," she added, winking at me before she filled the kettle.

"How long do you think she'll be out?"

She shrugged. "There's no set timetable. She could sleep until lunch, or she could sleep for two days. I've never seen one go longer than that," she added reassuringly. "Besides, she's young, so the process should go more quickly." As she pulled mugs from a cabinet, she paused, frowning. "The guest bed is pretty big, but I trust you'd rather not bunk with Sage while she's recuperating. The only other thing I can offer you is the den couch, and it's quite comfortable—"

"Oh, that'll do," I insisted.

"If it doesn't, let me know. I'll call Rose, and I'm sure she could arrange an invitation for you to Lord ti'Dana's place—*he* certainly has room to spare."

"Really, this is fine."

"Okay," she said, unconvinced, "but I hate it that you finally make it over, and the best I can do for you is the darn couch." She huffed a sigh and spread her arms. "Welcome to the Pactlands, I suppose. Now, I could pull together a bed—"

"So could I," I interrupted, "but where on earth would you put it?"

"True," she muttered, digging in a cannister for teabags. "And you make furniture? I know your father's been training you, but I didn't want to assume…"

"I'm probably behind on potions, and I'm sure I don't know half the theory I should, but I'm a decently competent sorcerer otherwise. It's Sage I'm worried about. She's just now discovering her abilities, and since she's so far behind across the board…I mean, I'm doing my best, but she needs remedial help."

"As my mother always says, we work magic, not miracles. How do you take your tea, dear?"

"Just sugar, please."

Canna doctored the mugs while the water quickly boiled—her range, I assumed, was souped up through sorcery—then carried our drinks to the table and sat beside me. "So," she said, and smiled.

I grinned back at her. "So."

"I can't believe you're here, Jane. And *legally*, no less."

Frowning, I said, "I thought this was some special dispensation from your boss."

"Well, *yes*, but I recall Rose sneaking in and out about a year and a half ago, so well done securing actual permission," she said dryly, raising her mug. "I wish I could introduce you to the rest of the family, but…"

"Not the right time for that," I finished as she trailed off. "And I'm probably supposed to keep a low profile while I'm here, so the reunion will have to wait."

Her mouth puckered as she mulled that over. "Would you like to see pictures, at least? Start putting names and faces together? Or not," she hastily continued. "I can't imagine what must be going through your mind. If I'm suggesting things that are too much, just tell me to back off."

"You're very kind," I said, reaching over to squeeze her free hand. "And I do want to know about my roots, but right now, with Sage…"

Canna nodded. "The director told me virtually nothing about her, just that she might have family here. How did you find a baby sorcerer out there?"

I sighed and sipped my tea, collecting my thoughts. "For starters, she's not fully a sorcerer. Probably half centaur under the mask she's wearing."

My cousin's jaw dropped, but she quickly collected herself. "That…*might* have been good information to know before I started testing her. Heavens know I don't want to make the child feel self-conscious, but…" She whistled softly. "So, she's masked? Yacovi had jewelry?"

"I made it, actually."

"*Really?* At your age? Good for you," she replied—and to my surprise, she sounded impressed. "I can barely manage it, but I've never had any talent for jewelry. That necklace she's wearing…"

"That's it. Best I could do with what I had—we needed to mask her quickly to start getting her out of the house."

Canna paused, wrapping her fingers around her mug. "Dare I ask what she looks like unmasked?"

"More or less, a bipedal centaur. Smash the horse bits together into a single pair of legs." Seeing her expression shift, I said, "Kid's had a *rough* time of it. Someone dropped her on a doorstep one town over from mine, and they couldn't have chosen a worse house. Guy who lives— *lived*," I amended, smiling to myself—"there pretends he has dark, mystical power," I said, widening my eyes in mockery.

"Why?"

"Eh, it's a type. Anyway, he raised her just long enough to put her to work for him around the place. Told her she was some sort of demon, and since she never spoke to another soul, she believed him. She still calls him 'Master,' but we're working on that."

One of Canna's hands had risen to cover her mouth. "*Jane.*"

"Yeah. She started developing talent, he got spooked, and since I'm locally rumored to be a witch of sorts, he showed up on my doorstep and intimated that he'd get rid of her if I didn't want to buy her off of him."

"Get *rid* of her?"

I mimed a pistol shot. "So, I bought her, and here we are." After another long sip of tea—I didn't recognize the blend, but it was *smooth*—I said, "She's thirteen, and she's smart—quiet and shy at first, but once she peeks out of her shell, there's a clever kid in there. But she can barely read and write, and I've done my best in the last few weeks to start working with her. It's been triage, you know? What do you do first, develop her talent, teach her vocabulary, put meat on her bones? And let's not forget the healthy dollop of trauma on top of everything else. Her father figure abandoned her with me, and he was such an abusive asshole that the poor kid walks on eggshells, trying not to displease anyone. That baby accidentally broke a bottle in the grocery store and had a complete meltdown. And now," I muttered, "Dad and Detective Birrid both think there could be *problems* with her parents, if you get my drift."

"Unfortunately, yes." Canna's eyes narrowed. "She's *thirteen?*"

"She was starved."

"Well, obviously. For someone of centaur extraction, she's tiny."

"Yeah," I said, "I saw one coming in today. Uh…Cennis, was it? She works at DOL."

"Oh, sure, I know her. She's actually pretty short." Lowering her voice, she added, "You didn't hear this from me, but around the Tribunal, she's known as the Pony.

Word among the counselors is that you underestimate her at your peril. But next to her...I realize Sage is still growing, but for her age, she should be at least my size. *If she were a full centaur*," Canna allowed. "I don't think we have enough data to make firm predictions for a child like her."

"Like I said, I've been feeding her and giving her vitamins, but I don't see signs of a growth spurt yet."

"Too soon, I'd think." She patted my hand. "You're doing the right thing, Jane. We have some supplements we can give her to jumpstart her growth, but I'd hold off until she's a little heavier—growing takes energy, and she doesn't have large reserves. But I wish you'd told me about her," she added with a hint of reprimand. "She needs to be under medical supervision."

"I know, I *know*," I replied, "but I didn't want anyone here jumping in until Sage had a moment to get her bearings. My pharmacist friend has helped where she can—we even got her some vaccines. But you didn't see her as she was when she came to me. I've tried to give her a chance to adjust before throwing the Pactlands at her, especially if there's a decent chance that her parents will reject her again."

"She could have been kidnapped..."

I held Canna's stare. "Do you *really* think that's likely?"

"No, but I won't rule it out just yet."

Grunting into my mug, I muttered, "At least Essa left me with someone decent. Assuming Sage wasn't snatched from her loving parents' arms, they've got a lot of explaining to do."

Canna waited until I'd drained my tea, her mouth tight. "Jane, honey...I'm so sorry about what your mother did to you. This...*business* with Sage can't be easy."

I shrugged and pushed the mug aside. "Hey, by comparison, I lucked out."

"I just wish I could figure out what would make her abandon you," Canna continued, scowling into the distance. "Of all my cousins, I'd never have imagined that Essa could do something like that. Not without good reason."

"Oh, I can think of one. I'm a living reminder that she threw away her life here for...let's see, widowhood, single motherhood, and poverty? Yeah, that covers it."

"But you're her child—"

"And she was broke," I interrupted. "She came to Dad with almost nothing. I'm sure she had some buyer's remorse about chucking her DPP career for a human who couldn't even give her five good years of marriage, and then she got saddled with one hell of a souvenir."

"*Jane...*"

"It's true. Essa left the Pactlands for my father. Once he was dead, how was she supposed to get by with me? No family support, no money, no credentials to get a good-paying job...frankly, if she started over somewhere else and landed on her feet, I can't entirely blame her for not coming back for me. Maybe she remarried, and husband number two didn't want to deal with husband number one's kid."

Canna squeezed my hand again until I met her eyes. "For Essa's sake, I hope she's healthy and happy somewhere out there, but should we meet again, she and I will have a *serious* talk. I can't imagine abandoning my kids, not even when the twins started teething."

"You're also part of a two-parent, two-income household, though, right? Essa must have decided she couldn't afford me and left me with someone stable she trusted."

"I...do understand," Canna replied, "and perhaps she was faced with a terrible choice when you were small. Grief certainly does awful things to people, too. But to go twenty-seven years without a word to her daughter? I'm sorry, but I can't imagine that. I don't know what you must think of us, but our family's not like that. Whatever happened to Essa..."

"Look, Canna," I said, gripping her hand in turn, "the things she did to me are between the two of us. I certainly don't blame *you*, okay?"

She smiled weakly.

"And maybe you're right to be optimistic. There could be something better here waiting for Sage."

Silence stretched between us, heavy with the truth that what I'd said almost certainly was a lie.

"And what about the worst-case scenario?" Canna murmured, rising. "Here, let me get you some more tea."

I mulled over the question until she returned to the table. "If Sage's conception was…nonconsensual," I began, "then I can't very well expect her mother to want anything to do with her. That would be completely unfair to ask a victim to raise her rapist's baby. But Sage has been though absolute hell, and I just want that kid to have a loving family." I picked up my mug and blew the steam off the top. "If she can't find that here, then I'll take her home and raise her. I'm not abandoning her. Don't suppose I could give her a world-class education, but Dad homeschooled me, and I've done all right for myself."

"You've got a good heart, Jane," my cousin replied.

I chuckled. "Tell that to the people whose houses I set on fire."

"I could be wrong, but it sounds to me like you've set at least some of those fires for decent reasons." She paused, then asked, "Have you started any since that Oil of Life mess?"

"Just the guy who sold me Sage. Burned down the family farmhouse and ran him out of town."

"Can't blame you for that." Glancing at the microwave clock, she said, "We've got a few hours of peace ahead of us. I'd be happy to take you for the driving tour, but—"

"Someone should be here in case Sage wakes," I finished. "Don't worry, I brought my computer. Do you have a power converter, by any chance?"

"Pars does. I'll get it for you," Canna offered, and

smirked as I stood to get my bag. "Enjoy this while it lasts. The kids are…a lot."

That was an understatement.

Around five-thirty, the front door slammed open, and in ran a tall, dark-haired girl with Canna's green eyes and a purple band-aid on her forehead. She slung her backpack into the corner of the den and called, "Mom? *Mom*! We're home!"

"Hi, Mommy!" squealed the slightly smaller girl who entered behind the first, another brunette with brown eyes and a pink dress streaked with dirt. "Can I have a snack?"

"We're about to eat dinner," said Canna, appearing from the kitchen with a dishtowel thrown over her shoulder. "Go wash your hands. Dieta, help your sister!" she said as the two thundered up the stairs.

In came the rest of the pack, the three-year-old twins in their matching overalls and their father, who carried both kids' little backpacks in one hand. Pars was a giant by sorcerer metrics, seven feet tall and built like an ambulatory suit of armor. He wasn't a model by any means—his nose had been broken as a child and healed with a far more pronounced twist than Liogh's had, and coupled with his heavy brow and crewcut, he looked like he might moonlight as a prize fighter. But his was a kind face all the same, especially when he smiled, which he did broadly when he spotted me loitering in the den. "Jane! Hi! Canna said you'd be staying over—"

"Mom!" the eldest girl—Dieta, I reminded myself— yelled down the stairs. "Who's in the guest bedroom?"

"Leave her alone," Pars called back to her. "Tell you later. Come on, let's eat…*ah*, not so fast," he said, catching the twins around the waist as they ran toward the table. Hoisting one in either arm, he said, "Hands and faces first, you dirty little monkeys. Let's get washed."

The two laughed and screamed as their father bounced

them all the way to the downstairs bathroom, and Canna smiled weakly. "At least they're past the 'flinging food' stage."

Soon, the elder children had seated themselves, and Pars returned to buckle the younger into their booster chairs. As I helped Canna dish out a chicken and rice casserole with a mouth-watering aroma, Dieta frowned at me and demanded, "Who're you?"

"Manners," said her mother without turning around.

"This," said Pars, taking the plate from me with a smile and putting it on Dieta's placemat, "is your mom's little cousin Jane. Can you say hi?"

The kids chorused their greetings—Colji even waved—but Dieta remained unsatisfied. "Where'd you come from?" she asked.

I looked at Pars, but he appeared to have planned for this question, as he smoothly said, "A long ways away. This is her first time in Beukal, so let's make a good impression, eh?"

"I went to Acori once," Maliul, her five-year-old sister, volunteered.

"You don't even remember Acori," Dieta replied with disdain. "You were *two*."

"Do, too!"

Dieta rolled her eyes. "Then where did we stay?"

"In a house," Maliul shot back. "And there were *mountains*."

"You don't remember them. You've just seen pictures."

"Let's not provoke your sister," said Pars in a low voice that tolerated no disagreement.

"I live in the mountains," I said, bringing the twins' smaller plates to the table. "In a tiny town."

Maliul brightened. "Near Acori?"

"Not quite," said Pars, coming in for the save. "And thank you, Jane. Didn't meant to put you to work..."

"And I didn't mean to crash on your couch," I replied,

"so thanks."

His brow knit. "We have a bed—*oh*, right. Of course."

I smiled. "Kid gets priority. Not a problem."

With dinner dished out, I slid into the empty chair beside Dieta, who'd already begun to attack her broccoli. She gave me a once-over, then stiffened in surprise. "You've got *earrings*."

"*Dieta...*" her mother warned.

"Uh, yeah. I do," I told the girl, tucking my hair behind my ear to give her a closer look. "Got this one when I was fifteen," I said as I tapped the largest of the silver studs, the one in the center of my earlobe, then moved up the side. "I had the second holes done with some friends when I was twenty, and the third two years later on a school trip."

She leaned closer to stare. "Did it hurt?"

"Not much. The cartilage down here is pretty squishy," I said, squeezing my lobe. "It gets tougher once you pierce higher up the ear, so I'm probably stopping with three pairs." Turning to face her, I showed her the matching trio on the other side. "See?"

"Why'd you do it?"

A question Dad had certainly asked with every new piercing. "Because I like them. My friends and I kind of made an experience out of it—most of us got piercings, but one girl actually got a tattoo."

Her mouth hung open, and I wondered belatedly if I'd complicated matters for Canna and Pars. Fortunately, it seemed that Dieta wasn't about to beg her parents for earrings. "That's so *weird*," she declared.

"Dieta," Pars snapped. "Manners."

"What? It's weird!" she protested. "Only fauns do that."

"And Aunt Rose," Maliul pointed out.

I glanced at Canna. "Aunt Rose?"

"Pars said you met in September..."

Her husband cleared his throat. "Yven's been an uncle

to this bunch for years, so this was the natural progression."

I supposed the kids didn't mind that the two of them were still engaged. "Got it. Sorry, I didn't pay any attention to whether Rose wore earrings—"

But by then, the tumblers had fallen for Dieta, and she blurted, "You're from *outside*, aren't you? Like Aunt Rose?"

Looking to her parents for the right answer, I bit my tongue and waited.

Canna took the lead. "Jane does very important work outside. So important, in fact, that you don't need to mention her to your friends or your teachers. Understood?"

"Why?" asked Maliul.

The twins, at least, didn't give a damn where I was from, since they were too busy playing with their casserole.

"Because we don't need to be talking about what Jane does. Pact business," their mother fibbed. "But she's visiting us now for a little while, and I expect best behavior. Understood?"

Pars might have been the muscular giant in the house, but the look Canna shot her daughters produced immediate assurances from them.

Still, Dieta wasn't finished. "Who's in the guest room?"

"That's my friend Sage," I told her. "She's looking for her family in Beukal, but your mom had to give her a language potion today, so she's sleeping that off first."

Dieta's face scrunched. "Why'd she need *that*?"

"Because…" I cast about for a plausible explanation and settled on something near the truth. "Because Sage was misplaced as a baby, and she didn't grow up here, so we're taking care of that now."

"So, she's also from—"

"You are *not* to discuss Sage, either," Canna interrupted. "I mean it. And leave her alone—she may feel sick when she wakes, and if she throws up on you, I won't be responsible."

With a chorus of *eww*s, the girls returned to their dinner.

It was Friday night, but routines being crucial in a house with four small kids, Canna and Pars went straight to work once dinner was over. While Canna bathed the twins and Pars cleaned up the kitchen, I sat in the den with Maliul and Dieta, who'd decided that although I was weird, I could still put on a blue feather boa and come to their tea party. After a few cups of pretend tea, Dieta started prying for information about the world beyond the Pactlands. I gave her little, but I obliged when she asked me to "speak Human," and a simple, "Hey, y'all," sent the girls into fits of giggles. I tried to explain that there were thousands of human languages, not one universal tongue, but this was only met with further demands that I say things, followed by their poor attempts to parrot them back to me.

By nine, even Dieta had been ushered off to bed, and Canna appeared with a set of sheets and a blanket to help me fix up the couch. "I'm sorry," she murmured. "You're very entertaining to the under-ten set."

"I didn't teach them any profanity, so don't worry about that."

"*Thank* you." Tucking in the oversized sheets, she said, "If Sage wakes, I'll hear her—I've been sleeping with one ear open for a while. Try to get some rest."

With the makeshift bed assembled, she brought me a glass of water, and I checked on the phone I'd plugged in to charge with Pars's spare converter. "So, what time do things kick off around here in the morning?" I asked.

"On Saturdays?" Canna grimaced. "Early."

This wasn't at all how I'd imagined my introduction to the Pactlands would go, I mused, staring up at the ceiling in the darkness. But the couch wasn't bad, the house quickly stilled, and with Canna's assurances to calm me, I rolled over and soon slept.

CHAPTER 12

By long custom, if Pars was home on Saturday morning, he singlehandedly took care of the children to give their mother a few precious hours to herself. Thus, manning the pancake griddle and promising that he'd call if he heard so much as a peep from Sage, he coaxed me out the door with Canna before the kids could drag me in for breakfast.

"He's a sweetheart," she said, backing down the driveway. "He's always been great about sharing childcare duties, but since his hours can be erratic, he tries to make it up to me."

I grinned. "Like September?"

"Oh, I got *several* mornings off for that."

Neither of us was particularly hungry, so as Pars had sent us on our way with travel mugs of coffee, Canna gave me the driving tour of the city. She made a quick pass through the small commercial strip in Old Farm, telling me it would be no inconvenience if I realized I'd forgotten something at home, then headed back downtown and began pointing out landmarks. DOL's tower I recognized, but she drove past the smaller one where DPP was headquartered—"My first post-internship job was in there, and it's really not as awful as Laws would have you believe," she said—then showed me a windowless stone building about half a mile away from DOL where the Division of Intelligence was headquartered. "Never been in there," she admitted. "It's an invitation-only sort of place. But Rose, Yven, and a couple of our counselors overnighted there during a big trial, and they said the sleeping quarters are like a hotel."

"With solid walls."

"Rose claims there's a spell that mimics windows. Personally, I wonder if it wouldn't have been simpler to use glass, but then I'm not a specialist in espionage."

As we rounded the corner past the relatively squat fortress—it couldn't have been more than ten stories tall, dwarfed by DOL—I asked, "That's where's Rose's great-grandfather works, right?"

"Mm-hmm. He's headed it since the beginning."

"Not a lot of upward job mobility when you're competing against immortals, is there?"

Canna chuckled. "More than you might think. Most of them get tired of whatever they're doing eventually and pursue something different. They'll change agencies or take up basket weaving or whatnot. You get a résumé from an older elf or nymph, and there's no telling what you'll find buried in there." Smiling to herself as she pulled up to a red light, she said, "We advertised for a junior healer a few years ago and ended up bringing on an elf who'd only recently finished his internship. I *thought* he looked a little older, but it's so difficult to be sure with them, so I didn't ask. Turns out he's four hundred years old, and this is his third career. Started as a blacksmith, taught math for a while, and now he's with us. Nice guy. *Crazy* stories."

"But DOI's never turned over?"

She shook her head. "They've got analysists and support staff of all kinds, but the problem is that you can't just train to be a farseer. That's a wild talent, and almost all of the best end up at DOI eventually. From what I've heard, Lord ti'Dana is peerless among them, but he's also been around long enough to understand how to manage that bunch. Plus," she added, "most of the top farseers are elves, and they'll defer to him for Hall reasons alone."

While Dad hadn't given me a thorough course in the elven Halls, I knew ti'Dana's current head was a Pact signatory. The Pactlands operated with a representative government, but still, the former king carried a fair measure of clout. I must not have been a grave danger to law and order, I reasoned, if he'd pushed for Sage and me to be brought over.

Canna's tour took us north to the museum complex, where a few early-morning visitors climbed the steps of the four massive buildings. I caught glimpses of children running around the grassy quadrangle as we drove by. "If we have time, I'll bring you back here for a proper look around," Canna told me. "History of Magic is my favorite," she continued, pointing to a grand building covered in slate-blue marble, "but Fine Art is also lovely."

We passed half a dozen parks and drove through a shopping area already lined with cars, and then Canna suggested brunch. "I'm guessing the restaurants here don't take Visa," I joked. "If you don't mind spotting me, I can give Pars cash, and…I don't know, maybe he can use it on his next trip or—"

"Nonsense. You're our guest," she said in her best mom voice, and that settled that.

The restaurant Canna chose was located in what she claimed was a trendy part of District 3, whatever that meant. The taller buildings around the public parking lot struck me more as apartments than offices, but by then, I was so turned around from the tour that I couldn't have pointed in the direction of Old Farm had my life depended on it. In any case, the eatery was already doing a brisk business, and even most of the tables outside had been filled. For a place geographically on par with Richmond, the Pactlands was far more temperate than I'd expected, but still, the patio heaters glowed, and I was grateful for my jacket as we walked up to the front door.

Luck was on our side, and we soon found ourselves at a cozy two-top in a back corner. After the waiter—a sorcerer, by the look of him—dropped off menus, I surveyed the space and tried not to stare too blatantly. Some of the diners could have made themselves at home at Mama Hen's Café back in Ragged Gap, though they might have gotten second looks for their clothes. Far more, however, would have sent people scrambling for either their cameras or the door. The six-top next to us was occupied by a pair of gnomes, a faun, a nymph, and a troll, a girls' brunch with a big pitcher of something colorful and certainly alcoholic at the center of the table. Closer to the door sat a trio of centaurs: a couple, who lounged atop padded mats in lieu of chairs, and a toddler, whose mat was considerably thicker and came with a pair of straps. The kid wore a bright green chest harness, to which the straps had been affixed—a high chair of sorts, I surmised. The little one was ignoring his plate in favor of playing with the troll couple next door, who pulled faces until their target burst into peals of delighted laughter.

"Jane," Canna murmured, and grinned when she startled me. "Decided what you want?"

"Oh, uh…sorry." I glanced at the menu, but nothing jumped out at me as instantly recognizable, and I missed the comfortable familiarity of Mama Hen's country breakfast special. "Um…tell you what, why don't you order for me?"

"Are you sure? Would you rather go somewhere else?" she asked, concerned.

"No, this is great," I hastily reassured her, "but I don't quite know what some of these things are, and besides, I'm sure I have an accent."

She raised one hand and shook it back and forth. "Somewhat. Your Pactish is very good," she said softly, leaning toward me to keep her voice down, "but you definitely don't sound like a capital native."

"Dad did his best…"

"It's not bad! It just…well, there's obviously something else mixed in. I can understand you with no problem, but I can hear the difference."

"Honestly, given the strength of my normal accent, that's close to miraculous."

She patted my hand. "You can understand us, though, yes?"

"Sure. It's weird," I admitted. "Hearing so much Pactish, I mean. My brain tends to think in English, so it's translating half the time, and…" I shrugged. "I guess this gets easier with exposure."

"Rose and Annie say so. Both got Pactish from a potion, so you're ahead of them on that count. Ah, hello," she said, straightening as our waiter returned. "Ready to order if you are."

From what I could gather, Canna selected several smaller plates to share, a sampler pack of her favorites. I was barely through my first cup of tea before the dishes arrived, crowding the table and making my mouth water with the novel but pleasant scents. Canna was thorough in her culinary tour guide duties, walking me through ingredients, preparation, and cultural origins, and I was deep into a plate of paper-thin fried eggplant slices when two nymphs approached.

Noticing them, Canna put down her fork and waved. "Good morning! I didn't see you sitting here!"

"We were hiding in the back," said one, bronze-skinned with blue hair and gray eyes.

The other, a shorter nymph with a pink complexion, gray eyes, and white pigtails, nodded. "I'm *stuffed*. Who's this?"

Without missing a beat, Canna replied, "This is Jane. She's a student, and we're talking about the ups and downs of making a career as a healer."

"She's a good one," the blue-haired nymph told me, thumbing one hand at Canna. "Seen *everything*. We make sure of it, right?"

"You certainly do your part to keep things interesting," Canna teased, and gestured toward the nymph. "Jane, this is Dal Gemellae, one of our agents, and this is her partner, Kirna Pannid, who's a counselor and thus *much* less demanding of my appointments."

I smiled at both, quickly trying to recall the elemental chart Dac had made me review as a teenager. Dal—she of the blue hair—had to be a metal nymph, a rather rare alignment. Kirna, the counselor, was an air nymph, who tended to be the lightest in coloration. But with the speed of Canna's introductions, I'd missed the more important information: their surnames, or at least their endings.

"We don't want to disturb you," said Kirna, and nodded to me. "Be nice to Canna, now. We need her back in the office on Monday."

"Nice to meet you," I said lamely, biting back the all-too-southern urge to drop a *sir* or *ma'am*, and concentrated on my food until I was sure they were out of earshot.

Canna mimed wiping her brow. "Sorry for the subterfuge."

"Oh, no problem," I replied. "We're doing the covert thing, aren't we? Are they friends of yours?"

"Close colleagues, I'd say." She paused, considering me, then chuckled at my discomfort. "Not great with nymphs, are we?"

"Liogh Birrid is the only one I know, so…"

"You could do far worse than Liogh. Now, you understand their naming conventions, yes?" she asked, spearing a well-seasoned potato wedge.

"In principle…"

"Dal is female. Listen for the *-ae* suffix. Kirna is nonbinary—they've got that *-id* ending going on, just like Liogh. Gemellae, Pannid," she repeated slowly, giving me a chance to absorb and process. "See? It's not difficult."

"Metal and air?"

"Exactly. Well done," she said with a hint of surprise. "I wouldn't necessarily have expected you to know that."

"Easier to figure out their elemental alignment than to gender them," I said, returning to the eggplant for another helping. "I couldn't have begun to guess with those two."

"Accidentally misgendering nymphs is a time-honored tradition, and most are very gracious when it happens. *They* can tell, but they know the rest of us are lost. The differences are subtle."

"Like with trolls?"

"Oh, no, far more nuanced than that. Trolls do actually have some physical differences between the sexes, and even if they're clothed, if you've been around them long enough, you can tell who's who. The problem with nymphs is that their differences are more in a matter of carriage and attitude, occasionally in dress—physically, they're all alike."

I frowned. "What do you mean?"

"They're hermaphroditic," Canna explained quietly. "Same equipment across the board, and any two of them can procreate. In the old days, or so I've been told, when they tried to map themselves onto a binary system, they decided that their males prefer to fertilize, females prefer to carry the young, and the nonbinary don't have a clear preference. Some of them tend to act more or less like what we'd think of as stereotypical male or female—they'll even exaggerate their behavior—but for most, if you don't know their name, good luck guessing."

I let that sink in while I chewed. "Okay...so what about their kids? How do the parents know how to name them?"

"Nymphs treat all of their children as nonbinary. They use standard childhood names—for instance, I must have seen fifty patients with a kid named Bele or Daga. And whichever surname the child receives, they only employ the root form—Gemel or Pan, to use convenient examples. Once they come of age and better understand themselves, they take on clearly gendered first names, and they add the proper suffixes to their surnames."

"That's...complicated," I muttered.

Canna shook her head. "Not after a while. Anyway, I've always found nymphic naming conventions fascinating. There's no other people like them here who so clearly delineate among three genders. Now, that's not to say we don't have a spectrum of presentation in other peoples, but none are as generally accepting of anything outside the usual binary as nymphs are."

Thinking of Sage and of my own peculiar circumstances, I asked, "So…if a nymph hooks up with, say, a sorcerer—"

She immediately shut that down. "Not possible. That is…well…" Briefly, she fumbled for the words, then murmured, "'Hook ups' like that, as it were, can and do happen. There are some *very* niche preferences, and that's all I'll say on the matter. But you never see children as a result of a relationship like that. The only person who can impregnate a nymph is another nymph."

And maybe a Greek god, I almost quipped, but feared the reference would be lost on my cousin.

"They're not unique in that respect, naturally," she continued as she picked at the leavings of a curiously flavored apple tart that had left me grabbing the lone cream sauce on the table to cool the unexpected spice burn. "Take any two species and throw them together, and if they're anatomically compatible, they still probably won't produce offspring, or the result will be infertile."

"A mule," I offered.

"Precisely. Why *any* of us are able to make viable, fertile hybrids is a mystery. Science can't explain it, though I've seen hypotheses from experts in theoretical magic."

I hesitated, hoping I wasn't about to step in it, then ventured, "A human–sorcerer cross might not be *that* surprising…"

Canna shot me a sly grin. "Careful where you say that, Jane, but I don't think you're wrong. We may be more like late-branching subspecies. None of my training was on human subjects, naturally, but we've collected biological samples over the years, and it really is shocking how close we are. There are some distinct markers you only see in each population, now, but we're *much* more alike than are, say, sorcerers and elves."

"But elves and humans—"

"It's still possible," she confirmed. "Heck, Rose is proof of that. The theoretical folks think magic has much to do with it, but that's not my specialty." She took a bite, winced at the heat, and chased it with a sip of tea. "Possible or not, crosses are rare. If people want children, they almost always stick to their own kind for partners— most have no choice. I mean, you can't get a cross from a troll, a naga, a gnome, a nymph…"

"Centaurs, though?" I murmured.

Her mouth tightened. "Oddly enough, they're fertile cross-breeders with elves, sorcerers, fauns—"

"Really?"

"Just…don't think about that too long. I'm no prude, but I don't want to consider the physics of any of those pairings if they opt to go unmasked. As I mentioned, there are some peculiar preferences out there. Anyway, while they *can* produce cross-bred children, they seldom do. It's considered grossly irresponsible, as the potential for catastrophic birth defects is so high. I mean," she continued, lowering her voice to a whisper, "you're taking a six-limbed parent and trying to match it up with a four-limbed parent. What do you *think* is going to happen?"

I smirked. "You haven't really seen Sage yet."

"No, and I'm concerned. Even if you don't see any problems, there may be hidden defects we need to address before she gets any older." Abandoning the tart, she held her teacup close and regarded me over the rim. "Generally, when a centaur cross happens, it's not a consensual event, and the majority of such pregnancies are terminated for a host of reasons. The fact that Sage exists is remarkable on its own, but I'm worried about what we may learn concerning the events that made her."

The waiter interrupted us before we could go too far down that trail, offering a dessert menu with a cajoling smile. As I considered the options, Canna's phone rang, and she apologized as she took the call. "Is anyone dead?

Do I need to come home?...*Oh*! Wonderful. We'll be there as soon as we can."

She beckoned to the waiter and said, "I'm sorry, but we'll have to skip dessert today and take our bill. Duty calls." He hurried off to get the tab, and Canna told me, "That was Pars. Sage is beginning to stir."

We almost didn't make it in time. While Pars was fluent in English, I didn't like the thought of Sage waking with no one but strangers around, and I was grateful for the application of Canna's lead foot as we sped through the winding streets of Old Farm. As soon as she stopped the van, I jumped out and ran into the house, then rushed upstairs to find Pars hovering in the doorway with the curious girls behind him.

I'd just made myself comfortable at the edge of the wide bed when Sage's twitching eyes fluttered open. "Hi, sweetie," I murmured as she blinked and focused on me. "How're you feeling?"

"Okay," she croaked. "Kind of tired..." She paused, perhaps realizing that she was no longer in Canna's office, and started to sit up. "Where—"

"Canna brought us to her house," I said, gently pushing her back to the mattress. "You've been sleeping off that potion for about twenty-four hours."

"Oh." She sounded dazed at the thought. "I'm sorry, I didn't mean—"

"Honey, *no*. This was expected. You haven't done anything wrong." Gesturing toward the enormous man in the doorway, I said, "This is Pars, Canna's husband. He's been keeping an eye on you, too."

Pars waved. "Hi, Sage. Are you hungry? Thirsty?"

"Yes, sir. A little thirsty, I mean. And, um..."

I sensed the source of her sudden reticence. "Bathroom's down the hall. Let me give you a hand, okay?"

Though she insisted she could make it on her own, Sage allowed me to help her off the bed and leaned on me as she tottered toward the door. She'd almost crossed the room when she spied the girls and froze. "Hello?"

Dieta, fearless, pushed past her father to intercept us. "Hi," she said in Pactish. "You're Sage, right?"

Sage looked at me helplessly. "I don't think that potion worked, Jane."

"It's still working," Pars explained. "Takes a few days before everything makes sense. And yes," he said, effortlessly switching as he addressed his daughter, "this is Sage. She can't understand you quite yet, so be patient."

Dieta huffed. "How long is it going to be?"

"Days. *Patience*," he said, tugging her dark hair. "And move aside, you're blocking the exit."

As Dieta stepped out of the way, Maliul waved shyly, and Sage waved back at her while we passed. I saw my charge as far as the bathroom door, then promised her I'd be waiting and gave her some privacy. Crouching to be closer to the girls' level, I said, "Everything's very new to Sage, and she still seems pretty sleepy, so if she's not up to playing just yet, don't be hurt."

They appeared to understand, and they scampered off while I helped Sage back to bed. "I'm sorry," she said, yawning, "I don't know what's wrong..."

By then, Canna had mounted the stairs with a glass of water in hand. Seeing Sage's drooping eyes, she smiled at her, then said to me, "Fatigue isn't uncommon at all. Let's get her back to bed. She should feel much more like herself in the morning."

I relayed the message and tucked Sage in, and she took a few sips of her drink and thanked Canna, who took up my spot on the bed and patted Sage's blanket-covered leg. "You sleep, dear," she said gently. "Don't worry."

I didn't suspect that needed translating, but I did so all the same.

As Canna and I started to leave, Maliul ran into the

room, her arms full of children's books. "What's this?" her mother asked.

She dropped them in a pile by the bed. "Since she can't talk yet, maybe she wants to read," she explained with the warped logic of the kindergarten set. "I can share."

"That's very nice of you," I replied, omitting the part about the patient's complete illiteracy in Pactish. "I think Sage is going to go back to sleep right now, but maybe she'll want to look once she's awake again, eh?"

Satisfied and having done her good deed for the day, Maliul returned to her own affairs, and I pulled the covers up to Sage's chin. "If you need me, just yell," I said, and took my leave. By the time I flipped off the lights, her eyes were already closed again, and not even the twins' afternoon tantrums could rouse her for the rest of the day.

CHAPTER 13

True to Canna's prediction, Sage was up with the chickens. I caught her when I heard the floorboards creak above the den, then hurried upstairs to find her groping her way toward the bathroom. With that accomplished, she was still a bit wobbly on her feet, which I chalked up to having not eaten in nearly two days. I didn't want to raid our hosts' kitchen, but before I could rationalize helping myself to the bread in the fridge, Canna peeked out of their room and spotted us. "Good morning," she whispered. "Are we hungry?"

"We can wait," I insisted. "Don't get up on our—"

High-pitched giggling from the twins' bedroom interrupted me, and Canna snorted in the twilit gloom. "Oh, don't worry about me. We're on an *early* schedule in this house."

While Canna started on breakfast, I got Sage situated at the kitchen table with a cup of heavily sweetened tea, then returned to the second floor to find Colji and Coltrane sitting on one of their beds, making a game of pushing each other over and laughing uproariously when one or the other toppled. With a little coaxing, I convinced them to take turns in the bathroom and go down to find their mother, who, in anticipation of their arrival, had already put out plates of diced fruit in front of the booster chairs. We strapped them in, and as the two went to town on their appetizer, running footsteps upstairs heralded the imminent arrival of their older sisters.

Sage was out to sea, unable to communicate beyond

miming but seemingly delighted with the flurry of activity the kids provided. She'd never been around children—hell, she'd barely been a child—but when Maliul slid paper and some crayons in front of her as a pre-breakfast amusement, she played along. By the time Pars descended to help control the chaos, Sage had done a surprisingly fair rendition of a house I recognized as Warner's, and I made a note to add art time to her studies.

It was Canna's suggestion that Pars take us for a drive, and though the older girls protested the loss of their new playmate, we made our exit later that morning, after Sage had a chance to wash off the funk. "I hope you don't mind hanging out," Pars told Sage as she slid into the back seat of his brown Jeep. "Canna would love to chat, I'm sure, but until that potion kicks in, you two aren't going to be great conversationalists for each other."

She had no objection to a trip around town, riding in cars still being something of a novelty, and she pressed her nose to the window as Pars retraced some of the route Canna and I had taken the day before. Instead of stopping downtown, however, he drove to a less built-up area of the city and headed toward what appeared to be a massive stone warehouse. Two lanes of traffic peeled off from either direction, joining into a four-lane driveway that, even on Sunday morning, was slow with traffic. Pars took the exit and joined the flow, which, instead of turning into a parking lot, drove straight into the building through a massive opening in the middle.

"Portals?" I asked.

He nodded. "Internal portals. I thought we might take a peek outside Beukal."

The inside of the building made the external portal building look small and sedate by comparison. Lined up within were what appeared to be ten toll booths, each with a name high above on the glowing marquee. For the five on the right, a wooden barrier arm in each lane blocked access to an open portal, a colorful, flashing vortex taller than a semi. The left-hand booths also featured portals, but the signs were dark, the barrier arms unmoving, and traffic was shunted away.

"We're set up kind of like your airports," Pars explained as he maneuvered into one of the narrowing lanes. "Major destinations offer portals to smaller destinations, and those in turn go even smaller."

"Hub and spoke?" I asked.

"Exactly. Those five over there are inbound, but during rush hour, the directions of some of the portals change."

As we neared the head of the line, I looked past the booths and saw vehicles emerging from the left-hand lanes, which merged into another wide road headed out the back of the building. "Where are we going?"

"Well, I thought we'd start with Green Lake. It's a recreational area not too far away from where Yven and I grew up. See? Tanaar," he said, pointing to the sign above our booth. "It's pretty close to Beukal."

"In real distance?"

"You mean if we drove it straight?" He made a face as he considered the question. "Don't know, I've never tried it. Maps to about Nashville, if that helps."

We made a roughly nine-hour trip in the time it took Pars to drive through the light show, and he steered us out of Tanaar's portal building into the morning sunshine. A short drive later, he turned onto a gravel track and slowed as we bumped along. "Here we go!" he said cheerily.

The trail wound through a mature forest of tall hardwoods, which were somehow still in vibrant leaf despite the lateness of November. Their branches stretched overhead into a tall tunnel, though not one so thick that the light-dappled soil couldn't support healthy undergrowth. We passed occasional emergency phones outfitted with red lights—"No one wants a fire in here," Pars said as I pointed one out—and after a time, the gravel road ended in a rustic parking lot, the ends of the spaces demarcated with logs. "Pretty nice, huh?" our driver asked.

"Want to talk a walk?"

Green Lake *was* nice, its trails marked and well maintained, but like Beukal, it was rather flat...and for someone who'd grown up in the Appalachians, its trees were less impressive than they were to Pars. Still, I appreciated the relative calm of the place, as did Sage, who alternated between running ahead to explore and holding my hand whenever a decidedly inhuman hiker passed us. Her confidence grew over the hour or so we spent in the woods, but I remained available for reassurance.

Pars ended our tour of the park at the eponymous Green Lake, which offered a fishing pier and boat slips. We stood back and watched as a female centaur, who'd made herself comfortable on a blanket with a book, yelled at her two sons to stop roughhousing in the shallows. The boys parted for a moment, but once their mother's attention had returned to her paperback, they resumed splashing each other until the larger brother managed to dunk his sibling. The little one came up sputtering, and their mother intervened, dragging both from the lake for a time-out.

"They're really *big*," Sage murmured.

"You'll grow," I told her, but I wrapped an arm around her shoulders and pulled her close, and Sage quietly sighed.

Canna's plan had been to host us until Sage's language potion took full effect, which she estimated would happen before the end of the week. She preferred not to work on patients with whom she couldn't directly communicate if at all possible—after a bad experience she would only hint about during her training, she lived in dread of some crucial piece of information being lost in the back-and-forth of relying on a translator. Plus, I could tell that she and Pars were doing their best to give me a taste of my mother's homeland, even if they did so surreptitiously by necessity

But the brass at DOL had other plans.

Liogh called on Sunday night with word from the director: Canna needed to bring Sage in on Monday for her physical and to take samples. Canna protested that Sage had only regained consciousness that morning and was acclimating—by which she meant flouncing around the den with a feather boa and oversized hat as the kids giggled—but Liogh's instructions were firm, and so Canna acquiesced.

The next morning, Sage held my hand on the elevator as Canna took us back to the healers' unit in the DOL tower. It would just be the three of us, Canna had explained; there was no need to involve Liogh until she had results back, and she assumed that Sage wouldn't want an audience for the proceedings. She ushered us down the corridors and into an examination room, then shut the door and said, "Tell Sage to close her eyes, please."

I did as she asked, and after a quick whisper from Canna, lights burst on from nowhere like a dozen flashbulbs, leaving weird afterimages in my vision for a few seconds while my brain caught up with what I'd just seen. That was a privacy spell, I gathered, and a *strong* one at that.

"A little something against eavesdroppers," Canna explained, perhaps mistaking my pained blinking for confusion. "All right, let's get to it. Jane, this may be tedious, but I need you to repeat everything to Sage, okay? If she doesn't understand at any point, let me know."

I conveyed this to the girl, who nodded and smiled nervously.

"Great." Reaching into a drawer, she pulled out a folded green paper gown. "Jane and I are going to step out for a minute. If you would, please change into this and unmask, and crack the door open when you're ready."

Sage regarded the paper garment with deep suspicion— I couldn't blame here there—but she had already slipped off her new shoes when Canna and I took our leave. A couple minutes later, the door opened slightly, and Sage peeked out through the crack. "I'm ready."

I translated for Canna, who led the way back in.

The gown Sage had been given was cut for someone of average adult human proportions. It fell halfway down her calves, the world's worst tea-length frock, and the extra material bloused over the belt, which was so long that she could have wrapped it around her waist twice. She hugged herself and backed up to the exam table, her hooves clicking against the tile floor.

Having been prepared, Canna didn't bat an eye. "Thank you, dear. I know those gowns aren't great. Here, let me turn this on," she said, tapping a button on the table's control panel. "That should help keep you more comfortable while we work. Why don't you hop up for me?"

Sage did, then patted the padding beneath her and turned to me. "It's heated!"

"Lucky you," I teased, and looked at Canna. "She's a fan."

With me standing beside the table to translate, Canna opened a computer and gently but thoroughly grilled Sage about her medical history. She got her height and weight, chatted with her about diet and exercise (the former to gain weight, the latter to build muscle), and then, as Sage grew more comfortable, Canna moved on to the full physical exam: ears and eyes, nose and throat, heart and lungs. She pulled up a chair beside the table and hoisted Sage's feet into her lap, one at a time, both to examine the hooves and to check the joints. Sage walked back and forth across the room so Canna could check her gait, and I explained the circumstances when Canna discovered Sage's closely cropped tail. Canna made note of the thin, dark stripe up Sage's back, the suggestion of a mane, and she spent time with the old scars around the girl's neck, pursing her lips and typing her findings.

"Let's start with the good news," she said as she

concluded her inspection. "Your vision and hearing are great. I don't see any spinal abnormalities, and based on centaur norms, your legs are short but fully formed. That tail is just going to take time to regrow," she added with a smile, and waited while I caught up. "Now, I know a dermatologist in the city who might have some ideas to help those scars along—you may always have traces, but if those bother you, they're easy enough to mask. There is, however, one thing I want to talk about before we get your blood samples."

Silently, I prayed that Canna wasn't going to launch into a discussion of the birds and the bees. While I didn't mind the topic, I didn't want to try to translate my way through *that* mess.

"You've never been to a dentist, have you?" Canna asked.

Relieved, I posed the question, and Sage shook her head.

"I didn't think so. Your teeth need professional cleaning—that's normal," she said, waiting while I reassured Sage—"and they're crooked. I'm no expert here, but I've got a lovely colleague down the hall who could help you out. Would you mind if I brought her in?"

"It's a good idea," I added.

Sage agreed, and after Canna collected two test tubes of blood from her skinny arm, she and I left again to let Sage dress and mask once more. "I'm going to call Liogh and get an okay before I grab the dentist," she told me. "Be right back."

Ten minutes later, as I sat with Sage and she inspected the neon blue bandage on the inside of her elbow, Canna returned with another woman in a purple lab coat. Her brunette pixie cut left no question that she was an elf, but even if she'd been wearing a hat to hide her ears, her high cheekbones and the unusually sharp teeth she revealed while flashing an otherwise warm smile would have given her away.

"Hello, there," she said, nodding to us both. "Canna said someone needs a checkup...so who's my lucky patient?"

Sage turned to me for a translation, but Canna slid in before I could begin. "This is *absolutely* a hush job, Jumie," she said, lowering her voice despite the protection of the privacy spell. "Director's authorized it, but word of this doesn't need to circulate until the investigation's closed."

The elf spread her hands. "Absolutely. What can I do for you?"

She gestured to us. "The young lady there is Sage. She was, uh...how to put this...misplaced outside the Pactlands as an infant."

Her colleague's manicured eyebrows shot toward her hairline. "What do you mean, *misplaced?*"

"Raised in Georgia," I volunteered. "Well, *raised* is stretching it—she was pretty badly abused, and she's never had much medical care. She's here to find her family."

Though Jumie seemed troubled, her face softened as she turned to Sage. "I see why Canna called me," she said in strangely accented but otherwise flawless English. "It's Sage, yes?"

Sage beamed. "Yes, ma'am."

"Lovely to meet you. I'm Jumie ti'Vir. Now, Canna said you needed someone to look at your teeth, is that right?"

She nodded.

"Little scared of dentists?" she asked gently.

"I...don't know, ma'am."

"She's never been to one," I explained.

"Oh, that's no problem," Jumie replied. "We'll go as slowly as you need, and you won't feel a thing. I guarantee it. We'll numb you up and have you clean in no time." Turning to Canna, she asked in Pactish, "Any potions in her system right now?"

"Traces of the language potion. She took it Friday."

The dentist waved it off. "That won't interact with the numbing agents." Beckoning to Sage, she switched back to

English and headed for the door. "Right this way, dear. Let's go to my office."

Sage slid off the table, but she looked at me uneasily.

"It's okay," I told her. "I'll be waiting for you. Not going anywhere. And if you get scared and want me to come hold your hand, just let Jumie know, all right?"

With that promise, Sage followed Jumie down the hall, leaving me to watch as Canna busied herself with Sage's samples and a piece of black machinery on the counter. "Dare I ask why your in-house dentist speaks English?"

"This is her second career," Canna replied, unwrapping a plastic pipette. "She started as a field agent here, made it to detective, then decided she wanted to give healing a try. I don't know what possibly drew her to dentistry, but we certainly need a dentist around here—I get the broken bones, but she gets all the broken teeth and jaws." Having freed the pipette, she opened one of the vials of Sage's blood, pulled a smaller container from a drawer, and began transferring the liquid.

"What're you doing?" I asked.

"This fits into *that*"—she nodded to the machine—"which will give us a basic health and genetic profile."

Having finished collecting her sample, she put an identical container of clear liquid into the machine and tapped a button, and it began to hum and whir. "Disinfectant," she explained. "Protocol says to clean after use, but a second wash doesn't hurt, you know?"

The machine soon beeped the end of its cycle, and Canna replaced the used disinfectant pod with the one carrying Sage's blood. "Here we go," she said, closing the drawer. "Let's see what she really is."

A computer sat connected to the machine, and Canna opened a window to show the program's progress. I couldn't make heads or tails of the data it was spewing, but she watched with interest. "Anemic," she said after a moment. "That's to be expected. Blood sugar and cholesterol are within normal range. Potion traces coming in…language and healing, standard fare."

"Really? She hasn't had a healing potion since we left Georgia."

"You'd be surprised how long some of those things can linger. Okay…no signs of active infection, which is good. I'd like to get her on a course of inoculations—I know she's had some shots with you, but we need to make up for lost time. Giving her a batch at once will leave her feeling crummy for a day or two, but all things considered…"

"It's the wise course of action," I finished. "So, what's her genetic mix?"

"Patience…*ah*. Standard markers present for sorcerer and centaur, both at fifty percent of expected levels. You're right. Half and half."

While it was nice to know I wasn't crazy, that information strengthened the case that we might be about to kick a hornets' nest. "Any clues about her parents?"

"That's a separate analysis," Canna replied. "Let me tidy up here first."

I waited while she discarded the dregs of Sage's sample and ran another round of disinfectant, and then she took the second vial of blood to a smaller gray machine at the other end of the counter. Once she'd prepared a sample, she plugged in the computer, opened a new program, and started the login process, which was more involved than I'd anticipated. As if sensing my bemusement, Canna said, "This is restricted information. We take samples from Pact personnel considered sufficiently high-risk, just in case of abduction or worse. Thankfully, we seldom have to access this database. It's still a pain getting in because no one wants unauthorized individuals playing around in here. I'm having to confirm that the director has requested this scan…and good, we're clear. All right, let's take a peek. It's possible her parents are in here with a missing child request…"

Canna and I sat back to wait as a progress bar slowly

filled with green. As it ended its search, the computer trilled a curiously peppy little fanfare.

"What does that mean?" I asked, leaning closer.

"Whoa," Canna murmured, scanning the output. "It means we've got a *double* match."

For a moment, my heart lifted. As both of Sage's parents were in the system, surely they had to have reported her missing...right? "Well? Who are they?" I pressed, envisioning Liogh making a quick and most welcome phone call that afternoon, possibly with a press conference to follow.

My cousin grunted as she read the results. "One donor is Mirrik Voln. Chance of false positive is less than one millionth of a percent."

"Unless...Mirrik? He, she?"

"He."

"Well, unless he has an identical twin..."

"He doesn't. The Volns are a prominent family of sorcerers, and he's the youngest of four, if I recall. Mirrik is one of our Forum reps."

"Oh, shit," I muttered.

She nodded. "And the other genetic donor is Relieg Tumari. Looks like she works for the Forum as well," she said, squinting at the screen, "but in media relations."

I frowned. "Why would they have taken a sample from *her*?"

"Because, prior to joining the media side, she was a Forum aide. They work in the representatives' offices," Canna explained. "And...yeah, this makes sense."

"It does?"

"Yep." Scooting her stool aside to show me the screen, she said, "This says Relieg started as an aide in 2003. Her rep was...*not* a favorite. There was an assassination attempt by one of his constituents in the late nineties, so to be safe, anyone who worked in that office got put in the database. He's retired now, but I guess the samples are never purged."

My guts clenched as I started to piece the puzzle together. "When did Mirrik become a representative?"

"Oh...2010, I think." Flipping to his profile, she said, "He started as an aide in 1980."

"So, he's a good bit older than she is?"

Canna consulted the notes. "He was born in 1902, and she...1963. Yeah. That's not a huge difference—"

"Sixty years!" I protested.

"Admittedly, that's a big gap for a sorcerer couple, but once you start dealing with nymphs and elves, all bets are off."

But I saw the picture coming into focus. Relieg, fresh out of school, young and probably pretty, crossing paths with older, more established Mirrik. Did he pressure her? Corner her? Slip her some sort of potion? I'd read enough mythology as a kid to have come across the "lascivious centaurs abducting women" trope, but here...

No, I did *not* want to think about the physics of that pairing, thank you very much.

"You don't think they had a relationship?" I asked Canna.

She shook her head. "Mirrik's never been in a long-term relationship—he's one of Beukal's most eligible bachelors. Relieg is...let's see...married, and 'Covana' is definitely a centaur surname. He's listed here as her next of kin."

While it was possible that the two aides had engaged in a quiet fling, the circumstantial evidence of a darker alternative couldn't be denied. In any event, my dream of a happy reunion that afternoon went sailing out the window and probably off a steep, rocky precipice.

"So...what do we do?" I murmured.

Canna reached for her phone, her mouth a tight line. "That's up to Liogh."

The detective took twenty minutes to arrive, having been

stuck in a meeting with their supervisor, and panted as they closed the door to the examination room. "We have matches?" they asked, formal robe swirling as they pulled up a stool by the computer. "I'm shocked."

"Oh, it gets *far* more interesting than that," my cousin replied, and showed them the report. "What does this suggest to you? Jane and I have theories, but—"

Liogh muttered to themself, their words sharp and incomprehensible, and I assumed I'd just heard something profane in Nymphic.

"My thoughts exactly," said Canna. "This is…well…"

"Sketchy as hell?" I suggested.

"And deeply disappointing," Liogh replied, turning to me. "Of the three sorcerer representatives, Mirrik is widely regarded as the best of the bunch. The most reasonable, at any rate."

Canna emphatically nodded. "Without doubt. Aniap's a pompous ass, and that new rep, what's her name—"

"Elm Carinar?"

"*Yes*, her. A pretty face with Aniap's money backing her campaign. So nice that he could afford a second vote, isn't it?" she said, her voice thick with sarcasm.

Liogh smirked. "Your cohort isn't unique for…shenanigans, shall we say? But yeah, that last sorcerer election was a farce."

I looked back and forth between them, but when it came to Pact politics, I was lost. "Sorry…who are—"

"We're each entitled to three representatives," said Liogh. "Each people, I mean, and we choose them by various methods. The most senior of the sorcerer reps has been a problem for years."

"Gerem Aniap," Canna added with distaste. "His grandfather was a Pact signatory, and to hear him talk, you'd think he was royalty instead of merely wealthy."

Liogh arched a brow. "*Merely*?"

"Okay, *very* wealthy. The Aniaps came in with money and resources, and they've done well for themselves ever since." Her mouth tightened as if she'd just sucked on a lemon wedge. "Gerem tried to rush Annie and her friend out of the Pactlands as soon as DPP's team found a cure for the potion that had mutated them. Thank heavens Wylan arrived in time—"

"Never thought you'd hear anyone say that about the freaking *Hunter*, did you?" Liogh teased.

"Oh, never, but he's a surprisingly nice fellow. Pars and I met Yven and Rose for dinner with those two a few weeks after they married, and he made great company. Self-deprecating and obviously smitten with Annie, and if she thinks he's good enough, then he'll do."

Cocking their head quizzically, Liogh asked, "You think that highly of her discernment?"

"All I know is that Pars and I kept working with her and patching her up, and she was practically ready to kill herself to save him, so there must be something redeeming there. But I digress," she said, turning her attention back to me. "Our illustrious senior rep makes pretty speeches that do little and throws his money around as needed, so he keeps his seat. To this point, I much preferred what I saw of Mirrik, but now…"

Liogh nodded. "This will take careful maneuvering, however we go about it. The director needs to know. While she's deciding our next step, could I impose on you to house Sage and Jane for a few more days?"

"No imposition at all."

"Come on, I'm sure you'd like your couch back," I protested.

She patted my knee. "I'll trade the damn couch for my wayward baby cousin."

It was nearly lunchtime when the dentist finished with Sage, but she returned to us smiling. "Did a good cleaning," said Jumie, "filled a couple small cavities, and tightened her alignment."

I marveled at Sage's teeth, which were considerably straighter and whiter than they'd been when I last saw them. "No need for braces?"

Jumie chuckled. "No, just some strong numbing and a bit of spellcraft." Giving me her fuller consideration, she said, "Sage told me all about the sorcerer who's been taking care of her. I don't mean any disrespect, but you're rather young to be out there, aren't you?"

"A special case," Canna interjected. "And another matter we're not presently at liberty to discuss."

"I'd assumed not. Anyway," she continued in English, pressing a familiar style of opaque plastic baggie into Sage's hands, "this is for you. Remember what we talked about with flossing, yes?"

"Yes, ma'am," Sage replied, then surprised the dentist with a firm hug.

Jumie patted her back. "You're very welcome, dear." To Canna, she said in Pactish, "Might I suggest a pain potion later this afternoon?"

Grabbing her purse, Canna said, "*Absolutely*. Come on, you two. Let's get something to eat before Sage's numbness wears off. Maybe we should start with ice cream."

*Tsk*ing, Jumie rolled her eyes. "The things you say in front of your *dentist*, woman."

CHAPTER 14

Sage was distractable, at least to a point. She eagerly answered Canna's questions about her time with Jumie—all passed through me—and stared around the restaurant to which Canna had escorted us with interest. Soup and sandwiches were familiar enough, a compromise before the promised ice cream, which Sage ate with gusto. By the time Canna dropped us off at her house, Sage's gums were beginning to throb, and so I was left with a selection of pain potions in small bottles and dosing instructions while my cousin returned to the office.

I convinced Sage to take a nap while the potion did its work and her lunch digested, and she proved amenable to the suggestion. But she couldn't sleep all day, and when she awoke mid-afternoon, no longer in pain, she wanted answers.

She sat with me in the kitchen while I raided the cabinets for mint teabags and sweetener, and I took my time, stalling the inevitable. I still wasn't sure what to tell her about Canna's findings. The last thing I wanted to do was crush her, but she was old enough to handle the truth…right?

When I could delay no longer, I brought our mugs to the table and sat beside her. "So. We got your results while you were with the dentist."

She took a sip. "And?"

"You're pretty healthy. Need more iron, and Canna wants to give you the rest of your vaccines."

Though she groaned, she didn't refuse.

"I know, kid, shots are no fun. And your genetic breakdown is just what we thought. You're *definitely* not a demon, so put that from your mind."

After another sip, she nodded, absorbing that information. "Master…*Warner*," she amended, "is kind of a jerk, isn't he?"

"That's putting it mildly, baby," I said, squeezing her free hand. "I'm sorry he lied to you for so long. Not an easy thing to work through, I'm sure, but you're doing great."

She flashed a small, brief grin. "Any matches to my parents?" she asked hopefully.

Shit.

"Yes," I admitted, wincing inside as her eyes lit up. "Both of them, actually."

A look of joy swept across her face. "They *were* searching for me! Just like Detective Birrid said, right? There's parents of missing children in the system." When I didn't immediately confirm, her smile began to falter. "Right, Jane?"

"Not exactly," I murmured, holding on to her hand. "Your father is a Forum representative—that's your sorcerer parent," I explained. "Mirrik Voln."

I paused while she mouthed his name, working out the strange syllables. "So, that's my last name? Voln? I've never had one…"

"It could be. Some kids get their mothers' names— Canna and Pars gave the girls his surname and gave hers to Coltrane."

"Huh. Okay, so who's my mom?"

"She's, uh…she works in media relations for the Forum. Relieg Tumari." I hesitated, then said, "She's married—"

"To my dad?"

"No, to another centaur."

"Oh." A note of anxiety crept into her voice. "So…they had an affair?" she asked softly.

That she was familiar with the concept wasn't a great surprise; while Sage certainly had gaps in her education, I'd learned not to assume that she was entirely naïve, and in fairness, Tabitha and I had exposed her to a *lot* over the last weeks. Sage was a sponge.

"It's possible they were dating," I told her. "I don't know when your mother married, but your father never has. Around the time you came along, they were both Forum aides. Coworkers."

"But they didn't report me missing?"

God, I hated the truth, but Sage trusted me. "No, sweetie. I'm sorry."

"They didn't want me," she mumbled, clutching her tea. "They threw me out."

"It…may be worse than that," I forced myself to say. "Canna says that centaurs *very* seldom pair up with anyone else. Your father's quite a bit older than your mother, and we certainly don't *know* what went on between them, but…"

"You think he hurt her?" she asked.

Sage was trying to be strong, I knew she was, but her lip had begun to wobble.

"Maybe. Again, we don't know," I stressed. "That's something for DOL to figure out. The important thing— the *really* important thing I want you to understand—is that whatever happened between them is *not* your fault."

She tried to blink back tears. "But they don't want me."

"Honey." I reached for her other hand, and she released her grip on her mug. "Hear me, okay? Whatever happens here, you will always have a home with me if you want it. I know it's not the same," I said as her face crumpled, "but you've got somewhere to land—"

Sage rose from her chair only long enough to throw herself into my arms, and I held her while she cried, murmuring reassurance that she wasn't alone.

From somewhere in the thoughts I tried to repress, my imagined picture of my mother floated to the fore, a woman somewhat weathered by the decades that had passed since Dad's last photo of her but still youthful and pretty. That was the face I saw in my nightmares, the ones in which I chased her and finally caught up, only for her to tell me to get away, that she didn't want anything to do with me, that she wished I'd never been born—

No. There was a time to deal with my own trauma, and this wasn't it.

And so I stroked Sage's hair and told her all the things Dad had told me about being wanted and loved and blameless in this mess, even if I had never fully believed him.

Sage was understandably subdued for the rest of the day, especially once her pain potion began to wear off, and she didn't protest when Canna suggested a warm bath and an early bedtime. I checked on her before retiring myself, once the house was quiet, and found her deeply asleep, her brow scrunched and one fist clutching the blankets by her chin.

Tuesday morning came without instructions from Liogh, and after breakfast, Pars and Canna took off with the children to divvy up the school and daycare run before work. Left alone in the quiet house, I texted Dad to assure him I wasn't dead—how the Pactlands had cell service remained a mystery to me—and I then tried to figure out what to do all day. Taking a walk could be problematic if we ran into unsuspecting neighbors, I didn't have my own car, and even if I knew of a taxi service in Beukal, I didn't have any money. Broke and out of options, I resigned myself to the television.

Around ten, I was again surfing through the channels on offer, hoping to find something Sage could understand. The one channel that played subtitled imports had just switched to an Indian film, and while I enjoyed the odd Bollywood dance number, I suspected the movie would be far less enjoyable for Sage if I had to constantly read her the subtitles. "This might work," I began, landing on a game show of some sort, when the doorbell rang.

Sage, who'd been doodling in a notebook on the couch beside me, looked up in alarm.

Kitchen, I mouthed, shooing her into hiding, then snapped off the TV and rose to answer the door. "Can I help—*hey!*" I cried, switching to English once I registered who was waiting at the top of the steps. "Aren't you supposed to be working?"

"It's called vacation," said Annie, though she sported a long-sleeved black T-shirt and black trousers that seemed suspiciously like a uniform. "Can't a girl take a day off?"

"How'd you know—"

She snorted. "Pars has been training me, remember? He told me what's going on, so I'm playing hooky. Mind if I come in?"

I stepped back to admit her. "Thought this was supposed to be all hush-hush."

"Laws can do what it wants, but no one told *us* what to do," she replied with a cheeky grin. "Besides, you know I'm not going to rat y'all out. Where's Miss Sage, anyway?"

"It's okay," I called toward the kitchen. "This is Annie—she's a friend."

While I wasn't sure if *friend* was truly the most accurate word to describe our relationship, I felt that surviving a hostage-situation-slash-arson together had left us more than mere acquaintances.

Sage peeked around the corner, and Annie waved and said, "Hey! Nice to meet you. How's it going?"

Annie hadn't masked that morning, but from a distance, she looked human enough, a brunette about my size but better toned. Only at close range did her oddities become apparent: amber eyes that reflected light in the darkness like a cat's, plus slightly pointed ears. Next to an elf, hers seemed almost dainty, the sort of ears easily hidden by a ski cap, should she have the need and her masking pendant failed. Unlike Sage's, hers was an elegant silver disc, obviously a professionally made piece. Given her work outside the Pactlands and the family she'd left in Virginia, she needed her own necklace; Annie had been human until about six months ago, and the abilities she'd gained upon joining the Wild Hunt hadn't included self-masking.

"Uh...hi," said Sage, stepping out of her hiding place. "Are you from DOL?"

"Nah, DPP—Plants and Potions," Annie clarified. "And I understand you're stuck inside, waiting for a language potion to kick in."

She nodded. "It's *still* not working yet."

"Eh, these things take time. Trust me—I got Pactish from a potion, too." Moving closer to Sage, she said, "I'm from Richmond, so if you're feeling a little overwhelmed right now, believe me, I get it."

"Part of the ex-pat club of two," I joked.

She slung an arm around my shoulders. "We're open to new members."

"Yeah, yeah," I said, freeing myself. "Want a cup of tea or something? I know where Canna keeps her stash."

"Actually, I've got a better idea." Turning her attention back to Sage, she asked, "Ever seen a flying horse?"

Sage's eyes widened. "No, ma'am."

"Mm. Ever been around a horse, period?"

She gestured toward her jeans. "I mean...kind of?"

"Touché. What I was thinking was that y'all might want to come up to the lodge for a bit, pet some horses, breathe some fresh air. We could do lunch. At least the trees around there look normal."

Though Sage had perked at the offer, I cut in before she could get too excited. "Sorry...*where* are we going, exactly? In case our detective comes looking for us."

Annie made a face. "See, that's a really good question, and I think Wylan may be the only one who could give you an answer. It's the family manse, so to speak," she explained to Sage, "and it's just the guys and me there, so I'd *love* some company of the female persuasion."

Dad had rarely ever mentioned the Wild Hunt, but Pars had given me a brief explanation back in September. Their leader, a sort of repository for a massive, ancient source of power, periodically went hunting with his band. Since then, I'd perused Dad's library for more information and instead found questions and theories. The Hunter was the embodiment of the primal hunt, the cycle of predator and prey—that much could be agreed upon—but no one knew when or where he had arisen. Hell, no one knew the guy's *name*, just that he was huge, sported a rack of antlers, and was particularly difficult to kill. The books had also disagreed upon the composition of the Hunter's followers: were they servants, conscripts, or something more? The Hunter had shown up uninvited to sign the Pact, then had apparently carved out his own little clubhouse within the pocket universe, inaccessible to anyone but the Hunt.

On one of our calls, Canna had clarified what the books could not: the ancient Hunter was a murderous, filicidal monster, and when he'd tried to kill Annie, his youngest son had brought him down, unexpectedly inheriting the role. "Wylan's at least somewhat social," she'd told me. "He's joined the Forum, which is more than his father *ever* did. Actually stopped by a team happy hour," she'd added with a grin in her voice. "Annie's in Pars's group, and partners are welcome when they go out...but I'm not sure they knew what to do when she arrived with *him*."

"Was it awkward?" I'd asked.

"Only for a few minutes, or so I heard. Wylan did a short stint at DPP, so it wasn't like none of them had ever seen him before. And then he and my brilliant husband apparently started a drinking game, and Pars ended up under the table, so now they're on solid footing." She'd sighed. "Men."

"Pars said that Liogh's attached to this case," Annie

continued. "They have your number, right?"

"Uh…yeah," I said, plucking my cell phone from the end table where I'd left it.

"So, there's no problem. If they need you, they can call, and I'll take you right in. Promise."

While I didn't want to annoy the detective if they caught us out of the city, Sage needed a distraction, and the TV wasn't cutting it. "Sounds great. If you're sure you don't mind…"

"Of course not," she replied. "But Sage, hon, you're going to want shoes."

One sprint upstairs for sneakers and a jacket later, Sage headed for the door, but Annie called after her, "No need to go outside. We can't drive there."

She frowned. "Then how—"

"I've got a trick. Give me your hand."

Sage did as she asked, and after making sure the door was locked, I did likewise, anticipating what was to come.

"This won't hurt, but it'll feel weird," Annie cautioned Sage. "Close your eyes and hold on, and we'll be there before you know it. Ready?"

"Ready," she mumbled, bracing herself.

I almost yelped as the world fell away around me, but before I had time to fully register my fear, my feet touched solid ground once more, and I was conscious of stronger light on the far side of my eyelids. Risking a peek, I found myself in a clearing surrounded by autumn-painted woods, stands of tall trees still in full golden and red leaf interspersed by long swaths of pines. The grass had faded to winter brown, but the forest could have been a snapshot from October.

"Your fall comes late here," I said, as Sage caught her breath.

Annie chuckled. "Not really. The trees in Beukal started turning weeks ago. I mentioned that they reminded me of home, and then I woke up the next morning, and voila, the pines around here had competition." Grinning, she added, "I *may* be mistaken, but I have a sneaking suspicion that Wylan's been postponing the leaf drop on my account." With that, she released us and gestured toward a massive wooden barn. "Want to see the horses?"

We followed after her, but I paused to get my bearings, looked around, and found an enormous building behind us, a sprawling construction of stone and logs the size of a resort. The wide wrap-around covered porch was hung with lanterns, ready for nightfall, and someone had left what appeared to be bows and quivers of arrows leaning against the wall. The wooden rocking chairs were a nice touch, though, and I wondered if they were a sign of Annie's recent influence on the place. Though I couldn't see anyone lurking around the lodge, I could hear the sound of deep voices raised in distance-muffled shouts, followed by the crash of a falling tree.

"Nothing to worry about," said Annie. "Some of the guys have been chopping firewood this morning. Come on, we should have the barn to ourselves."

The barn doors stood open on both ends, and the morning light coming through those openings and a series of skylights negated the need for lamps within the cavernous space. At once, my nose registered the overwhelming scents of a horse barn: the warm animals themselves, the straw, the leather tack, the old wood of the building and the stalls within, and, as was to be expected, the unpleasant notes of the horses' leavings—though fainter than I'd anticipated, which I suspected might be due to magic. Most of the stalls we passed on our way to the far end were empty, but the few horses inside peeked at us, their beautiful, sleek black faces curious. I was no expert, but even to my layman's eyes, the animals seemed *tall*.

"What sort of horses are these?" I asked.

"There's no official breed designation," Annie replied. "No one here seems to recall when the foundational stock was acquired, but the Hunt's been breeding this bunch for a *long* time."

"Is that…healthy?"

She glanced back at me, grinning. "Are they all inbred, you mean? Apparently not. They live a very long time, I've yet to see one need more than treatment for a bite or an upset stomach, and Wylan said that whenever they needed new blood, a stallion would just appear."

"Convenient."

"Totally. But since the old Hunter created all of his sons, I don't imagine that the occasional horse gave him too much trouble."

Before I could press her for clarification of *that*, she called, "Jimbo, sweetie! Where's my best girl?"

A gray head popped out of a stall near the end, and a whinny echoed back toward us.

"Jimbo?" Sage asked.

"I didn't name her, but that's what she answers to, so we're rolling with it," she replied, then raised her voice again as the horse's whinnies continued. "Yes, yes, I hear you! You'll get your fix!"

Concerned, Sage hurried closer to Annie. "Why is she alone in here? Is she hurt?"

"Oh, no, she's fine," Annie assured her. "Most of the horses are out in the pastures right now. I kept Jimbo in because I figured y'all would be by, and I went ahead and saddled her. Oh, my God, you big *baby*," she yelled back at the horse, "I'm *coming*!"

Two things other than her color immediately set Jimbo apart from the rest of the horses in the barn. First was her size: she was smaller, not a pony but petite by comparison to the Hunt's mares. Second was the pair of wide, feathery wings that extended from her shoulder blades, which unfolded and readjusted against her sides as Annie greeted her.

"Holy *shit*," I muttered.

"She's pretty, isn't she?" said Annie in the syrupy tone I generally associated with owners of cute puppies. "Yes, she's my good girl. She is," she said, rubbing the horse's nose. "Now for the bribe."

Reaching onto a shelf beside Jimbo's stall door, Annie pulled down a sealed plastic box, which she opened to reveal several dozen sugar cubes. "We have a sweet tooth," she explained, plucking a cube from the box. "Sage, honey, hold out your hand…that's it…"

The horse eagerly took the proffered treat, and Sage giggled as Jimbo's lips searched her palm for crumbs.

"So," said Annie, giving Jimbo's nose another rub as the horse tried to check her shirt for hidden snacks, "would anyone be interested in going up?"

"I don't know how to ride," said Sage.

Annie patted her shoulder. "Know what? I've only been riding for about a year, and Jimbo is *very* patient. How about going with me? I'll make sure you don't fall."

Though Sage regarded the horse somewhat warily, she agreed.

Annie bustled around the barn, returning with a pair of nylon harnesses like those a rock climber might use and two coils of rope. "The guys laugh at me," she said, adjusting one of the harnesses to Sage's slight body, "because none of them would be caught dead with a safety tether. But they've been riding for decades, at *least*, and I'm still a newbie by comparison, so harnesses it is. Okay, that's tight…now, let's get you up into the saddle…"

Annie quickly followed her and clipped both of them in. "You're not going to fall," she insisted, "but if you did, this would catch you. I've had my share of fall training, and believe me, it holds. Jimbo knows that if someone starts dangling, she's to land. Just try to run away from her hooves, got it?"

With that safety briefing behind them, Annie unclipped a silver collar from around the horse's neck, then led her out of the barn. "We won't go far," she told me, then nudged Jimbo onward. The horse took a few trotting steps, spread her wings, and rose, and I heard Sage's sharp gasp turn to delighted laughter.

The day was nice, and I saw no need to stay in the barn, so I walked outside and shaded my eyes as I watched the trio rise and bank. From the back of the building, I could see a fenced pasture dotted with grazing black horses, a few of which raised their heads with interest as Jimbo soared past. I headed that way to entertain myself while I waited, and I'd almost coaxed one of the mares to come to the fence for petting when I heard a baritone voice behind me: "You must be Jane."

Startled, I wheeled around and found a large man standing a few feet away. He was a bit shorter than Pars, I estimated...well, if you didn't count the impressive rack of antlers rising from his skull. Though he wasn't so heavily muscled as my cousin's husband, what I could see of him was certainly toned, more like a swimmer's body than, say, a linebacker's. His light brown hair was unbound and fell around his shoulders, and through it, I could see the tips of ears much like Annie's poking through. Same amber eyes, I noticed. While Pars favored a closely shorn chinstrap beard, this man sported what looked like a three-day scruff, which managed to come off as rugged instead of lazy. I wasn't quite sure what to make of his getup—boots, dark leather leggings, and an off-white tunic that laced up the front instead of buttoning—but at that moment, I was more concerned with apologizing for wandering somewhere I wasn't meant to be than criticizing his wardrobe.

"Sorry, I didn't...Annie went up..."

He chuckled at my babbling. "You're fine," he said, and to my surprise, switched to English. "Didn't mean to sneak up on you. You *are* Jane, yes?"

"Guilty."

"Thought so. The number of blonde rogue sorcerers I've found roaming around here is...currently one."

"Wylan, right?"

"What gave it away?" Grinning, he stepped to the side

and found a spot to lean against the fence. "I'm guessing the youngling's with Annie," he said, shading his eyes with his hand as he peered up at the circling winged horse.

"Nice of her to bring us here," I said. "Canna and Pars have been great hosts, but there's only so much TV you can watch, especially since Sage's language potion is still taking effect." I hesitated, trying to gauge his reaction, then said, "If we're being an inconvenience—"

"Certainly not. I'm working from home today, and Annie needs to take the odd day off, so I should probably thank you for that." He flashed a smile but quickly sobered. "I *am* curious what you're doing here."

"Uh…Annie invited me—"

"Not *here*, sorry. The Pactlands, I mean."

"Moral support and translational services for Sage, more or less."

"Mm." His brow furrowed. "My understanding from Annie, though, was that you were being kept a secret. Incidentally, she said you're an impressive pyromancer, so it's a pity you're stuck outside."

Shrugging, I said, "I'm okay, I guess. And yeah, I'm still a secret, but DOL has said they won't prosecute my dad, so I'm…I don't know, testing the waters? Sticking a toe in?"

"*Ah.*" He nodded, then laughed to himself as Jimbo banked sharply and Sage screamed like a roller coaster rider. "Annie said the girl is searching for her parents."

"Annie says a lot, doesn't she?"

"Only to me," he replied with a teasing smirk. "What's her background?"

I sighed and braced my hands against the fence behind me. "Abandoned as a baby. Father's a sorcerer, mother's a centaur, and Sage is—"

"Unique?"

"That, plus malnourished and abused. We're working on it."

"So, Laws has identified her parents, then?" Wylan

asked.

"Yup. Got a double match in the blood database. Her mom works for the Forum...communications or some such...and her dad's a freaking *rep*, so—"

"*What?* Don't tell me Gerem has been sleeping with the staff!"

"Not him. The other guy—Mirrik, I think?"

"Mirrik Voln?" He sounded shocked. "That's difficult to imagine. Does Laws think he..."

He didn't need to finish that thought. I nodded. "That's what we're afraid of. If he forced himself on her..."

"Honestly, I'm not sure *how* that would work, but..." He whistled softly. "I might expect a stunt like that from Gerem, but not Mirrik. He's been nothing but cordial to this point, but perhaps I don't know him as well as I'd thought."

"Man," I weakly joked, "how bad *is* this Gerem guy?"

Wylan's expression darkened. "He's an asshole of the first order, and he almost cost me Annie, so I've little praise to heap upon his head."

I frowned. "Canna said he tried to kick her out—"

"Yeah, and with a mind wipe. Had I arrived five minutes later than I did, she'd have taken a potion that could have erased her memory of the Pactlands."

"Sheesh," I muttered. "I know folks here are *particular* about humans, but..."

"If Annie had just been a random human who hung out at DPP and waited for a cure, that might have been one thing. But she risked her life over and *over* during that wait. Almost killed herself," he said, his voice rising with his indignation. "She's still scarred from that time, you know? I've offered—I *think* I can remove the scars—but she's kept them to this point."

Trying to be delicate, I said, "I was wondering about those. She showed them to one of our would-be witches back in Georgia, said they were from the wrong potion or something."

He huffed a low grunt. "That's putting it mildly. Did she mention Roulette?"

"Yeah. Said she was drugged with a potion."

"Essentially, and a nasty one. With that in her system, other potions and magical items often didn't work properly Painkillers were less effective, that masking pendant she wears now left her with a scalp condition, her arms turned blue for a time…" He shook his head. "Anyway, the scars largely come from her first trip here. My father had abducted an elf to hunt down."

"*Shit.*"

"Yeah. Annie sneaked in there," he said, pointing to the storage barn, "and got her out. But she'd taken a scent neutralizer, see, and when she added an invisibility ring to the mix, she was left with a burning rash all over. She carried the elf out on her shoulders to keep her invisible as well, and the chafing battered her skin. I mean, that was a secondary concern to the kidney failure…"

"Wait, what triggered *that*?"

Wylan shrugged. "Something in the combination. Your guess is as good as DPP's. Annie's fine now," he continued, "but that's where most of her scarring originated. The rest is from an explosion back in May. The parents of that elf she rescued are…something," he said with distaste. "Her father tried to blow up Annie. He's on a penal farm now. And *that*," he said with a soft chuckle, "is the long explanation for why I have as little to do as possible with Gerem. Annie did things DOL wouldn't dare to try, and he repaid that with cruelty."

"Sounds like a real prince," I replied, watching Jimbo make another pass overhead.

"Perhaps he fancies himself one. He's wealthy enough, and he has a pedigree of sorts. Suppose that's how he got his wife…" Turning to me, he caught my blank look and laughed. "Annie taught me a phrase, cradle robbing?"

I winced. "Ooh. How bad is it?"

"Well, in all honesty, I can't talk, but if we're limiting this to sorcerer norms, his current wife is a child beside him. Gerem is a hundred sixty-five or so, I think, and the woman on his arm is all of sixty."

"Married him for his personality, I'm sure."

"Of course. I'm certain her looks and his money had nothing to do with the union," he deadpanned. "But that's Gerem. I wouldn't be surprised to learn he'd cheated on his wife, and if you told me he'd done something worse, I'd probably consider it. *Mirrik*, though?" Wylan sighed. "He's not a hideous man, but I find it hard to believe that a centaur would willingly bed him. And you said she's a Forum employee?"

"It looks like they were both aides at the time."

"Still…if he did, in fact, force her, and with him a representative now…" Giving me a long look, Wylan said, "I'm glad that DOL has decided not to prosecute your father, but do you have any such guarantee from the Forum?"

A cold worm of doubt began to coil up in my gut. "What do you mean?"

He hesitated, then said, "When I joined the Forum, I thought it'd be wise to familiarize myself with their rules. Some are seldom invoked, but there *is* a provision that allows us to initiate prosecution without DOL's involvement. It takes two-thirds of the representatives to proceed," he quickly added as I stared at him in dawning fear, "and I don't believe it's been used in some time, but—"

"What if Mirrik retaliates?" I interrupted. "What if he finds out about my involvement in this mess and comes after Dad?"

"I certainly wouldn't vote for prosecution," he murmured, "but I'm only one vote. Jane, I don't mean to alarm you—"

At that point, I'd breezed past mere alarm all the way to the cusp of panic, but I tried to stay calm, even as short flames licked along my arms. "I can't leave. Sage needs this, and I…hell, I don't even have a *car* here. Detective Birrid drove us over and got us through the checkpoint."

"And they're the one who told you all was well because DOL had agreed to look the other way?"

"Uh-huh."

"Disappointing, but from what I've heard, DOL tends to forget that other agencies have options beyond their control. Listen, now," he said, gently gripping my shoulders before the fire could reach that high. "You're not trapped. Annie and I can evacuate you at any time, understand?"

I took a few deep breaths to calm myself, then managed to mumble, "Really?"

He released one of my shoulders to snap his fingers. "Like *that*. Please don't burn me."

Muttering an apology, I extinguished my flames, and Wylan stepped back. "Annie was right about your pyromancy," he said.

"I've got it under control, it's just—"

"Stress reaction, I know. I've seen that before. The elf Annie carried out of here, Fellora, is a pyro as well."

Before he could elaborate, Jimbo came in for a running landing, and Annie pulled her to a stop a few yards away. "Hey!" she called as the horse walked toward us. "Look who decided to see daylight!"

"My eyes were crossing over committee reports, so I took a break," Wylan replied, stepping forward to meet them and take the reins. "Have fun?"

"Still in the saddle, so that's a yes. Hang on, hon," she said to Sage, "let me get down, and I'll help you."

Sage stared at Wylan in silence, her green eyes round with anxiety.

"Here we go," said Annie once she'd unhooked and hopped off the horse. "Jimbo's not going anywhere. Just unclip, atta girl, and you're going to get off like you got on. Use the stirrup…"

She landed in the grass and sidled closer to Annie, still gawking, but Wylan seemed both unsurprised and unoffended by her reaction. "Hi, there," he said, dropping to a crouch as one might with a small child. "You must be Sage."

"Yes, sir," she whispered.

He smiled. "Glad you could come. Are you hungry?"

Her mood brightened at the offer of food, and Annie laughed. "Well, *I* am," Annie said. "Let me get Jimbo collared again before she flies off without me, and…" She paused, giving me a curious look. "Everything okay, Jane?"

"Fine," I lied.

Unconvinced, she looked to her husband, eyebrows raised in query.

He straightened and handed her the reins, and Jimbo nudged Annie's arm, presumably hunting for hidden sugar. "DOL may have decided not to pursue Jane's father," he said quietly, "but has anyone over there considered the ramifications of pinning a paternity scandal, much less rape charges, on a representative?"

"I don't follow…"

"The Forum can bring charges on its own. It's rare, and it requires a significant majority, but…"

Annie made the same rapid calculus as I had and hissed, "*Shit.* You don't think—"

"I wouldn't have dreamed of such from Mirrik, but if he's capable of *this*…"

"What's wrong?" Sage interrupted, looking at each of them in rapid succession. "What happened?"

"Nothing for you to worry about, sweetheart," I said, forcing a smile. "Let me—"

"*Tell* me, Jane. I'm not a baby," she insisted. "What's going on?"

Though I didn't want to put one more thing on her plate, I relented. "Wylan pointed out that there's a slight chance that if Mirrik gets upset about being called in to DOL concerning you, he might find out about me, then

Dad, and get the Forum to bring charges against Dad as payback. Even if DOL won't touch Dad, he's not safe yet. But that's not a strong possibility," I said, trying to convince the irrational part of myself as much as her, "and—"

"Why didn't Detective Birrid *tell* us?" she demanded, aghast.

"They probably didn't think of it," Wylan replied. "And Jane's right, this is an unlikely scenario."

"But Yacovi's not safe. Not if I..." She shook her head, then grabbed my hand. "Let's go home, okay? Tell the detective to stop looking. It doesn't matter."

"Sage, of *course* it matters," I protested. "You have a right—"

"I know who my parents are. That's what I came here for, isn't it? And they don't want me," she said with a sad smile. "I was hoping that, you know, someone had kidnapped me and they'd want me back, but that's not true, and I...I can accept that."

"Honey—"

"You've been *really* good to me, Jane. The best. And I don't want to be the reason you lose your dad," she said as her eyes welled. "That's not fair. So, can we go home, please?"

I pulled her into a long, tight hug. "We can stay and see this through," I murmured into her hair.

But she shook her head, and I looked up at Annie and Wylan. "I'm sorry to ask, but could we bum a ride?"

CHAPTER 15

Ten minutes later, after a quick trip by Canna and Pars's house to pack, Annie, Sage, and I reappeared in my kitchen.

"I'll go see Pars as soon as I get back," Annie promised. "They'll understand." She paused, then asked, "Are y'all going to be okay?"

"Absolutely," I replied more confidently than I felt. "Thanks for everything."

"No problem. And listen, if things go sideways, give me a call. If I've been there, I can find you."

I assured Annie we'd be all right, and she vanished, leaving Sage and me alone in the quiet house.

"So…" I said, flipping on the kitchen lights, "that, uh…"

"I'm sorry."

I turned to Sage and found her hugging herself, looking as if she were trying to hunch into nothingness. "You didn't do anything wrong."

"You were having a nice time with your cousin—"

"I'll talk to Canna again. What I'm more worried about is your future." Leaning against the counter to give Sage space, I said, "You're welcome to stay with me—that hasn't changed. But I don't have to mask here. You do, and I…I wanted you to have the chance to be yourself."

Sage shrugged. "I'd have to mask there, too. You saw how the detective and Canna looked at me. Wherever I am, I'm a freak," she mumbled. "But if you don't want me here, if you're worried about your dad—"

"I want you, Sage."

Her jaw trembled as she looked at me. "I don't want to hurt you…"

I held her as she cried in earnest, the culmination of a long, strange few days of anxiety and disappointment, then stopped her as she tried to apologize. "Why don't you go wash your face and unpack?" I suggested. "I'll make lunch, and you can tell me all about Annie's *freaking* flying horse."

Sage swiped a hand over her eyes. "You didn't get a turn—"

"It's okay. Here," I said, pulling a can of ginger ale from the fridge, "take this with you. Can't hurt, right?"

Once I heard the water running, I released a slow breath, then set about pulling a meal together. Having divided the Thanksgiving leftovers between Dad and Tabitha, I didn't have much around, but the bread looked mold-free, and there was peanut butter in the cabinet…

My phone rang in my purse, and my stomach knotted as I dug it out, expecting to have to explain myself to Canna. Instead, I saw an unfamiliar but local number and tapped the screen. "Hello?"

"Jane? Hi, it's Connor Willow. From the Whitford PD?"

"Connor!" I made a mental note to save him to my contacts list. "Uh, hi. If something's on fire, I didn't do it."

"If something's on fire, it's news to me, but thanks for the heads-up. I'm sorry to bother you," he said in a rush, "but I hadn't seen any activity by the Cavanaugh place, and I, um…I just wanted to make sure everything was all right. Do y'all need anything? I don't mind helping with a cover story."

I started to tell him that we were fine, but instead, I heard myself say, "Things are kind of messy right now. We got back to town a few minutes ago, and I don't want to get into the details, but it's possible I'm going to have at least one irate detective on my doorstep tonight."

"Y'all in danger?"

"Nothing I can't handle."

"Uh-huh," he replied, sounding unduly skeptical, I thought. "In that case, I've got a proposition for you."

"Oh?"

"Seeing as my colleagues in Ragged Gap don't need any more mystery fires to deal with, why don't y'all come over to my place for dinner tonight? That way, if someone should come looking for you, they'll be out of luck, and you won't have to charbroil anything."

"That's...really nice of you," I said, taken aback by the offer, "but we'll be okay."

"I'm sure you will, but now *I'm* worried, and although my peace of mind isn't your responsibility...please?"

And there went my resolve.

"Counteroffer," I said. "You host, I bring pizzas."

"Addendum: would you be upset if I provided beer to accompany said pizzas?"

"Depends on the beer. Natty?"

"I'm thirty, Ms. Fortune, not thirteen," he said dryly. "Would Yuengling do?"

"I could agree to those terms. What do you want on your pizza?"

"Where are you ordering, Gino's?"

"That's where I normally go," I replied. "Something wrong with that?"

"Not at all. There's a place over my way that does decent pizza, but I have real concerns about the meat they use. Anything's fine at Gino's. I'm not picky."

"When? Six?"

"Works for me. I'll text you the address."

He did, and I saved his information that time.

Connor was waiting at the front door as Sage and I pulled up that evening. For once, he'd changed out of the uniform, opting for jeans and a brown cotton sweater roughly the same hue as his eyes...

Reminding myself to focus, I stepped past him into the warm house, pizzas and cheese sticks in my arms, and took stock of the place. Connor's home wasn't massive, but for a single guy's starter house, it was enormous...and surprisingly well decorated. The furniture spoke more of Sears than of Target or IKEA: a maple-stained dining room suite in the room to the right of the foyer, a floral-printed couch and coordinating solid-colored stuffed chairs in the room to the left, both rooms heavy on the brass lamps and wallpaper borders. Overall, the house had an unexpectedly feminine touch, down to the porcelain angel I saw peeking out of the china closet.

"You've got a lovely home," I said as Connor took the pizza from me.

"Thanks. Let's unpack this in the kitchen," he replied, cocking his head toward the back of the house, and I followed him down the faux Oriental runner.

"Did you decorate all of this? I don't mean to be nosy," I said, "but the guys I knew back in college mostly furnished their apartments with thrift-store finds and beer paraphernalia, so..."

"It's a little better than that, I hope." Putting the boxes on the square kitchen table, which had already been set for three, Connor murmured, "This was my family's house. I haven't done much to it since I inherited the place, but—"

"Oh. Oh, *God*," I said, retreating a step as my hand flew to my mouth. "I'm so sorry, I didn't know—"

"You're fine," he insisted with a little smile. "I didn't tell you. And if there's anything you like about the décor, it was my mom's doing. She'd be happy that someone still appreciates her taste. Little frou-frou for me, but...you know."

I held up my hands and slowly exhaled. "Okay, can we please start over? Hi, thank you so much for having us, and I'll try to keep my foot out of my mouth for the rest of the night."

He chuckled and opened the fridge. "Beer?"

"Please."

Connor passed me one, then handed Sage a Coke— "You wouldn't like the beer, and I really can't be a party to underage drinking," he told her—and jokingly clinked his can against mine. "To avoiding the fuzz, eh?"

"If that's the goal, I'm doing a terrible job of it," I replied, cracking open my drink.

"I *am* off duty unless all hell breaks loose, which, given that this is Whitford…" He took a long swig of beer. "Not much risk of me having to drive drunk tonight, know what I'm saying? Come on, let's dig in before the pizza gets cold."

Sage didn't need to be told twice, and she said little as we ate, leaving Connor and me to chat like locals, piecing together points of overlap in our pasts. Though he'd attended the county schools and I'd been homeschooled, we were close enough in age to share commonalities in our childhood memories of the area. We'd just finished reminiscing about what a pain it had been—and still was— to drive to North Carolina to see any new blockbuster when he asked if I'd like another beer. I wasn't opposed, and so Connor turned around in his chair to mutter and motion at the fridge until a pair of cans floated to the table. "My one good party trick," he said with a slightly embarrassed grin, "and I can't really pull it out at parties, so…cheers."

"I bet you can do a lot more than that," I said, popping the top of my beer. "You probably just need training. Let me guess: you got little flashes of talent in grade school, and you've been figuring it out on your own ever since?"

He nodded. "More or less. I learned a bit from some of my kin out at East Branch, but there's no, like…*manual* for the touch."

Considering the bookshelf full of grimoires back at Dad's house, I begged to differ, but Sage jumped in before I could. "So, you're a sorcerer, too?"

Connor paused, can halfway to his mouth, and gave me

a long look. "There's that word again. Your detective buddy asked me if I had sorcerers in the family...Beard, wasn't it?"

"Close enough. And, uh..."

As I waffled, Connor said, "If this is something top-secret, you don't have to tell me. I'm a big boy."

"It's not that—I'm trying to think of the best way to do it," I replied. "So, um...in the place where Sage is from, where we've been lately, there's a community of people who look human but aren't. They can live for a few centuries, and they've got power. Sorcerers. It's not a profession—it's what they are."

"Uh-huh." He rubbed his chin, then took a sip of beer. "And you think that I might be one of them?"

"Maybe in part...like me."

To my relief, he didn't recoil at the revelation that I wasn't of pure Georgian stock. "I don't know. There've been people with the touch at East Branch as far back as anyone can remember, but no one's ever mentioned *sorcery*."

"How long *has* your family been there?"

He hissed as he consulted the ceiling for answers. "Shoot, I don't know. Generations. Before the Civil War, I know that much...maybe back to the Revolution."

I thought quickly, trying to find a delicate way to phrase my hypothesis, then said, "You said everyone out there is related. If you had a sorcerer or two among the early settlers, and you've had a couple centuries of cousins.. intermingling..."

"You're talking about a 'Blue Fugates' situation?"

"A what?" Sage asked.

Connor grunted and put his can aside. "Let's just say that as the product of a rather close-knit family and the butt of one too many 'Paddle faster!' jokes, I've always been interested in similar communities. There was a family in eastern Kentucky not too long ago that carried a recessive gene...don't ask me the medical specifics, but it screwed up something in their blood, and they looked blue. You know how it went with little mountain towns in the nineteenth century," he said to me. "Big families, not a lot of options, few coming or going, and almost everyone ended up marrying cousins after a couple generations."

"Small gene pool," I replied.

"Bingo. The last of that family have dispersed now, so you don't see a cluster of blue people, but at the time, they were notorious in the area. So...you're thinking East Branch might be something similar? Like, we've got a double recessive for sorcery or some such?"

I laughed. "When you put it like that..."

"Stab in the dark," he said.

"Fair." I drank my beer. "One thing I can tell you is that talent doesn't rely on some sort of recessive gene. My mother was—*is*—a sorcerer, and my father wasn't. You see the result," I concluded, and before I quite thought it all the way through, I sent pale flames licking up my left arm.

Connor scooted back in his chair on instinct, eyes almost bulging, but recovered quickly enough when he saw that I wasn't panicking. "*Damn*, woman. Doesn't that hurt?"

"Nah. It's not actually making contact with me—it's just above my skin and clothes." Extinguishing the fire, I said, "I'm fifty percent sorcerer and still have the talent. Same goes for Sage, though she's a late bloomer."

The girl heaved a sigh and stole more cheese sticks.

"We don't have to figure out exactly what you are tonight," I told Connor. "But once things calm down, if you want some tips or anything...you know, the talent's innate, but spellcasting is taught. I could give you some pointers."

He grinned. "You're not awed by my remote beer retrieval skills?"

"Impressed, but I'm confident that you could do more."

Those pretty eyes crinkled, and I realized with a sudden flash of self-awareness that I was *flirting*.

My mind skipped ahead several large steps to the awkward conversation I'd have with Dad about a new man in my life, but I derailed that train of thought and sipped my drink to give myself a chance to focus. "So, uh, thanks for having us over tonight," I said. "I don't want to monopolize your evening, so let me clean this up—"

"Are you okay to drive? That's a legitimate question— I'm not trying to pull the cop card," he insisted. "The Breathalyzer's out in my vehicle. It's just dark, and the roads ain't exactly wide and straight, and the deer don't always mind their manners…"

"And my DD is thirteen," I said, nodding to Sage.

"Slightly too young for night driving," Connor replied with faux solemnity. "Maybe a little TV before y'all go? I'll make coffee," he offered.

We let Sage choose, and she settled on a nature show, giving Connor ample opportunity to deploy his best— albeit still somewhat lacking—Attenborough impression. Sage giggled as he offered ever more ridiculous running commentary, but shortly after the second episode began, I glanced over and found her asleep, curled up with a mauve corduroy throw pillow.

"She's out?" Connor murmured as tropical birds squawked on the screen across the room.

I nodded. "It's been a rough few days."

"Mm. Want to tell me what's really going on?" When I hesitated, he said, "I know I probably can't do anything to fix it, but on the off chance that I can…"

He seemed sincere, and frankly, I wanted to talk to someone who wasn't deeply involved in this mess, but there remained the tiny problem that in so doing, I'd be ripping back the curtain once more. Granted, if Connor were indeed of sorcerer extraction, he'd need to learn the full truth sometime, but could I trust him to keep his mouth shut?

He hadn't spread the news about Sage, had he? Or about my history of arson? Hell, I doubted that even Dad had heard of the potential sorcerers at East Branch until I told him about Connor's visit.

"There's this place called the Pactlands," I said, and Connor lowered the volume on the TV. "A pocket world, if you will, separate from ours but still attached. It was created by sorcerers as a safe haven for persecuted non-humans."

He nodded, digesting that. "Okay…"

"We took Sage over late last week to do some testing, and she matches with two people in a blood database. Her mother is a centaur."

"I'd kind of assumed something along those lines."

"Apparently, they don't typically hook up with non-centaurs"—Connor grimaced at the notion—"but the problem is that Sage's father is a sorcerer. Her parents worked together, but he was a more senior employee. Our fear is that he forced himself on her."

"Not to be crass," said Connor, "but how the hell do you force yourself on a *centaur*? I would think a hoof to the crotch could stop that."

"If he were human, sure. But he's a sorcerer. There's no telling if he drugged her or…or did something more physical. The folks at that cabin back at Labor Day, the one I burned down? The potion they were using isn't the only thing out there that can override someone's will. There's plenty of shit—*illegal* shit mostly, but if you've got money and connections…"

"Sounds familiar," he muttered. "So, this has turned into a probable rape investigation?"

"And that's only part of it." I pushed my hair out of my face and sighed. "Sage's father is now a representative—part of the top level of government over there. Another rep raised the possibility that if Daddy Dearest learns of my involvement, he might try to retaliate against me."

Connor's brow furrowed. "What does he have on

you?"

"It's my dad," I said softly. "Not my bio-dad, but the man who raised me. He broke Pact law, and I'm the result."

"Sorry, I'm not following…"

"Because I haven't explained it. They're pretty particular about keeping humans out of the Pactlands—"

"Figures."

"Yeah, but they take it to an extreme. Say you're a sorcerer who has to come out here for some reason, and you meet a local and fall in love. That's what happened to my parents," I said with a brief, tight smile. "Relationships like that are forbidden, so the sorcerer in that scenario has two options: break it off or take the death draught."

"The *what*?"

"Death draught," I repeated. "It neutralizes talent and kills the drinker in a few decades, tops. They wanted a potion that gives the drinker a more human lifespan, but it works too well. Anyway, my parents met, they hooked up, and they wanted to be together. Dad—my adopted dad— was my mother's boss, and he was supposed to give her the draught. He didn't. Fudged the paperwork or whatever."

"Good man," Connor murmured.

"Yeah, Dad's pretty great. And he's my dad because my bio-dad died when I was two weeks old, and my mother went to Dad for help. He let us stay for a bit, and she bailed on me in the middle of the night."

Connor's eyes softened. "Jane…"

"It's okay," I said, which was far from true but seemed like the right thing to say. "She's not in the picture, and Dad's been great, so no complaints about him. But the problem is that I'm talented, whereas if my mother had taken the draught, the effects would have been seen in her children."

"In other words, you're walking proof that your dad lied."

"Exactly. I've been here all my life, and I made contact with folks in the Pactlands for the first time in September. Extenuating circumstances," I said, declining to mention the dead faun I'd found in my backyard. "Once all of this with Sage came up, I reached out again, but I didn't go over there without a guarantee from the Division of Laws that they wouldn't prosecute Dad. He *should* be off the hook—word from the top is that they're overlooking this. But apparently, the Forum can bring its own charges, and no one bothered to mention that until this morning, so we got the hell out of Dodge."

He nodded slowly. "What's going to happen to Sage?"

"I'll keep her, try to raise her. Honestly, she'd have more opportunities in the Pactlands, but now that she knows she probably wasn't a consensual baby, she's not keen on reconnecting. Can't say that I blame her. In any case, now I'm worried that our detective is going to come around, and if they go forward with the investigation and Sage's father finds out about me…"

Whether from the recent stress or the beer in my system, I felt my eyes begin to prick, and I blinked the tears back before they could fall. But Connor was more perceptive than I'd have liked at that moment, and he reached for my hand. "Why don't y'all stay here tonight? Your detective won't find you, will he? We can move your truck into the garage if you're concerned that he'll go hunting for it."

"Oh…oh, that's really nice of you to offer, but—"

"I'm serious. This place has plenty of beds, Sage has already conked out, and if you stay, I can bring in the last of the six-pack. Maybe it's just me, but you seem like you could use it."

That *was* tempting, but I tried to hold firm. "I don't want to get in the way. You weren't planning to have houseguests tonight, and I'm okay to drive now."

"It's no problem, Jane. I mean it. Besides," he said with a little grin, "should someone come looking for trouble,

I'm a decent shot."

The hand he wasn't holding flared, but Connor didn't flinch that time. "I can take care of myself."

"Never said you couldn't. But to keep the arson in the area to a minimum, why don't y'all camp here? As backup plans go, I'm not the worst."

With that, my resolve crumbled. I followed him upstairs, and he flipped the lights on in a pair of rooms flanking a small and rather dated bathroom. "My old room," he said, nodding to the one on the left, "and the guest room. I don't think that comforter's been touched in five years, so, uh…"

"You grab some sheets and let me handle it," I told him, and centered myself as I moved into the doorway of the guest bedroom. With a muttered incantation, the dust rose from every surface and coalesced into a gray sphere the size of a tennis ball, which I deposited in the empty trash can by the pine dresser as Connor reappeared.

"Now, *that's* useful," he declared. "Got a spell to make the bed, too?"

I smirked and took the stack of folded sheets from him. "Half the fun of being a sorcerer is making housework easier."

He stood beside me as I mumbled, coaxing the fitted sheet around the mattress, tucking in the rest of the layers, and sliding the pillowcases on. "Can you teach me to do that?" he asked.

"Not tonight."

"Fair enough."

While Connor found clean towels and dug some extra toothbrushes from his dentist stash, I made short work of the second bedroom, which actually appeared to have been redone since the turn of the millennium. In lieu of the wallpaper accents and large florals, Connor's former room had sandstone walls and navy bedding. The furniture was decent but utilitarian, the sort of wooden pieces one might acquire for a teenage boy, and I thought of my own room back at Dad's house.

I gently shook Sage awake and coaxed her upstairs to sleep, and she kicked off her shoes and fell into Connor's old bed without complaint. After tucking her in, I slipped back downstairs with Connor to finish off the beer, and we drank in companionable silence while the nature documentary switched to scenes of the white Antarctic and a doomed seal. As the orcas moved in for the kill, I said, "Thanks again for having us over. And, um...I'm sorry for bringing up your folks."

"You didn't know," he said kindly. "It's been a while, too, so it's not like I'm in deep mourning."

"How long?"

He sipped his beer and watched the hapless seal vanish beneath the waves. "My dad died eight years ago in July. Colon cancer."

"I'm so sorry."

"At least he didn't suffer long after his diagnosis." Connor paused, studying me, then seemed to reach a decision. "I was born and raised in Whitford, yeah? Dad worked at that hardware store that caught your license plates on your way to that strange act of God that took out the Cavanaugh house"—I grinned—"and Mom was a short-order cook at Betty's down the block. They pushed me to get out of town once I finished high school, but I got my Associate's and came back. Got on with the police—it was good money, and it's not like we're the murder capital of Georgia. So, I did that for a few years, and I was considering putting in for a job in Atlanta, trying to get more experience, when Mom finally dragged Dad to the doctor and he got the bad news. It was already late-stage by then, and he didn't see much point in going through chemo."

He paused for a long drink.

"We buried Dad that summer, and Mom...she faded. I'd been renting, but I moved back home to look after her. She wasn't eating much, not taking care of herself. In

October, I came home after an overnight shift and found her in bed. Heart attack," he said simply. "She loved Dad something fierce, you know? I don't blame her for wanting to be with him, but that's not to say I don't miss them."

Having never known either of my progenitors, I didn't miss them so much as I missed the *idea* of them, but I knew how broken I'd be without Dad on the other end of the phone. "Connor, I'm sorry for dredging this up——"

"No, don't apologize. I coaxed you through the wringer tonight, so this is only fair," he said, flashing a lopsided smile. "Anyway, once Mom was gone, I stayed here. Kept on at my job, forgot about Atlanta, and now I'm chief of a three-man, one-dog operation."

"Three? I thought there were only two of you."

"I hired a guy after I got the promotion. Sam's a very good boy as German shepherds go, but he can't cover a shift alone, and his spelling is *atrocious*."

The joke was unabashedly terrible, but I laughed way too long, a combination of alcohol and exhaustion, and Connor ended up laughing with me as he flushed.

I could have stayed on that couch. Mrs. Willow had selected a comfy one, and my slightly intoxicated libido was suggesting that I do the wise, ladylike thing and jump atop the pretty cop like a velociraptor before he knew what hit him. But prudence, that old killjoy, won out, and as the TV shifted to the credits and the countdown to the next episode, I made my excuses and dragged myself to bed. And whether he was too much of a gentleman to follow me or too concerned about fireballs to take the risk, Connor bade me goodnight and slept alone.

CHAPTER 16

While my phone didn't have much juice the next morning, it had power enough to ring in my purse as I skulked around Connor's kitchen at five, looking for a water glass. I fished it out, if only to silence it, then saw Liogh's number and decided to face the music. If I talked to them, I reasoned in my pre-caffeinated haze, then maybe they wouldn't come hunting for me.

"Hello," I mumbled in Pactish.

"Jane?" Their voice bore an unfamiliar edge, though whether it was concern or anger, I couldn't tell. "What the hell?"

"I could be asking you the same."

"I sent Canna a message late last night saying we're ready to bring Relieg in to talk, but now I hear that you've *left?*"

"Safety reasons."

The detective sputtered briefly, then said, "Putting aside the matter of *how* you two sneaked out—and I suspect I'll be having a strong word with Humphries—what's going on? You were perfectly safe here!"

"Dad wasn't."

"The director has assured me—"

"And that's great, but what if Mirrik takes this to the Forum?"

"Jane," they said, sighing, "what are you talking about?"

I wondered if Liogh was likewise waiting for that first cup of the day. "Wylan told me that even if DOL doesn't want to come after Dad, the Forum could."

"Well...yes," they allowed grudgingly, "but I haven't seen them deploy that option in years. It's an administrative headache, and without support from us, most of them don't know what they're doing. The last time the Forum brought a case to the Tribunal without DOL, it was tossed on technicalities."

"But it *could* happen," I pressed. "And if you go after this Mirrik guy and he finds out about Dad and me—"

"You're catastrophizing, youngling. I don't want to see Yacovi before a judge any more than you do."

"I *seriously* doubt that!"

"Okay, okay," they said, adopting a more placating tone. "You're right, I'm sorry. But what about Sage? What am I supposed to tell Relieg—'We found your daughter, but she's on the run'?"

"Maybe you shouldn't tell her anything."

"Come again?"

"Look," I said, filling a glass at the tap, "Sage knows this won't end well. She's not stupid. As much as I'd like to bring someone to justice for what she's been through, even putting the matter of Dad's safety aside, I don't want to drag her back into this just to break her heart."

Liogh paused before answering me. "I understand that impulse. I do," they insisted. "I'm not a complete monster. But as difficult as this process may be for Sage, you need to think about what's best for her in the long run."

"Yes, because rejection will do *so* much to help her—"

"Past that. Even if her parents aren't an option for her going forward, she's entitled to Pactlands citizenship, and she could be maintained until she reached majority. We have a few children in similar situations, 'wards of the Forum.' There's an excellent school in Beukal with boarding facilities, and she could live there and get the remedial education she needs."

"She can get an education here, too," I said.

"And what about therapy? You *know* she needs to work with a therapist. Can you give her that in Georgia?"

I knew I couldn't—if Sage were honest here, the counselor would either think her a liar or call the cops as a mandatory reporter.

When I hesitated, Liogh said, "We have resources that you can't touch, Jane. I'm not saying this to diminish what you've tried to do for the girl, but we should be practical. Sage needs more than you can give her. Besides, is it fair to ask her to live masked for the rest of her life? That's what she'll have to look forward to out there."

"She seems to like it well enough," I muttered.

"Perhaps she does. But there's always the *what if* to consider. If her pendant breaks, if she's caught unmasked…and she doesn't have any real identification, does she? You want to condemn her to live with forged paperwork?"

"Works for Dad."

"An experienced agent who knows what he's doing and made the choice to live outside. She's a child. Let's bring her back," Liogh said. "It'll be simple to formally establish her parentage, and if they don't want her, they'll be charged for her upkeep—"

"Whoa, whoa, *wait*," I snapped. "If Relieg is indeed a rape victim, are you telling me that you want to bill her for Sage—"

"Not Relieg. That's not the plan," they hastily explained. "Assuming the worst, if she testifies against Mirrik, we should be able to clear her of responsibility, legal and fiscal. If he fights it, we can call in a farseer from DOI to snoop around at the time of Sage's conception. Relieg will be free to go on with her life, Mirrik can pay, and Sage can start fresh. No one is trying to punish a victim."

The plan they were laying out made sense…but there was still the matter of Dad's safety to consider.

"I'll think about it," I told Liogh. "Talk to Sage, see what she wants to do. But I'm not making any promises right now."

"Please consider it. I know you care about her, and the odds of the Forum initiating charges against Yacovi are incredibly slim—"

"They're still odds, not a guarantee," I retorted. "You can't give me that. I'll call you," I said firmly, and hung up.

Sighing, I reached for my water glass, only to hear Sage's voice behind me: "I understood that."

I turned and spotted her on the threshold of the kitchen, barefoot and rumpled from the night in her street clothes but smiling. "Yeah? You did?" I asked in Pactish. "Is this making sense now?"

She hesitated, then answered me in kind. "It's so weird. The words are *there*, but they don't feel quite right…"

"Give it a little time, and I bet you'll be in good shape. We'll ask Dad—he's taken that potion before."

Sage nodded, then sobered and switched back to English. "Was that Detective Birrid?"

I followed her linguistic lead. "Yep. They're not happy with me. They were planning to bring your mother in for questioning before they realized we'd sneaked out."

"Glad they found out we were gone first. That would have been awkward if she'd wanted to meet me…I mean, she probably doesn't," Sage mumbled, absently rubbing her arms, "but if she was curious or something…"

The flame of hope for a happy reconciliation hadn't entirely died, I noted, though that was no great surprise. Sage was young and desperate, and I remembered being her age and dreaming about my absent mother, alternately hating her for running out on me and longing for an imagined maternal ideal that surely bore no resemblance to reality, a loving, soft-voiced figure who would sweep back into town and somehow make me whole. If I were truly honest with myself, though my hopes had long since burned down to embers, they still glowed.

"Liogh says there's a boarding school you could attend in Beukal," I told her. "Get a better education than you could with me. They'd make your father pay if…you know, if he hurt your mother. It's not a bad offer—"

"I don't want to go to school alone, Jane. Would they let you come, too? I mean, *would* you come with me?"

"They wouldn't allow me to stay. But they'd help you with your reading and math, and teach you magic...it wouldn't be bad."

But she emphatically shook her head. "Please don't make me go alone. *Please*. I don't want to be alone—"

"I'm not going to make you do anything," I soothed, hugging her to calm her fear. "We can tell Liogh to go jump in a lake, if that's what you want. But we need to think and be smart about this."

"What about Yacovi?"

"That's part of what I have to think about." Hearing footsteps, I looked up and saw Connor appear in the doorway. "Immediate danger is past. I had a chat with the detective, and we're going to mull over our options."

His eyes narrowed. "You're sure?"

"Pretty sure. And doesn't someone need to superintend Whitford's Finest instead of babysitting us?"

"Y'all are welcome to stay..."

"I appreciate it," I said, holding his gaze. "Really. But I need to go home and straighten myself out."

"Okay," Connor replied, though he sounded unconvinced. "Will you do me a favor and not call me a sexist jerk if I make the occasional pass by your house, just to be sure you haven't been kidnapped by, uh...I don't know, fairies?"

I laughed. "My place is kind of out of your jurisdiction, isn't it?"

"I don't mind using the gas. Town pays for it."

When an incredulous look didn't deter him, I said, "Fine, if it'll make you feel better."

"Thank you." He paused, seemingly realizing in that moment that he was still hosting and we were clustered in the kitchen, and pointed to the freezer. "Uh...anyone want a Toaster Strudel?"

Not wanting to put Connor to any more trouble—and silently considering that I could do better than frozen pastry—I thanked him for his hospitality and loaded the truck. As we backed out of his driveway, I asked Sage, "How would we feel about Waffle House?"

She ran a hand through her mussed hair and made a face. "I don't think I'm clean enough to eat out somewhere."

"Oh, trust me, hon, there's no dress code where we're going."

I explained the concept of the diner, talking up the many hashbrown options and the possibility of a chocolate chip waffle, and by the time I reached the Whitford town line, Sage was on board with the excursion. She tidied herself with the comb in my purse and the visor mirror, and as I steered us south toward the highway to larger pockets of civilization, she said, "I like Chief Willow."

"Yeah, he's all right," I replied.

"He's nice."

"For a cop, sure."

Sage hesitated. "Kind of handsome, isn't he?"

I stared at the road. "And what do you know about that subject, young lady?"

"I've watched TV," she protested. "He's a lot better looking than Warner, anyway. At least he doesn't seem scary when he smiles."

Warner. A little thing, yes, but progress all the same.

"He's not hideous," I allowed. "Satisfied?"

From the corner of my eye, I caught Sage's all-too-knowing grin.

We took our time at breakfast, lingering at the booth while I made up for the previous night's sins with coffee in a chipped white mug and Sage ate eggs and potatoes until she groaned. When we made it back to the house, I sent her to the shower, then sat down with my neglected computer to look over my delivery schedule. I hadn't planned to be gone quite so long, and though Tabitha, that saint, had made a post office run in my absence, I had plenty more to pack and ship. I wrote up a list, then took my turn in the bathroom, pulled my wet hair into a ponytail despite the December chill, and headed out to my workshop to pack boxes and try to clear my head. I still didn't know what to do about Sage, but I could fret while either staring into space at the kitchen table or being useful in the shed, and at least working would give me something to do with my hands.

With several batches of candles to pour, I lost track of time, breezing right through lunch, and might have kept working until sundown had Sage not opened the door to a blast of cold air around two and rapped on the wall. "Jane? Your dad's here."

Message delivered, she skedaddled back to the house as Dad stepped into the shed. "Hi, Janie," he said, and latched the door behind him. "Sorry, how much am I interrupting?"

"Nothing that can't wait." While my workshop boasted decent insulation, the day had a bite, especially after the more temperate Pactlands, and I eased closer to the space heater I'd plugged in on the floor. "What's up?"

Dad obviously wasn't in the middle of a brew—he sported his "going to town" clothes, jeans and a sweater that lacked the stains and burn holes of his work attire, and I suspected he'd stopped by to check on the house on his way from the grocery store. He soon disabused me of that notion, however, explaining, "I got a call from Liogh."

Figured that I'd been tattled on.

"We're considering our options—" I began, but Dad shook his head.

"There is no better option for that child than taking her to the Pactlands," he murmured. "None."

"That's debatable," I countered, "and did Liogh mention my concerns about Sage's father and the Forum?"

Dad joined me by the space heater and held my hands. "I'm not going to stand here and tell you that a Forum prosecution couldn't happen, but they're *so* rare, and they usually fizzle. Liogh's right."

"That's not a guarantee."

"There are precious few guarantees in this life, girlie, and the sooner you learn to make your peace with the odds you're given, the better. Now," he said, tightening his grip, "I appreciate your concern for me more than you'll ever know, little one. But part of being a parent is doing the right thing by your kid."

I frowned. "You've been great, Dad—"

"Not me, you. I know you haven't officially adopted Sage or anything, but you've been her guardian all month, and you're the closest thing she has to a parent right now. She doesn't know what's in her best interest yet, and so that responsibility falls to you."

"I'm *trying* to help her."

"Honey, I know that," he said, giving my hands a squeeze. "I'm not here to criticize you—I believe you've stepped up admirably, all things considered. I know you think you're grown, and most of the time, I agree, but this is one of those situations in which you're still very young, and I've got experience."

"You didn't dump *me* alone at some boarding school in the Pactlands," I murmured.

"You would have had a better education had I done so."

"Yeah, and you'd be locked away."

Dad offered a weak shrug as he released me. "There were…extenuating circumstances in our case. More than just my general desire to avoid a penal farm."

I smiled sadly. "You mean that definite chance that my mom might come back for me?"

"That's part of it, too," he replied. "Sage is in a very different position. She *needs* support—tutors, medical experts, a good therapist. And while I know you and

Tabitha have been doing what you can for her, you're just not equipped for this, Janie. Not if you want her to have the best possible future."

"Let's not forget the present with all this talk of the future, huh? She's not even a month free of Warner, and right now, she wants to stay with me."

"Sure. You're the first person in her life who hasn't beaten her. No surprise there. But if she stays here, she's going to be masked forever. She'll never be able to see a doctor because her numbers will come back *all* kinds of messed up. I mean, we had a faun who wound up at the ER following a car wreck at the end of my tenure in Virginia, and we had to check her out of there against medical advice and rush her back to Beukal before the specialists could come in." He shook his head at the memory. "What if Sage breaks a leg? She'd need to unmask for it to be set properly. Or what if she gets pregnant? If she stays here, she'll have no option but to remain single. I mean, how would she explain a baby with hooves?"

"I'm not exactly spoiled for choice when it comes to available sorcerers," I pointed out.

"No, but if you were in love, you could pass as human. Sage doesn't have that luxury. So, to recap: she's not going to get the education she needs here, she's not going to have medical or psych support, and she'll ultimately be alone, either working whatever job she can get without real ID or going into business like you and hoping for the best. And even if she somehow finds passable ID," he continued as I started to object, "she'll have to start over eventually, just as you will. She can't live in Ragged Gap for the next three centuries, and neither can you."

I waited in silence as Dad put his thoughts in order.

"You're so young," he said after a moment. "I've prepared you as well as I can, but the reality is that this life you've built will have to be abandoned at some point. Even if you mask to match your age, you can't stay here forever. You'll have to create a new version of Jane from scratch. Cut ties, uproot yourself. I...I've kept you out of the Pactlands to this point for several reasons," he said slowly, "but if it's time for me to face a tribunal, then so be it. I've been selfish, Janie. You're getting to the age that you should start thinking about moving there."

"My *life* is here," I said, "and even if I wanted to, I don't have Pactlands citizenship."

"I know. Liogh and I talked about it, and they're willing to help you through the process."

I clenched my teeth, trying to find the perfect counterpoint and coming up emptyhanded.

"It's your heritage," he continued, "and it's high time you claimed it. I want more than this for you—"

"I *like* my workshop, thank you very much."

"Oh—no, honey, not your business. I meant Ragged Gap," he clarified. "I'm damn proud of you—*so* proud— but someday, when I'm gone, I don't want you to be the witchy recluse living halfway up a mountain in some podunk town. With a little more training, you'd be one hell of a sorcerer. Now, you don't have to leave Georgia today," he stressed, gripping my shoulder. "I'm not saying that at all. But just like I'll need to vanish at some point, so will you. It's inevitable. And when that time comes, I want you to have all the opportunities of the Pactlands."

Dad wasn't *wrong*, exactly, about my eventual need to leave town—I was realist enough to accept that—but the notion of throwing away my life in Ragged Gap felt like giving up on the woman I'd become, on my business, on my relationships here...

On my mother.

Essa wasn't coming back for me. I hadn't believed in fairytales in a long time, and I knew with the wisdom born of bitter disappointment that only a fool would keep waiting for her. But as long as I stayed here, somewhere she could find me, nothing was quite final. In that liminal space in which I lived, she probably would never darken my doorway…but she *might*. She might show up one day with an extraordinary story about why she'd been away for so long and how she'd missed me terribly, and the little piece of me that still went to bed on the night before my birthday hoping that *this* would be the year she returned clung to that possibility.

But this wasn't the time for me to deal with my hangups.

"We can talk about that later," I said to Dad. "Today, we've got two problems. One, I don't want to put Sage through the trauma of getting rejected. That's the last thing she needs. Two, I don't want to be the reason you spend the rest of your days in custody. I was stupid and stubborn enough to drag Liogh out here—"

"You weren't stupid. Baby, listen to me," he insisted, lowering his voice as he held my stare. "I should have prepared you for the Pactlands years ago. I…failed you there, and I'm sorry. I told myself you were safer here, and you were, but you're growing up, and I'm not so afraid for you as I was. Don't worry about me."

"Daddy…"

"I love you, Janie, and I hope you know that. If the Forum comes for me, then so be it. I'll make the best hooch in the prison, no contest," he joked. "As for Sage, even if her parents want nothing to do with her, she'll have support. I'm not saying it'll be easy for her at first, but this is one of those 'eat your veggies and thank me later' situations. Be the parent she needs and do the right thing."

With that, Dad reached into his back pocket and dug out his phone. "Call Liogh. Get this ball rolling."

Though Dad held it toward me, I didn't take it from him. "What if you're wrong?"

"Then I'll own it, and I'll do what it takes to get Sage out of there. But I'm not wrong about this. She may argue with you now, she may swear up and down that she wants nothing to do with the Pactlands, but you need to be her advocate."

I looked down at the phone in his hand, trying to juggle a thousand variables and land on a result offering more than possibilities and heartache, then sighed and pulled my own phone from its charger on the counter.

CHAPTER 17

To no one's surprise, Sage wasn't thrilled when I told her we were going back. She didn't yell or argue, but she was withdrawn all evening, and she only picked at her dinner. That night, as she slunk off toward her room, I followed her and sat on the edge of her bed before she could roll over and pretend to be asleep. "I am not abandoning you," I told her. "We're just going back to see what we can learn. This could go *really* well," I said, though I was fairly certain that neither of us believed it. "And if it doesn't, we'll work through the next steps together. But whatever happens tomorrow, I am *not* dropping you at the door of some damn boarding school and walking away."

"You said that's the best thing for me," she retorted.

"I said that the *education* you could get in the Pactlands would be the best thing for you." I held out my hand, and after a brief hesitation, Sage clasped it. "Here's the thing, hon: you're not a baby, and you're not stupid. I'm taking Dad's advice for now because he's an old fart, and he's seen things."

She grinned at that.

"But even old farts don't know it all," I continued. "So, if we go back and everything goes wrong, and Liogh is still pushing boarding school for you, then we'll have a serious talk. Pros and cons, both sides. And whatever you choose, I'll be here as a backup plan. Okay?"

That satisfied Sage enough to allow her to sleep, but I stewed in my uncertainty and my own unresolved issues all night, until finally, around three, I slipped out and drove down the road to Walmart. Sage was awake by the time I returned and anxious at my absence, and I offered a bag of fast-food biscuits as a peace offering. "Got you a little something," I said as she tucked in, then produced a small box and slid it across the table.

Sage dropped her biscuit in shock. "For *me*?"

"It's nothing fancy," I cautioned. "That's a pretty basic smartphone. But since mine works in the Pactlands, I know this one will, too. We'll save each other's numbers, and if you ever want to call me, you'll have this. I can add money to the account from here—"

My chair rocked with the force of impact as she lunged from her seat and hugged me, and I squeezed her in turn. "I swear I'm not abandoning you," I murmured. "Now finish your breakfast, and I'll get this bad boy charged."

She seemed to be in much better spirits by the time Annie arrived to collect us. I'd called her the day before and apologized for the change in plans, but she'd told me not to worry. "It's really no trouble to get to you," she'd said, "and if it'll save you the drive and the portal trip, I don't mind." When she appeared Thursday, we were packed and prepped, with me doing a final check of the lights and Sage waiting at the kitchen table, listening to my MP3 player and eagerly tapping at one of the games I'd downloaded for her.

A moment later, we arrived in an echoing space of white marble walls that gleamed in the sunlight spilling through the windows behind us. Blinking, I noticed a few empty wooden benches, then a desk in the corner, staffed by a startled elf. "Morning!" Annie called, giving him a cheery wave, and made a beeline toward him. "Here to see Detective Birrid. We're expected."

"Where..." Sage mumbled, looking around at the people passing through in colorful formal robes or more casual black shirts and pants.

"DOL," Annie replied over her shoulder. "This is the lobby, since *someone* gets twitchy when I let myself in. Can't imagine why."

The elf, who'd apparently heard this complaint before, smirked at her. "Director Erenani prefers to keep a log of visitors to the building, Agent Humphries. This isn't a great hardship to you."

"It slows me down," she protested, and he rolled his eyes as he called for Liogh.

The detective soon emerged from the bank of elevators, sporting a violet robe that fluttered behind them as they speedwalked across the lobby. "Thanks for coming back," they said, looking Sage and me in the eye in turn. "She's due to arrive in about ten minutes. Let's get you upstairs."

Liogh shepherded us to the fourth floor, which reminded me of a doctor's waiting room at first blush. Stepping off the elevator, I found myself in a comfortable space with neatly arranged institutional couches and chairs, the sort of furniture that served a purpose but enhanced no style. Low end tables slotted between and around them offered a selection of magazines, while a TV mounted to one wall had been tuned to a news program but nearly muted. A full coffeepot squatted on a table in the corner, ready for guests. I'd expected the detective to tell us to make ourselves at home, but instead, Liogh led us around the sitting area and down a long, far less homey off-white hallway lined with gray doors, each identical to the others but for the number on the wall plaque. They opened one, revealing a windowless room more welcoming than I'd anticipated: a blue loveseat and a pair of matching chairs, a television, a few more magazines of questionable vintage, and a minifridge whose clear door showed shelves stocked with bottled water and cans of other beverages.

"I'll ask you to stay here," they said as I dropped my overnight bag by the door. "In case Relieg wants to speak with Sage, you'll be close by. Do you need anything?"

I glanced around the room and spied the remote. "No, I think we're fine."

"Great. I'll collect you in a while. Should you get hungry, there are usually some snacks in the back of the fridge," they added, giving Sage a conspiratorial wink, and closed the door behind them as they left.

Sage flopped onto the loveseat, glanced at the unfamiliar program, and wrinkled her nose. "I wish we didn't have to sit here. We came all this way to watch TV?"

"I mean, there are worse fates," I replied, handing her the remote. "Your choice, kiddo. I'll be right back."

"Where are you going?"

"Ladies' room. I'll scope it out for you," I joked, and let myself into the hallway.

The restrooms were halfway down the hall, labeled *Male*, *Female*, and *Unisex*. I opted for the women's room and…well, was underwhelmed. I don't know what I was expecting—the bathroom at Canna's house had seemed pretty standard—and the DOL facilities were recognizable as such. Tile floor, beige walls, a bank of sinks, then a bank of cubicles, all fairly ordinary but for the size options. One of the sinks hit around knee height, while another rose to my chest. Some of the cubicles looked ordinary enough, but the half-sized one at the front was enclosed on top as well, presumably to prevent taller visitors from looking in. Two in the middle were slightly wider, while the stall at the far end—what I'd have assumed to be the handicapped option outside the Pactlands—was *enormous*. Curious, and finding myself alone in the big bathroom, I peeked into the massive cubicle and found not a toilet, but rather a substantial pit in the floor, half-filled with water. A handle on the wall behind the pit appeared to be the flush mechanism, and below it were two nozzles—judging by the signage, water and air. Sitting beside the toilet paper was an opaque jar the size of an umbrella stand, nearly filled with a clear liquid. Translucent gray plastic handles rose from the top of the jar, and I pulled one out to find that it belonged to a thin stick that ended in a sort of pincer, manipulated by a button by the handle…

And suddenly, as I realized the purpose of the plastic claw, I knew far more than I'd ever hoped to know about centaur hygiene. I hastily suck the stick back into what I prayed was some form of disinfectant, then availed myself of the more familiar end of the bathroom.

As I was running a brush through my hair, my phone beeped, and I dug it from my purse.

Everything okay, Firebug?

Connor—even if I hadn't saved his contact info, I'd have known.

Just fine, I wrote. *Went back with Sage.*

I waited while he tapped out a message: *Are you safe? Do you need help?*

No, we're good, I reassured him. *No guarantees yet, but I hashed it out with my dad. Det is about to bring in Sage's mom.*

Okay, came his quick response. *If you need something, CALL ME. No fires.*

Just a little one?

His answer that time was a familiar GIF of Elmo with his arms upraised before a wall of crackling flames, and I snorted as I put my phone away.

Thus tidied, I returned to our waiting room and opened the door...only to find the place vacated but for our luggage.

"Shit," I hissed, and ran down the hallway toward the main waiting room. Had Liogh already come for Sage? Had she gone exploring on her own? Did she get lost? She couldn't read well in English, so if she managed to turn herself around, could she read the Pactish signs enough to find her way back?

The waiting room was empty, and I darted down another hallway, looking for hints of life. A door about a third of the way down was closed, and a circular light above it glowed red. But the door to the adjacent room was cracked open, and when I peeked inside, I found my charge. "What are you doing here?" I whispered. "Come on..."

My order died on my lips when I saw what Sage was up to. The room she'd chosen held two rows of plastic stackable chairs, definitely not the sort of furniture intended for visitors, and a low table against the wall offered notepads and a cup of pens and pencils. Between her room and the one with the red light was a wide one-way mirror, and through it, anyone in this apparent overflow space could watch the proceedings next door.

The space on the other side wasn't a standard police interview room—there was no table bolted to the floor, no place to lock handcuffs. Instead, it had been outfitted with a pair of upholstered chairs much like those in the waiting room on one side and a thick, coordinating mat on the other, with a wooden coffee table between them. A box of tissues and a quartet of coasters awaited atop the table. Sitting in one of the chairs was Liogh, legs crossed, seemingly at ease. Sitting on the mat was a brunette centaur.

"Honey," I whispered, "we shouldn't—"

"Please," Sage whispered back, and I saw the longing in her eyes—eyes, I noticed, very much like those of the woman next door, who'd crossed her forelegs at the hoof and was sipping from a small bottle of water. "*Please*, Jane."

I knew we had no business being there. Prudence told me to drag Sage away and let Liogh work in peace. But if that had been my mother in there, with only a window between us and a speaker in the ceiling allowing me to eavesdrop on her secrets...

Sighing, I closed the door, then sat beside Sage and wrapped my arm around her tense shoulders.

Relieg Tumari was, by either human or equine standards, a pretty woman. Her hair was thick and glossy, and it fell down in her back in a carefully constructed arrangement of soft curls and pinned braids holding sections in place. While she and Sage shared large green eyes, Relieg's were lined in charcoal and fringed with dark lashes. She seemed young by my estimation, but as centaurs aged more slowly than sorcerers did, my baseline was poorly calibrated. After all, Canna had said she was nearly sixty. Like Liogh, she wore a sleeveless formal robe, one cut from thin, royal blue wool out of respect for the season. But unlike the full-coverage robe I'd seen on Cennis, the centaur counselor, Relieg's split at her waist and fell to either side of her...hips? Her shoulders? Unfamiliar with the nuances of centaur anatomy, I settled on "front legs." In any case, the robe framed her torso but left her equine bits on display. As I'd expected from having seen Sage, Relieg's hair was the same dark brown all over, all the way to her coiffed tail.

She and Liogh had been making small talk, giving Liogh a chance to assemble their notes and Relieg a moment to settle in, but shortly after my arrival, the detective got down to business.

"Thank you for coming, Ms. Tumari," they began with a tight smile. "I know your schedule must be packed..."

She laughed softly and put her water bottle on one of the proffered coasters. "They certainly keep me busy, but at least I have help in the media office. They can spare me for an hour or so," she said, and clasped her hands in what would have been her lap. "So, Detective, what can I do for you?"

They paused, shuffling through their thin folder of papers, and I wondered whether the move was a psych-out tactic or Liogh's way of stalling the inevitable.

"About a week and a half ago," they finally said, "I was made aware of the existence of an unusual child outside the Pactlands. Considering her anatomy and her apparent ability to cast, she was brought in for testing." They gave Relieg a long look, then asked, "Do you know where I'm going with this?"

She shook her head, but her frozen expression made a liar of her.

Liogh proceeded as if they hadn't noticed her reaction.

"We tested her against the database, trying to determine whether this was a child abduction case. She didn't come back flagged as an abductee, but we *did* receive positive results for both of her parents. You and Representative Voln."

Liogh had only let that hang for a few seconds before Relieg's face screwed up and she burst into tears. They waited while she covered her face and sobbed, then rose and offered her the tissue box once she managed to regain a modicum of control. "It's all right," they murmured. "I'm not here today to throw blame, Ms. Tumari. I'm just trying to get to the bottom of this."

Slowly, she pulled herself together, dabbed at her eyes, and finished her water bottle. Liogh brought her another from the minifridge in the corner, and she mumbled her thanks.

"Why don't you start from the beginning?" they suggested, settling back into their chair. "Did you and the representative have a relationship?"

"No," she replied, emphatically shaking her head. "Mirrik worked in another representative's office. I barely saw him outside of committee meetings and the odd staff mixer."

The detective waited, allowing the silence to stretch.

Relieg took a long, shuddering breath. "One night, I was working late alone, and he…he came into my office. I asked him what he needed, and he…*did* something to me, a spell of some sort. I couldn't move. Couldn't scream. And he…he…"

She began to cry again, and Liogh gave her time before asking, "He assaulted you?"

Relieg nodded, her face a blotchy mess. "He said he'd ruin me if I told anyone. My career, my prospects…he'd been an aide for so much longer than I had, and people liked him, and who would believe me? He said his family had contacts at DOI, and they'd make sure that no farseer was ever brought in. So, I kept quiet."

"Was it only the once?"

"No. He must have caught me six or seven times. I tried not to be alone in the building with him, I locked the doors, but he always found a way to get to me."

Liogh's expression softened as they watched Relieg wrestle with her composure. "I take it you weren't on birth control."

"Not then. My fiancé and I weren't intimate, and I wouldn't be unfaithful to him, so there wasn't any need. I've never told him," she said, her eyes welling again. "Mirrik said he'd find a way to ruin Grantis, too, if I said a word."

The detective frowned. "Your fiancé had political aspirations?"

She laughed mirthlessly. "Not at all. He's a healer, but one of Mirrik's relatives is on the grievance board, and I was afraid they'd bring false charges against him."

"I see. Did Mirrik stop once you became pregnant?"

"No—I don't think he ever knew I was pregnant, to be honest with you. His attention was on another woman by then. A sorcerer. I suppose he'd satisfied whatever awful urge led him to me. But I suspected soon enough and tested, and I realized he'd left me with a parting gift," she said bitterly.

My arm tightened around Sage.

"Why didn't you just terminate the pregnancy?" Liogh asked.

"Because Grantis would have found out," she replied, and reached for the tissues again. Dabbing at her mascara-smeared eyes, she said, "Call it paranoia if you want, but I knew it would get back to him if I bought a potion or went in for removal."

Liogh's brow furrowed. "Why would you think that?"

"Because he's an obstetrician. He was already practicing when we were engaged."

"You...do realize that healers have a code of privacy, yes?"

She regarded them incredulously. "You don't think they talk among themselves? And what if someone he knew learned that I was ending a pregnancy? If you thought your friend's partner was cheating on them, wouldn't you say something?"

They acknowledged the question with a slight tilt of their head. "The temptation would be strong, I suppose, but surely you could have gone to a healer who didn't know your fiancé."

"I didn't exactly have a list," she retorted. "And I couldn't risk him finding out. He'd either believe that I'd cheated on him or else I'd have to confess what Mirrik had done to me, and I knew that Grantis would never let *that* lie, so…I hid my pregnancy and kept hoping I'd miscarry."

"A difficult thing to conceal, especially from an obstetrician."

"Not so difficult as you might think," she muttered, and paused for a long gulp of water. "I'm not what you would call tiny to begin with," she said, cocking her thumb over her shoulder toward her broad back and hips, "and I switched to full-cut robes for a while. They were fashionable that year, thank heavens, and they covered what little swelled. I exercised more and ate less, trying to keep my weight down. Thought perhaps that would end the pregnancy for me, but no such luck. Fortunately, Grantis and I had a long engagement planned while he finished an internship, and he was so busy during that time that we seldom saw each other, and he never saw me without a robe on."

Liogh nodded, making notes. "You delivered alone, then?"

Relieg sighed. "No. My older sister did a stint in the Mountain Patrol and had training for emergency situations, including childbirth. She'd taken a job as a portal attendant by then—bad knees and old injuries were keeping her at a desk, anyway—and I knew I could trust her. I delivered at home, and she helped." Her voice started to wobble as tears threatened once more. "It was…small. Horribly misshapen. I didn't think it would live long, breeds often don't, and I…I wanted it *gone*. So badly," she said, beginning to cry. "Mirrik did that to me, and I just wanted it to be over, and…and…"

"Take your time," Liogh soothed. "How did she get outside? The baby?"

She, I noticed, not *it*.

If Relieg caught Liogh's choice of pronouns, she ignored their suggestion. "My sister offered to take it. She's got portal credentials, see, and she could get out without the system logging the trip. So, she dried it off and gave it a few drops of a potion to make it sleep, and she took it away. I cleaned myself up, destroyed the evidence, and went on with my life. Until now," she said, staring across the table at Liogh.

They didn't look up from their notepad. "Did your sister ever tell you what she did with the baby?"

"No. I assumed she left it in a wild place outside the Pactlands—it would die of exposure, if nothing else, and the body would be lost. Guess not."

Liogh finished writing, then looked up at Relieg. "The baby was left at a house, but your plan might have been kinder. The man who found her mistreated her horribly, and she only gained her freedom in the last month. She's been unofficially fostered since then. We're trying to bring her home." They hesitated, then asked, "Would you like to meet her? Or see a picture, perhaps? I realize this is asking you to revisit old trauma, and it's not fair, but the fact of the matter is that I've got a child on my hands who could use a little compassion."

But Relieg shook her head. "No. I'm sorry, no. I can't do that. I *can't*," she said, her voice breaking. "How would I explain that to my husband? My boys?"

"Perhaps if they knew the full circumstances of her conception—"

"No," she said again, hugging herself in her distress. "I

don't want to return to that time. I don't. Please, *please*, don't make me…"

With a sudden sob, Sage pulled away from me and out of her seat.

"Sweetheart?" I asked as she hurried to the door. "Sage, baby…"

She ignored me, and all I could do was run after her as she headed back toward our abandoned waiting room. Instead of turning in, however, she continued to the bathrooms, found the correct one, and came apart in my arms.

That child wept, the sort of deep, anguished cries that only come from heartbreak, and I kicked myself for ever agreeing to this plan. Knowing her parents probably wouldn't want her was one thing; sitting there while her mother explained how she'd anticipated that Sage would die in the woods somewhere was another matter entirely, a senseless cruelty atop the shit heap of Sage's many abuses. At least my mother was still a fuzzy ball of probabilities somewhere in the vague distance—my childhood fantasies of a maternal relationship had faded, sure, but they'd never been shattered in front of me.

Sage cried until she made herself sick, and while she clung to the gnome-sized toilet, I held her hair back, trying to console her. I might as well have been talking to a wall for all the good I did, as she was still kneeling at the bowl, crying her eyes out, when Liogh poked their head into the restroom.

"Jane?" they said, noticing me at the cubicle door. "Is everything okay?"

"What do you think?" I snapped.

"What *happened?*"

"Sage found the viewing room."

Liogh's jaw went slack, and they let themself in. "How much did she see?"

"Enough."

They hesitated, wincing as Sage's wracking sobs echoed

off the tile, then mumbled, "I suppose I should call Canna. We're finished for today."

CHAPTER 18

Canna gave Sage a mild sedative as soon as she got us home and sent her to bed. "You'll feel better tonight," she said, tucking her in with practiced hands. "Take a little nap, eh? Clear your head."

Exhausted and helped along her way by the potion she'd knocked back, Sage was soon asleep, and I followed Canna downstairs to fill her in. She'd come as soon as Liogh had called, then taken one look at the situation and packed us into her van, telling the detective that she'd be working from home for the rest of the day. How, precisely, a healer in her position could work from home was unclear to me, but Liogh said they'd make her excuses.

Given Sage's state, I'd barely had a chance to say hello to my cousin, and I owed her far more than that. "I'm sorry," I said once we were in the kitchen and Canna had put on water for tea. "For running out on you—"

She cut me short. "It's fine. Annie explained everything, and while I think you *might* have given the Forum too much credit, I do understand the impetus. Are you okay? Well," she amended, pointing to the ceiling, "besides *that*."

"Shoot, I'm all right," I replied. "My dad's the one who talked me into bringing Sage back. And she was okay until the interview…"

Canna sighed and shook her head. "How did that *happen*? That child shouldn't have been anywhere near an interview room!"

"Uh…" My face began to heat. "She went exploring

when I was in the bathroom, and by the time I found her, Liogh and Relieg were getting set up, and Sage wanted to see…"

"But why did Liogh have you there?"

I shrugged. "In case Relieg wanted to meet Sage, I guess. Maybe they were hoping for the best."

"Foolish," she muttered. "If that poor woman was raped—was she?"

"That's what she told Liogh."

"Then I'm sure the last thing she wanted was to be reminded of that trauma. Liogh should have known better."

I waited while she pulled mugs from the cabinet, then asked, "Does Liogh *do* many cases like this one? I know they don't handle much in the way of murder, and this is a fairly niche field, yeah?"

"Liogh," she said, stepping into the pantry for a box of tea, "liaises with DPP. Drugs, potions, and all the things that can go wrong when unauthorized people start brewing and distributing. They should have handed this case off to someone better versed in such…*delicate* issues, but I'm sure they're trying to protect your father, and the fewer people who know what Yacovi got up to, the better. Of course, that doesn't make this any easier for Relieg," she muttered, ripping open a foil-wrapped teabag. "Poor thing. What happened to her?"

While Canna fixed our drinks, I recounted what I'd witnessed, and my cousin's face twisted. "No good options," she said, cradling her steaming mug. "I mean, abandonment like that certainly wasn't right, but I can't entirely fault her…"

"Could Mirrik really have destroyed her career?" I asked. "As an aide?"

"It's possible. The Volns aren't as prominent as the Aniaps, but they're close. The right people could have applied the right pressure if one of their own were accused of rape."

"And now?"

She sipped as she thought. "This is going to be messy, whatever happens. The truth needs to come out, regardless, but there won't be any winners here." As I reached for my mug, she cupped her hand over mine, staying me. "How are *you*? Really?"

"I'm fine—"

"Are you?"

I hesitated before answering her, trying to make sense of the amorphous blob of unease and anxiety in my chest. "Between us?"

"Absolutely."

"In a way, I'm happy for Sage. At least she understands why her mother isn't in her life. I know that kid is going through hell right now," I quickly added, "but once the shock wears off...it's nothing *Sage* has done, you know? It sucks for her, but there's a good reason why Relieg can't be the mother she wants."

Canna nodded, her grip on me tightening. "Jane, dear...whatever made Essa leave, you did nothing wrong. You know that, don't you?"

Despite my best efforts, my vision started to blur. "If she'd just *tell* me why...I don't need her, but a little closure..."

My cousin gave excellent hugs, I mused, finding her arms around me. Guilt flashed through my mind—this mess wasn't about me, this was about a parentless child who'd just had her hopes dashed—but Canna was a well-practiced mother, and even if she wasn't mine, something in me responded to the murmured assurance that it was all right, it was going to be all right.

I apologized for soaking her shoulder once she released me, but Canna waved that off and muttered at her shirt until it dried. "No harm done," she said, and patted my arm. "You know, a nap might do you good, too."

So it was that I soon found myself fixing up the couch bed with fresh sheets, and Canna closed the blinds to throw the den into twilight. "I'm going to work on my charts in the kitchen," she said as I kicked off my shoes. "Let me know if you want lunch."

I snuggled down, thinking I'd catch a half-hour snooze, maybe a bit more, but the next thing I knew, Pars was walking in with all four children, and the sunlight that sneaked past the blinds had faded toward the gold of evening. The kitchen smelled like herbs and chicken and baking bread, and I sat up as the older girls ran over to investigate, momentarily wondering what planet I was on.

"Welcome back," said Pars, grinning as I blinked blearily up at him. "Feel better?"

He laughed when I grunted, then herded the kids away while I got up and reassembled the couch. "What time is it?" I croaked.

"Almost dinner. Hungry?"

"Starving, actually." Looking around the room, I counted heads but came up short. "Where's Sage?"

"Still in bed," Canna replied, popping into the den. "Why don't you rouse her, Jane?"

"Oh, let me," said Pars, plucking one of his daughters' many boas from the dress-up box against the wall and wrapping it around his thick neck. He led the way upstairs, trailing hot pink feathers, and sashayed into the guest room as Sage turned dry but groggy eyes on the large silhouette blocking the door. "Hello, dear. Welcome back," he said, slipping into English. "Dinner is served, and after that, we're doing our nails. Have you ever had a mani-pedi?"

"Um...no, sir," she mumbled. "What...what is—"

"Fingernails and toenails, and I have *just* the thing to buff away calluses. You'll join us, won't you? The girls would love it."

Though bemused, Sage agreed, and after dinner, Pars set up shop in the den with a stained drop cloth, bubbling foot tubs, an array of polishes, and a movie. Now that Sage could understand them, Dieta and Maliul talked her ear off, interspersing questions with stories about their school and commentary about the film, which was heavy on princesses. Dieta deemed it too babyish for her, but Maliul stared raptly at the screen while her feet soaked.

Happy to see Sage distracted and in good company, I gave Canna a hand when she began readying the twins for bed. "Thank you," I said as the bath filled and Canna wrangled her children's soiled clothes off. "Sage needed something silly to take her mind off...well, everything."

"Oh, no troub—hey, get back here, you little monkey," she ordered, grabbing giggling Coltrane as he made a half-clothed dash for the door. "You need to be clean!"

"No," he shouted, though he laughed as he did so, and I suspected I was privy to a well-established game.

"I don't know," said Canna, turning grave. "If you don't take a bath, the Tickle Monster might get you...like *this*!"

He squealed as she tickled his chubby tummy and covered his face in kisses. "Give up?" she asked.

"No!"

The playful fight escalated, with Colji jumping in to help her cleanliness-averse twin, but soon, Canna had both of them pushing plastic boats around in a bubble bath. "Pars and the girls have a nail night at least once a month," she explained. "It's been daddy–daughter time for years, and adding one more girl to the mix is no problem...as long as Mali doesn't do Sage's nails. She wants to help, but her hands just aren't steady yet."

I sat on the counter, out of the way, while Canna washed the twins' hair. "What do I do?"

"You take it a day at a time. Make yourself available if she wants to talk, and don't take it personally if she wants to hole up in her room alone. And you get her into therapy," she said, giving me a look over her shoulder. "She needs it, that's obvious."

"I can't do that in Georgia."

"No, I would think not."

"But I also can't stay here."

Canna plucked a cup from the side of the tub and began rinsing the suds away. "There *is* a process. Liogh and I had a chat this afternoon—"

I wasn't sorry to have slept through *that*, as I suspected Canna hadn't held back on them.

"—and they've spoken with one of our counselors about you. Each of our peoples handles citizenship requests differently," she explained. "Ask Rose about elves—she was out in the cold until the head of one of the Halls acknowledged her in. Did all right for herself in the end, now," she continued, chuckling, "but that poor girl went through a mess. Our way is much simpler: you just make your case to our representatives."

"Your *Forum* representatives?"

"Yes."

"So...which one would I need to contact? The rapist, the jerk, or the one who does whatever the jerk says?"

"Your particular case could be somewhat complicated," she admitted, "but I understand that there's little love between Mirrik Voln and Gerem Aniap, so even though Gerem's a jerk, he might approve your application just to spite his colleague."

"Or there's the boarding school route for Sage," I said.

"*You* should be in school, too, you know."

"Yeah," I said, laughing, "*no*. I graduated at twenty-two, and I'm not going back. I mean, can you imagine me in a classroom here? They wouldn't know what to do with me!"

"Mm. Maybe private tutoring would be the way to go," Canna allowed, as Coltrane turned his boat into a submarine. "But you should apply for citizenship. You know I'd vouch for you, right?"

Before I could answer that, the doorbell rang. "Would you mind?" Canna asked. "Pars's nails are probably still wet."

Hoping Liogh wasn't on the welcome mat, I hurried

downstairs and unlatched the door to find a stranger standing there, a youthful woman about my size in a loose-cut gray tunic and black leggings. Her blonde hair was pulled into a high ponytail, revealing unmistakably elven ears, and when she smiled, her teeth were sharper than I'd expected. "Hi," she said, rubbing her bare arms against the December chill. "You must be Jane."

"Uh...yes—"

"Come on in, Fell!" Pars called from his spot on the couch, and I stepped aside to admit her.

Spotting the homemade salon, she grinned and waved at the girls. "Why did no one invite *me* to nail night?" she teasingly groused.

"Because this is a very *select* group," said Pars, indicating his daughters and Sage with a turquoise-tipped finger. "And interagency cooperation only goes so far."

"Oh, please, you sleep with one of us."

"Canna was at DPP first."

"She's not anymore!"

Pars rolled his eyes. "Jane, this is Fell ti'Mal, one of DOL's trainees. Fell, that's my wife's cousin, and Canna knows how to hurt you, so behave."

"Naturally." Turning to me, she said, "I was informed this afternoon that a little gym time would do you good. Do you have anything to wear? If not, I've got clean spares in my bag."

"I...um...well, I was helping Canna—"

"Go with Fell!" she called down from the bathroom. "I've got this!"

"You heard the woman," said Fell, and so, with assurances from Pars that Sage would be perfectly fine in my absence, I dug a T-shirt and leggings out of my duffel and slid into the stranger's car.

"Where's the gym?" I asked as she backed out of the driveway. "And thanks for coming to get me, but you didn't need to."

Fell chuckled softly. "You know what's more

dangerous than a baby pyro?"

"Uh…no?"

"A *stressed* baby pyro," she replied, removing one hand from the wheel as a white fireball bloomed in her palm. "Which, incidentally, I know something about."

Suddenly, the pieces fell into place. "You're Annie's friend, right? The one who…um…" I paused, recalling *how* the two had met, then finished with, "The pyromancer?"

"That's me. Annie said you needed to…how did she put it…'blow off steam.' Yeah?"

"She's not wrong," I muttered. "How'd she know?"

"Canna called. Now, I trust your cousin's judgment, but Annie has seen me at my worst, and when *she* asked me to collect you, I listened. As for where we're going," she continued, rolling through an empty four-way stop, "DOL has a set of reinforced practice rooms in the basement, some designed with people like us in mind. I thought you might show me what you can do, eh?"

"Can't hurt," I replied. "Do you, uh…did Annie tell you what's going on?"

"Nope. All she said is that you're a pyro, you're going *through* something, and Liogh screwed up magnificently today. Not my place to pry, but if you want to talk, I can keep my mouth shut."

While I appreciated the offer, I didn't take her up on it right away, and Fell didn't press me.

She parked in the DOL deck, then scanned her badge and ushered me into the elevator. "The training area is actually lower than the garage," she said as we descended. "Safer this way."

We stepped out into a hallway lined with imposing metal doors, all of them left halfway open. "Looks like we have the place to ourselves," said Fell, and led me into the last room on the right. "This one's my favorite. Let me set the alarm…"

She scanned her badge again at a panel inside the door, and a red light in the wall illuminated. "User authorized," said a female voice from a speaker in the high ceiling. "Locks engaged. Please proceed with caution and follow all system prompts."

"What's that all about?" I asked.

Fell cracked her knuckles. "In case someone needs to interrupt us, the computer will warn us before the door unlocks. That way, no one is accidentally incinerated."

"Good plan."

"No fatalities yet," she replied, aiming a pair of finger guns at me. "Now, for targets."

She tapped at a small console beside the scanner panel, and with a soft whir, hidden mechanisms in the walls and floor sent forth a dozen or so metal posts topped with basketball-sized wooden circles. "I set it to randomize the placement," said Fell, "and nothing's going to shoot back at you, so destroy at will."

"Really?"

"Sure. Show me what you've got."

Fire came instinctively to me, but I'd learned though experience that the most impressive flames arose when strong emotion fanned them—anger, usually, though fear worked in a pinch. With nothing facing me but a touch of stage fright, I reached in to tap the churning mass of my feelings, looking for fuel.

Warner, sitting on my couch, his feet propped on the coffee table, casually discussing his familiar.

Bitsy Prescott, who I'd thought was my friend until she kicked me out of her store and her life.

Sage, sobbing in the DOL bathroom.

And then a face rose in my mind, one I knew only from pictures: blonde and brown-eyed like me, her mouth curved into a laughing smile. It faded even as I tried to sharpen its features, leaving me with nothing but formless mist and the ghost of those crinkled eyes, and...

Flames burst to life along my arms as if I'd touched a lit match to a jet of gas. With a cry I barely recognized as my own, I shot my right arm forward like I was grabbing for the nearest target, and a blast of fire rocketed forth from my palm. Another target caught my eye, and I spun and released, pouring more power than I needed to into my shots but riding my anger and worry and loss. The room grew smoky, and strong fans in the ceiling clicked on to clear the air…and when the haze thinned, I found myself standing in the middle of the practice room, panting, a fireball in each hand and my arms taut as wound watch springs.

"Nice work," said Fell as the smoldering targets crumbled around me. "Feel better yet?"

I shook my head, not trusting myself to speak.

"Didn't think so," she replied, and with a command to the system, a fresh set of targets appeared.

By the end of my fifth set, much of which I'd torched with a sort of bullwhip of flame, my burning anger was spent, leaving me hollow and empty. I sank to my knees, exhausted and nearly in tears, and looked up when Fell knelt beside me and patted my back. "It's all right," she murmured. "That's the worst of it, yes?"

"I think so."

She waited until I pulled myself together and sat back on my heels, then said, "One of my instructors here taught me that it's dangerous for people like us to repress our feelings too often. You can only pour so much into a bottle before it overflows, see? It's good advice in general, but if a non-pyro gets upset, they might cry or yell, maybe smash something. When we reach our limit, we *flare*." With a wry smile, she told me, "I repressed for most of my life. Having a place like this, an outlet, has been a welcome change…and I suspect my husband sleeps better for it," she added. "Do you have somewhere you can go to burn off the buildup?"

"Not exactly, but…thank you. This does feel better," I said, and slowly exhaled. "I'm sorry for taking up your evening—"

"Happy to do it. Annie's found me down here many a

time," she said. "The least I can do is help a fellow pyro with…whatever it is you're going through." Glancing around us at the ash and embers, she said, "I can tell it's not easy."

"Just got a lot on my mind."

"I know the feeling." She stood, then offered me a hand and pulled me to my feet. "Not trying to pry, but have you considered an agency career? Your control is fantastic, and if you wanted to speak with someone about joining the trainee program here, I'd be happy to make the arrangements…if you're old enough, I mean. I'm sorry," she said with an embarrassed chuckle, "I'm not great at estimating sorcerers' ages, and Annie didn't tell me…"

"Twenty-eight in February."

"That's *it*? And you're that controlled? Please tell me your career counselor has been nudging you toward Laws. *Please.*"

"I, uh…I don't have a counselor. Got my bachelor's a few years ago, and I make soaps and candles and such."

Fell frowned, and then her dark eyes widened in comprehension. "You don't live here."

"Nope."

"If I may ask…"

"Ever been out the Central portal?"

"Not yet…Virginia?" she guessed, the word strange with her accent.

"Georgia. We're southwest of Virginia."

"Your family are growers, then?"

Hesitating, I questioned how much to reveal, then decided that if Fell was friends with Annie, surely she wouldn't grab a torch and pitchfork. "My mother briefly worked for DPP. My biological father was human."

To my relief, she seemed perplexed, not horrified. "But…I thought the draught affected the drinker's children as well."

I tilted my head and smiled. "Who said anything about the draught? Half-blooded, fully talented, only pyro in town, and in legal terms, fucked."

Her expression shifted toward pity. "Surely there's something that can be done for you. It sounds like you have family ready to claim you, yes?"

"Canna's the only one on my mother's side who knows about me," I replied. "And Liogh thinks it's up to the sorcerer representatives, which…is a whole situation I won't bother you with tonight. But thanks again for letting me toast some shit."

Fell set the system to clean up, and the drive back to Canna's was quiet. But before I got out of her car, she said, "Let me give you my contact information."

"Yeah?"

"Absolutely. Should you need another pyro to talk to before you crack and burn down a city, you know…I have portal credentials."

Friday morning, after dropping the twins at daycare, Canna delivered Sage and me to Liogh's office.

While they weren't the leader of their section, the detective still commanded sufficient seniority to merit a space with walls and a door instead of a cubicle. It wasn't anything to write home about, a space half the size of my kitchen tucked away on the back side of the fourteenth floor, but it was large enough to hold a decent wooden desk, a pair of tall cabinets designed for hanging folders, and two guest chairs with cream-colored upholstery. Aside from some framed certificates on the walls, the only piece of décor of note was an electric fountain, a resin piece designed in a series of cascading pools, which burbled at the edge of Liogh's desk.

"White noise?" I asked, pointing to the fountain.

They smiled, then flicked their fingers until the water within rose and formed a perfect sphere, which landed in Liogh's palm. "Stress toy, you might say," they replied, squishing the ball into a pancake and reshaping it like putty. "I picked that up in Pennsylvania some years ago. Have a seat," they said, and sent the water back into the fountain. "We're expecting one more…"

"Sorry, *sorry*," came a voice from the doorway, and I turned to see a naga in a black robe quickly slither into the room. "Our rookie counselor is having a come-apart with her first trial, and she cornered me in my office as soon as I arrived this morning."

Judging by her voice and her delicate features, the naga was female, but I wouldn't have staked my life on it. Her head was shorn—nagas could grow hair, Dad had told me once, but most chose to do without it—and her golden complexion was smooth and youthful. She wore a red blouse beneath her open robe, which only fell slightly below her waist. From that point, her body transitioned to a muscular tail scaled in a pattern of brown and black bands, which she pulled into a tight coil as she shut the door behind her.

She turned to Sage and me and mimed wiping sweat from her brow. "Hi. Sorry. Daffodil venGiep," she said, extending her hand.

I shook it, biting back the many questions I had concerning her name. One of her parents had probably worked outside the Pactlands, I reasoned, but I certainly wasn't going to ask.

"Jane Fortune," I replied, "and this is Sage."

"Daff is one of our counselors," Liogh explained. "And since she specializes in family law, the director has brought her in on this case."

"Pleasure to meet you both," she said, and settled into her coils. "Sage, I suspect you have concerns about what comes next. I'm here to give you the broad contours, if you will."

Sage nodded and slid forward in her chair, the better to see her.

"So, first, the good news. Citizenship is *not* an issue for you. You've got confirmed matches to both parents, and if my recollection of Liogh's notes is accurate, you were born in the Pactlands." Spreading her hands, she said, "If no one has already, then let me be the first to welcome you home, dear."

"She doesn't have to go to a Forum rep or anything?" I asked.

Daff shook her head. "No, that would only be necessary if she had human ancestry, and I *will* help you navigate that process," she insisted. "My thought was we deal with this one at a time. You're both minors, but you've reached adulthood, Jane, so I figured we should start with the child."

"Wait…"

"The age of majority here is thirty-five," Liogh offered. "That's why education is compulsory until then. But once you reach twenty-five, you're legally considered an adult—"

"In some respects," Daff murmured.

"You can work part-time, sign contracts, rent an apartment, initiate lawsuits…marry, though that's rare…but you can't vote or hold office until thirty-five, you're stuck in school, and good luck applying for a mortgage."

"I can practically see your hackles rising," Daff told me with a little smile. "Relax. We've had a couple interesting cases of late—"

"Rose and Annie," said Liogh.

"Yes, so there *is* precedent for making certain allowances. I can imagine that for someone your age, in your circumstances, it must chafe to be considered a minor. But that's a matter we can address later. Right now, we need to decide the path forward for Sage." Looking past me at the girl, Daff said, "Detective Birrid here will be checking some of the statements your mother made yesterday, but assuming she was telling the truth, you won't be suing her for support. Abandoning you as she did was certainly not the right action to take, but given her probable state of mind, it's not entirely inexplicable. In any case, she's a victim in this as well, and the Pact is not going to seek to punish her for that."

"So," Sage murmured, "that leaves Mirrik?"

The counselor nodded. "I'll help you assemble and file a suit for parental support. We don't have many abandonment cases here, fortunately, but we do have a protocol to follow. Assuming all goes as it should before the tribunal, Representative Voln will be billed for your upkeep—a percentage of his income and assets, so you'll be in good shape. Legally, you'll be a ward of the Pact, and you'll have a caseworker to oversee your education and housing situation."

"Boarding school?"

"That's a good option. Or there might be a foster placement for you, perhaps with relatives."

Sage brightened at that. "How about Jane?"

But Daff grimaced at the suggestion. "At this time, legally, Jane can't remain here. She's here because of the extenuating circumstances, but once we have you settled, Jane will need to petition for citizenship if she wishes to stay."

"Okay, so once Jane gets that—"

"You still wouldn't be placed with her," Daff said gently. "She's underage. But this isn't an issue that needs to be worked out this morning—"

"I want to stay with Jane," Sage interrupted. "If she still wants me..."

A responsible person, I suspected, would convince Sage of the opportunities she'd have while living in the Pactlands. But whatever hypothetical responsible person reached that decision hadn't held that girl while she cried.

"Of course I want you," I told Sage, reaching over to take her hand. "And until things are settled here and you're satisfied, you're staying with me."

Daff seemed taken aback at this. "We can get her into school on Monday. She'll need testing and tutors—"

"She's coming home with me," I interrupted. "*I* am her guardian for now, and until I know that she's safe and at least somewhat happy, I'm not leaving her."

I couldn't see Sage's face when I made that pronouncement, but her grip on my hand tightened.

"Now," I said to the counselor, "if you want to start proceedings against Sage's father to get funds for her, be my guest. This kid deserves anything you can squeeze from him. Detective Birrid has my phone number, and you can keep us apprised."

She frowned. "But—"

"This is not up for discussion. I'm sorry, I don't mean to be rude, and I know you're doing your job, but Sage is coming with me."

Quirking a brow, Daff said, "Not if the director puts a hold on her. She won't get through the external portal without permission."

Releasing Sage, I stood and folded my arms. "Try me."

Daff cut her eyes to Liogh, who cleared their throat and rose from their swivel chair. "I'll come upstairs and work through the details with you later this morning, if that's all right. These two need to be on their way."

"Liogh," the counselor protested, "you *cannot*—"

"If I've learned anything about our…recent arrivals, it's that they share a bond. They protect each other. And if I'm not mistaken, they consider Jane one of their number."

I smiled to myself. The expat community in the Pactlands might have been tiny, but they made solid allies.

"And since one of them is a Huntsman…Huntswoman?" they amended, then shrugged. "A member of the Hunt, call her what you will. If Jane says she's ready to leave, you won't be able to keep her."

"And the director approves of this?" Daff retorted.

"She's aware, and she is choosing her battles," said Liogh, then nodded to me. "My investigation is going to take a few days. Why don't you go home for now, and I'll be in touch?"

"Why don't you take us to Canna's office first so we can say goodbye like civilized houseguests?" I replied.

"That's fair. Daff, I'll be up shortly."

I'd pulled my phone from my bag and messaged Annie for a lift before the frustrated counselor had fully slithered out the door.

CHAPTER 19

We didn't call Dad or Tabitha when Annie brought us home. After I'd sent her on her way with a bottle of Dad's aged 'shine—it was the least I could do for her chauffeur services, though she insisted it wasn't necessary—Sage and I hung out together for the rest of the day. We unpacked, and then she helped me clean the cabin before settling in with her books and MP3 player. Finding her curled up on her freshened bed with her accoutrements, I thought about the logistics of downloading some audiobooks and synching them with the old equipment. Surely she'd prefer something meatier than the beginner readers through which she was working. The alternative was putting them on her phone, and while Sage had learned the basics quickly enough, I didn't feel up to giving her a full course in data usage and Internet safety that day.

That afternoon, Sage joined me in my workshop, where she helped me pack orders and sniffed her way around my product line. "I *can* be useful, Jane," she said as she tucked bottles into the shredded paper nest of a gift box, a new option I was offering for the holidays. "Warner said I'd be working for you, anyway."

"As long as you're here, your job is to get an education, and maybe keep your room cleanish." I told her. "Everything else is on me. If you want to help me out here sometimes, I wouldn't mind a hand, but we'll factor that into an allowance."

Her brow furrowed. "Allowance?"

"Spending money for you."

Sage huffed. "That's really nice, but you've given me so much already, and I haven't done——"

"Horey," I murmured, stopping her with a hand to her shoulder. "You're the kid here, and I'm the grownup. We take care of y'all, not the other way around. Now, I wouldn't be doing you any favors if I didn't teach you some baseline skills along the way—cooking, cleaning, checking your car's fluids, laundry—but I'm not asking you to earn your keep."

She returned to work, but I could tell she remained troubled. "What's on your mind, Sage?"

"Nothing."

"Liar. Tell me."

With a sigh, she finished tying a raffia bow around the box before she spoke. "What if they make me go back?"

"To the Pactlands?" She nodded, and I brushed my hair from my face. "I think Liogh understands what a bad idea that would be, and I bet their director does, too. And look, I'm no troll, but I ain't a pushover."

She grinned at that.

"Now, here's the truth," I continued, leaning against the counter. "From a medical, psychological, and educational standpoint, the folks in the Pactlands can give you more than I can, and I need to make that clear. That said, you deserve a voice in your own future. If you want to stay here, you're welcome. If you want to stick around for a few months, then maybe try school in the fall, that's fine, too. Maybe, if Annie's willing, we could shuttle you back and forth to let you chat with a therapist, start figuring yourself out. You've been through hell, baby," I said, holding her stare. "They can talk about protocols and best outcomes all they like, but I guarantee you there's no set playbook for how you go forward from here."

Sage's eyes began to turn glassy, and I pulled her into a hug. "It's going to get better. Maybe this is the part where the band-aid is ripped off, you know? Hurts in the moment, but then it's over." Pulling back slightly to see her face, I said, "I'm proud of you, hon. You've been a trooper. And whatever comes next, it's going to happen with your consent."

I thought I'd put her mind at ease, and she seemed to be in good spirits that night when we watched a movie and ate pizza on the couch. But around three the next morning, I woke to hear Sage yelling incoherently in her sleep. I rushed down the hall to rouse her from her nightmare, and she lay there panting in the darkness amid her tangled blankets, sweating despite the chill in the house. She didn't want to talk about what had so terrified her in her sleep, but when I invited her to spend the rest of the night in my room, she took me up on the offer.

While Sage slept in on Saturday morning, I stepped outside with my phone to give my posse the update. Both were already at work, Tabitha finishing Friday night's inventory and Dad with a brew. Once I assured them that we were okay, I hesitated just long enough to chide myself for the nervous flutter in my stomach, then called Connor.

He picked up almost immediately. "Tell me you haven't been kidnapped by fairies yet."

"I'm *pretty* sure they don't exist."

"You know, I thought the same thing about centaurs until recently. How're you, Firebug?"

His voice sounded distorted—a speaker. "You're on the road?"

"I'm picking up the morning shift. Radio's off, so lay it on me."

I filled him in, and though he had some *thoughts* about Liogh leaving Sage in a position in which she could spy on an interview, he quickly put professional matters aside. "I'll be off by dinnertime. If you'd like company, I could pick up food."

My stupid stomach fluttering intensified, but I reasoned that Sage could use a distraction, and so we made plans.

Connor pulled up around six with an assortment of takeout containers from Los Amigos. While the restaurant wasn't going to win any awards for authentic Mexican cuisine, it being the sort of establishment that offered "cheese dip" instead of queso on the menu, it was Ragged Gap's lone option for enchiladas, and it scratched the itch. "I probably should have called to ask what y'all wanted," Connor said as he unpacked a pair of loaded plastic bags on my kitchen counter, "but I figured nachos were safe enough."

Indeed, he'd bought a small buffet of the house specialties, and Sage, who'd never had so much as a taco, eagerly sampled them all. We talked about everything but the Pactlands while we ate, and then Connor suggested going out for ice cream—not my first choice on a cold December night, though Sage jumped at the notion. I offered to drive, but Connor insisted. He'd brought his patrol vehicle, gas wasn't a problem…and he put Sage up front, where he could show off the bells and whistles. Admittedly, I wasn't thrilled to find myself in the back of the Explorer, seated behind the reinforced panel and enclosed by doors that wouldn't open from the inside, but Sage cheered when Connor threw on the lights and siren for a moment, and I laughed to myself as she peppered him with questions about the controls.

We wound up at Dairy Queen, and as I started on my dipped cone, I noticed fat snowflakes falling outside the window. "Shit," I muttered, "I should have looked at the weather today…"

Connor chuckled. "That's the other reason why I wanted to drive. When did you last buy tires?"

I made a face. "Uh…"

"Thought so. I noticed your tread was low when y'all were at my house. Got a guy in Blue Ridge who'll do it for a little above wholesale, if you need someone."

I could have told him off. I was a strong, capable, independent woman who could manage her own life and wreck others' with a well-placed fireball...but yeah, he had a point.

"I'll go to my usual place, but thanks," I said. "Maybe we should take this to go—I'd hate for you to end the night sliding down the mountain."

"You should stay over," Sage suggested, all innocence. Before Connor or I could speak up, she added, "The couch is great."

"It's not bad," I told him, and was strangely gratified to see his flush rising.

"Appreciated, but how about a rain check?" he replied. "I'm taking the day shift tomorrow, and if I got stuck in Ragged Gap, there would be *questions*."

I let it go, but I most certainly caught the teasing grin he shot me in the parking lot as I slid into the back of the SUV, ice cream in hand.

I'd imagined that Sage would be disappointed when she didn't wake to a winter wonderland on Sunday—early snows were letdowns like that, especially when the ground wasn't cold enough to encourage accumulation—but she seemed almost relieved to see the brown grass and bare trees the next morning. Then again, I reminded myself as I made oatmeal and Sage sipped cocoa at the table, when one lived in an old barn, winter weather was nothing to be celebrated.

The roads were barely slick, and so Tabitha came by midmorning to check in and bring Sage a fresh load of books. As they chatted and Sage recounted the previous evening's dinner, Tabitha flashed me an impish little smirk. "And where is Connor today?" she asked.

"Working," I said, trying to discourage further enquiries with a look. "He's been very...helpful."

"I'm sure," she replied, though her eyes told me she knew *exactly* what I wasn't saying.

As it turned out, Tabitha had an itinerary in mind, and

she lured Sage out of the house with the promise of bowling. "I thought you could use a break," she murmured when Sage ran back to her room to pull on socks and shoes.

"You don't have to babysit," I protested, keeping my voice low.

"It's not babysitting. She needs enrichment, and I happen to like bowling. Ta-dah."

"Really?"

She snorted at my incredulity. "I'll have you know that back in college, my team won our rec league *three* semesters in a row," she said, buffing her nails against her sweater.

"Didn't know Tech had bowling."

"It wasn't an official league or anything, just a bunch of us who organized ourselves and chipped in to buy this horribly gaudy trophy to pass around. Some of the frats had teams, a couple sororities…the physics majors were surprisingly good."

"Where did yours come from?" I asked.

She grinned. "All Wiccans. We called ourselves the Crystal Balls. My friend Micah actually had a custom ball, clear with a skull inside…it made a statement. The Bowling Baptists were *not* amused."

Thanks to Tabitha and Sage's long lunch out and an afternoon at the lanes, I had plenty of time to clear my backlog of orders, prep my local deliveries, and even go grocery shopping. I called Dad and brought him dinner— as usual on a long weekend project, he'd holed up in his brew room and forgotten to eat—and I had a fire going and a frozen lasagna in the oven when Sage returned, much to her delight. Tabitha joined us for dinner, then stuck around for a game of Trouble, at which Sage excelled.

Monday dawned clear, cold, and without a peep from Beukal. I made my delivery rounds while Sage worked through her new books, and I was beginning to ponder dinner plans when Connor called. "Any interest in Chinese tonight?" he asked. "And if so, do you have any clue what Sage might like?"

The closest Chinese restaurant to Ragged Gap was ten miles outside of town, a mom-and-pop spot that had been in operation longer than I'd been alive. The faded pictures on the menu over the counter bore little resemblance to what one received in the white takeout cartons, but the food was cheap, filling, and excellent with soy sauce, so the locals kept the place alive.

"How about a family meal for four? I'll pay."

"Nah, my treat."

"You just bought dinner!"

"Jane—"

"I will find you, and I *will* Venmo you."

Eventually, Connor conceded defeat, and I had the table set and ready when he arrived. He'd stolen time to change clothes, swapping the uniform for jeans and a navy sweater over a white button-down, and I bit back a smile. True, my customary "eating fried rice with Netflix" uniform was pajamas, and I'd stepped up my game to real pants that night, but Connor was blatantly *trying.*

I could have told him that he needn't have tried so hard, but where was the fun in that?

He and I unpacked the boxes and explained the dishes to Sage, who ate with gusto and went back for more. She laughed and talked through dinner, telling Connor about her bowling outing, and he told her about the time when he was a teenager that the sheriff had to remove a guy on mushrooms from that alley during Cosmic Bowling night, complete with a wide-eyed and stumbling impression of the overwhelmed fungus aficionado. I'd just brought over the fortune cookies and was about to caution Sage not to eat the paper when the doorbell rang.

Connor immediately tensed. "Expecting someone?" he asked quietly.

"Not tonight."

"Want me to get it?"

"If there's a sorcerer out there, I'll have better odds of disarming him," I replied, pushing back my chair. "Sage, stay with Connor, and if things go south, run out the back and down to the creek."

"But—" she began.

"No buts. You can follow that creek off the mountain."

Nodding to Connor, and trying to exude more confidence than I felt, I peeked out the window and saw a lone woman standing there, a tall brunette in a black windbreaker. Her vehicle, a nondescript dark sedan, was parked at the end of my driveway, blocking us in. Hoping she wasn't armed, I unlatched the door and cracked it open. "Can I help you?"

She smiled nervously. "Uh...I'm sorry, I'm looking for a girl..."

Switching into Pactish, I asked, "Who are you, and what do you want?"

Her shoulders sagged with apparent relief on hearing that language. "My name is Enne Tumari. I'm looking for my sister's daughter."

That certainly answered the question of whether she was masked. "How'd you find this place?"

Slowly, she reached into her jacket pocket and withdrew a compass, which pointed straight past me and glowed blue. "Borrowed a tracker. It's set to locate my sister, so her daughter would be the closest hit here. Um..." She tucked it away, then showed me her empty hands. "No tricks. May I come in?"

"Not until you tell me how you got out here."

Rubbing the back of her neck, she said, "It's simple enough when you're a portal attendant. And since I did a brief stint with Laws when I was in my early forties, I have some familiarity with customs in this region. The language, at least."

"And your own masking ring," I said, glancing at the silver band on her right hand.

"Seldom used, but just in case." She took a step back, giving me a little room. "I mean you no harm. Is she here?"

A small fireball flared to life above my open palm. "She is."

To her credit, Enne didn't turn tail and flee. "I didn't realize I'd left her with a sorcerer."

"You didn't leave her with me." Glancing over my shoulder, I found Connor blocking the doorway to the kitchen, and he gave me a sharp nod. "Come in, I guess," I said in English, stepping aside. "Unmask, if you like. But put one hoof out of line, and I'll run your ass off this mountain and back to Beukal so fast, you won't know what hit you."

"To prove there's no deceit," she said, moving into the most open part of the den, then rubbed her ring and muttered under her breath. An instant later, her mask fell away...and yes, that was clearly a centaur in my house, dark-haired like her sister. Somehow, her trousers and boots were part of the illusion, as I didn't wind up with shredded clothing on my floor when Enne's true form manifested.

I glanced at Connor, whose only reaction was a slight widening of the eyes. Whatever else could be said for him, at least he didn't jump for his gun at the smallest odd development.

"I'm sorry to interrupt your evening..." Enne began, then gasped. "Is that...are you..."

Turning around again, I saw that Sage had appeared behind Connor, curious but hesitant. "This is Sage," I said. "Sage, honey, this is your aunt."

Enne took two steps closer, her hooves clicking on the wooden floor. "She's masked?"

"Jane made it for me," Sage replied, staring up at her. "I'm not taking it off for you."

She held up her hands in placation. "No, that's fine, youngling. I can imagine—"

"I don't think you can."

Wisely, Enne bit her tongue.

"Why are you here?" I asked. "Did Relieg send you?"

"No. I came on my own. She..." Enne's face worked briefly as she put her thoughts in order, and then she said, "My sister is beside herself."

For a split second, my heart lightened.

"She came to me in hysterics," Enne continued, stuffing her hands into her jacket pockets, which I suspected did nothing to put Connor at ease. "Said that DOL had found the baby and were going to come after her for support." Looking quickly at Sage, who continued to lurk behind the cop, she turned her attention back to me and said, "She's got a beautiful family. A husband who adores her, two wonderful sons. If this comes out, her life will be ruined—"

"Whoa," I interrupted, cutting short her plea. "No one's going after Relieg for money. Maybe she misunderstood."

Enne frowned. "She told me that the detective said—"

"They're pursuing Sage's *father*, not her. DOL isn't demanding money from a rape victim."

"Rape?" she echoed, stepping back. "What are you talking about?"

I eyed Enne for a long moment, but before I could recount what Relieg had told Liogh, Connor asked, "What did your sister tell you about Sage's origins?"

She sighed deeply. "She never mentioned rape. I...I mean...that is..."

"Take your time," he coaxed. "Let's start at the top. When did you learn she was pregnant?"

"When she was already in labor. She showed up on my doorstep late one evening, crying and panicked...she said she had no idea she was pregnant, but she recognized the signs of imminent delivery, and I confirmed that pretty quickly."

Connor's eyebrows rose. "She didn't *know*?"

"No. Once she and Grantis were engaged, she decided she wanted to lose some weight before the wedding, so she'd been dieting and hitting the gym every day. She'd complained to me about how the scale didn't seem to move, but we'd just thought it was stubborn fat. Apparently not," she mumbled. "Now she was in labor, and she'd taken no measures to protect the fetus—no supplements, no medical checks, nothing of the sort. She'd been drinking less alcohol than usual—dieting, right—but I know she'd been taking stimulants. Her job was so demanding…"

"And who did she say was the father?"

A guilty expression flickered on Enne's face. "One of her colleagues, a married guy in her office. She'd told me she was having an affair months before—she was frustrated because Grantis was taking his time in making things official with her, and I suppose she wanted a little fun before settling down. She played with fire—she should have been on birth control, but she was afraid that Grantis would ask questions if he found out. I told her it was a bad idea, but she's always done her own thing, and she ended the affair once she was engaged. Anyway," she said, her tail flicking with her discomfort, "when the baby was born, we saw how deformed she was, and I didn't imagine she would live long. A dead baby was the last thing Relieg needed. Relieg was crying, asking me to take it away, and…she's my little sister," she said, almost pleading. "She needed me."

"What about your *niece*?" I snapped.

"Honestly, I thought she was dying. I gave her something to let her sleep, then bundled her up and sneaked her outside the Pactlands. I didn't know what to do, but if we'd had to report a dead infant, my sister's engagement would have been over. I wasn't going to ruin her life like that."

"So, you dumped Sage out here."

"I didn't *dump* her," Enne protested. "I drove aimlessly

for a long time, trying to think, but I knew I needed to get back to Relieg, and then I saw a house set off by itself with lights in the windows, and I...I thought that someone would find the baby. Take care of her until she passed."

"You thought she was dying," I said slowly, staring at Enne, "and you couldn't be bothered to hold her until the end? Make sure she wasn't in pain?"

"I know how it sounds—"

"*Do* you? Did you even check to see if someone was home before you dropped Sage on the doorstep and ran?"

"I heard noise inside. And there were lights—"

Connor folded his arms and grunted. "Come on, have you never turned on some lights and the TV before going out at night? Pretty common trick."

"Look, I could have done better, I realize that, but...you're all right, yes?" she said, gesturing to Sage. "You were found and raised and—"

"Abused," I interrupted. "She was abused. You left a helpless child with a fucking monster. Also," I said as Enne's mouth flapped open, "your sister lied to you. Maybe she was trying to protect you, I don't know, but Sage's father is Mirrik Voln."

Enne stiffened in shock, momentarily silenced, then licked her lips and anxiously pawed at the floor. "That...would explain the deformities."

"She's more or less healthy, just underdeveloped because she's been starved all her life," I said. "Because *wow*, you picked a real winner of a house."

"I didn't know—"

"No, you didn't," I said, "because you didn't take the most basic of precautions for that child! You could have brought her to a...a hospital or something, right? Surely you have adoption in the Pactlands, yes?"

"It's not that simple," said Enne. "Grantis is a healer, and if he'd learned of this—"

"Of *what?* Either his fiancée was assaulted, in which case the perpetrator needed to be brought to justice, or else she's a cheat, and he should have been informed of that before marrying her. In neither case did Sage deserve what you did." When Enne didn't immediately argue with me, I pressed my case. "She was treated worse than a junkyard dog. Chained up by her neck in a *barn*. Could barely walk, her hooves were so overgrown. And if I hadn't paid off the asshole who 'raised' her..."

I paused to glance at Sage, stopping myself before I could blurt out exactly what Warner had planned to do with her in case his plans for me fell through.

When I turned back to Enne, I was surprised to catch her on the verge of tears. "I'm sorry, little one," she said to Sage. "Truly, I am. It wasn't my intention that you be..."

"Tortured?" I suggested. "You know, she grew up calling that man 'Master.'"

She had the grace to wince, but that was all. "None of this is your fault," she continued, holding Sage's gaze, "and I know it's a lot to ask, but please think of my sister, *especially* if she was raped. If you sue for support—"

"I'm not asking her for anything," Sage cut in, hugging herself.

"No, and I'm sure she'd appreciate that, but she will have to testify. If she doesn't swear that she was...*forced*, then the tribunal could order support from her as well." Finding nothing from the three of us but silence, Enne said, "Relieg is far from perfect, I know that. But as I said, she's got a wonderful family, two little boys who love their mother, a doting husband...if she's compelled to go to the tribunal over this matter, what will happen to all of that?"

I frowned. "You think her husband would leave her if she were raped?"

"*No*, no," she said emphatically, "Grantis is a good man. But she'd have to explain everything to him, to the boys—how is she supposed to tell them they have a half sister? Especially one—"

"Like me?"

There was a steel edge in Sage's tone that I hadn't

anticipated, and the doubt and fear in her eyes had burned away.

Enne paused, choosing her words. "It's a...it's a *complicated* matter..."

"You dumped me here to *die*. Like...like a kitten dropped on the side of the road. You and Relieg didn't give a damn what happened to me, just so long as her precious fiancé didn't find out. And now you expect me to care that she might have to *tell my brothers what happened?*" Her voice rose to a shout. "They go to school, don't they, these little brothers of mine? They have beds, right? Food? Do they get toys? You know, I always wanted a doll—"

"Sage—" Enne began.

She ignored her aunt. "They're not beaten, are they? Chained up? Do they get blankets and coats when it's cold?"

"I—"

"*He told me I was a demon!*" she screamed at her aunt, furious tears streaming down her face. "I thought that's all I was, and it's your fault! It's your...*fucking*...fault!"

Connor pulled her into a hug, rubbing her shaking back as she sobbed. Enne watched, momentarily stricken, but before she could try again to reason with Sage, I shut her down. "I'm going to do everything I can to see that Sage gets what she needs," I said, and walked to the door. "If your sister *was* raped, then I'm sorry. No one deserves that. But she can have an uncomfortable conversation with her family if it means a better life for Sage. And I think it's time you headed back."

But Enne had one last angle. "She could stay here, couldn't she? Make a life for herself? If she's masked—"

"Get out," I growled, throwing the door open with one suddenly flaming arm.

Enne quickly masked and departed, and I slammed the door behind her once she drove off. I stood in the foyer for a moment, collecting myself and coaxing my fire to retreat, before I turned to find Connor and Sage watching me. "Sorry," I muttered. "Temper."

"You didn't set her on fire," said Connor. "I'm impressed."

"I've *never* set anyone on fire...but she was looking mighty flammable, there," I admitted, and sighed. "Sage, honey..."

I don't know who needed that hug more, her or me, but I held her until I didn't feel quite so ready to watch the world burn.

CHAPTER 20

The evening ended soon thereafter. I coaxed Sage into the bathroom to wash her face and brush her teeth while Connor cleaned up the leavings from dinner, and once I'd put her to bed, I returned to the kitchen to find him picking at the pieces of a fortune cookie. He offered to stay in case I feared Enne would return, but I insisted we'd be fine.

As I walked him to his SUV, he squeezed my hand and pulled me to a stop in the driveway. "You call me if you need backup, okay?" he murmured. "I'll come. Promise."

"You've been a help already," I replied.

"My pleasure." He hesitated, then released me and opened the driver's-side door. "I mean it, Firebug. I can't do much with magic, but I'm a damn good shot."

I smirked as he slid behind the wheel. "You're all right, for a cop."

"Not exactly high praise, but I'll take it," he said, grinning back at me. "Don't go setting the county on fire, now. Count to ten first."

Once Connor had departed, I checked on Sage and found her asleep—exhausted, I suspected. That was the angriest I'd seen her, and I knew damn well there was plenty more in the well from which that outburst had boiled forth. Expressing her anger was good, especially since Sage's didn't result in flames, but I could understand why she was so worn out after the unexpected meeting.

Still wired but reluctant to disturb her, I took my phone to the shed and considered the time. True, it was past eight, but surely Liogh would want to know about our visitor.

They picked up on the second ring. "Jane? Is all well?" they asked, their voice tense.

"Fine," I insisted, quickly adding, "Sorry to call so late, but I've got some information for you."

"No apology needed. Let's hear—no, wait just a moment."

When they spoke again, I could tell I'd been put on speaker. "Can you hear me?"

"Uh, yeah. Are you busy? I can call back—"

"No, this is fine. I was actually discussing Sage's case with one of my colleagues from DOI, and I thought he should hear whatever you have to offer."

"Oh?"

"The director cleared it," said an unfamiliar male voice, his Pactish bearing a trace of the lilt I was beginning to recognize as an elven accent. "Ganti ti'Van. You're Jane Fortune?"

"That's me."

"Ganti is a farseer," Liogh explained. "Past-oriented. He's been invaluable in some of our more difficult investigations."

"Considering the politics of this situation and the allegations Sage's mother has raised, my director brought me in," said Ganti. "While I'm sure Liogh and their crew could handle this case, since we need to be sure and to move expeditiously…"

My stomach clenched. "Have you seen…you know, the assault?"

"Why don't you tell us what you've learned first, and then I'll share my findings."

When Liogh didn't protest, I said, "Sure. Dinner tonight was interrupted when Relieg's sister stopped by—"

"Her *sister*?" the detective blurted.

"Yeah. Enne Tumari. I don't know who her boss is, but she needs to be looked into. She's a portal attendant."

Liogh groaned. "On my list. Tell me you didn't set her tail on fire."

"I behaved," I protested. "Anyway, Enne said that Relieg never told her she was raped. Relieg claimed she was having an affair with a married coworker, and she didn't use birth control. Had no idea she was pregnant until she went into labor, and she ran off to Enne for help with the delivery. They thought Sage was too messed up to live, so Enne drove her out here and dumped her. Didn't want the fiancé to find out Relieg had been two-timing."

One of the two on the other end grunted.

"She tried to convince Sage to drop her suit," I continued. "Said Relieg's freaking out about the whole thing because she'll have to confess her dark secret to her perfect little family. I kicked her out when she started suggesting that Sage could stay here permanently."

"Reasonable," said Liogh. "Ganti, thoughts?"

"Before you do," I cut in, "I'm not saying that I don't believe Relieg was raped. I watched that interview, and—"

"We have a saying in Laws," Liogh interrupted. "'Nod but confirm.'"

"Huh?"

"You're not an investigator, and I'm not surprised that you took her at her word, especially considering how she reacted in the interview. But I've done a few of these, Jane, and I have a decent sense for when someone's not being entirely forthright."

I paused. "You think she lied?"

"Well...it's curious. I had our tech team retrieve the door records from the Forum offices. Those go back *decades*. Given Sage's age and her likely gestational period, I was able to limit the search to a few months. And it's peculiar: I can't find any instance of Mirrik and Relieg being alone together. Each representative's suite has a set of locking doors, and since they were in different offices, their movements would have been obvious if they'd visited each other."

"Unless they used someone else's credentials," I pointed out.

"Unlikely if they weren't carrying their colleagues' hands around. Those doors are on palm locks."

"What if Mirrik masked? The door—"

"Would still register him," said Liogh. "It would be a poor security system if something as simple as a mask could thwart it. So." I could almost see them leaning toward the phone. "If they weren't being intimate in the office, then where were they? Which is, I hope, a question Ganti can answer."

"Not definitely," the farseer replied. "I've yet to catch Mirrik and Relieg together."

"Not at all?" Liogh asked, sounding disappointed.

"No, not outside normal Forum business. *But.*" His voice grew louder as he, in turn, moved closer to the speaker. "What I *can* tell you is that he had a girlfriend."

"Mirrik?" I asked.

"Mm-hmm. Pretty woman, a blonde sorcerer. Lovely blue eyes, a little pout, an...*impressive* figure, if you know what I mean. The sort of woman who seldom lacks male attention."

"Why do you think they were together?" Liogh asked.

"Well, any number of reasons. I keep finding them at Hearthstone, for one."

"Hearthstone?" I interjected.

"Probably the nicest restaurant in District 1," he explained. "About two blocks from the Forum. It's an institution in Beukal—representatives have hosted meals or drinks there for two centuries. Mirrik must have met the woman there ten times, possibly more. And he paid. She mentioned working as an artist, so I don't suppose she was flush was cash. Forum aides aren't exactly wealthy on their salaries, but Mirrik probably had access to the family money."

"Is that your only proof?" Liogh pressed. "Dinner dates?"

"I saw what followed those dates, too," Ganti said dryly. "In explicit detail."

I cringed. "Ugh. That's awkward."

"Exactly. I try not to peek in on intimate moments unless the case calls for it, and unfortunately, this one does."

"Your poor eyes," Liogh joked.

Ganti chuckled briefly. "I'll admit, I've seen worse than those two, but it's rather difficult to look someone in the face after you've spied on him with his pants off. But that's my proof," he continued. "No sign of Relieg, but Mirrik was quite content at the time."

"So, who was she?" I asked him. "The blonde."

"Ah. And *that* is the mystery. Mirrik called her Joviff. Nothing odd there"—I took his word for it—"but I've yet to find any records of her, either current or contemporaneous."

"Huh." Liogh mumbled. "None whatsoever?"

"No, which strongly suggests—"

"An alias, yes," the detective finished. "Who ended it?"

"I believe she did, though I haven't spotted the breakup just yet. Now, I can widen my search," he offered. "If you want me to look at a broader range of dates, I'm happy to do so. But if you think this child's conception happened during the time I've been searching...well, I haven't seen direct evidence of it, unless..."

Ganti left that thought unfinished, but I saw where he was going with sickening clarity. "She was masked. Relieg masked herself and posed as a sorcerer."

"So far, that's the only conclusion that matches what I'm seeing," he slowly replied.

It was, I reluctantly admitted, possible. While Enne's mask included built-in clothing, Sage's did not. If Relieg had access to a suitable piece of masking jewelry, she could have gone home, adjusted her body, slipped into something cute for date night, and sneaked out to see Mirrik...who called her by another name. Was he in on the caper and aware of her true identity, or had she tricked him into wining, dining, and sleeping with her? And if so, *why*? She obviously wasn't trying to baby-trap him.

"We need to hear from the representative," Liogh muttered. "See what he says about his girlfriend. Jane, can you be on standby with Sage?"

"I'm not putting that kid through another interview like Relieg's—"

"No, of course not, but...let me see how this plays out," they said. "Depending on his reaction, Sage may want to come over."

"We'll see. Anything else you need from me?"

"Not tonight." They paused, then asked, "How is she?"

"Sleeping it off. She had a rough time of it with Enne. Maybe not the most healthy expression of anger, but I think it's progress all the same."

Ganti grunted. "How bad *was* it?"

"Let's just all be glad I'm the lone pyro in this house."

We said our goodbyes, and I stood alone in my workshop for a long moment, staring into space and letting the disturbing puzzle come into focus.

Liogh was right: they needed to chat with Mirrik. But would the representative voluntarily come in, or would he smell the stench of a brewing scandal and clam up?

And in either case, where did that leave the girl sleeping on the damp pillow in my spare room?

I woke around six on Tuesday morning to a check-in text from Connor. Assuring him we were fine, I rose and shuffled to the kitchen, where I slumped into a chair with my phone and absently gestured a mug from the cabinet, the tea from its box, and the kettle under the spigot. I'd just put on the water to boil and was deciding whether I should make toast when my phone rang.

"What's up?" I asked in Pactish, seeing Liogh's name appear.

"We've got Mirrik in the building," they replied, not bothering with the niceties of greetings. "One of my colleagues goes to his gym and called me in, and I got him off the treadmill. He wants to talk."

"Does he know what Relieg claims?"

"*Vehemently* denies everything. He's willing to take truth serum to clear his name."

That took me aback. Truth serum was seldom used because of the nasty side effects, and I'd only seen Dad brew it once. While under the influence of the potion, which typically lasted half an hour or less, the drinker would be unable to lie. According to Dad, the potion's developer had intended for it to be used in tribunal proceedings, as the other method of ensuring reliable testimony, a spell, inflicted pain if the witness fibbed. But as it was quickly discovered that truth serum would at best leave the drinker sick from both ends for a week, and at worst trigger organ failure, it was shelved as a last resort. Outside of *very* particular circumstances, administering the potion was a crime.

"Lousy way to start the morning," I said.

"Yeah. He changed out of his sweats before coming in, but I'm sure he's had better days. Anyway, we're getting authorization for the potion now. If Sage wants to be here, I'll slip her in."

Glancing up at the sound of footsteps, I found Sage in the doorway, sleep-rumpled and puffy-eyed, frowning at me.

"I'll ask her," I told Liogh, "but I make no guarantees."

They quickly ended the call, and I beckoned Sage toward the table. "So, I called Liogh last night and told them about Enne's visit. They were sitting there with a farseer—"

"What *is* a farseer?" she asked, sliding into the chair beside mine.

"Farsight's a wild talent like pyromancy, but rarer. They can see forward or backward in time—only one direction—but Dad says they're handy in investigations. The guy Liogh called doesn't think Relieg's story holds water." Quickly, and as delicately as possible, given the hour and my pre-caffeine fog, I filled Sage in on my conversation from the night before and Liogh's news. "It's up to you," I told her. "If you want to watch the interview, I'll call Annie or drive you over. If not—"

"I want to see."

The kettle began to whistle, and I motioned it off the eye. "You're sure?"

She nodded. "Even if it's bad, even if he doesn't want to meet me, I want to know what he has to say." Her eyes narrowed. "*Especially* since I can't trust Relieg."

When Annie arrived about twenty minutes later, she brushed off my apology for the early call. "It's really no trouble," she insisted. "I'm not even due in the office until eight. Incidentally, I'm going to need more of that hooch you sent home with me."

"You've got it," I said, pulling another bottle of Dad's aged moonshine from its hiding place. "Seems like a fair price for the taxi service—"

"What? Oh, no, I don't want *payment*." She stepped back and shook her head. "No, Wylan really liked it, and he shared it with the guys, so they wanted to know if we could buy more."

"*Ah*. Well, take this one, anyway," I said, pressing the bottle into her hands, "then let me know how many bottles you're after, and I'll get y'all on Dad's list..." Turning at the sound of heels, I found Sage ready to go, having chosen a corduroy skirt and boots for the occasion. "Want some breakfast, hon?"

"I'm not really hungry, thanks," she replied, smiling tightly, and with that, we were on our way.

Protocol aside, Annie brought us straight to Liogh's office, and the detective, who'd been frowning at their computer, almost fell out of their chair at the shock of our appearance. "Stars above, woman, *warn* me before you do that," they said, clutching their chest, but quickly closed the computer and rose to smooth their robe. "You made good time," they continued, calming. "Mirrik is being prepped by the healers, so I can sneak you into the viewing room."

We hurried ten stories down, and Liogh led us to our hiding spot. "Do us all a favor and stay here until we've got Mirrik in position next door," they said, and slipped away.

As we waited, Sage swung one leg for a time, then stood and began pacing the viewing room, agitated and anxious. "It's going to be all right," I murmured, catching her arm on a pass. "Whatever happens, I'm here, okay? You're not alone in this mess."

A faint smile and a nod were her only reply.

After a time, I detected voices and footsteps on the tile outside our room, and I motioned Sage back into her seat, putting a finger to my lips. She did as I asked, perching on the chair beside mine, and I held her clammy hand as the lights came on in the interview room next door.

The man I took to be Mirrik arrived with an entourage. I could see why he'd made the list of the capital's most eligible bachelors: he was a classically handsome man who appeared to me to be in his thirties, with a thick black ponytail and worried brown eyes. He wasn't huge, especially not next to Liogh—maybe a hair under six feet, I estimated—but he seemed trim beneath his dark formal robe, not scrawny. While Sage certainly had her mother's eyes, I mused, there was no denying her paternity; much of her face seemed like a scaled-down echo of her father's.

Along with Mirrik and Liogh came an agent in black, a pair of healers—I recognized them by their purple lab coats—and a tiny woman with a youthful face, neatly coiffed white hair, and an embroidered robe that probably cost more than anything in my wardrobe. She was a gnome, I realized, but no one I'd met.

As Mirrik took a seat, the gnome looked up at Liogh, who easily made two of her, and asked, "Are you ready?"

"Yes, ma'am," they replied, sitting opposite the representative. "If our videographer is prepared…"

The agent—an elf, I could see, catching him in profile as he fiddled with the equipment in the corner—nodded. "Ready."

"Good. Let's begin the recording," said the gnome, and waited until he gave her a nod before commencing. "This is being recorded on December seventh in the four hundred eighty-fourth year of the Pact, approximately seven-fifteen in the morning capital time. I am Kabno Erenani. Present with me for this interview is Detective Liogh Birrid of…DPP Affairs." She sounded almost amused at the detective's presence in an interview so far beyond their usual cases. "Also present are two of our healers to monitor the subject and a videographer. This is the interview of Representative Mirrik Voln."

Turning from the camera to Mirrik, she said, "I've been informed that you've requested truth serum for this interview. Is that correct?"

"Yes, Director," he replied.

"And you have been made fully aware of the risks and potential complications of taking this potion?"

"Yes."

"Has anyone attempted to compel you to take it?"

"No."

"You do so of your own free will?"

Mirrik nodded. "I do."

"Then good luck to you," the director replied, and beckoned toward the healers. "He's all yours."

One of them handed a small bottle three-quarters full of a dark orange liquid to Mirrik, while the other placed a far more mundane plastic bucket beside his chair. Grimly, he uncapped the bottle, raised it in a brief salute to the camera, then shot it back.

"It will take about two minutes to full effect," the bucket-bearing healer told him. "Try to breathe deeply. The nausea won't kick in right away."

As I watched, Mirrik began to turn pale, and a sheen of sweat broke out across his forehead. The other healer, who'd been consulting her watch, weighed the lapsed time against his reaction until she was satisfied and said, "I think we're in business. Make this brief, Detective."

Liogh lost no time. "Name?"

"Mirrik Voln."

"Mr. Voln, are you acquainted with Relieg Tumari?"

"I am," he said, swallowing hard.

"How?"

"We were Forum aides together. Uh…different offices, but all the aides knew each other. She works in Forum media relations now, so I see her on occasion, but that's the extent of our interaction."

"Have you ever been in an intimate relationship with Ms. Tumari?"

"No. Not to my knowledge," he amended with a weak chuckle.

"Have you ever had sexual contact with Ms. Tumari?"

"Again, no, not to my knowledge. I suppose it could have happened, considering what I've been told this morning, but I have *no* memory of such."

Liogh paused briefly, considering their notes. "Are you attracted to Ms. Tumari?"

"She's pretty," said Mirrik, "but she's also a centaur, and that doesn't do it for me."

"Let's go back about fourteen years. Were you and Ms. Tumari aides during that period?"

"Yes."

"Were you in a relationship with anyone?"

Mirrik pressed his fist to his mouth and scrunched his eyes closed, then fought past the apparent wave of nausea. "Yes. Jovif Nemar."

"And who is she?"

"She's an artist. We dated for a few months."

"Sorcerer?"

"Yes."

Liogh's pen scratched at their notepad. "How did you meet?"

"Oh, gosh…I went to Hearthstone one night after work to relax, and she approached me at the bar."

"By 'relax,' do you mean you were drinking alcohol?"

"Ordinarily, sure, but not then," said Mirrik. "My healer had found cancerous colon polyps, and I was being treated…do you need details about that?"

"No, that's fine," said Liogh. "But you weren't using alcohol?"

"Not with the potions I was taking. Healer forbade it, and I trust her judgment. And the cancer's gone, so…" He spread his hands. "Hearthstone has a nice non-alcoholic menu, and I liked to sit at the bar and watch TV."

"I see. So, Joviff approached you…"

Mirrik nodded. "She'd drawn a sketch of me and said she knew it was creepy, but she wanted me to have it. I thanked her—it's really good, I keep it on the wall at home—and since we were both alone that night, we started talking."

Well, that explained where Sage's artistic talent came from.

"A relationship developed?" Liogh asked.

"Absolutely. She was funny, clever…*gorgeous*," he said, chuckling, "and I thought she was great. We met up at Hearthstone for the first few weeks, and then we tried other restaurants, went for walks, and after a while, I invited her to my place."

"Did you ever go to hers?"

"No. She said she had roommates and no privacy, and since I had a nice apartment, I didn't force the issue. She started staying over some weekends."

The detective's expression gave away none of their thoughts. "Would you characterize your relationship as serious?"

"*I* would," said Mirrik, who was looking paler by the minute. "I was considering bringing her home to meet my parents "

"And you two were intimate?"

"Yes."

"Birth control?"

Mirrik made a face. "Joviff said she had an allergy to the potion, but I've been taking it for most of my adult life, so I didn't think we had a problem. I learned after my cancer treatment was over that it *considerably* weakens the potency of the birth control potion, but since I never heard from Joviff about a baby, I assumed we'd been fortunate."

Nodding, Liogh asked, "You didn't want a child with her?"

"Not immediately. I wanted to be in a better place financially before starting a family, and Joviff had said she wasn't ready, either. But if we'd stayed together, then yes, I'd have wanted children with her. I'd like to be a father someday," he said, unable to be anything but sincere. "It's never been the right time, and I've had poor luck with partners, but I like kids, and I'd love to have some of my own."

"So, what happened to you and Joviff?"

Mirrik's face fell. "She came over one Saturday afternoon. We were supposed to go to dinner that night, and I remember I was still in my sweats, but she looked put-together. She *always* looked nice," he murmured. "I'd barely said hello before she told me she was ending things. There was someone else," he said with a sad—and honestly, queasy—smile. "And they were moving out to the country to make a start together. I begged her to reconsider, but she said her mind was made up, and she wished me the best…and that was the last time I saw her."

"You've never looked her up?" asked Liogh, one blue eyebrow rising.

"I tried a few years ago, just to see how she was doing," he replied. "Couldn't find her. I don't know if she changed her name or died...I *hope* she didn't die. I mean, maybe it's silly, but I do still care about her..." Cutting himself short, he reached for the bucket, but his stomach decided to play nice for a bit longer. "Sorry, this stuff really is terrible, isn't it? Now, let me get this straight: DOL found a child outside the Pactlands who's genetically mine and *Relieg's*?"

"You see where we would have questions," said Liogh.

"And assume the worst, but I assure you that if I had sex with Relieg Tumari, I know nothing about it. I wasn't getting black-out drunk, I don't recall any instances of lost time..."

"We've got a farseer on the case, but the current thought is that your Joviff may have been heavily masked."

Mirrik's forehead furrowed. "But *why*? I don't understand...Relieg's never shown any interest in me, even when she was single. Why go through an elaborate charade like that?"

"We're still investigating," said Liogh, shrugging, "but between our farseer and your interview today, I can say with confidence that her rape accusations were false. And I'd be remiss in my duties if I didn't mention that if she *was* intimate with you under the circumstances coming to light, that would turn the question of assault right back on her."

"If you figure it out, call me," Mirrik muttered. "But the child. You're *sure* she's mine?"

Liogh cut their eyes to the director, who said, "I've read the report. The odds of you not being her father are astronomical."

"Is she here now?" he pressed. "In the Pactlands? Can I meet her? I...I mean, if she's got a good family, I don't want to rip her away from people who love her, but if she needs someone..."

"Our plan was to sue you for support," said Liogh, "but with Relieg's story falling apart—"

"You don't have to sue me—I'll take her. Gladly."
Leaning toward Liogh, Mirrik said, "I've been thinking
about this all morning. I'm not an experienced parent, but
I can give her a home...*does* she need a home?"

"She's...had a difficult childhood," Liogh began, but
that was as far as they got before Sage jumped from her
seat and ran for the door.

I followed after her, trying to put the brakes on her
apparent plan. "Honey, this might not be the best time—"

"I've got to see," she said, and threw open the door to
the interview room.

I arrived behind her in time to catch Mirrik's eyes
widen with surprise. "Oh!" he said, startled by the
interruption, and then he beamed and rose from his chair.
"Hello. Are you, um..."

"I'm Sage," she said softly, ignoring the healers'
shooing motions. "Hi."

Though he was surely feeling awful, Mirrik's smile
grew. "Sage. It's so nice to meet you," he said, stepping
out from around the coffee table. "What a beautiful young
lady you are."

"I'm masked," she mumbled. "You should know."

"That's fine. Or you can take it off, if you prefer."

She stood there for a moment, nervously licking her
lips as she wrestled with her next step, then grimly
removed her boots and socks, and touched her pendant. I
caught the flash of regret in her eyes just before she
whispered her mask away.

And there she was, exposed from the knees down and
quite clearly not the product of two sorcerers. "Sorry. So,
um..." she said with a tremor in her voice, "this is me..."

Mirrik cocked his head. "You know, that's different,"
he said—possibly the understatement of the morning—
"but you're still beautiful, Sage. And if...well, if you're in
the market for a father, I'd love to have you."

Her eyes misted as she stared at him. "Really?"

There was so much doubt in that word, so much pain,

but also a tiny spark of hope—and to my relief, Mirrik nodded, his smile returning. "Absolutely. Mask or not, that's up to you. I'm just so pleased to learn that you exist. I was telling the detective here that I've wanted kids..."

Sage's face crumbled as she ran toward him, and Mirrik caught her in a tight hug. "We'll get acquainted," he said, patting her back as she sniffled. "I promise. But, uh...*oh*, sorry..."

He freed himself and stepped away, then barely managed to yank the bucket into place before he was violently sick. "It's not you, sweetie," he said between spasms. "Potion...oh, *damn* it..."

Glancing my way as the representative puked his guts out, Liogh said, "We need to get him to the healers' suite. Want to call Canna?"

"Is he going to be okay?" Sage asked, eying her heaving father with concern.

"Probably," Liogh told her, "but he's not going to be in any condition for guests for a few days. Trust me, he's not in for a pleasure cruise."

"I'm sorry," said Mirrik, barely lifting his face from the bucket. "This is..."

"Only the prelude," Liogh muttered to me. "Seriously, youngling, you should go before his day gets any worse."

CHAPTER 21

My initial thought was to call Annie and take Sage home to wait out Mirrik's convalescence, but the director caught me in the hall before I could pull out my phone. "Do you have accommodations in the city, Ms. Fortune?" she asked, her voice almost childlike in its timbre. "Would your cousin be an option, or do we need to arrange a hotel?"

"I was thinking we could head back to Georgia...ma'am," I said, looking down at her.

"That is an option," she admitted, "but it would be helpful for Sage to remain here."

Sage gripped my hand, but I kept my eyes on the director. "For what purpose?"

"Well...there is the matter of her permanent custody to resolve." Cocking a thumb in the direction of the elevators, she suggested, "Let's take this to my office, hmm?"

I wasn't sure what to expect when we reached the top floor, but to my relief, the director had opted for guest furniture scaled for people larger than human kindergarteners. She gestured toward the couch, then closed and locked her door and hoisted herself into a coordinating chair, from which her feet dangled. "We've yet to be introduced," she said as Sage and I settled in. "Kabno Erenani. Welcome back to Beukal," she added with a knowing half-smile.

"Thanks for not hauling my dad in here," I said quietly.

She nodded. "Sometimes, the strict application of the law does not result in *justice*," she murmured, "which is a truth I've seen borne out over a long career. That, and I have a certain counterpart at DOI with...*firm*...thoughts about prosecuting Mr. Hewt."

"Sorry, uh..."

"Let's just say you haven't escaped the farseers' notice. We try not to unduly interfere in each other's domains, but on occasion, I do listen to the oracle," she said, rolling her eyes. "Who could certainly be *plainer* but does things his way. Ah, well. Now, about Sage—"

"If she wants to stay with me, that's her decision," I interrupted. "Kid's been through enough."

"I appreciate that," said Kabno, softening as she looked at Sage, who, having masked again, sat close to me on the couch, tense and silent. "Legally, here's the situation. Her father didn't know of her existence but should have had parental rights. Sage has never been formally adopted, correct?"

"No," I murmured.

"Not that I have any clue how we would manage a shared custody situation with citizens of a country that doesn't know we exist, of course, but the fact that we don't have an adoption to deal with does simplify matters. You've been her guardian for...a month?"

"And change."

"Mm. And you don't yet have citizenship rights." Scooting forward in her chair, Kabno said, "I'm going to be straight with you, girls. Both of you should be in school here. The fact that there's a self-taught pyromancer walking around in *Georgia* is giving me an ulcer. Now, yours is a complicated problem, Jane, and it'll take work to unravel. But Sage has a clear path forward. She has citizenship, and she has a biological parent here who has stated he'll support her. What I'd like to do today is appoint a caseworker for her, someone who will start coordinating the services she needs while her father recovers, and who will then supervise to ensure she has a stable, healthy living situation. How does that sound?"

I glanced at Sage, then asked the director, "Could we have a minute, please?"

She acquiesced and slipped out of her office, and once the door had clicked closed, I turned to Sage and took her hands. "I am not kicking you out, and I need you to understand that, okay?" I said, slipping into English for privacy. "Got it?"

"Uh-huh."

"You are welcome to stay with me. But what she's suggesting makes a lot of sense, baby. I...I think you should give Mirrik a chance."

Her eyes welled, and I hugged her. "This is *not* goodbye," I murmured into her hair. "If things don't work out, if you're unhappy, or God forbid, if he hurts you, then you'll have a place with me. All you have to do is call. You know that phone I got you works here, right? I'll keep it paid up, and you can call whenever you like."

"What if I stay here and they don't let you back in?" she murmured.

"That's not going to happen," I said with feigned confidence. "And anyway, do you think Annie really cares?" As Sage sat up, I smiled at her. "If you need me, I'll find a way. Promise."

"And...you really think I should stay?"

"I think you should try it out. In a year's time, I bet you won't even recognize yourself," I said, tucking her hair behind her ear. "But know that as long as I'm out there, you've got a backup plan."

Once Sage had dried her face—she'd had a long morning already—I opened the door to find Kabno leaning against the far wall, arms folded over her chest. "Well?" she asked, straightening. "How are we feeling?"

"Unsure but willing to see how this goes," I replied. "What's our next step?"

"I'll make the necessary calls." Reaching up to grip my arm before I could step back into her office, she whispered, "You're doing the right thing, Jane. She'll thank you for it."

Perhaps, I mused. Perhaps not. In any case, I felt no need to point out to the diminutive director that Sage had an exit strategy.

Then again, if she had farseers shooting her intel, she probably knew that already.

Once again, my cousin and her husband graciously opened their home to us. "You're not an imposition," Canna insisted as she drove us toward Old Farm.

"I'm literally monopolizing your couch," I countered. "And eating your food."

"Well, you're welcome to it," she replied, softening. "Glad to see you two again."

Sage grinned from the back seat. "It's only been four days."

"And the girls have been asking about you, so there." She peered into the rearview mirror and stuck out her tongue, and Sage laughed.

While Sage entertained the elder two children upstairs and the twins played underfoot in the den, I filled Canna and Pars in. "Glad to know Voln's not completely awful," said Pars, "but what's the plan? You're stuck here until he's back on his feet?"

"And what's going to happen to Relieg?" Canna asked, crossing her arms. "Or that sister of hers? Liogh's planning to do *something*, yes?"

"They're keeping me in the dark for now," I told her, "and yeah, the plan is for us to wait around until Mirrik's able to get out of bed. Sage's caseworker has a few appointments lined up for her, but other than that..."

"Make yourself at home," said Canna, and Pars nodded. "And should you need to run back to Georgia, just let me know before dinner, eh?"

That night, once Sage had crashed in the guest room, I called Dad and Tabitha to give them the news, then hesitated only a moment before calling Connor. "Hey," I said when he picked up. "Want to guess where I am?"

"Jail?"

I groaned. "You and my father, I swear. Guess again, Officer Smartass."

"Ran back to Neverland, did we?"

"You want the skinny?"

"You know I do."

I summarized for Connor the chat I'd had with Liogh and Ganti after he'd left the previous night, then told him about Mirrik's statement under truth serum. "Damn, that's useful stuff," he said.

"Except for the part where Mirrik's now, like, on bedrest while his system recovers from it."

"*Shit.*"

"More than just that. Anyway, we're here while he recuperates, and then Sage will go home with him."

"So...no goodbyes, then?" he asked.

I smiled to myself. "Kid's going to be busy over the next few days, but...what'd you have in mind?"

"How about dinner? I'll take care of everything. That friend you mentioned, Tabitha, find out when she's available. And your dad, if you want."

As Connor and I weren't even dating—yet—I wasn't sure how I felt about introducing him and Dad, but at least this would be a low-stakes meeting.

"That's sweet of you," I told him. "Let me coordinate schedules—send me your shifts so I know when not to plan it. And, uh...could you do me a favor? I'll pay you back for that and dinner."

"Whether I want it or not," he said, chuckling. "Sure, what do you need?"

"Do you know that store downtown called Evangeline's?"

"The one with the frilly dolls?" he asked bemusedly.

That was putting it mildly. The proprietress, Evangeline Winthrop, was a creature born into the wrong era, the sort of woman who sported an Edwardian pompadour and a cameo brooch like she was cosplaying her grandmother. I'd dragged Dad into her shop a few times as a kid because she sold beautiful collector's dolls, porcelain creations with painted lips or more rugged rubberized numbers with glass eyes, all in the sort of lacy gowns Evangeline probably wished were still in vogue. Dad had bought me my share of dolls, but he'd been unable to justify paying the sort of prices Evangeline's commanded for what amounted to a pretty art piece, best left on a shelf to collect dust.

"Exactly," I said to Connor. "Could you pick one out, please? I don't care about the cost."

"I, uh…I've never bought a doll before…"

"Much easier than buying fishing gear or a gun. Just take a look around and pick a pretty one. Or ask Miss Evangeline for pointers. She probably talks to the damn things."

I held my breath, waiting for Connor to balk, but to my surprise, he laughed to himself. "All right, I'll do it. Is it okay if I tell her you sent me?"

"If it'll make you feel manlier, then sure. You know, my cousin's husband's built like a brick shithouse, and he's currently rocking a turquoise manicure because his girls did it for him."

"Mm. Was that meant to shame me or to build up my confidence?"

"Just putting that out there. Take from it what you will."

"Uh-*huh*. You're a complicated woman, Firebug."

"And yet you keep coming around," I teased.

"Arson prevention, you know?"

I scoffed in mock offense, Connor laughed in earnest, and he signed off, marching orders in hand.

The rest of the week was a whirlwind of appointments for Sage. Wednesday morning, her caseworker, a middle-aged sorcerer named Solla Kentri, drove us to a pediatric specialist for a full workup, and though the healer briefly gawked when Sage unmasked, she kept her tone light and friendly, putting the girl at ease. Wednesday afternoon was free, but Thursday was spent shuttling among a cadre of remedial teachers for hours of testing. Their conclusions were positive—though woefully undereducated, Sage was bright and showed promise—but the poor, exhausted kid was a zombie at dinner and fell asleep as her head hit the pillow that night.

On Friday, Solla took us to a child therapist, a sweet faun with vibrant red curls who ushered Sage into a room outfitted with bright, plush furniture and a box of toys. As I took a chair in the waiting room, Solla quietly said, "She specializes in trauma. Probably the best in the city. Don't worry."

Still, I fretted, unable to hear through the apparently soundproofed door and worrying that Sage was upset in there. I knew therapy could be emotionally challenging, but surely Sage had cried enough for one month. When they emerged at the end of the session, Sage's eyes were red and puffy, but she smiled at us and didn't complain when Solla took her over to the secretary to set up her next appointment. I was about to follow when the therapist asked, "Could I speak with you for a moment?"

I followed her into her office, and she closed the door. "So," she said, looking up at me—she couldn't have been five feet tall—"I take it you're Jane."

"Yes, ma'am. Is Sage—"

"We've got a long way to go," she said gently. "I received her file yesterday, and..." She shook her head. "The good news is that she seems fairly resilient. Once she opens up, she's a sweet child, but I'm going to push her. Make her confront some emotions she may not yet feel safe enough to express."

"She lost her temper Monday night, but that's the first I've seen of it. She...I don't know everything that the man who raised her did to her," I murmured, "but she's kind of…brittle, you know? It's gotten better, but she's not, uh…"

My voice faded, but the therapist nodded. "You can't undo a lifetime's programming in a single month, dear, no matter how much you try. And I do believe you've tried," she said, holding my gaze as I tried not to fixate on her rectangular pupils. "She's obviously very fond of you."

I smiled, though it felt weak. "You didn't see her when she arrived."

"The detective on her case has taken fairly good notes. I have some idea. By the way, *nice* work on that masking pendant."

"Best I could do…"

"I mean, it's not a ti'Cren piece, but goodness, child, you should be proud of yourself."

"Did Sage, um…unmask?" I asked.

"She did, briefly. She's not entirely comfortable in her own skin, and I'm not shocked by that. But, uh…" She gestured at her goatish lower half, the dark red curls of which perfectly matched the hair around her horns. "Perhaps I can put her a little more at ease. We did talk hoof care," she added with a grin. "Her father presumably doesn't know the first thing about that."

"Probably not. So…you think she's going to be okay?"

The therapist patted my arm. "I have high hopes for her. Don't worry. You've done well."

On Saturday evening, framing the outing as a chance to pack Sage's belongings, I had Annie slip us back to my place just as Connor drove up with pizza and cake. Tabitha, still in possession of my spare key, had already prepped with balloons and a bouquet, and Sage goggled, slack-jawed, as she stood in the corner of the kitchen while the rest of us bustled to set up. "Is this…is this for *me?*" she finally managed.

"You didn't think you were getting away without a sendoff, did you?" Tabitha asked, leaning over the box of garlic breadsticks to take a deep sniff. "Oh, yes, these will do nicely."

Tabitha's other contributions to dinner were fresh bruschetta—a slightly classier appetizer for those with an older palate—and another of her cousin's praline pecan pies with a bowl of bourbon-laced whipped cream, as one simply could not have too many dessert options. Annie couldn't stay, having her own family dinner plans, but when she looked appreciatively at the pie and Tabitha learned she was a Virginian, Tabitha cut her a thick slice to go. "Seeing as you're practically a neighbor and all," she teased, covering a paper plate with plastic wrap. "There, a little something for the drive back."

Smiling, Annie took it from her. "Good thing there's no drive involved. I've got to get this home and hide it from my brothers-in-law."

"Oh, if you've got more people, I can get you another slice—"

"Thank you for the offer, but, uh…that pie ain't big enough. I'm going to enjoy this one in my office," she said with a wink, then vanished.

Tabitha and Connor stared at the place she had been for a few seconds before turning to me. "How, exactly…" Connor began.

"It's complicated, but it's been convenient for us. Is Dad—"

The front door opened, and Dad swept in on a blast of cold air, dragging a wheeled pink bag. "There she is!" he said as Sage waved from the kitchen. "Will this do you?" he asked, showing her the suitcase. "Figured you should have luggage of your own."

Delighted, Sage hugged him, then happily helped herself to the spread. I pulled up a folding chair to squeeze five around the table, and soon, the conversation stilled while my company tucked in.

Once the pizza had largely vanished and Tabitha headed to the counter to see about dessert, Connor asked me to step outside, and I followed him to his Explorer. He pulled a giftwrapped box from the back seat and grinned sheepishly as he handed it over. "Miss Evangeline said it should be wrapped, and she wouldn't take no for an answer."

"You didn't want to argue with an old lady?" I teased.

"Frankly, she's a little creepy."

I swatted his arm. "She's eccentric."

"She started going on about how dolls make great friends, and...I don't know, all those glass eyes were staring at me, so I let her do her thing. All that's to say the paper wasn't my choice."

It wasn't terrible, periwinkle with ornate snowflakes, but it did seem slightly fusty. "Don't worry about it. What do I owe you?"

"You don't have to—"

"*Connor.*"

He huffed a sigh in mockery of my annoyance. "Okay, if it means so much to you...I was going to go to the Christmas tree farm next weekend and get mine. Help me pick one out and chip in a bit, and we'll call it square."

A slow smile crossed my face as I considered the subtext of that too-casual suggestion. "A Christmas tree farm? Do you watch Hallmark movies, by chance?"

"*Hell*, no. The farm just has better trees than the ones at the church lot, and my folks used to make a morning of it with me. Tradition, I guess." He paused, brow knitting. "Do you not do Christmas?"

"Dad never made a big deal of it, but, uh...I suppose I could help you find a tree to kill."

He snorted. "When you put it like that..."

"*Festively* kill?"

"It's okay, you don't have to go—"

"No," I interrupted, grabbing his wrist. "No, I'd like to."

He eyed me beneath the security light. "You're sure?"

"Positive." I started back toward the house, then paused. "Do we call this a date?"

"Would you *like* to call it a date?"

"Yeah," I replied, smiling up at him. "Yeah, I think I would."

Despite being creeped out by Miss Evangeline, Connor had chosen well. The doll in the wrapped box was eighteen inches tall, with soft brown curls, long-lashed sea-green eyes, and a flouncy green confection of a dress poofed with tulle and bedecked with sequins. Sage stared for only a moment of open-mouthed silence before she squealed and threw herself into my arms, then hugged Connor for making the purchase. When he, Tabitha, and Dad departed with the leftovers split among them, Sage was still clutching her doll, absently smoothing its hair while I wiped down the table. She kept it within her sight as she packed, and by the time Annie arrived to take us back to Canna's, Sage had named her Marigold, which seemed as good a moniker as any.

Canna was waiting with tea when I returned from seeing Sage off to bed. "Looks like someone had a good night," she said, passing me a mug. "And she'll want to keep that doll away from Maliul."

"Heck, I'm tempted," I replied, and sipped. "Connor did a nice job."

"I should say so. If you don't mind, how much did that run? Maliul will be six in April, and if I might enlist your services…"

"I don't mind, but I can't tell you. Connor bought it, and I'm reimbursing him by buying him a Christmas tree."

"Come again?"

"We're going on a date to a freaking Christmas tree farm. Cliché small-town romance, but hey, I owe him—"

"*Date?*" Canna interrupted with a gleam in her eye.

"Yes," I said, lifting my mug, "one of those things. Might even be fun."

Her lips curled impishly. "In that case, little cousin, I'd advise you not to set any trees on fire."

CHAPTER 22

On Sunday afternoon, Solla called with the update we'd been awaiting. "Representative Voln isn't at full capacity, but the healers say he's sufficiently recovered to be discharged. He's eager to collect Sage," she told me.

"You've approved it?"

"Yes, but with the understanding that I'll be regularly checking in. Her therapy *must* continue, and I want to be certain that she receives the educational support she needs. And part of the arrangement is that the representative must take a few basic parenting classes."

I was glad that DOL, in its infinite wisdom, wasn't just dumping a traumatized teenager on an inexperienced parent and sending them on their merry way. "What about family therapy?" I suggested.

"It's an option. I want to observe for a few weeks and see how they begin to adjust to each other, but I've got tools in reserve if needed. No one expects this process to be entirely smooth."

"And he's not giving you any pushback?"

"Not yet, fortunately. He was shown a copy of her file while he recuperated, and I think he understands that he needs help. This isn't like sending new parents home with a baby," she said. "This is a child with a lifetime of abuse, and on the cusp of puberty, no less. He may be in for a rough ride."

My guts began to knot. "Is he having second thoughts?"

"No," Solla said emphatically, "he's not. Not that he's

expressed, in any case. He's nervous, but he's legally claimed her. She's in the system as Sage Voln now."

Mirrik wasn't the only one with nerves. On Monday morning, Canna packed Sage's luggage into her van and drove us to DOL, where we found Mirrik waiting with Liogh, Solla, and Kabno in the director's office. The representative looked *rough*, pale and sunken-eyed, and I suspected he'd lost a few pounds over the last week, but he smiled when Sage walked in, pulling her suitcase and clutching her doll.

"Hi, Sage," he said, pushing himself out of his chair with a wince. "How are you?"

"I'm okay," she mumbled. "How are *you*?"

He laughed weakly. "Felt better, but the healers let me escape, so…"

"Why don't you two sit down?" Liogh suggested, pointing to the couch.

Though Sage left her bag by the door, she clung to the doll as she took a seat beside me. As she looked up at her father, I saw her anxiety mirrored on his face.

I thought Mirrik was going to join us on the couch, but to my surprise, he took a knee in front of his daughter. "I am *so* sorry," he murmured. "If I'd known you existed, I'd have come for you. Please believe me, I would have come."

"It's okay," she whispered.

"No, it's not. None of this is okay." As he took her free hand, his eyes began to mist. "The detective told me how you got out there and what that monster did to you, and I…I'm sorry, I didn't know…" He swallowed hard, pulling himself together. "I'm not perfect, and I don't entirely know what I'm doing, but if you'll give me a chance, I'd like to be your dad."

Sage nodded. "I…I'll keep the mask on…"

"Sweetheart," said Mirrik, leaning closer to her, "I do not care. If it makes you happy, wear it. If not…well, I know a good tailor. We'll make it work."

At that, finally, she smiled.

Mirrik had to brace himself against the couch as he stood, but he managed to get back on his feet. "Want to go see your new home? You've got a bedroom dearly in need of decoration."

Sage turned to me then, and I read the questions in her eyes.

"You're safe," I said softly, switching into English, though I suspected it wouldn't give me quite as much privacy as I'd have liked. "You're always welcome with me, and I'm a phone call away. I *want* you to call, all right? Let me know how you're doing."

"Thank you, Jane," she said, tearing up in turn, and dropped her doll to hug me.

"Go be great," I whispered into her hair. "You've got this, kiddo."

When I looked up, I saw Mirrik watching us with a stricken expression. "Something wrong?" I asked in Pactish over Sage's shoulder.

"Language," he said. "I didn't even *think*—"

"I'm sure it's been a difficult few days," Solla smoothly cut in. "Sage can understand you, this is not an emergency—"

"Can I get a potion?" he asked, turning to Kabno.

"*Mirrik*," she said, planting her fists on her hips, "you'll get nothing but healing potions for *at least* the next week. Be reasonable."

"I've handled language potions well to this point—"

"And my healers will kill me if I ask them to give you one today. Absolutely not."

"But—"

"It's okay," Sage told him. "I took a potion, so we're fine."

Mirrik offered her his hand, and Sage collected her doll and let him help her off the couch. "I'll fix this," he promised. "As soon as I can. For now…back to the house, and maybe we could go out for lunch?"

"Sure," she said, and grinned shyly.

Looking past her at me, he said, "Young lady, the file didn't say much about you, but I'm in your debt."

"It's no trouble," I replied, and nodded to Sage. "Bye for now, hon. Don't be a stranger."

Mirrik collected Sage's suitcase at the door, and an escorting aide waiting outside rushed to assist. "Thanks, but I'm not an invalid," he said to the nymph. "Lead on."

As they started off, I heard Sage ask, "Could you tell me what my chores are, please?"

"Chores?" Mirrik echoed. "Uh…school, I guess. And maybe you could make your bed. Would that be all right? Oh! We need to go wand shopping, don't we?"

Solla slipped out after them, closing the door and leaving me alone with Liogh and the director. "Just out of curiosity," I asked, "what *did* you tell him about me?"

Liogh smirked. "That you're a baby-faced master grower. Good enough?"

"Sure. So…what happens now?"

Kabno crossed her arms over her elegant pink robe. "Detective Birrid has been busy, and I'm sure they have more to do."

"Going after Relieg?"

"*So* hard," they replied. "I'm actually bringing her back in tomorrow. With any luck, she has no idea—we explained Mirrik's absence as a novel stomach virus. If she's wise, she'll show up with a counselor tomorrow, but something tells me she thinks she's pulled this off. Should be interesting—"

"But nothing for you to worry about, dear," Kabno interjected. "Your part in this affair has concluded unless we go to a tribunal, which I *sincerely* doubt will be necessary. Will you need a ride home, or can Agent Humphries do the honors?"

And that was it. My usefulness having been exhausted, it was time for me to get out. While the logical part of me understood that my presence in the Pactlands was highly irregular and had been permitted only to assist in Sage's case, the part much closer to my heart felt the sting of rejection all the same.

I suppose my expression must have betrayed me, as Liogh quickly said, "I don't mind driving you—"

"It's okay," I told them, forcing myself to smile. "Don't worry. I'll give Annie a call."

I'd started to step into the hall and was rooting in my purse for my phone when Liogh said, "Jane."

"Yeah?" Turning, I willed myself to come off as collected and unbothered, though the look on Liogh's face suggested I hadn't quite managed it.

"It's not fair," they murmured. "There's nothing fair about this, youngling, and I *will* do what I can to make it right. *We* will," they added, looking pointedly at Kabno, who nodded. "Not today, but soon. Yes?"

"Sure," I said, my throat constricting too much for me to manage a more eloquent response. "Yeah, okay."

They walked up and gripped my shoulders. "You've done a good thing. Twice, now, if you consider September. That doesn't go unnoticed."

I shouldn't have to do anything, I wanted to yell at them. *How much will it take for you people to forget the taint on me? Sage walked right on in. She's wanted. Why am I not fucking good enough?*

But I held back my anger and my tears alike until Liogh released me to call for a lift home.

The quiet cabin gave me some inkling of how Dad must have felt when I first went off to college: suddenly conscious of how much space one person doesn't need, of how silent solitude can be, of how the ear strains to hear the familiar sounds of the missing even when they're miles away. I wouldn't say my house was too big, but it felt hollower, somehow.

I closed the door of the spare bedroom, leaving it intact

in case Sage needed an escape but not yet ready to look at the empty place where my strange little houseguest had been.

And she *was* a houseguest, I tried to convince myself. I'd never intended for her to stay permanently...right? That would be silly. I was closer in age to her sister than her mother, and I didn't know the first thing about raising a kid, much less one with Sage's baggage...

But she'd become so familiar to me, a presence lurking at the edge of the room, anxious but beginning to blossom, and...

Well, damn it, I missed her.

I didn't want to interrupt her bonding time with her father, and so despite my unexpected melancholy, I didn't call her. But on Wednesday night, as Netflix queued up the next episode of the true-crime documentary I'd chosen for the evening's entertainment, my phone beeped with a message:

hi am gud mis u

I miss you, too, I wrote back, proud of her attempt at texting. *Happy?*

She responded with a smiley face, which needed no attempt at spelling.

Sage had a family, and that was as it should be. True, her maternal side wasn't so great, but at least Mirrik had stepped up.

I was thrilled for her, honestly, but as I lay on the couch that night and watched snippets of witness interviews, I couldn't help but wonder yet again why my mom had never come back for me.

I hadn't expected to hear from Connor until the weekend, but on Friday morning, he called me as I was mixing up a batch of bath soak in the workshop. "Could we get a tree today?" he asked. "Beat the Saturday crowd? It's always more fun without screaming children."

"Don't you need to serve and protect or something?" I teased, more grateful than I let on to hear his voice.

"Eh, that's overrated. Also, I have underlings."

"Tell me you didn't leave Sam in charge."

"He's a very good boy," he replied with a pained sigh, "but alas, no. So, can I pick you up?"

I was only slightly disappointed when Connor didn't roll up to my house in a tacky Christmas sweater, having opted instead for a Carhartt jacket and well-worn jeans. A flash of red plaid peeked out above his zipper—more hipster than lumberjack, I thought, but I kept that to myself. He seemed almost giddy at the outing, and I was laughing at his impression of the previous night's intoxicated driver, who blew a point-two but still thought he could bluff his way out of trouble, when my phone rang.

"Secret admirer?" Connor asked as I fished it from my bag.

"Hardly. It's Liogh." Tapping the screen, I switched into Pactish and asked, "Everything okay?"

"That depends on who you ask, doesn't it?" they replied. "I'm fine. Relieg…less so. Thought you might want the update."

"Please."

"Well," they began, chuckling low in their throat, "she was foolish enough to come without a counselor to hold her hand and shut her mouth. The director and I put her in a room, showed her Mirrik's questioning under truth serum, and then sprung Ganti's latest findings on her."

"Oh?"

"Yeah, he caught her masking in her apartment. She had a back entrance, so no one saw her when she went out as Joviff."

"Ooh, *busted*."

"Exactly. She crumbled. Told us everything."

"So, what really happened?"

"Mirrik's an innocent party, that's certain," they

muttered. "Relieg was impatient to be engaged, and she thought Mirrik was handsome. Decided she'd mask and give it a try, and apparently, she liked it well enough to keep up the charade for months. But once she and Grantis made things official, she broke up with Mirrik."

"And then she realized she was pregnant?" I asked.

"Not until the very end—it sounds like Enne had the right of it. Sage was small, Relieg was dieting, and she didn't even suspect until her final few weeks. Told herself she was imagining things until her labor began, when she went to her sister's house for help. *She* knew that her baby had to be Mirrik's, but she didn't tell Enne that she'd been sleeping with a sorcerer, so Enne genuinely believed the baby was deformed and dying. I spoke with her, too," they explained. "At least she was smart enough to bring counsel to the interview."

Connor pulled into the parking lot at the tree farm but made no move to shut off the engine, and I mouthed *Sorry* at him. To Liogh, I asked, "Are you charging Enne?"

"Yes, but only with child endangerment and unauthorized portal use. She's already been fired, and I suspect we can work out probation for her."

"*Just* probation?"

"You sound disappointed."

"She dumped Sage with *Warner Cavanaugh*," I protested.

"True, but there are mitigating circumstances, and I want to use her against Relieg. Child abandonment carries a stiffer penalty, plus there's the matter of Relieg's false accusation...and if she balks and tries to take us to a tribunal, we can always charge her with rape. We might only win on sexual assault, but what she did to Mirrik is criminal."

I grimaced as a Subaru drove by with a ten-foot pine lashed to the roof rack. "How does *he* feel about going through a rape trial?"

"I haven't asked him yet," said Liogh, "as I don't think we'll get to that point. If Relieg wants to see her other children, she doesn't need that sort of conviction—and she *will* have a fight for custody."

"What do you mean?"

I could almost hear the detective smirk. "Solla called me last night. It seems Relieg tried to get ahead of this matter by confessing to her husband. Didn't go so well. Grantis is horrified, and he took the boys and went to a hotel. He called DOL yesterday morning and got through to Solla, and he's offered to let Sage meet her half brothers. Solla doesn't seem convinced that Sage is ready for that quite yet, but perhaps there's hope for a relationship someday."

"That's...decent news," I said. "Thanks for filling me in."

"Of course," Liogh replied. "Now, once we work out a settlement, there's the matter of your citizenship to consider. Can you give me until early next year?"

My heart beat faster. "Uh...yeah, certainly. No rush."

"No, there needs to be a rush on this," they insisted. "And whatever happened to that officer I met, the one you think might be part sorcerer?"

"He's fine," I said, and smiled at Connor, who raised his eyebrows in query. "Got to go, I've got someone waiting on me."

"Is everything okay?" Connor asked as I put my phone back into my purse.

Grinning, I said, "I'll give you the recap later," and opened my door. "Come on, let's look around before all the good trees are gone."

Given the acreage of the tree farm, we were in no real danger of ending with a three-foot fir, but I didn't want to dwell on the Pactlands just then—the cousin I'd grown fond of, the little girl I was missing, the rolling prairies and glass skyscrapers and vibrant populace of the place I was never meant to see because my mother fell in love with a no-prospect Virginia boy. I didn't want to think of the missing mother and dead father who'd left my life before I was old enough to form memories of their faces or voices.

"Are you all right, Jane?" Connor asked, pausing at the end of a row of apartment-scaled trees. "You're awfully quiet."

"Just taking it all in," I fibbed, then threaded my arm around his and nodded to the taller pines ahead. "Lead on."

A few steps later, Connor stopped in his tracks and groaned. "Axe is back in the truck. *Damn* it."

"I could always burn through the trunk for you," I offered.

He shot me an incredulous look, and I fluttered my eyelashes and tried not to crack.

"I swear, Firebug, you're going to be the death of me," he said, and turned toward the parking lot. "Tell you what, you don't burn down the tree farm, and I'll buy lunch."

"Hm. I suppose I can live with those terms," I replied, and laughed as he escorted me through the ersatz holiday forest, our breath puffing as the distant clouds massed, bearing with them whispered promises of snow.

ACKNOWLEDGEMENTS

We meet again, friend! Thank you so much for reading. I hope you've enjoyed, as this story isn't over yet...

The Novel Chicks continue to let me hang out with them, and for that, I'm grateful. My sincere thanks also go to Adam Domby, whose suggestions always improve these stories.

And yes, here's to you, Mom and Dad.

ABOUT THE AUTHOR

When not writing fiction, Ash Fitzsimmons is an appellate attorney and an unrepentant car singer.

Find her online:
www.ashfitzsimmons.com